CHASING CLAY

THE DEWITT AGENCY FILES #3

a novel by
LANCE CHARNES

WOMBAT GROUP MEDIA — ORANGE, CALIFORNIA

Wombat Group Media
Post Office Box 4908
Orange, CA 92863
https://www.wombatgroup.com/

First Printing November 2019
Second Printing December 2020
Third Printing September 2021
Fourth Printing September 2025

ISBN 978-1-7333989-0-9

This is a work of fiction. Names, characters, businesses, places, events and incidents are either the products of the author's imagination or used in a fictitious manner. Any resemblance to actual persons, living or dead, or actual events is purely coincidental.

No animals were harmed in the writing of this novel.

Printed in the United States of America

For Betty

Who's decided this really is a thing

For bonus chapters from **Chasing Clay**, reading group questions, an interview with the author and an art gallery, check out <u>https://www.wombatgroup.com/dewitt-agency-files/chasing-clay/chasing-clay-bonus-material/</u>

Chapter 1

My phone rings. This doesn't happen a lot these days; not many people call me other than Chloe, my roommate. The number's blocked. "Hello?"

"Where are you right now?" A voice like coarse sandpaper on steel. Gotta be Len, my federal probation officer.

It's nine-ish on a cloudy, cool Monday morning. I sigh. "At work." I opened the store at five, and since then I've been dealing vente Caramel Macchiatos and other caffeinated candy drinks to the usual going-to-work and post-gym crowds.

"You sure?"

I'm sitting at my usual place on the sidewalk along Hill, two tables up from Santa Monica's version of Main Street, with a cup of two-percent milk and a marked-out onion bagel from yesterday's baked goods. Breakfast.

When I got out of prison in 2014, I was ordered into three years' supervised release—kind of like probation, but different—with a few special conditions of supervision, including community service and paying restitution. I'm a few weeks away from finishing my second year. Len had been slacking off on me until a couple months ago when some of the Central District of California's probationers violated out spectacularly. Now he's doing these random spot-checks to see if I'm secretly cooking meth on the side.

Because he's my PO and he's been okay until this mess started, I don't say the first four or five things that come to me. "Let's see. I'm wearing a green apron. I'm sitting here in Ocean Park where I have no other reason to be. I had to get up at *four in the fucking morning* to help open." *Bring it down…* "Yeah, I'm pretty sure."

"I don't see you."

"You're *here?*" I look around in a near-panic, but all I see is some woman in a crop top and yoga pants walking away with a trenta something that's mostly whipped cream. Len must be in the store. Grilling my boss comes next. "Is this the start of my audit?"

"It is if you don't sell me some coffee in the next five minutes…"

"I'm on break."

"You going with that, Friedrich?"

The new employment audit's got me crapping cinder blocks. Some of those violators were slaving away in jobs that apparently didn't exist. Len tells me he has to look at work product, time cards, and the other bread crumbs you leave behind when you have a real job. I really work for Starbucks, but the money I use to pay my fiscal debt to society supposedly comes from a New York City architectural/engineering firm I supposedly do freelance design work for. The firm exists, but I've never seen it and I've never drawn a single plan for them.

Len's waiting next to the cashier station, arms folded, doing his bulldog imitation. He's only five-nine and looks like a bald Sam Waterston, but I know he's made of old steel cable and iron filings. He growls, "Finally."

This is getting old. "I'll ask again—is this my audit?"

"Not yet. Like I told you, I'm doing the real shitbags first. Your time'll come. You're a felon—shit happens to you. But while I'm here, I'll watch you pull my drink."

"Like you haven't seen that before." He ordered a grande Americano with an extra shot of espresso. Not hard to do unless you're being graded. I think about slipping him an extra extra shot so he'll have a heart attack. With my luck, I'd end up with a real asshole for a PO.

He sips and nods. "Good enough."

"You gonna interrogate my boss next? She loves that shit, you know." *Not.* I always get crappy shifts afterwards.

"Not this time." He leans over the serving counter toward me. "Color inside the lines. They're looking for reasons to twist our shorts. You got a year left—don't fuck it up."

Another year of this. It was just about tolerable until recently. I'm back to reporting by phone three times a week (I'd been down to once a week) and (a new wrinkle) monthly in-office interviews. I still have to file monthly written reports, get permission to leave Southern California, and I can't leave the country… legally, at least.

And now this employment audit's heading my way. This is bad... *real* bad. Like, going back to prison bad. I have no idea how I'm getting past that.

I fill a few more orders, then get the boss to let me take the last ten minutes of my break. I stew about Len's visit and the short leash he's put on me again. At least in prison you know where you are and what the rules are. Outside, it's almost like being free until they remind you you're not.

I get into such a dark place that when my phone rings again, I bark into it, "What do you want now?"

Silence. Then, "One-Seven-Nine?"

This is so out-of-context that it takes me a moment to figure it out. "Olivia? How'd you get my number?"

"Do you truly need to ask?" Olivia has this creamy Oxbridge accent on a smooth mezzo voice that usually makes me feel all warm and safe. It's not working right now because she's calling me out of the blue on my personal phone. "You didn't answer your agency mobile."

"That's because I'm not working for you right now."

"Nonetheless. When can you be at the airport in Santa Monica? Allyson wants to see you immediately."

Oh, shit. "What'd I do?"

"Nothing... yet."

Chapter 2

I cover a lot of ground over the next three hours.

I don't leave work until 12:30—I have a full shift, and Allyson won't pay me for leaving early—then go home, change into my new slate-gray Canali Siena suit, and pick up my agency phone and laptop. Olivia's arranged a town car for me so I don't have to take the bus everywhere. Allyson's Cessna Citation XLS is waiting at the Santa Monica airport when the limo drops me outside the executive terminal. I've never been on a business jet before—it's a pretty sweet ride, with a bar and snacks and everything. Not having to deal with TSA is a bonus.

A limo collects me at the Eagle County (Colorado) Regional Airport and hauls me to the Sonnenalp, a huge *faux*-Bavarian hotel/resort in the eastern half of Vail's ski village. I have an impression of stone facias, heavy-timbered balconies, and tiled hip roofs on my way from the limo into the lobby. Allyson left me a present at the fake-half-timbered front desk: a key card to a room.

The room's on the third floor. An entry hall lined with paneled, stained doors; an arch into the white-plaster bedroom; a king bed facing a large pine armoire and matching cubbyhole desk. It's nice, quiet, and comfortable. Am I staying here tonight? It's past six and getting dark out.

Then I notice a royal-blue Vail Executive Forum registration folder on the desk with most of its guts taken out, and a black roller bag stowed between the desk and armoire. I catch a whiff of jasmine and sandalwood when I open the closet. Allyson's perfume. The closet's full of women's clothes—*nice* women's clothes. The kind she'd wear.

This is Allyson's room?

Allyson DeWitt owns the DeWitt Agency. She's my other boss. We "fill needs" for people or organizations rich enough to hire us to fill them. The things I do for her aren't always legal, but that's where

I really get the money I use to pay off the banks and the feds. I've worked for the agency off and on for a year and I'm not in prison again. I must be doing something right.

The white-painted washstand in the bathroom is crowded with all the magic potions Allyson uses to keep herself from looking like the portrait she hides in her attic. The armoire holds the TV, safe, and minibar. The desk's also a three-drawer dresser. Allyson still wears very nice lingerie. The other two drawers aren't as interesting.

While I wait, I look up the Vail Executive Forum on my work phone, a big quad-band Samsung. It's an annual by-invitation "gathering of corporate and public opinion leaders" put on by the Vail Global Coalition toward the end of April, when the resort's between winter and summer seasons. A pit stop between Davos and the Milken Global Forum, I guess, so CEOs can avoid going back to work.

I startle when the front door lock clicks and the door swings open.

It's Allyson. Her eyebrows jump. "Mr. Friedrich. You're here… finally." A little irritated, not fatally.

Allyson's in her late-ish forties. She's everything I love in a woman: almost black hair, dark eyes, olive skin, great cheekbones, better legs, and a smooth alto voice that's stuck in my dreams for years. Not beautiful, but striking, with the kind of presence that makes you look when she comes into the room. Like now.

"They had us flying in circles around the airport for, like, forty-five minutes. Some dude had to have his jet towed off the runway. That's gotta be embarrassing, you know? You're out there trying to impress last year's Miss Universe and your airplane dies." *Stop babbling*. Allyson does this to me.

She plops her purse—a black D+G Sicily top-handle satchel that costs only 170 hours of me pushing coffee—on the green-and-white plaid bedspread. "I'd planned for you to arrive *before* cocktail hour, not after." Her tone says miffed, not mad. Mad's not a good look on her.

"Sorry."

Another thing I like about Allyson is that she wears clothes well. I had to learn a *lot* about fashion at the art gallery where I used to work so I could tell how much money our clients had. Allyson's outfit is a long-sleeved, above-the-knee sheath with red, white, and black geometric print blocks by Prabal Gurung, one of Mrs. Obama's designers, and black Prada ankle boots with cone heels. She's wearing a few months of my Starbucks pay.

She hauls in a deep breath, then lets it out slow. She waves away my sorryness. "Can't be helped. My apologies. This conference always brings out the worst in me. Did you have a pleasant trip?"

"Yeah, it was good. Thanks. Why am I here?"

"Yes, of course." Allyson steps to the armoire, opens the safe, and pulls out a slim manila folder that she hands to me. "Please read the top document. I'll change while you're at it. They never schedule enough time for the women to change for dinner." She tosses her conference badge and lanyard onto the bed as she quick-steps to the closet.

"Why change? You look great." A little flattery never hurts.

The corner of her mouth turns up. "Thank you. It's formal." She braces a hand against the closet doorjamb and unzips her left boot.

"Would you like me to step out?" Not that I object to watching Allyson undress; it's just good form to ask.

She drops the left boot and goes to work on the right. "That won't be necessary. You won't see anything you haven't already, and I'm confident you can control yourself."

Wow. That's the first time since my job interview that she's referred to… that night.

I've lusted after Allyson for the almost six years since our one-nighter. My little brain still wants a replay. It's arm-wrestling my big brain, which knows a black widow when it sees one.

The other boot clunks to the floor. She starts fiddling with her zipper, which is apparently in an especially awkward place.

The little brain wins a round. "Here, let me get that."

She gives me a look. Not *The* Look, which is lethal, but *a* look. "Read."

It's on Department of Justice letterhead from the United States Attorney, Northern District of California. Nothing good ever comes from DOJ. Addressed to a federal judge at the courthouse in downtown San Francisco. Re: United States v. Matthew Benjamin Friedrich.

I stop breathing. I've seen too many of these. They were never good news.

It's the typical legalese written by somebody who's never been exposed to standard American English. The first paragraph's the usual throat-clearing and recitations. The second paragraph...

Seriously?

I read it three times. Some of it is *blah blah blah*, but one line explodes in my brain: "...recommend to the court a modification to the terms of the sentencing agreement under Rule 32.1(c)(2) to effect early termination of the supervised release judgment order..."

Early termination.

Freedom.

With this letter, I wouldn't have to care about that employment audit anymore. I'd be free. I'd get my passport back. Len wouldn't come randomly to where I live or work to ambush me, my landlord, my boss, or my roommate.

I know: it could be worse. But seriously? I want to be a grownup again.

I skim to the end to see if there's a part where they say "just kidding." There isn't, but there's no date and no signature. "Ally—um, Ms. DeWitt?"

"Yes?" Her voice echoes out of the bathroom.

"What's with this letter? And how come you have it and not my lawyer?"

"Does it please you?"

"So far. I need to read it carefully. They forgot to sign it."

"That wasn't an oversight."

I read the rest of the page-and-a-half letter carefully and finally spot what I'd missed the first time: Mr. Friedrich is supposed to render valuable service to the Department of Homeland Security. "If this' a quid, what's the quo?"

"What you read is the reward for successfully completing the project I intend to assign to you."

She doesn't explain. I lean against the wall next to the bathroom door. "Can I read the project description?"

"Not yet. Our client has become interesting to one of your federal law enforcement agencies. He—"

"Arrested?"

"Not yet, but possibly soon. He's been negotiating with the two lead agencies and has come to an understanding with them. He's agreed to fund a discreet private adjunct to their investigation and supply information to them. In return, they'll grant him immunity.

He's been a steady client of ours, which is why he hired us to manage the investigation."

Alarm bells started ringing somewhere around *private adjunct.* "Hold on. We're gonna run an off-books operation for some three-letter agency? That's nuts."

"We've done just that before, though not recently." The calm in her voice makes it sound like she thinks this is just business as usual. "I want you to be project lead."

Another explosion in my head. "Don't I have to be an associate to do that?" I'm a junior associate now, the lowest of three pay grades in the agency.

"Yes. That's why in addition to the gift from your government, I intend to give you a provisional promotion to associate, with this project as your probationary period." That's a €500-a-day pay bump. She *really* wants me on this thing. "You did excellent work on the Portsmouth project, though a bit... unconventional. Understandably, the client is less than pleased by the outcome. The client's representative, though, is extremely pleased with how you worked with her and saw to her needs."

I wonder if she told Allyson about the... *personal* services I provided that weren't about burgling museums and forging paintings. "Thanks for the feedback. I'll assume this project has something to do with art." What I learned at the gallery gets me Allyson's art-related projects.

Right then, I realize something's missing from the offer letter. I comb through it word-by-word while I try to listen to Allyson.

"In a manner of speaking, it does. The client may have done something... *irregular* with antiquities from Southeast Asia. Pottery, in this case."

I don't know anything about pottery, and most of what I know about Southeast Asia came from watching *Apocalypse Now.* I'm about to mention it when a little voice whispers "early termination" in my ear. I'll lay off on the honesty for now. "He's in trouble with ICE?" That's Immigration and Customs Enforcement, part of DHS. If this guy's smuggling, they're the ones who care.

"Among others, yes. I believe your IRS is also interested. Our investigation is to identify the people trafficking this pottery and relay the information to the client."

It's not here, it's not here... "Why doesn't ICE do it? They've got investigators."

Allyson doesn't answer right away. Was that a trick question? Then she says, "Excuse me. Lipstick. I'm told that host-nation cooperation has been almost nonexistent. Your government would get better cooperation if it wasn't so squeamish about paying commissions to foreign officials."

Commissions = bribes. "Allyson... is there another letter?" Shit. I called her *Allyson*.

"What do you mean?" Apparently she didn't notice, or care.

"Another letter, offering immunity."

The door opens and Allyson finally emerges. Amazing. Her emerald-green, sleeveless floor-length column gown skims her bust and hips, just enough to let you know what's there but not so tight that she looks like she's wearing a sausage casing. Sequins cover the upper bodice's back and sides, flashing like little green stars in the hallway light. Her outfit doesn't show much skin, but it's sexy as hell.

She hangs up her day dress, bends (*ohhhhhhhh*) to scoop up a pair of black patent pumps, then turns to face me. The dress isn't as modest as I thought; the skirt's slit about two-thirds of the way up her right thigh. "No, there are no other letters for you."

My heart stumbles. *No other letters* for you. "For the agency?"

"Why do you ask?"

She must've thought of this. She's nothing even close to dumb. "Look, the only reason the feds would want an off-books, deniable investigation is because they expect us to do illegal stuff they can't. Information from informants is admissible even if they get it illegally. If we get caught, the feds don't know us. If we don't have immunity, we're targets." One of those sneaking suspicions sneaks up on me. "Did *you* get immunity?"

She finishes slipping on her shoes and sweeps off toward the safe. "That's not your concern. Your concern is—"

"That's *exactly* my concern." Her non-answer tells me the real answer is *yes*. "If there's gonna be line-crossing, *I'm* the one who'll be doing it, not you. They know about me now. You'll be reporting to the client, right?"

"Of course." She's at the desk, rooting through little figured silk pouches for jewelry. Her freshly lipsticked lips are getting thinner.

She doesn't see it... or, worse, she doesn't care. That scares me even more than the situation itself. "And he'll hand it to the feds.

They'll have a paper trail with *my name* on it. If anything goes sideways and they need a scapegoat, all the fingers'll be pointing at the ex-con."

Allyson straightens and plants a fist on her hip. "Be reasonable. Why would they prosecute an operation they created? They'd only embarrass themselves."

"They won't be there forever." Somehow I got to only a couple paces from her. "Look at the crazies running for president right now. What if one of them wins in November? What if they do something incredibly stupid, like fire all the USAs and put in a bunch of zealots? They'll be looking for dirt to throw around."

Her lips are gone now. She folds her arms. "You weren't worried about this in Portsmouth." The ice is back in her voice.

"We weren't telling the feds about Portsmouth." I turn tight circles on the carpet to try to vent a little steam somewhere other than in Allyson's face. "We weren't inviting them to *watch* in Portsmouth. Can't you see it?"

"I can see that you've let your paranoia get the better of you."

That stops me. I stare at her for a few moments. Her face is tight and closed. "Paranoia? I'm an ex-convict. A felon. Have—"

"Interstate transportation of stolen property." She almost sneers.

"A felony. I still served time." I wrestle my voice down. "Have *you?* Ever been to prison?"

"Not in this country."

"I have. I've seen the system from the inside. You can't trust these people." I rush her, my hands up, pleading. "Please. For all our protection. Go back to them. Get immunity for you, for me, for the agency. Or walk away from it. It's not worth the risk."

Allyson's arms are folded tight enough to leave bruises. Her neck and ears are turning scarlet. "Do you think I would walk away from this after everything I went through to secure this project? To get *that*"—she stabs a finger toward the file in my hand—"for *you?* How many thousands of dollars it cost to bring you here so I could tell you about this personally, thinking you might be *grateful?* There's no renegotiation, Mr. Friedrich. No going back for more. The deal is what it is." She closes the gap between us, radiating heat, and glares through my skull. "You can let me pay you a lot of money and regain your freedom. All you have to do is complete the project." Her fingertip bores a hole through my breastbone. "Don't you dare tell me it's not enough."

She's not listening. I give it one more shot. "If the feds decide to take me down, I'm going back in the hole. This time, it won't be a nice, safe prison like Pensacola. They'll put me in with the animals. I won't survive that. Fourteen months in stir with crooked execs almost drove me nuts. Drug dealers and mobsters? I can't do it. I won't."

Allyson sniffs and shakes her head. "You're scared?"

"I'm terrified. This setup terrifies me. Yeah, great upside... but the downside's a bitch."

Her eyes slash my face. Her knuckles are white. I've never seen her so angry. "You refuse to do this?" Her voice is low, like the growl a panther makes before it bites through the neck of a deer.

Think hard. Think fast. "Unless there's immunity—"

"*There is no immunity.*"

"No. I won't." God help me. "I like breathing. I like being outside. I can't risk that."

The points of her jaw glow white. I expect to hear teeth breaking.

Shit. I can smell the freedom that letter can give me, but I can also smell prison disinfectant. What'd I just do?

"Coward." She thrusts a loaded finger toward the door. "Get. Out. Of my room."

Chapter 3

It gets real dark after the limo passes the west edge of Vail. Scattered window lights here and there, mostly on the south side of I-70, like square yellow stars. The moon's not even out yet, or it's behind a mountain.

It's dark inside me, too.

Did I totally fuck up, or dodge a bullet? Or both? My brain's been going back-and-forth on that since I walked out of the Sonnenalp. I can't even tell anymore if I was right. Was all that me being paranoid? Was it me being smart for a change?

Smuggled pots. How bad could it be? I don't know how that trade works in Vietnam, Cambodia, wherever. In southern Europe, a lot of the trafficking goes through one mafia or another. If it's that way in Southeast Asia, I could end up doing deals with some seriously bad dudes while one of our endless number of police agencies looks over my shoulder. Thailand's got a military dictator now. Myanmar's full of ethnic militias that double as drug gangs. There's been a guerrilla war going on in the southern Philippines for about a century. Some descriptions of the corruption in the area include "endemic," "all-pervasive," "spectacular," and "inescapable." Is there a line for bribes on my expense report? Do I have to report kickbacks? I should check that out.

The short answer: it can get pretty bad. At best, I'll be papering the place with bribes; at worst, I'll be playing games with mobsters and drug runners. And if I pay off the wrong person (or don't pay off the right one), I end up in a hellhole Third World prison where I'll be the protein supplement for dinner.

Maybe I dodged a bullet.

But... early termination. Freedom.

I've been in the system one way or another for five years. They've controlled my life even when I wasn't in prison. If you've never experienced it yourself, you have no idea how demeaning and infantilizing it is. It's like having World's Strictest Parents, except they can ground you for real.

What would I do differently if they cut the cord? I don't know. Maybe nothing. Just knowing that Big Brother isn't watching anymore might be enough. I won't have to get Len's permission if I decide to change jobs, or if I manage to develop a girlfriend and want to spend time at her place. I could travel more for the agency and not be scared out of my wits that TSA's going to throw a flag on the play. Skip the crazy spy-vs.-spy shit I do on projects to keep from violating out.

The agency. Allyson.

I've pissed her off before, but never this bad. The look on her face when she threw me out won't stop looping in my head. Do I even still work for her?

Why's she so hot to have me do this? She's gotta know we didn't do ceramics at the gallery. The closest we ever got to Asian art was a few Russian Impressionist canvases we sold. The antiquities market was too dirty even for us.

I think back to something she said at the hotel: *after everything I went through to secure this project*. What was that exactly? Why did she work so hard to get this? Or… was this done *to* her? Did some spooky agency put the screws to her? The Mob?

I shake my head hard to derail that train of thought.

Freedom. Yeah. *Think about that.*

Freedom.

There's nothing outside. No lights, only the dark shapes of hills or mountains blocking the stars. I close my eyes and let my head fall against the headrest. My brain throbs from the fight and the tension and all the questions.

Do I play, or do I sit it out?

Even if I want to play, will Allyson let me, or did I slam that door?

Those questions have a cage fight in my head for I don't know how long. Along with my headache, my stomach starts to tie itself in knots. *Make a decision, idiot.*

My work phone rings. Allyson calling to say *sorry?* Yeah, right. "Hello?"

"Matt? Carson."

Carson was my partner on two of my three projects. She's a

tough, smart Canadian ex-cop who's built like a Bengal tiger and has roughly the same disposition. We're past the I-hate-you stage and we get along okay... but not okay enough for this to be normal. I open my eyes and sit up. "Carson? Why are you calling?"

"What. The *fuck*. Did you do?" This buzzsaws through my ear. "Allyson called. Almost fucking melted my cell. What'd you say to her? She wants to kill you."

Seriously? I mean, I know it's usually a figure of speech, but with Allyson... does she do that? "Why'd she call you?"

"She thinks you listen to me. What happened?" Her voice is flat Midwestern vowels with a little Canuck twist.

The thing is, Allyson's sort-of right. I do usually listen to Carson. When I don't, I often regret it. "What did she tell you?"

"You turned down a project. An important one. Says she busted her ass to make it good for you. You said no. What the *fuck?*"

There's lights ahead to the left. A green highway sign zooms past: "Eagle 1 Mile." We're almost at the airport. I lean forward to ask the driver, "Can you stop?"

"On the highway? No. There's an exit up there. That okay?"

"Yeah." I pull the phone away from my chest. "Hold on a sec. I need to get rid of the audience."

"Where are you?"

"In a limo in the middle of the Rockies. Hold on."

A minute later, we pull off the freeway and turn right into a gas station and convenience store called (I kid you not) Kum & Go. I bail out of the limo as soon as it stops. It's freaking cold out. I button my coat while I un-mute my phone. "Still there?"

Carson growls, "Still waiting."

I tell her the story. The whole thing start to end. Just having to put it into words brings it into focus, though I still don't have a solution.

Carson listens without interrupting until I'm done. She mutters something I'm sure I don't want to hear clearly. Then, "Doesn't matter."

"What?"

"Doesn't. Matter. That letter real?"

"I'm pretty sure. I've seen enough of them."

"Know what that is? A fucking *gift*. You get one of those a *lifetime*." Her voice singes the hair around my right ear. "You blew it off? You fucking *idiot!*"

"Whoa! Wait. Did you listen to the rest? ICE? No immunity? Paper trails? Did—"

"Shut up and listen." She takes a very audible deep breath. "Never heard of Allyson doing so much to make a project look good to one of us. For us? She forks over the shit sandwich, tells us to eat. *You?* She covers it with *candy*. Lights a *candle*. Don't know what you got on her, but…" Carson breathes hard a couple times. "Know what I'd do to get one of those? What I'd give to get kicked loose from Rodievsky? Anything. I'd do any*thing*, doesn't matter."

Rodievsky's her other boss: a Russian mafia don or whatever they're called. Carson owes him a scary lot of money. When she's not working for Allyson, she works for him. "Would you really? If you got thrown back to him, he'd kill you."

"Think I don't know that? Still worth a try. What's your excuse? Your feds get you, they put you in jail. Boo-hoo. You've been there."

"They'll put me in with the freaks this time. I won't come out."

"Don't fuck up, then."

"What's so hard about immunity? The feds give that out like parking validations."

"She say she doesn't have it?"

"She said *I* don't."

"Bet she does. That's how she rolls. Get over it. Another thing. You spit in Allyson's face. You don't make it good; you never get another project. Good luck paying off your tab."

I haven't even thought about that. My past sins left me with over $500,000 in mostly non-dischargeable debt: restitution, student loans, interest, and my ex's credit card and medical debts. At $10 an hour at Starbucks, I'll be dead before I dig out. It goes faster at €1500 a day.

My driver's smoking by the limo's nose. I watch a trickle of cars fill up under the flat canopy over the pumps. I'm getting seriously cold out here, but I can't move. "I don't know what to do."

Carson sighs. "Sort it out. Told you what not to do. You throw this away; I'll never talk to you again. I don't talk to fucking idiots."

Great. "You'll come visit me in prison?"

She snorts. "Go inside for something you do for Allyson? You got a job when you come out. She'll square it with you. Seen her do it. Look. You're smart—*use it*."

Then she's gone.

I drift between the store and the mini-carwash out to the sidewalk at the edge of the slope above the freeway. Headlights and taillights streak by below me, though I don't really see them.

Listen to Carson, or listen to myself? She knows how Allyson's system works, but I know how the criminal justice system works (or doesn't). Which do I trust less?

As an ex-con, my job with the agency is my only way to earn enough money even semi-legally to get out of debt. But if enough of Allyson's people get convicted for her to have a policy for what to do with them when they get out? No. Not going there.

I wake up my phone to tell Olivia I'm out. There's a missed call and a voicemail waiting for me. Len's number. The timing doesn't give me a good feeling. I reluctantly tap the "play" triangle.

"Friedrich? Len. Where the hell are you? Some woman called, said you left the state. Your roomie doesn't know where you are. Call me ASAP or the flag goes up."

Allyson called my PO. I didn't see that coming. That's like calling SWAT on my house for a fake hostage situation.

It's a warning.

Chapter 4

It's a long wait. Over two hours. I'd go to dinner, but the thought of eating makes me sick. So I sit and watch the numbers change on the digital clock in Allyson's room. Call my boss at the store, tell her I won't be in tomorrow. Try to rehearse my lines.

The door clicks open at ten. Allyson stands there, silent, her right hand holding the door open, her left gripping a beaded clutch that matches her gown. She stares at me for a long time. As usual, I can't read her, and I'm pretty good at that with other people. Normal people.

She finally paces slowly through the hall, sits decisively in the armchair against the wall opposite me, throws her right leg over her left. The dress falls open at the slit. She lets me look for a few moments, then flips the skirt over her knee.

There's a long, *long* silence.

I swallow. "I'm sorry."

Allyson's left eyebrow ticks up a notch. "That bought you ten minutes." How a voice like hers can be arctic, I don't know, but it is. "Use it well."

Another great thing about the Citation is that it has real tables, not those useless folding things in airliners. That means I have room for my Burger King dinner while I go over the project description on my laptop.

It's all about pottery.

Your mom's china vase is a tchotchke. Your great-grandma's favorite stoneware urn's an antique. Your great-great-etcetera-grandma's best earthenware amphora is an antiquity. The same general arrangement of baked mud goes from garage-sale reject to priceless cultural heritage object after a couple millennia. And while you might not be able to give away mom's vase, you're not supposed to sell great-great-etcetera-grandma's amphora—it's illegal.

In general, I approve of this. Some of the poorest places on Earth are the richest in cultural heritage goods. But think about how the world works: if a poor country has something a rich country wants—oil, timber, minerals, labor, women, art—the rich country just swoops in and takes it. Sometimes richer people in the poor country organize this—the government, a warlord, a mafia (often all the same thing). Maybe a few locals get paid a couple bucks to dig up or cut down their own savings account; otherwise, they get nothing. All the upside goes to well-off people selling the loot to richer people in rich countries.

It's a global industry. One expert I read said that 90% of the antiquities in private hands in the U.S. are looted. The client's in good company.

According to the project description, somebody discovered what's left of an eight-hundred-year-old culture on the northwestern Thai/Myanmar border. It's called Nam Ton, after the local river. They made pots—lots of them—and they're gorgeous. They're coming into the U.S., probably illegally, and getting bought by people who can afford to lay out high four or low five figures for pots with missing pieces.

Our client's arrangement with ICE—the customs cops—is that he'll turn over the entire supply chain from start to end. That means whoever takes it out of the ground, whoever gets it to port, whoever ships it to California, and how it gets into the hands of the gallery the client bought it from.

Three big problems jump out from the beginning.

Problem #1: the client wants the project done in sixty days from the time it starts. I don't know if this is his idea or the feds'; either way, it's too short.

This project's basically a long con. I learned during my fourteen-month, government-paid vacation at its all-inclusive facility in Pensacola that the thing that kills long cons most often is speed. I can't just grab people by the throat and say, "Tell me where the pots come from." I have to work my way in. That takes time. If ICE has been on this for two years (like it says in here) and hasn't found out this stuff yet, why does anybody think we can do it in two months?

Unless they don't think we can and they're setting us up to fail.

By "us," I mean "me." Then ICE gets to bust the client and perp-walk him to show everybody that even a rich white dude can get arrested every once in a while.

Problem #2: the client bought his pots in San Francisco. That's in the same state I live in. I was in the news four-to-five years ago... a *lot*. My name, my picture. If I walk into any gallery in the state, it's better than even odds somebody'll recognize me, no matter what name I'm using. I have to be very careful, but not too careful, because I have only sixty days.

Problem #3: the client's lending us his art advisor to introduce me to the two people the client thinks are running the smuggling scheme on this end. That's a person I can't control getting a front-row seat to whatever I do. Also, it's somebody who gets a lot of time to figure out I'm maybe not my cover identity. Unless she's involved and she's a future defendant, she sounds like a perfect witness for the prosecution.

Given what the client's paying, I guess he gets to call the shots.

These problems are why I asked to read the project description right there in Allyson's room after she handed it to me on a little blue thumb drive. She threw me out instead.

I probably shouldn't turn the plane around and go back to Vail. Talking to Allyson is out for now. But when we land, I can go to the next best thing.

There's no town car waiting for me when I get to Santa Monica. The nice people at Atlantic Aviation, the bunch who takes care of the business jets, let me sit in their remarkably generic conference room while I wait. I dig out my agency phone and hit the contact labeled "Mom."

Two rings later, Olivia says, "Good evening. How may I help you?"

Allyson owns the DeWitt Agency—it's her last name, after all—but Olivia runs it. She keeps track of us associates, helps us get things we need, processes our expenses, and makes sure our pay gets to our offshore accounts. She's our psychologist, mother-confessor, and concierge. I'm told none of us have ever met her.

"Hi. One-Seven-Nine." My employee number. "I got my

assignment."

"So I hear. Are you still in Vail?"

"No. Santa Monica. Will there be a car, or do I take a taxi and expense it?"

"I'll arrange for something. In future, when your plans change, please inform me—I can serve you better." I think that was a scolding. "How else may I help you?"

"I need to talk to Allyson. How do I reach her?"

She pauses. "You've not had your fill of that for the year?"

"Guess you heard. She's putting me in a bad position."

"I know. Knowing her as I do, I'm certain she was less than sympathetic. That must have been frustrating for you. Nonetheless, one mustn't bait the bear."

Tell me about it. "I apologized. A lot." *Groveled* wouldn't be totally inaccurate. "I still need to talk to her. I read the project description on the flight home. There's a few things I need to know before I start."

Olivia pauses again. "May I offer you a spot of advice?"

"Okay."

"Avoid Allyson for a spell. Several days would be a good start. She's quick to anger and slow to cool. You ought not remind her of your existence until she's recovered. If you insist, though…"

"No, that's okay. Can you relay some questions to her and let me know what she says?"

"I can try. I'll not guarantee anything. What do you need to know?"

"The client's lending his art advisor to us. To Rick Hoskins. Does she know who I am really, or does she think Hoskins is a real person?"

"Right. Go on."

"Does the client know my name? I want to know if Allyson negotiated with DHS directly or if she did it through the client. If it's the first one, that's one less opportunity for my name to get out."

"Right. What else?"

"Is the sixty-day limit from the client or the feds? It's too damn short. If it's the client's thing, it would be great if she could get him to stretch it. Ninety or 120 days would be better."

"Right. Anything else?"

I saved the best—or worst—for last. "I need to know the client's name."

Olivia lets out a little cough. "You know that's—"

"Against the rules, yeah, I know. Except it wasn't last project. And this time around, he supposedly referred Hoskins to the art advisor. If somebody asks me where I found her or how I got into this game, I need to give them a name. If somebody asks me about this guy, I need to recognize his name so I can answer. I can't wave my hands around this. I'll find out who he is when the indictment's filed, but it's too late then. Get my drift?"

"Clearly. Allyson will not be pleased."

"She's already not pleased. I doubt she can get any less pleased. We might as well take advantage of that."

"More easily said than done. I'll do my best. You haven't any more questions, have you?"

I'll take the hint. "That'll do it for now. I've got a couple for you, though. Requests. I need to buy a bunch of books in the next day or two. Probably a few hundred dollars' worth. Can I expense them even though the project hasn't officially started yet?"

"They're related to the project, yes?"

"Yes. Call it homework."

"I see no problems with that. I'll not look too closely at the dates."

Phew. "Thanks. Also… it'd be real useful if I didn't have to work this coming week. It's an extra eight or ten hours a day I'll have available for studying. Is there any way I can get a stipend or something? I can't not have money coming in."

I can hear her breathing and a keyboard clicking. "For a week? Is that necessary?"

I was hoping to not tell anybody else about this, but it's a reasonable question. "If I tell you something in confidence, can you keep it from Allyson?"

"Well… it depends, of course. If you're plotting to kill her, I've an obligation to warn her. Anything less dramatic is situational."

"It's nothing that dramatic." Deep breath. "This project's all about pottery and Southeast Asia. I don't know a Krishna from a Ganesh, and I don't know shit about pottery." Actually, I *do* know Krishna from Ganesh—Ganesh is an elephant—but that's as far as it goes. "I need to do some serious homework so I don't sound like an idiot. That means a lot of reading and visiting museums. I really need to do this right." The downside looks worse the longer I stare at it.

"I understand. I assume you'd rather Allyson not know. How much are you asking for? What *are* you paid for a day of work?"

"On a full shift—which doesn't happen all the time—I get eighty bucks minus taxes."

"Good God. That's pathetic."

"It's good for counter service. Welcome to America."

Olivia sighs. "Let me see what I can do. I may be able to juggle some accounts to beat out a few dollars. I'll let you know."

"That'd be great. Thanks. Um… can I get a partner?"

"Only as needs must. If this is a veiled way to ask if One-Two-Six will be joining you, she will not. She's unavailable." One-Two-Six is Carson's employee number.

"Okay." Not okay. I'd hoped she could help. It'll feel weird without her. This will be my first time working a project alone. "That lawyer of Allyson's—does he do criminal?"

"There is no one solicitor. She has several. As for criminal law, I understand a number of her solicitors have a great deal of experience with it." One thing that makes it hard to get irritated at Olivia is that she's always so calm, no matter what's falling from the sky. Shit, in this case. "Please keep in mind that Allyson will review your performance at the end of this project and decide whether you may keep your temporary promotion."

As if I didn't have enough to worry about. "Is there a test?"

"The project is the test. Good luck."

Chapter 5

Achara Asian Art is on Sutter Street, a block north and half a block east of San Francisco's Union Square, next to Caldwell Snyder, a contemporary art gallery. It's too far from Market Street to be swarmed by the tech crowd—young people of various genders in hoodies and backpacks, loping by with their eyes locked on their phones. All the buildings on this side of the street except for Caldwell are older low-rises with cornice detailing, fire escapes, and multi-lite windows. I'm the only human in sight wearing a suit.

Savannah touches my forearm with her fingertips. "I hope you'll like this, Rick."

Savannah Kendicott's the client's art advisor, and now she's mine. Actually, Richard Hoskins'. He's an L.A. commercial property developer who's worth nine figures or so and likes to spend it on art. This is my second go-round as him. It's kind of a philosophical exercise to figure out whether Hoskins really exists. I exist, so when I'm Hoskins, does he exist? I never took philosophy in college, so I try to stay away from questions like that.

Another philosophical exercise: is this where I step over the legal line? I'm not going to take anybody's money. I'll actually buy something if they let me. Still, I was all nerves while I waited for Savannah this morning. It would help if I trusted the feds to not screw me, but being in the system cures you of that fast.

I shake it off... for now. "This is where you've been buying for your clients?"

"That's right." She brushes back a swoop of honey-blond hair from the corner of her eye. "This is really why you're here, isn't it? Not the gallery this morning."

"Not entirely." I'm lying; Achara's totally why I'm here. "I needed an idea what the market's like here. It was also a way to get to know you, and for you to figure out what I like."

One of her perfectly plucked eyebrows perks up. "My audition?"

I have to assume Savannah thinks Hoskins is real; Allyson hasn't answered my questions yet. "We'll see."

A New York art dealer once said that anybody with an iPhone and a pair of Louboutins can call herself an art advisor. When I was in the art business in L.A. five years ago (that long now?), I got to see a lot of art advisors and "art advisors" in action. The first kind—the ones who'd been at it for a long time, who'd done something real in the market before printing their new business cards—were like walking grad courses in art appreciation. I'd follow them around when they came to my gallery and just listen and learn. The second kind? Well…

I haven't figured out yet which bucket Savannah falls in. She must have a trust fund, a rich daddy, or a sugar daddy behind her to be as young as she is, doing this, and still be able to afford the cap-sleeved, black-and-white Escada knee-length sheath and the Louboutin open-toed black pumps. She's in the last half of her thirties (like me), a cheerleader-pretty, well-designed, French-braided blonde (though it doesn't match her eyebrows). She's named after a city and even has a shiny new iPhone. If I stopped there and decided to be judgmental, I'd decide the New York art dealer was right.

But Savannah has the resume (advanced degree, Sotheby's), seems to know what she's talking about, and the gallerist at the last place didn't roll her eyes when we walked in. Maybe she's the real deal. Not that it matters a lot. She doesn't know it yet, but I need her for only two things—and one of them is to get me through Achara's front door.

She gives me a smile that's so perfect, it must've built her orthodontist a ski cabin at Squaw Valley. "Shall we?"

I stare through the glass door and suck in a deep breath. We visited a by-appointment-only gallery this morning, and I was in full fight-or-flight mode from the moment I walked in the security door. Nobody said, "Hey, aren't you…?" or "You look just like…" *that rat bastard who destroyed part of the L.A. art scene.* The day's still young, though.

Gulp. "After you."

The door chime sounds like a gong. The floor's paved with

Saltillo tile—rough-hewn, foot-square terracotta—instead of the usual pale hardwood strip in most galleries. It warms what could be a chilly space. We pass the obligatory gilded Buddha (in rough-enough shape to really be a few centuries old) on a pedestal and the usual pot of incense sticks in pebbles. No gamelan or sitar music, thank god.

Savannah leans close and lays her fingertips on my sleeve. She's a toucher, not that I mind. "Achara's the only Bay Area gallery that specializes in classical Southeast Asian art." Her voice's low and soft in my ear. "Lorena's wonderful to work with—I hope you'll like her."

We're surrounded by things that look like things I saw in the books I've been inhaling since last Tuesday. I can even place a couple in time, thanks to last week's trips to the Norton Simon and the Asian collections at the Los Angeles County Museum of Art. But it's mostly a smear of Hindu deities and Buddhas and bodhisattvas on cream pedestals or ledges against sanded white walls. The *ikebana* arrangements seem like a mixed metaphor. Savannah murmuring in my ear things like "Shakyamuni, Ayutthaya" is only marginally useful. I get a lot of practice in nodding knowingly and smelling her perfume (woody and understated).

I spent the past week studying eighteen hours a day. I bought (and expensed) over $400 worth of books (not as many as you might think) at Hennessey+Ingalls in downtown L.A. I have this trick memory where if I read something three or four times, I can remember it more-or-less forever. Too bad I only had time to read a couple of the most important books once or twice. My head's full of random facts with no connecting tissue. Feeling completely unprepared is hateful, but here I am anyway.

"Good morning, Savannah." The voice is gentle and slow and warm, like a good kindergarten teacher's.

Savannah breaks away from me and hurries toward a willowy woman draped in a verdigris silk *áo dài*. "Lorena! You look lovely." The women hold each other's elbows and do the two-cheek air-kiss thing. "I was just about to come looking for you."

"I'm sorry. I was on the phone. I love that dress on you."

I've heard enough fake-affectionate cocktail-party greetings to tell that these two aren't acting—they don't actually hate each other.

Savannah steers Lorena by the arm in my direction. "Lorena, this is my new client, Rick Hoskins. Rick, this is Lorena Montford.

She owns Achara."

Lorena wraps both her long, delicate hands around the one I give her to shake. Her face is fine-boned, almost fragile, with plenty of definition. Deep-set, pale-blue eyes, laugh lines, freckles from the sun. Her center-parted black hair has a fair amount of gray in it. Late fifties?

"Nice to meet you, Ms. Montford."

"Oh, please, call me Lorena. I'm glad Savannah brought you to me." She squints, then purses her lips. "Have we met, Mr. Hoskins? You look familiar to me."

Of all the things she could say, that's the worst. Luckily, I've had a week to prepare myself to hear it, so I don't have a heart attack. Much. "I'd remember if I met you." When in doubt, try flattery.

A pink glow shows on each of her high cheekbones. "You're too kind. But I'm sure I've seen you before."

Aw, hell. On the first day here. "The news, maybe. *Real Estate Forum*. The business section of the L.A. *Times*."

"Of course." But she's still peering at me. She'll be thinking about it. I hope I'm a long time gone when she figures it out. "I understand you're just getting started with Asian art."

"That's right." We're done shaking, but she hasn't let my hand go and there's no polite way to pull it loose. "Be gentle with me."

She squeezes my hand. "I'm always gentle. You won't feel a thing." She finally lets me go. "Does anything you've seen here speak to you?"

Here's where I steer us to the reason I'm here. "You know, you have a lot of gorgeous pieces, but..." I shrug. "Having somebody else's god in my living room doesn't work for me."

Savannah says, "Rick's really interested in ceramics."

"Really?" Lorena's smile gets bigger. "You've come to the right place. Follow me."

Her dead-straight hair falls like a curtain to her waist. The calf-length *ao dai* ripples when she moves. Its skirt's been slit to her hips, and it trails out from her loose black slacks. It's like somebody's pouring her hair and outfit over her while she walks.

The store's U-shaped, surrounding an enclosed stairway that leads to the architect's office upstairs. We cross from the sculpture gallery to the everything-else gallery. I stop. "This isn't what I'd expected."

Lorena looks over her shoulder. "I hope it's a pleasant surprise."

I'd expected vitrines and shelves and more pedestals. Instead, there's over a dozen pieces of old, tropical-looking furniture placed artfully throughout the space—sideboards, tables, kitchen and manuscript cabinets—displaying ceramics and bronzes. I recognize teak but not the other woods, and the closest I can get to pinning down the furniture's origin is "not Europe." But when I take a moment to let it sink in… "Actually, yes, it is. It's warm. Comfortable. Not like that museum we went to this morning."

Savannah says, "King and Company."

Lorena nods. "They have such a beautiful gallery, but it doesn't appeal to everyone. Did you see anything there that you liked?"

I bob my head side-to-side. "A couple pieces. Nothing I had to have right away. May I?" I don't wait for permission to cozy up to a distressed, dark-stained console table and the half-dozen pots peppering its top. Each sits on a low, square plinth covered with figured scarlet silk.

Lorena glides my way. "Of course. Is there anything special you're looking for?"

"I'm sure there is." In fact, I know there is: Nam Ton ceramics. The client says he bought his here, and Savannah confirmed that (sort of) outside. It's the only style I can recognize without a book in front of me. "I'll know what it is when I see it."

I browse the displays, trying not to blow past the ones I don't care about. I can't afford to be obvious this early in the game. I see lots of different shapes (kendis—a kind of Southeast Asian teapot—mortuary pots, water jars, bowls of different sizes and depths) and lots of finishes (glazed, unglazed, painted, incised, cord marked, sgraffito). None of the right ones, though.

Savannah appears at my elbow. "Come on. I'll show you something I think you'll like."

The significant look she gives me tells me to let her tow me by the sleeve to the room's street end. We stop in front of a well-aged cupboard. Its doors are open, and there are almost a dozen pots on its shelves. I ask, "Which one?"

She glances behind us—Lorena's at the room's other end, watching—then murmurs, "Any of them. Just 'ooh' and 'aah'."

"Ooh. Aah. What?"

"I get that you don't want to tell Lorena what you're interested in." Savannah stretches to get her lips next to my ear. "Sometimes I tell my clients to hold back. But you need to tell *me*. I can't help you if you don't. I mean, I don't mind taking your money, but I'd rather help you buy something with it."

Usually the first step an art advisor takes with a new client is a meeting where they talk about the client's goals and tastes. That talk never happened for us. I met Savannah this morning at the Bancarella coffee pavilion on Union Square. After we finished our lattes, we jumped in my town car and took off. The conversation never went deeper than *first time here?*

Maybe we didn't have that "what are you looking for?" talk today because Our Client already filled her in. Maybe not. But she's just an overpriced tour guide if I don't let her do her job.

"Something fresh and new. Surprising. Something I won't find in every other collection."

She frowns at me. "I'm not sure I understand. Should we look next door?"

At the contemporary art, she means. "Not that kind of new."

As my bought-and-paid-for advisor, her first loyalty's supposed to be to me. If she's part of the scam—a possibility I can't dismiss—showing her what interests me may be too much, too fast. Or—worse—she'll smell a rat and bolt.

But I have to get things rolling or the project's dead.

I pull my work phone, sort through the open browser windows, and show her a picture. "I ran across this a while ago. I couldn't find out much about it. It's Thai, right?"

Savannah's ocean-blue eyes widen a few ticks. She gently takes the phone and studies the photo. "It's *from* Thailand. There wasn't such a place when it was made, though." She glances up at me. "Why didn't you show this to me earlier?"

"I wanted to see what you'd come up with on your own."

She nods. "Okay. A test. I get that." She doesn't seem put out by it. "I don't see anything like that here right now, but Lorena's handled it before." She gives me my phone with both hands, like it's a big business card. "Let me talk with her. You look around; see if there's anything else that catches your eye."

I do that while the women have their sidebar in the back of the gallery. There really is some pretty stuff here. I like the pieces where the artist didn't try too hard—simple, clean lines, unfussy decoration.

Like that Nam Ton water bottle in the picture I showed Savannah.

They leave me alone longer than I would have in my gallery. Both women eventually join me, one on each side. Lorena asks, "Have you found anything you like, Mr. Hoskins?"

A little aw-shucks usually knocks down defenses. "There's so much to choose from. I don't know where to start."

Savannah, on my right, is texting like crazy. "Well, Lorena had a great suggestion."

"Buy one of everything?"

Lorena lets out a you're-the-client-so-everything-you-say-is-witty laugh. "That would work, too. No, I told Savannah that she should take you to the Norris Museum. They have an excellent collection, and she'd be a wonderful guide. You can learn a great deal in a short time. It might help you pick a period or a style to concentrate on. You can never have too much education when you're starting to collect in a new area."

The Norris Museum. James Bandineau. The other guy the client mentioned.

Yeah, I should go there.

Chapter 6

San Francisco has two Asian art museums. The bigger one calls itself the Asian Art Museum of San Francisco, like there's only one. It's supposed to be very nice, and Savannah tells me it has a little something for everybody. "That means," she tells me in the back seat of a town car Olivia arranged, "you don't get a lot of depth in the galleries."

We don't go there. We go to the Norris Museum of Southeast Asian Arts in the area called South of Market.

I watch the mutt-mix roll by: newish apartment buildings, slightly scruffy older mixed-use buildings, and the occasional scraper. The walkers are way more downmarket than a few blocks back near Barney's and the Ferrari Store. It's frayed but not scary… much. "You know, when I was a kid, I'd come up here with my folks for long weekends. This out here? This was the place tourists weren't ever supposed to go."

Savannah nods. "I remember that. It's crazy how much it's changed." She waves toward her window. "This part hasn't, but when we turn on Folsom? That's the new SoMa. The galleries are moving here from Union Square." She points out the driver's side. "Gagosian's three blocks that way."

"Seriously?" Gagosian's a megadealer with sixteen branches around the world. When somebody drops eight or so figures on a lot at a contemporary art auction, there's a good chance the artist is part of Gagosian's stable.

"It's a whole different city up that way, and it's moving down here."

Creeping hipsterization doesn't seem to bother her much. I suppose it wouldn't concern Hoskins, either, since he causes it. "You're a local?"

"I grew up on the Peninsula."

I'll figure that out later. Like most Angelenos, I can locate San Francisco, Oakland and maybe San Jose on a map. The rest is all here-be-monsters. People from the Bay Area think L.A. goes all the way to the Mexican border.

The Norris is a handsome three-story, red-brick building taking up half a long block on Folsom. If you don't look hard, you can believe it's a cleaned-up turn-of-the-century warehouse. It isn't.

The driver lets us off at the main entrance on the corner of Sixth Street. We arrive just as they open at ten and breeze through security after Savannah flashes a card at the guard.

I say, "I guess you're a regular here."

She almost blinds me with her smile. "This is like Disneyland for me."

The galleries start on the third floor. They're arranged chronologically rather than thematically or by nationality. We bust through "The Hunter-Gatherers" to get to "The First Farmers."

It's like jumping into one of those books I'd slaved over in my hotel last night. Statues, figurines, jewelry, pottery, nicely displayed in airy vitrines lit by grid-mounted LED spots below an open ceiling. The labels are big and contrasty, easy to read in the subdued lighting. I like this place already.

Savannah parks next to me. She's in Escada again, a sleek, closely-fitted knee-length black dress overlaid by a tone-on-tone broken plaid pattern. "This is where we start. I'm your audioguide."

"You're too big to wear around my neck."

She peaks an eyebrow. "You're sure about that?"

Women flirt with Hoskins. They haven't flirted with me since I started working counter service. I've missed being Hoskins.

I follow Savannah through the next several galleries as she teaches me about the objects. I listen just enough to tell if she's asking me a question or wants a comment; most of my attention's on the labels, which is what I'll remember. My memory's visual, not aural. It's interesting to see contemporaneous objects from different cultures displayed together—it provides some context I don't have yet. I didn't really come for that, though.

I came for Nam Ton. I came for James Bandineau.

We've just entered the first Northern Thailand gallery—where the Nam Ton works should be—when a man slips through the doorway at the other end. I recognize his hair from a picture on the museum's website: thick, mostly gray, brushed back from his forehead into what a romance novel would probably call a mane.

He pads up behind us a minute later. "Well, look who's here. Savannah! What a surprise."

I doubt that. If she didn't warn him, Lorena did.

Savannah spins and claps her hands together. "Jim! Hi!" They do the two-cheek air kiss. "What are you doing out in public?"

"I like to see what our guests are seeing." He turns toward me and holds out a hand. "We haven't met. Jim Bandineau. I work here."

"Rick Hoskins."

We shake. He has a good, firm, Chamber-of-Commerce handshake, which isn't always the way with guys working in the arts. He's my height—just shy of six feet, some of it hair—and looks like the romantic-hero professor in a Hallmark Channel movie. There's hardly any correction in the rimless glasses. A prop?

Savannah explains me to him (the other thing I needed her for), then tells me, "Jim's the museum's chief curator. Everything you see here is his work."

Bandineau waves that away. "Hardly *all* mine. Is this your first visit?"

We do the polite first-date chat for a couple minutes. He wears a V-neck, long-sleeved sweater in heather green over an open-collar white dress shirt. At least there's no tweed jacket.

According to the client, he's Lorena's partner in the looting scheme. He's certainly in the right position to do it.

He says to me, "Let me show you some of my favorite pieces. I'm sure Savannah's been talking your ear off."

"She's a lot more charming than the audioguide." That makes her smile. It's not hard to do, but it's nice to see.

Bandineau leads us around the gallery, pointing out objects here and there. He talks about the makers like he knows them personally. Sometimes he tells us about the people who found the artifacts—"the real heroes of the story"—making bread-and-butter archaeology sound like high adventure. His favorite phrase seems to be "This is fascinating…" What he says next usually is. No wonder he's done so much publicity for the museum.

I finally find what I've been looking for. "Jim? Can you tell me about this?" Yeah, we're on a first-name basis now.

He nods as soon as he sees what I'm looking at. "Ah, yes. One of my current favorites, too. Aren't they extraordinary?"

They are. The vitrine holds eight Nam Ton pots. The shapes are crisp and streamlined. They're thin-walled, symmetrical, and well-formed. Five of the eight are intact, not 3D puzzles glued together out of sherds like most of the pots here.

But the most striking thing is the decoration. The makers used only two colors—a pure-white slip and cobalt blue—and kept the designs as understated as the forms. A single sharp, uniform blue band below the rim of a bowl. A single blue stripe reaching from the mouth of a tall water bottle to the base, hugging the swell of its body. A vase split exactly in half, the bottom blue, the top white. Five wares have an extra design element: one or two complex, curving blue-line figures that seem to have been dashed off with a single gesture. The colors still pop even after 700 years in the dirt.

I've seen a lot of pictures of Nam Ton over the past couple days, but seeing them in person and in context is almost overwhelming. They're not the thick-walled, lopsided things I expect from jungle tribesmen. They're not like the pots in the other cases around us. There are no clumsy drawings of fish or birds or flowers. A lot of technical skill went into making these. It took a sophisticated design eye to come up with the decoration and not overdo it.

It's like finding a 700-year-old iPhone. Something that shouldn't exist but does.

I don't even notice Bandineau arrive until he says, "You could put those on your dining table today and they'd look perfectly at home."

"Yeah." I finally look up. "How did they...?"

"Do this? No one knows for certain." He turns up a hand. "We have a good idea how they *made* these, of course. It's likely a variation on how people make pottery in northern Thailand and Laos today. They use a simple spinning platform on a stick..."

If you're like me and all you know about making pottery is from date night watching Demi Moore and Patrick Swayze play in the mud... well, that ain't it. There's no potter's wheel, for one thing. I soak up the labels while staying partly tuned to Bandineau's wavelength.

Savannah stands at the end of the vitrine, listening to the lecture while watching me. What does she see? What does she know?

When Bandineau stops, she says, "They could've used wheels. India and China had wheels three thousand years before these were made. It'd explain the symmetricity."

I'm impressed she can make words like "symmetricity" sound perfectly normal.

Bandineau makes a circling motion with his hands. "Well, yes, that's possible. But we have to look at the record…"

They launch into a debate that gets seriously out there after a minute or so. They've done this before—the playful jabs they take at each other seem almost practiced. Since Savannah keeps glancing at me, I figure she's showing off for a new audience.

They both stop for air. I say, "What about the decoration? The patterns could be mid-20th century, not mid-fourteenth century. That's what makes these special."

Bandineau nods like he's heard this before. "Exactly. I'd argue that the most remarkable thing is the level of craftsmanship in the basic fabrication. I'm sure you've noticed—it's close to what we see with classical Greek ceramics. But the colors do catch the eye, don't they?"

"They do. Why isn't there anything else like them? Where do they come from?"

He steps to a mounted poster-sized map of mainland Southeast Asia covered with numbered red dots. "These pieces came from around here." He points to a spot along a dashed blue line showing the border between modern-day northern Thailand and Myanmar. "The archaeologists have been deliberately vague about exactly where to protect the sites from looters."

It must not be working.

"As for where the Nam Ton *culture* came from… well, we don't really know. These wares have been trickling out of Thailand for years, but the first scientific excavations happened only eight years or so ago. The scholarship's thin so far. I've seen only two papers."

Savannah says, "They're not as unique as you think. Don't get me wrong, they're lovely, but…" She drifts around the case's corner toward Bandineau. "The forms are pure Southern Song Dynasty. That's thirteenth-century Chinese. The Song made thin-bodied whiteware in the twelfth century. *Qinghua* wares—blue-and-whites—started being mass produced at the beginning of the Yuan Dynasty." She finger-circles the three pots to my right. "See that squiggle? It looks a lot like a form of very abstract calligraphy that developed in China at the end of the thirteenth century."

I say, "So you're saying these are Chinese?"

"I'm saying that Chinese potters trying to escape the Mongols may have kept running until they reached northern Thailand. There wasn't anything to stop them. Once they got there, they started making ceramics again."

Bandineau says, "There's no proof of that, though."

As they bicker, I start thinking big-picture.

Like I told Olivia, I never had to pay attention to ceramics. I dealt with flat art: oils, watercolors, the very occasional litho. The only pottery I had any serious exposure to in art history class was Golden Age Greek. Sculpture's greatest hits—another "fine art"—showed up in class but always seemed like an afterthought. Art to me was something you hang on a wall. That's what pulls down the serious money on the market.

Seeing hundreds of pictures of pots over the past few days didn't make a dent on me. It took seeing ceramics in person yesterday and this morning to make me finally get why they're different, and special.

They're real. I can touch them. Even if a piece is a grave good—a lot are—it still has a familiar form and purpose. People have made cups and teapots and jars with their hands for five thousand years. If Bandineau let me, I could pick up one of these bowls and hold it exactly the same way somebody did eight hundred years ago. That's a direct connection with the past you can't get with a painting.

"Rick? Are you still there?"

Savannah's voice breaks me out of my head. I take another long look at the Nam Ton pieces. They're still amazing even if they aren't as unique as I'd thought. Then I look up—I want to see their reactions when I ask this question. "Do these come on the market? Can I buy any?"

Savannah stifles a smile and glances at Bandineau.

He purses his lips for a moment like he's thinking. "Well, I don't see why not."

Chapter 7

The rest of Wednesday and the first half of Thursday are about studying. I brought two suitcases with me: one with clothes, the other with books (it weighs a ton).

I've studied in way worse places than a suite in the Westin St. Francis next to Union Square. (I know… Hoskins would stay on Nob Hill. All the galleries are down here, though.) For one thing, it's bigger and way nicer than the ex-pool house I live in. It's called a City View Suite because of the primo view from the 28th floor of the tower's northeast corner. When I look up from my laptop or the books on the suite's round, polished wood table, I see the postcard shot of Coit Tower on Telegraph Hill with the bay behind it.

I read what I can find about the places and things Savannah mentioned, especially at the museum. But whenever I concentrate enough to remember her words, I start thinking about her. Not in a she's-so-hot-I-want-her way. More along the lines of, what's her connection to this?

Savannah's clearly very friendly with both Lorena and Bandineau. That's not suspicious all by itself; I was friendly with half a dozen advisors who brought clients to Heibrück Pacific, the gallery where I worked. It's not unknown for museum curators to work as consultants on the commercial side or be resources for people who do.

The real question is: could she represent a client who claims to have seen (read: participated in) shady doings without her knowing about them? Anything's possible. It would help to know exactly what kinds of mischief the client was involved in. All I have are non-specific references to trafficking and tax fraud. I guess he didn't trust Allyson enough to confess his sins to her. Smart man.

What would Savannah get out of being part of whatever scheme this is? Kickbacks? She'll get those anyway, only they're called "commissions," and they're legal. If anything goes south, her name would be on the indictment next to Lorena's and Bandineau's. Based on what I know—which isn't much—I don't see the upside for her.

That pings around in my head while I stare out the east-facing window at the forest of glass boxes crowding the Financial District a dozen blocks away. I'm not ready yet to call Savannah an unindicted co-conspirator. I'll keep it as an option in case I get smarter on all this. I don't need to trust her completely, either.

Our visits to King and Achara and the museum convinced me of one thing, though: I can't possibly absorb enough from these books to hold my own with specialists. The history's different, the languages are alien (written Thai looks like Martian runes), the medium's the polar opposite of canvas and paint. If somebody wants to make me into a mark, I'll be the perfect one—I won't know enough to keep myself out of trouble.

I hate that.

Something I hate more than that? Savannah's the only thing standing between me and the sharks. Even though I can't trust her, even though my original plan was to cut her loose after our first meeting with Bandineau, I can't get rid of her now even if I want to. I have to hope that her duty to her client (me, not Our Client) will beat out her relationships with the two maybe-villains we know about.

And that's a really stupid thing to hope for.

I check in by phone with Len, my PO, on Wednesday afternoon, the first time during this project. I'd had to get his permission to take a supposed new freelance job with a San Francisco architecture studio and to travel here. Len's cool, but I'm reminded why I want to get off my leash for good.

Olivia emails late Thursday afternoon. It's a forward of an email she sent to Allyson with my questions.

1. Does the art advisor know 179's real identity, or does she believe he is really Mr. Hoskins? *She has been told he is Hoskins.* (Good. That's easier.)

2. Does the client know 179's name? *No. I negotiated directly with ICE for his early termination agreement.* (Whew. One less person who knows who I am.)

3. Did the client or the government set the sixty-day limit for the investigation? *ICE did. They need a swift conclusion.* (But why? Never mind.)

4. What is the client's name? *179 should know better than to ask.*

Three out of four. Not bad. Except that the one she didn't answer is the most important.

At least she didn't get blisters from all the typing.

I'm eating a luscious swordfish steak at Farallon, a restaurant across Post Street from the St. Francis that looks like the inside of Captain Nemo's submarine on acid. It's my reward for spending all afternoon at the big Asian art museum in the Civic Center. It was very pretty, but other than teaching me more about Buddhism and Hinduism than I strictly needed to know, it wasn't as helpful as I'd hoped. The book selection was pathetic.

Another benefit of being Hoskins is that I can eat well enough and often enough to gain back the weight I lose between projects. And there are tablecloths.

As I disappear the steak, I try to figure out how to drive this project forward in a way that won't set off alarm bells. In real life, building a trusting relationship with Lorena or Bandineau might take months. I don't have months. But pushing too hard might make them bolt. Any way I look at this, I lose.

I wish I had somebody to hash this out with. I really miss Carson right now.

My phone vibrates. It's Savannah. "Hi! Oh… did I catch you at dinner?"

She must've noticed the background noise. "Yes."

"I'm sorry." She doesn't sound sorry. "Where are you?"

I'm about to say *none of your business* but decide a little bonding might be useful if she's supposed to keep me from becoming shark bait. "Farallon. The seared-scallop appetizer and the swordfish steak."

"Ohhhhhhh. I'm *so* jealous. I love that place. Those big jellyfish things hanging over the oyster bar are wild. Uh… the reason I called is, Lorena wants to invite you to lunch tomorrow if you're available."

Huh. And here I was wondering how to keep things moving. Still, I need to play at least a little hard-to-get. "Why lunch?"

"Well, she doesn't tell me everything. I think this is about getting to know you, and she thinks it might be more relaxing over lunch than in the gallery. Can you make it?"

"Will you be there?"

"Of course. I won't let you go in there alone. I have interests to look after."

Sure. "I have a meeting in the Financial District at one-thirty."

"That's perfect. Eleven-thirty, then? She'd like to meet at Zero Zero on Folsom between Fourth and Fifth. Should I tell her yes?"

"Tell her yes." I have more research to do on Lorena Montford.

Lorena's fifty-eight—a friend of hers posted a picture from her fifty-fifth birthday party on Facebook three years ago—apparently single and doesn't get into trouble. Which is disappointing.

She's had a fairly normal career path for somebody in her position: art degree, junior curator at an obscure museum, gallery assistant, bigger-gallery assistant, gallery manager, owner. Achara's been open for fifteen years, a long time for a single gallery in a small market niche.

I'm about to tell myself *move along, nothing to see here,* when I stumble across another Achara, this one in Chelsea in Manhattan. Born 2005, died 2009. In between, it became the only East Coast gallery caught up in the Ban Chiang scandal.

Ban Chiang artifacts—not just pottery, but bronzes and other cultural heritage bits—started pouring into the U.S. from east-central Thailand in the '80s. Some knuckleheads from Southern California smuggled in container loads of the stuff and pushed it into museums and private collections. The whole bunch of them got busted in 2008 after looting *ten thousand pieces* from what's still a UNESCO World Heritage Site.

The Chelsea Achara had to send sixteen pots and three bronzes back to Thailand and pay the government $46,000 in fines. The gallery closed a few months later.

"Achara" means "beautiful angel" in Thai. It's not an uncommon name. It takes me almost an hour to find a smoking gun. A post on a New York City art-watcher's blog talking about the galleries killed by the 2008 crash says:

```
Achara Asian Art, the West 26th
St. branch of a San Francisco
gallery (who thought THAT would
work???), in February 2009.
```

Aha.

It probably made sense at the time. The economy was booming, Asian buyers were starting their stampede into the art market, and rich people always need new décor ideas. But it costs a lot to open a gallery in Manhattan. It's a tough audience. How much did Lorena sink into that? How much did she lose? Did the crash kill it, or getting caught with hot pots?

And: why do it again? She should be older and wiser now. Unless… maybe, like me, she owes so much money from her past sins that she can't pay it off honestly.

However it went down, I know now that Lorena isn't a saint. She might have debts. She might have a useful amount of ethical flexibility. Maybe—for the promise of enough money—she might get sloppy again.

Chapter 8

Zero Zero is a two-story space on Folsom Street under, next to and across from newish-looking apartment complexes. This is the "new SoMa" Savannah talked about on Wednesday. The restaurant's a tangle of one-way streets away from Achara. I wonder why we're here until I realize the Norris Museum's a block west.

Savannah's waiting for me beside the seater's podium inside the front door. She's in a Michael Kors knee-length white sheath with a thick black X across her midriff. She wears it well.

She gives me a big smile and a lingering handshake. "I'm glad you could come. We're upstairs."

I follow her up the stairs (nice view). The legs of the X wrap around the waist of her dress like twin black belts.

The mezzanine is all warm woods, burgundy upholstery, and flame light pendants. The place's buzzing even though it's just past eleven-thirty. I see more grown-ups than I have anywhere else in this city except at Farallon last night. Not a hoodie anywhere.

Savannah leads me to a round banquette in the back corner under a mural of… Pinocchio? Lorena's there, wearing an eggplant silk *áo dài*. Bandineau's next to her, looking all business-semicasual in a black blazer and open-collar, pale-blue dress shirt. Once again I'm overdressed, this time in the gray Canali suit. My afternoon meeting, you know.

Bandineau pops off his seat. "Rick! Good to see you again."

We shake. "Jim. Can't say I'm surprised you're here. Having lunch next door to the museum kinda gives the game away."

He gives me a you-got-me smile. "I suppose so. Unlike the ladies, I have office hours."

I lean a hand across the table. "Lorena, thank you for the invite. That's a lovely color on you, by the way."

Again with the pink bloom on her pale cheeks. "You're so kind, Mr. Hoskins."

I slide into the banquette next to Lorena; Savannah settles in next to me. Her hip and thigh press gently against mine. It's tight; luckily, Lorena doesn't take up much room.

We make the usual what's-good-here chat while we scope out the menus. It's not until our waiter brings our drinks that I say, "So, other than sharing lunch, what's this all about?"

Bandineau says, "Straight to business, is it? I appreciate that."

Lorena folds her arms across her stomach and gives me a smile that's a few degrees cooler than the last one. "This is a way for us to get to know you better, and for you to learn about us. We'd also like to tell you what we're doing and see what part you might have in it."

That sounds promising.

There's a pause while Lorena waits for me to say something. I don't. She shifts in her seat. "When Savannah told me that she was bringing you to see me, I naturally tried to find information about you. I like to know something about my clients." I'm impressed that she can keep her kindergarten-teacher voice going while she asks whether I'm a figment. "I wasn't very successful. Why is that, Mr. Hoskins?"

Because Hoskins doesn't exist? Let's not go there yet. "Have you seen anything good come from being an internet celebrity?"

"No, I can't say that I have."

"Me neither. I spend a lot of effort making sure I have as little online presence as I can."

Savannah says, "No Facebook, no Twitter."

"Exactly. You know how I recognized you Tuesday morning? When you were looking for me on Union Square? Your website picture."

"You found it? Oh, good. There's a few Savannah *Endicotts* out there, no K. It can be embarrassing sometimes—one of them's a real kook."

"That's not the point. The point is, I didn't know you, but I looked at your website and your Facebook profile. You should do something with your privacy controls. I know what you look like, what you do, where you go, what you like to eat, and roughly where you live. Explain why it's a good idea to hand strangers all that detail."

She concentrates on her Negroni more than she needs to. When she finally puts it down, she says, "I'm my product. I mean, if we're talking about brands and marketing, I sell me. I have to be out there."

"Yes, you do. But frankly, unless we're dating, do I really need to know about your thing for mocha ice cream?"

If the lighting was just a skosh dimmer, I wouldn't notice the flush in her cheeks. Savannah sits for a moment staring into her glass, her lips doing complicated things. "I mention that a lot, don't I?"

"You do." I squeeze the hand she's resting on the table. If she can touch, so can I. "It's okay. I've been known to eat mocha ice cream too."

She squeezes back. "You see? Now I know you're a good person." She twists toward me and rests her arm on the banquette's back. "I'm surprised you're not on LinkedIn."

"I was, for a while." I turn toward Lorena and Bandineau. "I took down my profile when I made my first hundred million." Now's when I uncap the egomaniac rich guy lurking inside Hoskins. "When you get to the place I'm at, online buys you nothing. My company gets opportunities from firms that already know what it's done *in real life*."

Savannah says, "That explains your company website. One page, a phone number, and a contact form? That's old school."

"What more does it need?"

She shrugs. "Pretty pictures of all the things you've built?"

"The people who bring us work already know about that. If they don't, we have a very nice package that one of my project managers takes to their office when he goes to talk to them about what they want. In real life."

I got into this discussion with one of our clients at the gallery. I asked him roughly the same question Lorena asked me. I'm giving her the answer he gave me, cleaned up a lot. We tried not to look too far into our clients' backgrounds—we'd run a credit check, and as long as they had the money, we didn't care where it came from. I'd thought that would be the deal here. I didn't expect an interrogation.

Lorena says, "I find it interesting that the only picture I can find of you is the one attached to your Wikipedia page. It's an awful picture."

Bandineau waves his wine glass at me. "Is it accurate? Your Wiki page?"

"More or less." I wrote it. The picture's a doctored dark-and-slightly-blurry still from *Woman in Gold* of Ryan Reynolds in a suit. Not that he looks so much like me, but he doesn't look so much *unlike* me that people won't buy it when they see me in person. I give Bandineau and Lorena my best serious stare. "The rules change when you hit nine figures. That's when you go from being wealthy to being rich. I can afford to buy something very precious— anonymity. That's why you won't find much about me online. I like it that way." I notice the waiter approaching. "Here come the appetizers. Just in time." *Subject closed.*

Zero Zero is set up for family-style eating. We share the avocado bruschetta and the fried chicken thighs, which are both very good. So's the *margherita di bufala* pizza. Lorena nibbles on her arugula salad with a very serious expression, like something I said gave her indigestion.

Back to business. "Lorena, you said something about telling me what you and Jim are doing. What is that?"

She throws a look to Bandineau. He nods, wipes his mouth on a white linen napkin. "We've both noticed that you're interested in the Nam Ton wares. As I said in the exhibit the other day, I completely understand why—it's some of my favorite work, too." His hand gestures look confident and purposeful. Planned? "The challenge we face is that the museum community is pushing back against including Nam Ton in their collections. There's just not enough scholarship around it yet. They don't feel comfortable spending limited acquisition funds to bring it onboard."

He's given this speech before. Either that, or he naturally thinks in complete sentences.

Bandineau takes a sip of water. "What we're trying to do is find a few serious collectors who are interested in being pioneers in bringing on and donating Nam Ton wares. To—"

"When you say 'we,' who's 'we'?"

He nods once. "Myself, of course. A few curators in a small number of museums that have the... *vision,* let's call it, to invest early. Gallerists like Lorena who are committed to growing the market without sacrificing its integrity. Rick, I'll assume you're aware of the state of the antiquities market these days. Forgeries, looted artifacts, restrictive cultural heritage laws, restitutions. Museums are becoming gun-shy about taking anything. But we can't let our collections stagnate. When something new and extraordinary appears—like Nam Ton wares—we have to move quickly before it all disappears into private collections. So we have two choices." He holds up an index finger. "We can read the tea leaves and buy what we believe to be legal pieces that we think will be important in the future. This isn't always popular with our trustees." He adds the middle finger. "Or, we can work with collectors like you, guide your purchases so you get the best pieces with good, clean provenance, and maintain an ongoing relationship to earn your donations and your bequests."

This doesn't shock me. Museums have done this for years. Their trustees tend to be rich people who collect art. The development staff's main job is to make sure the trustees and their friends give money and art to their museum and not the competition. They're not above staging vanity exhibitions for their most promising donors. Of course, these days you just build your own museum if your pockets are deep enough. Eli Broad and the Marcianos did that in L.A.

"So today's about figuring out if I'm worthy of being one of your pet collectors?" Rude, maybe. Exactly what somebody like Hoskins would say if one of the little people suggests he hasn't passed enough tests already.

Bandineau winces. "That's not the way I'd put it at all. I apologize if I gave you that idea. We'd like to know if you're interested in building your legacy as a patron of the arts by helping us bring Nam Ton wares to this country."

Nice climbdown. "Lorena, how's this work? Will I be buying pieces from you?"

She holds her napkin to her lips until she swallows. "Yes, that's right. Jim and I work together. He's graciously volunteered to come to the gallery, talk with you about the wares we have, perhaps guide you toward the ones that would be best for your tastes and for investment potential. I handle the commercial side of things."

And he gets a piece of the action? It's convenient there's no public market for Nam Ton yet.

Lorena lofts her eyebrows at me. "Are you interested, Mr. Hoskins?"

Savannah hasn't said much since the food arrived. I don't doubt for a minute that she's heard every word. I hover my mouth over her ear. "What do you think?"

Her breath's warm on my cheek when she leans in. "I think we shouldn't talk about it here." She pulls away to give me a significant look.

"Got it." Normal voice. "You're a brave woman."

She gives me crunched eyebrows. "Why?"

"You're in a white dress, eating pizza with tomato sauce."

That brings out a sly smile. "This business isn't for wimps."

I turn to Lorena. "Let me eat on it. We'll talk in a few."

"A few" turns into almost half an hour, after we've disappeared the food and nobody has any blood left in their brains. Once the waiter's cleared the plates and we've waved off the dessert menu, I tell Lorena, "I'm interested in learning more. Hearing your goals. What you think my place in it is."

"Excellent." She leans forward far enough to see past me to Savannah. "Savannah, dear, could you please excuse us? We need to discuss some things with Mr. Hoskins."

Huh? "Wait." I put up both hands, palms out: *stop*. "She's my advisor. Anything you have to say about art, she gets to hear."

Savannah's hand touches my shoulder. "Rick—" I wave her off.

Bandineau takes a first sip of his post-lunch coffee. "It's nothing about art."

"Whatever. Savannah works for me. I decide whether she stays or goes, not you."

Lorena presses her palms together and holds her thumbs against her breastbone, almost like a Namaste. "Of course. The discussion may bring out some… *personal* information. But if you want her to be here—"

"Rick, it's okay." Savannah's hand squeezes my shoulder, then it's gone. I turn to find her standing. "I get it. I'll just go down to the bar. I need another Negroni anyway. Come down after you're done and we'll talk." She turns to the others. "Lorena, Jim. Thanks so much for the lovely lunch. Don't hurt my client, okay?"

Bandineau says, "We wouldn't dream of it."

I watch Savannah shimmy her way through the still-crowded tables. I notice Bandineau watching, too.

Lorena says, "You should be careful, Mr. Hoskins. Savannah

likes older men."

I laugh. The joke is, she's no more than two years younger than me—I did the math on her LinkedIn profile. I just *look* like I'm ten years older because of the premature gray (thanks, Dad).

"Let's cut to the chase here." I pull my wallet, slide out the American Express Centurion card, and hand it to Lorena. "You're a vendor. Call the vendor number. Get my limit." There isn't one. I could buy a car with the thing. Maybe a house.

Her lips get flat for a moment, then she hands the card back to me. "I'm certain you have money. The fact remains that we don't know who you are." If anything, she's speaking slower.

This is when the real Hoskins would walk. I don't have that option, but that doesn't mean I have to be nice about it. "My money's green. How much more do you need?"

Bandineau pushes his open hand toward the tabletop. "This isn't personal, Rick. Please don't take it that way. We need to know— now more than ever—who we're doing business with." He touches one hand to his chest, and the other to Lorena's bicep. "I'm sure you've checked into our backgrounds, or you will. We wouldn't expect anything less, and I hope you'll be satisfied with what you find. We need to do the same."

Lorena says, "This isn't a simple purchase, Mr. Hoskins. We want to establish a long-term business relationship with you"—out comes a wan little smile, no teeth—"but we need to do that with our eyes open. Surely you understand that."

I lean my elbows on the tabletop and figure whether I can push back more. I don't want to scare them off, but I also need to stay in character. And Hoskins would rip them both a new one for this.

The waiter comes with the bill in a black vinyl folder. Bandineau takes it before I can even reach for it. I hold my hand out to him— *give it here*—but he shakes his head. "I wouldn't hear of it. The museum's development budget'll pick this up."

Do they know that? Not my problem. I turn toward Lorena. "Look. I don't *have* to prove a damn thing to you. My privacy's more important than your comfort." They both wince when I say that. "If you *need*—absolutely, no-shit *need*—something from me, tell me what it is, why you deserve it, and how you'll protect it. Because if something I tell you in confidence gets out, you're both out of business. Understand?"

Bandineau and Lorena exchange indigestion-related expressions. Their eyes and jaws have a short conversation. Then Lorena says slowly, "References. Galleries you've worked—"

"You don't need that. Who I've worked with before doesn't concern you. Next."

Lorena gulps. "We'd like an idea of what your collection looks like now. Also, how will you keep the pieces you buy? We want them to be safe."

I give her a sour look, but don't object. It's not too unreasonable an ask.

Bandineau clears his throat. "You mentioned LACMA." He places the check holder upright on the table with a credit card sticking out of the top. "One of the few things we could find online was a press release about a long-term loan you made to the museum." *Wait, what?* "I'd love to know who you worked with there. I've wanted to talk to someone about getting Nam Ton into their Asian collection, but I'm not having any success."

It takes a few beats to remember—that press release was a setup for something Allyson was working on a few months ago. I never found out what. I guess she's got hooks into somebody inside the museum's administration. "You're lucky you found that. I've been after them to take it down." I lean back and pretend to think about his request. "Asking me to share a contact is like asking me to share a mistress. I'll have to think about this and talk to my contact. Not all our arrangements are… official, let's say."

Bandineau's got the look of a cat that got a big, fat pigeon for Christmas. "I understand. It would be a huge help, and a gesture of goodwill on your part."

Sure.

Hoskins has to turn into a real person.

Chapter 9

I tell Savannah the abridged version of what happened as we wait on the sidewalk in front of Zero Zero for my town car to show. "What the hell do they think they're doing? I'm looking to buy pots, not nuclear codes."

She smooths my sleeve. "It's not personal. It's almost exactly what they told three of my other clients."

She's got three clients in this thing? So much for figuring out who Our Client is. "Doesn't matter. How many Twitter followers do I need before I can buy in?"

"It's not that." She's using her calming-the-angry-dog voice. "It's strange to find someone prominent, like you, who doesn't have a social media presence. They're just being careful. My clients are all in tech and they're everywhere. It's really easy to check up on them." A skeptical look. "Unlike *some* people I know. Tell me the truth— did your ex really try to rob a museum in England?"

Ah. The Portsmouth project. It's… a long story. "You know the great thing about exes? You don't have to keep track of them. But if she did, I'm sure she had a reason, good or not."

"I'm sure." Her face turns serious. She folds her arms and glances at the sidewalk. "Rick… uh, thank you for defending me in there. You didn't have to."

"Yes I did, and you're welcome."

"No, really. It was very thoughtful of you, but—"

"If you don't draw lines, people don't know where to stop." More wisdom I picked up at the gallery. "Jim and Lorena know where to stop now."

"They're friends. It's really not a problem."

"You work for me. Nobody kicks my employees out of a meeting without my say-so. You're representing me, right? You're on my side *only*, friends or not. Right?"

"Well…" She sputters a little, then lets out half a laugh. "Yes.

Of course."

"Good." The town car's finally trundling down the street toward us. "The chariot's here. Can I give you a lift?"

Savannah holds her hands palms-up and moves them up and down like a balance scale. "Hmm. Limo, Uber. Limo, Uber. Let me think." The black Lincoln purrs up to the curb right in front of us. "This'll do."

I open the door for her. She knows exactly how to gracefully get into the back seat of a limo while wearing a tight skirt. I think she's done this before, and not just with me. I get in and tell the driver, "Fifty California."

Savannah quizzes me on the L.A. art scene for a couple stop-and-go blocks. After a while, I ask, "This sounds like more than just curiosity. What's your interest?"

She swivels toward me and plants a hand on the seat an inch or so from my hip. "You're right. I'm thinking of branching out. I love it here, but... well, it's still a small market. L.A. seems so, I don't know, wide open. Is it?"

I'd been wondering if she'd make this pitch. Now that's it's out in the open, I know exactly what her next ask is going to be. "It depends. There's a lot of art, and a lot of buyers, and a lot of galleries. But there's a lot of advisors, too. You'd have competition."

"I have my niche."

"Yeah. There's a lot of Asian money there, so that might work for you. Do you do Asian contemporary?"

"I can. I've met a few artists. I don't like it as much, but I work that space here." She settles into her seat. Here comes the pitch... "Maybe next time I go down there, you can show me around? Maybe introduce me to some people you know?"

"We'll see. You'll pay *me* then, right? Because I'll be the advisor?"

Savannah giggles. "You're funny."

She checks her phone after it makes a popping-bubble sound. While her head's turned, I notice what looks like shadowing on the back edge of her dress' left arm hole. It's not, though; it's wear. I'd never guess that she'd keep dresses long enough for them to start falling apart.

She asks, "How long does your meeting go?"

"Two to three hours. Why?"

"Lorena just texted. She wants me to bring you to the gallery after you're done."

So soon? "Why?"

"She doesn't say."

"Ask her."

Are they going to let me in the tent without passing their test? That would be great, but I don't think so. Maybe they'll tell me to get lost. I doubt that, too. Lorena's going to drill Hoskins some more about his background? More likely, and a conversation I'm not prepared to have yet.

After a few moments, there's another popping bubble. "She says it's a good thing and you'll like it."

There's no graceful way to skip it. "Tell her I can make it by five."

More skittering; another dead soap bubble. "She'll be waiting."

We eventually reach 50 California, a towering concrete-and-glass skyscraper in the Financial District. Good thing there's no 1:30 meeting—it's 1:31 now. I get out, then lean into the open door to tell the driver, "Take her wherever she wants to go."

Savannah says, "Tahiti, please."

I say, "Continental U.S. only."

She pushes out her lower lip. "I knew there was a catch."

I pull up a table at Peet's Coffee at Battery and Bush after the town car disappears. Yes, Peet's. I can't sit in a Starbucks for more than ten minutes anymore without needing to wipe down tables and sweep.

The next three hours give me time to review what happened at lunch and catch up. I check in again with Len. Will I miss that if everything works out? That would be ironic.

The Smithsonian's Freer and Sackler galleries have an amazing website about the ceramics of mainland Southeast Asia. While I go through every page on my phone, I think about how to prove that Hoskins exists.

Richard Danforth Hoskins has a paper trail. He's got a California driver's license, a well-used passport, a few high-value credit cards, and a smorgasbord of bank and investment accounts. He's got very nice credit histories with all three big agencies. There's the Wikipedia page I wrote and the company website somebody else put together. The company has a real L.A. County business license. Hoskins had some semi-coherent things to say in a newspaper piece about urban mixed-use development (it was early, and they caught me off-guard) and a couple brief mentions in trade publications late last year. His ex-wife was famous in Europe for a few days last December.

This apparently doesn't make him tall enough to go on the ride with Lorena and Bandineau.

So what does?

Chapter 10

Savannah's waiting for me at Achara's front door. "Did you walk?"

"It's only ten blocks. I've been sitting on my butt all day. Walking felt good."

She folds her arms and peers at me like she's looking over glasses. "Are you sure you didn't just lose your car?"

I like her spirit, but Hoskins needs her to know her place. "How I get here doesn't matter to you." I pull open the door. "After you."

Lorena greets us in front of her desk—an old teak trestle table with a glass-covered top—in the back of the non-statue gallery. When we get done with the pleasantries, she says, "Savannah told me what caught your fancy at the museum the other day. I'd like to show you something."

She steers me to an antique sideboard against the long wall. There are three pots on it, each on its own red-silk plinth. The overhead spots reflect on the smooth, polished black surfaces. I bend to take a closer look. "Phimai Black."

Savannah says, "You're learning."

"I'm teachable."

Lorena stands to my right with her hands folded in front of her hips. "Is there anything you'd like me to tell you about them?"

I can't count how many times I was in that same place next to a client, waiting to do the same thing. "Not now. Just let me look at them."

"Of course."

If I didn't have to be all about Nam Ton, I could get to like these. I studied the Phimai Black tradition after I saw it at the Norris. It came from the upper Mun River valley in northeastern Thailand during the Iron Age. Not all the pottery from there is black, but the blackware's the most striking work. The shapes are simple and streamlined, and the decoration's tastefully minimalist.

The left-hand ware's a voluptuous round-bottomed urn, maybe a foot wide, with an everted rim (it curves out rather than in) and a cylindrical neck. The shoulder and body meet at a soft angle, like the crease in a luxury car's fender. There's some repair on the neck and rim. The burnished surface glows in the soft light. I want to rub my palms all over it.

"That one is lovely, isn't it?" Lorena's slipped on latex gloves. She gently rolls the pot on its display ring so I can see inside. "Wares of this form are typically funerary vessels. They were used to bury infants."

Gag. "You had to tell me that."

"It's important that you know how these were used."

"Did this one…?"

"I have no idea."

Moving on. A shallow bowl is the center piece, maybe nine inches in diameter. A smooth curve, a small shoulder, an indented rim. The inside's polished in a way that left a swirl of shiny black lines against the matte-black field. Nice. "Please don't tell me they ate the hearts of their enemies in this."

Savannah giggles. Lorena says, "Oh, no, nothing like that. That would be Mesoamerican. This is a simple bowl."

"Good." On the right side is a tall jar with a lid. The jar's charcoal-gray body is nearly spherical with matte horizontal bands burnished into the glossy surface. The neck and rim are shaped like a cone with the point cut off, flaring up from the body. The lid's like the bowl next door, except slightly deeper and obviously reconstructed from sherds. Very nice.

I turn to Lorena. "These are awfully pretty. Thanks for showing them to me."

She nods. "Would you like to take any of them home?"

Just what I thought. Get me hooked on the process so I'll go along with her test to get to the Nam Ton wares. Well, I can play. "I'd like that a lot."

I scan the pottery again. The bowl's kinda *meh*. The funerary vessel's pretty and in good shape, but the idea that it's a baby coffin squicks me out. That was never an issue with paintings. That leaves the lidded vessel, my favorite. "What's the provenance on this piece?" Meaning, *what's its history?*

"I can show you that now." Lorena glides to her desk and returns to carefully hand me a typewritten sheet. "Of course, I'll give you this and the documentation."

"Sure." There's not much to it:

```
Phimai tradition, est. 500-600
C.E.

Excavation date & place unknown

Acquired at Non Sung market in
March 1960 by Maj. & Mrs. David
Johnson, U.S. Air Force
```

The Thais passed their foundational cultural heritage law in 1961. Exporting these pots became illegal then. Is the 1960 date just a coincidence? And the buyers might as well be Mr. and Mrs. John Smith. "How good is this?"

Lorena gives me an opaque look. "As good as gold, Mr. Hoskins."

Meaning it's bought and paid for? If the provenance really is sketchy, this is where I become an accomplice to trafficking in protected cultural heritage items. A minor felony, but that's all it takes to put me back inside. But that's why I'm here. "Starting price?"

"Four thousand. Very reasonable for a piece this special."

Even though this stuff is super old, it's not all that expensive. Last night after reading had made my eyes cross, I started looking for auction records to see where prices are. There aren't any. I went through the 198 past lots that came up when I searched for "Thai" at Sotheby's; three were ceramics. Bonhams had *nada*.

To find prices for Thai pottery, you have to go to a few off-brand online storefronts and... eBay. Seriously. The asking prices are all over the place, and of course you can't tell what anything actually sold for. The most expensive piece I found was a Ban Chiang pot for $2600.

Bottom line: the prices for the ceramics here are exactly what Lorena says they are, with whatever room there is for bargaining, if any. And I thought the valuations of *paintings* are opaque...

I aim an eyebrow at Lorena. "Seriously? I thought it'd be expensive. I'll take it."

Lorena gently lifts the pot and plinth. "I hope you'll enjoy it. Let's go to my desk. If you don't mind, I'll need some information for the receipt."

The door gong interrupts as I give her Hoskins' phone number and email. Lorena glances up from her computer and finds Savannah scoping out a pair of small bronze dancing Shivas on an upright cabinet. "Savannah, dear, could you please see who just came in? And please lock the door—it's past closing time."

"I can do that." Savannah hurries off to the other side of the gallery.

We finish the ritual of paying for the pot. For $4,750, including sales tax and Savannah's commission, I become the owner of a 1,500-year-old relic of a lost culture. Somehow it's not nearly hard enough or expensive enough. This seems wrong.

Lorena hands me the receipt. "Would you like for me to wrap it for you so you can take it home?"

"That'd be great. Thanks."

She hefts the pot off the desk and disappears through a semi-hidden door. I wonder—what's back there besides butcher paper and packing peanuts?

I drift into the statue gallery. Savannah stands close to a tall, rangy guy wearing a beat-up brown-leather bomber jacket over boot-cut jeans. Judging from the miles on his face and the sprinkles of gray on his temples, he's probably somewhere in his late forties or early fifties. They're laughing at something.

Savannah notices me and pulls the guy's elbow to point him in my direction. "Trey, this is my new client, Rick Hoskins. Rick, this is Trey McCarran, one of my old clients."

"I ain't that old." Good god: the man has a Texas accent.

We close the distance. He has big hands and a handshake that could probably flip a bull or something. He nods to me. "Good to meet you, sir."

"Please, call me Rick. You're not from around here, are you?"

One side of his mouth smiles. "Nope, sure not. Fort Worth. You?"

"L.A. How long've you been with Savannah?"

Savannah's parked herself face-on to the two of us. "He's not anymore. I taught him all he knows, then he decided he didn't need me." She says this while her mouth tries to keep a grin under wraps, so I guess she's not too upset by it.

McCarran scratches the back of his neck while he shakes his head. Just like cowboys do in the movies. "Now darlin', that ain't the way it was." On top of the accent, he talks almost as slow as Lorena does. "The way it was, Rick, is if I spent any more time with this here girl, I'd've had to marry her, and the missus wouldn't cotton to that."

"Savannah?" Lorena's voice rings from the back of the room. "Who came in?"

"It's Trey. He's here to pick up something?"

"Yes, of course. Could you please help me for a moment? Mr. McCarran, I'll be with you very soon."

"Yes'm." We both watch Savannah rush off. He turns to me and hooks his thumbs on the front of his belt. "How long you been with Savannah?"

"This is the first week. I just bought my first pot. Phimai blackware."

He nods again. "Congratulations. I got me a couple of them. Reminds me some of San Ildefonso pottery. Pueblo in New Mexico? Maria Martinez?" I shrug. "Beautiful work. Prettiest thang I've seen that ain't female."

Is this guy for real? He's like a younger Sam Elliot without the moustache. But I wonder what a Texas cowboy's doing here, in this place. So I ask.

"Well"—it's a two-syllable word—"I used to collect Pueblo pottery. But then I saw some Asian work and thought, 'I gotta get me some of that.' So I started coming here. Lorena's got a new piece waitin' for me."

"What style?"

Before he can answer, Lorena glides around the corner carrying a foot-square white cake box that probably doesn't have a cake in it. "Mr. McCarran, it's so good to see you again." She hands him the box carefully. "I hope you'll enjoy this."

He hefts the box a couple times. "If it's even half as purty as the pictures"—*pitchers*—"I surely will. Thank you, ma'am."

Savannah marches in, cradling a box about half again as big as the pot I bought. She hands it to me like an award. "Your very first pot. Are you excited?"

It's heavier than I thought, but not enough to be annoying to carry. "I'll be excited when I get it home in one piece."

She holds out her hand. I trap the box against my chest with my left hand and shake with my right. She says, "I've had fun. I hope you have, too."

"Sure."

"Call me when you're coming back. I'll work out something for us to do." She lets me go and points to the box. "Your pot needs a friend."

That gets a chuckle out of me. "We can't let it get lonely. I'll be in touch."

Savannah scurries to unlock the front door. After a final round of goodbyes, McCarran and I hit the sidewalk at about the same time. He's almost half a head taller than I am. "It's almost six. You got someplace you need to be?"

"Why do you ask?"

He shifts his box to under his left arm, like it really is full of pastry. "Well... how's about I buy you a drink and we can chat some?"

Hm. If he's been around Savannah and Lorena for a while, he might have some useful info. If he's seen both of them, maybe he's dealt with Bandineau, too. It's worth a shot. I don't have anything planned. "I never turn down a free drink. You got a place?"

He nods. "As it happens, I do. A few blocks thataway." He points toward Union Square over his left shoulder. "Rough area, but nothing the two of us cain't handle, I reckon."

The middle of upmarket shopping heaven's just two blocks away. How rough can it be? "Lead on."

Chapter 11

It's only eight blocks from the gallery, but we take a cab. I see why. Once we get about three blocks west of Union Square on Geary, we leave the happy tourists packing Saks and Neiman's shopping bags and enter *Blade Runner*. We pass homeless people dragging filthy blankets or roller bags covered with duct tape. Dark bundles of humanity or stuff (sometimes it's hard to tell which) crowd the sidewalks along Jones. When we climb out of the cab, some collection of rags across the street is yelling about killer alien hipsters.

Bourbon and Branch is behind an unmarked wooden Craftsman-style door at the corner of Jones Street and O'Farrell. The sign at the corner says "Anti-Saloon League." Cute.

"This here's called the Tenderloin," McCarran tells me as we wait in line. (Yes. A line to get into a bar.) "Reckon you can see why."

"Jesus. This is worse than back home." Which is saying something, given all the homeless in Santa Monica.

"This' just the edge." He points west. "Few blocks thataway, it gets real ugly."

Hard to believe. For a complete contrast, everybody in line with us is a millennial and dresses like it. We creep forward like arthritic snails, I finally ask, "What's this line all about?"

"Reservations."

"Seriously? For a bar?"

"Yup."

We get to the front of the line. The black guy in a fedora at the door pushes a buzzer on the wall. The door opens. A woman in a white dress shirt, red suspenders, and hair the color of drying blood says, "Name?"

"McCarran."

She gives me the side-eye. "Your reservation is for one."

"I don't reckon that'll be a problem tonight, Eleanor." He must be a regular.

She scans me up and down. Maybe I'm too square to come in. "Yes sir, Mr. McCarran. Password?"

"Ballantine's." He just about doubles the syllables.

"Right this way, sir."

It's seriously dark inside. Once my eyes adjust, I see a narrow but tall space with a pressed-tin ceiling and a white chandelier that looks like the mother ship for a race of alien dandelions. We pass between small booths on the left and the bar to our right and slide into a booth against the back wall. It's nearly big enough to keep us from knocking knees. As busy as the place is, it's strangely quiet.

We order from menus pressed between polished, laser-cut wood planks. There's a whole page of absinthe varieties. I'm not liking the vodka choices, so I throw the dice on a Clase Azul Plata tequila while McCarran goes for a flight of bourbon.

Once the waitress leaves, I ask, "So Trey, what's your business?"

He gives me the crooked smile. "Software."

"Seriously?"

He puts up his hands. "I know. Don't look much like a tech tycoon. Surely don't sound like one. But there you go."

He gives me a long, down-home story about how his company makes management systems for farmers and ranchers, which sounds like it's more complicated than counting the cows. He's here because Google bought him out. I tell him my company does project design and management consulting with smaller A&E firms doing specialized urban development projects. It strikes me that both our stories are the kinds that shut down the "what do you do?" party conversation pretty fast.

The drinks arrive: mine in a large snifter, his in three small snifters set in hollows in a wooden block. Mine smells like honey and tropical fruit and it's sweet on my first sip. Not what I expect from tequila.

McCarran asks, "How'd you come by Savannah?"

The Art Nouveau-style table lamp throws just enough light through its mica shade to make McCarran's face a pale shape across the table. His accent still throws me, but I get this spidey-sense feeling the question isn't as casual as it sounds. "One of her clients referred me."

He takes a sip, then rolls it around in his mouth before

swallowing. He waves the snifter at me. "This is some fine liquor. Who referred you? I might know the man."

I know tech's a small world, but I doubt it's that small. "He asked me to keep it quiet. I guess he's not very public about his collecting. Do you know a lot of her clients?"

"A few. That is one hard-workin' girl, let me tell you. Ain't hard to look at, neither. What's she done for you so far?"

Here I thought I'd be asking the questions. "She took me to Achara and another gallery, then to the Norris Museum." He nods knowingly. "You too?"

"Yup. First thing. You meet Bandineau?"

"Yes, I did. What's your take on him?"

McCarran blisses out on another draw of bourbon, which takes a few moments to pass. "Well, I reckon you could dress that ol' boy in a shiny suit and drop him in a used car lot in West Texas and he'd do just fine for hisself."

"You think he's a huckster."

"I do. What do you think?"

"I'm surprised he's not running the museum."

"Ain't gotta have the title to do the job, y'know."

"You want to explain that?"

McCarran finally finishes off his first snifter and settles into his bench. "Not too long after I started with Savannah, I went to the museum to see the director. By my own self, not with Savannah. I told him I wanted to chat a bit about the donations I'd made and what else I could do to be of service to that fine institution. 'Course, first thing that ol' boy does is call Bandineau."

"Not the development director?"

"Nope. Bandineau. Once he showed, he did all the talkin'. The director just set there noddin' and smilin'. And I thought, well, now we know who's got the bit in his mouth, and who's holdin' the reins." He leans his elbows on the little wooden table. "Y'know, before this, Bandineau told me I should talk to him if'n I had any questions or wanted somethin' from the museum. He was just a mite riled that I went to the director and not him."

Interesting. I know only about five percent of what's going on, but even I can tell this is news I can eventually use. "Makes you wonder if the director knows what Bandineau's up to." Whatever that is.

"Don't it, though."

He watches me like he expects me to say something else, so I do. "What's in that box?"

He stares into my eyes for a few moments, glances at the box on the bench beside him, then back to me. I can see him make a decision. "Ever hear of the Nam Ton culture?"

Score. "Yeah. We saw it at the museum. That's what's in there?"

"Yup. A bowl, eight inches across maybe. Beautiful piece of work. That what you're interested in?"

"Yeah. Today at lunch, I got the speech about how they're looking for collectors to be pioneers, yadda yadda yadda."

McCarran nods along with me. "Yup. Heard that one too. But they sold you Phimai ware. Why's that?"

How much do I want to tell this guy? It sounds like he's been down at least part of the road I'm on; maybe he's got some bright ideas. But he asks a lot of questions and I can't tell yet why. Okay, I'm asking questions too, but I know why.

"I'm not sure. I said some nice things about it at the museum— maybe they thought I'd like to buy some. But I said nice things about the Nam Ton stuff too. Maybe not enough."

McCarran starts in on his second snifter. I can't tell if he buys what I just said. "You got a Savannah in L.A.?"

"No. I was collecting in a medium and period I understand, so I didn't need one. How'd you find her?"

"Weren't hard."

Right. We sit there watching each other drink. I get the feeling he's told me all he's going to tonight. I don't think it's anywhere near all he knows, though.

He swirls the last hit of bourbon in his glass. "How much d'you know about what Montford and Bandineau are doing?"

There's a couple ways I can go with this. I could pretend to know more than I do and play all mysterious while I try to dig more out of him. I don't get the feeling that'll work this time around. So I go with Door #2. "Some, not much. How about you?"

He shrugs. "Some more, I reckon."

"Anything you should warn me about?"

"Nope. I survived. Reckon you will, too." He reaches into his jacket, pulls a business card, and spins it like a playing card into the hand I've got on the table. "Let's me and you keep in touch. Compare notes, like. Maybe one of us'll need to warn the other down the road. What'd'ya say?"

Do I need somebody else maybe poking into Hoskins' life, especially when I can't figure his angle? No. Blowing him off may make him more curious, which is worse. I take my business-card case out of my inside pocket—it's a 1920s stainless-steel cigarette case with Art Deco enamel trim—and toss a card next to his drink caddy. "Send me a picture of your pot when you get it unwrapped."

"Will do." He holds my card so the lamp's yellow light can brighten it enough to read. It doesn't say much: *Richard Hoskins, Topanga Development Partners,* a phone and an email. It disappears into his inside pocket. "Send me one of yours, too. I always like me some blackware."

"Sure." I pocket his card without looking at it, then finish the rest of my tequila. "Trey, thanks for the drink."

He shakes my hand. "Been a pleasure. I hope we can help"—*hep*—"each other out down the way sometime."

We'll see about that.

Chapter 12

I order a crabcake sandwich at the Clock Bar off the St. Francis' lobby and check out Trey McCarran on my phone while I eat. His card is as minimal as Hoskins': *Trey McCarran, President and CEO, Demeter Systems, Ft. Worth, Texas, USA*, an email and a phone. His is white text on leaf green; Hoskins' is black text on heavy cream stock. Otherwise, they're equally uninformative.

He's got a Wikipedia page that tracks his story, even with his real picture. I guess the federal probation system isn't interested in him. There's plenty on the wider web about Demeter Systems—a bunch on the one in Bangalore, but a fair amount for the Texas one. The company's site is nice, mobile-friendly with lots of pictures of happy farmers with happy cows. There's even a photo of McCarran out in a field with a bunch of geeky-looking guys and one hottie (not Savannah). Another hit's for a press release on the Google website announcing Demeter's buyout.

The Trey McCarran I met seems to get around. He appears semi-regularly on the company's Facebook page, though he doesn't have his own profile. He's quoted in magazines with exciting names like *Progressive Farmer* and *Dairy Today*. He pops up now and then in *Fort Worth*, the local lifestyle magazine. I spend $49 of the client's money to get McCarran's data from an aggregator I used at the gallery to get the dope on clients. What they give me is more detailed than Hoskins' sheet but not nearly as messy as some of my ex-clients'.

Is McCarran for real? I wonder about that while I finish my sandwich and my Drake's 1500 pale ale. He seemed awfully curious about me and not too anxious to talk about himself. The normal rich guy's favorite thing to talk about is himself.

Maybe the Cowboy Way is to not brag.

Am I so used to people having an angle that I see shadows where there aren't any?

Something else crawls out of my brain while I'm in the elevator.

Bandineau said something at lunch that didn't make an impression until now. *We need to know—now more than ever—who we're doing business with.*

I wish I'd caught that right then so I could've asked. Why "now more than ever"? What's changed? Does he know the feds are looking at him? Does he think I might be an undercover fed? Not that he'd tell me the truth, but even the lie would've been interesting.

I stand at one of my suite's windows and watch the forests of lights blink and shimmer. Watching but not seeing. My head's busy with the Hoskins problem.

How do you know somebody's really who they say they are? ID? That's easy to fake. Talk to their friends? They may not be real friends, or even real people. Social media? Real people cook up fake profiles (ask anybody on a dating app); why can't a fake person?

I can probably get Olivia to get the client to vouch for me. I can maybe get Olivia to dig up other random people who'll be willing to say they know Hoskins. They'll just be voices of people Lorena's never heard of. Probably not enough.

Plus, Lorena wants to know about Hoskins' collection. I had to design one for him on my first project, so at least I have that already. A list is one thing, though; seeing canvases on walls is another.

Bandineau's hot to talk to my "contact" at LACMA. It sounded like it could be a deal-breaker for him. How'll that work?

One by one, my options fall on the floor and break. By the end of my second minibar beer, there's only one option left. It's hideously complex and it's got at least a thousand different ways of going wrong. But it's the only thing I can think of to get the job done.

And it has to happen in Los Angeles.

Hoskins lives in L.A. So do I. So do a lot of people who know me: FBI agents, ex-clients, people whose businesses or lives I destroyed with my testimony, vendors who got screwed out of money we owed them when the FBI shut down the gallery. If one of them recognizes me, it's game over.

The whole game. Hoskins' identity, his credibility with Lorena and Bandineau. I'd never get another shot at them. The project would be over.

I can't risk that. Too much is at stake.

Freedom.

Yeah, that. I'm like Pavlov's pooch; I think of that word and I start to drool. If I do this thing and it goes bad, I won't get that freedom. I'll be lucky to keep what I have. If I don't do it, the project's basically over. I won't get any farther with Bandineau or Lorena, won't move on to the next link in the chain, won't get the client what he needs. What *I* need.

I spend a lot of time grinding this over, coming at it from different angles. I pace a couple miles around the suite's living room. I pick up the discarded options, try to piece them together, see if they've changed since I threw them away. They haven't.

Finally, it comes to me: *you can't think your way out of this.*

I remember a scene in *Indiana Jones and the Last Crusade* where Indy is trying to get through some insanely lethal puzzle palace in Petra and he comes to a point where the clue is, *make a leap of faith.* It looks like he'll fall into a bottomless hole if he does anything. Indy solves the puzzle (not a spoiler—he always does) in his typical sideways manner and moves on, but he does have to make a leap of faith.

Maybe I do too.

But it's a long damn way down.

Olivia asks "How may I help you?" once we get past the usual greetings.

"Three things. Can you ask the client if anything's changed with this project recently? I heard something today that makes me think it has."

"Change of what sort?"

"I don't know. Something that'd make the two subjects jumpy." The "two subjects" being Lorena and Bandineau.

"I'll need to ask Allyson. Only she can speak with the clients. By the by, she would like a progress report."

Great. "It hasn't even been a week yet."

"I'm certain she's aware of that. Please send it to me this evening unless you fancy an impromptu visit."

Given how we left things after Vail, a visit's the last thing either of us needs. "I'll send you something in a while. Second: the client needs to vouch for me with the gallery. They made it clear this isn't optional."

"Oh, dear. Right, noted. And your third wish?"

"Three more wishes?"

"No. That violates the rules of magic. Choose wisely."

I explain Lorena's challenge and Bandineau's need to talk to LACMA. Olivia waits until I'm done before she pelts me with questions. Can you do X? Did you consider Y? Everything I'd already thought of and dropped in the trash. She runs out of ideas after a while. I'm not looking forward to the obvious next question because she won't like the answer.

"What do you propose?" *That* question.

I make my leap of faith. My brain's been working on this for a while and it's filled in a lot of details while I've dealt with other things. It still feels like I'm describing a movie while I lay out the plan.

Olivia's ominously quiet after I finish. She sighs, clears her throat. "This will be… expensive." Her accent makes even bad news sound good. Not that this is news.

"It's gonna cost a mint. It all depends on how happy the client wants to make the feds."

"This is, of course, vital to the success of your project."

"If we don't do this, the project's over."

"I see."

More silence. The longer she doesn't say anything, the more nervous I get. Just asking for this could end the project—or my part in it.

"I'll have to ask Allyson, of course. But it does sound like a spot of fun. Tell me more."

I'm up by seven the next morning—sheer luxury, considering I usually have to be out the door at four to get to work—and run a three-mile loop that takes me down to the waterfront (called "the

Embarcadero" here), through the Financial District, and back to Union Square. I see boutique coffee places setting up their outside tables and sandwich boards next to bushes homeless dudes are sleeping in. I pass well-scrubbed human whippets out doing their jogs or power walks in their Under Armor and high-end Nikes, dodging street crews power-washing barf off the sidewalks. I spot a ragged guy snoring at the foot of the palatial glass-and-granite Apple Store overlooking Union Square.

The local TV news is all about some tech dude who ODed on some kind of high-powered heroin, the third one this month. I guess they're not as smart as they're supposed to be.

My work phone rings while I'm shaving. It's Olivia. "Allyson's convinced you're barking mad."

"She's not the first one. What else did she say?"

"The client has approved your proposal. Allyson will be watching very closely, so you'd best make a good job of it." It may be interference on the line, but I think I hear a little chuckle. "Let's make Mr. Hoskins a living person, shall we?"

Chapter 13

Frank Petri once told me, "Ya gotta have a story, kid. The mark buys the story."

During my stay at Federal Prison Camp Pensacola (a.k.a. PEN, and yeah, we laughed about that), I worked in the library with Frank, who was doing seven-to-ten for a lot of charges that were different ways of saying "con man."

According to Frank—who'd gone twenty-six years on the grift before getting sent up, so I figure he knew his stuff—a con is like an advertising campaign. You have to hook a mark's heart, not his brain. Why else do you think Budweiser has so many ponies and puppies in its ads? Why do charities use pictures of babies? That charity should run a picture of the number 429,000, because that's how many people died of malaria last year. Instead, they have some cute little girl with dirt on her face, crying. "Esperanza's mother died of malaria last year. Help save her father. Give to…" And the wallets open. Stories do that.

What I really need is to tell Bandineau and Lorena a story to stoke their warm feelings toward Hoskins. Giving Lorena a look at Hoskins' Amex card? Tactical mistake. That's like showing her a bank statement. It may satisfy her brain, but not her heart.

Hoskins needs a narrative.

Like, why's he interested in art? Why does he want the Nam Ton wares so much? What will he bring to Bandineau's scam? All very personal, and all best shown rather than told.

While that swirls around my head, I think: Bandineau alone? Invite Lorena, too? That feels wrong to me for a reason I can't put my finger on. Maybe she's not as invested as Bandineau? I can't take that chance.

Savannah? Hmm. *She's* invested. I think she's playing her own narrative involving Hoskins. She's been flirting with him since they (we?) met. If she buys into the tale I'm telling—and she's already partway there—she can help convince Bandineau.

Maybe I should've been nicer to her. I can still fix that.

I need to drop them into an ongoing story about who Hoskins is and why they want him on the team. There's only one setting where I can do that.

That's why I proposed to Olivia that we invite Bandineau into Hoskins' home. He can see some of Hoskins' collection, then meet the LACMA guy.

Two things about this idea absolutely scare the shit out of me.

I've already mentioned the L.A. thing. I still don't know how that'll work. I have to stay away from any vendors or workers we used at the gallery. I need to stay out of Beverly Hills entirely or somebody might try to run me over with their Bentley. I'll be on red alert every time I go outside.

The other problem: Bandineau's certainly been in rich people's homes and knows what they look like. Likewise Savannah. Luckily, so have I.

Unfortunately, we don't have time to meticulously prop the venue. I'm at fifty-five days and counting, which can go by like *that*. We need to surround the marks with activity to keep them from looking too closely at things. Distract them, play on the social inhibition against tossing somebody else's drawers in their own house. Which means a lot more people involved, and a lot more moving pieces.

So all I have to do is build Hoskins a home, write a play… and make sure nobody in the real world knows.

The house is key. If the house and its location aren't perfect, the rest doesn't matter.

Hoskins—like me—is an ex-architect. He won't live in some nasty McMansion or an overblown Versailles replica. He'd probably design and build his own home. We can't do that.

If he bought a house, it'd have a good design, and probably an interesting one. He likes old things, so it's probably an old house with character rather than some white cube on a hill. Since he's not into publicity, he won't have a famous house. People keep track of buildings designed by Wright or Schindler or Neutra or Gehry; they know who owns the Chemosphere (the UFO-looking place on Mulholland) and the movie-star homes. So as much as I'd love to score a Case Study House, it ain't happening.

The house needs to be big enough to be credible. The bigger it is, the harder it'll be to prep it, and the better the odds that somebody will get into places they shouldn't. I decide that Hoskins doesn't do big parties at this home (I'm sure he has others; I need to figure out where); anything with more than a dozen guests goes to an event space.

We can trade off size for view and keep the apparent price high enough to get our point across. This means the Hollywood Hills, Laurel Canyon, Beverly Park, Beverly Glen, and Bel Air, all in the Santa Monica Mountains where the other Masters of the Universe have the whole L.A. basin at their feet literally as well as metaphorically.

It's possible to rent mansions (and everything else) in L.A. Some agencies book them by the night, like Airbnb for the one percent. We can't use those. The last thing we need is for Bandineau or Savannah to leaf through a *Los Angeles* magazine, see an ad, and realize it's Hoskins' house in the picture.

Likewise, it'd be useful if the deed's held by a corporation or trust in case somebody gets the bright idea to research the ownership.

I email Olivia my longish checklist. After a few minutes, she replies, You neglected to mention the color of the drapes.

It's good to know she can do sarcasm. Not purple. It's a wish list. Do the best you can.

Once I'm back in L.A., I send McCarran a picture of my pot, then repack it carefully until I have some reason to display it. Too bad; it's just as pretty here as it was in the gallery.

McCarran sends me a picture that evening. His Nam Ton bowl is gorgeous. The ghost-white sides flare out from a narrow footring to a slightly everted rim; the interior is entirely cobalt blue. It surprises me how much I want it. All his email says is, "Keep in touch."

◪

While Olivia's trying to nail down a house, I work on the second most important part of Hoskins' story: his collection.

We don't need the whole thing at his home; just enough to convince the marks he has one. The list I made almost a year ago included all real paintings that had sold at auction to corporate or anonymous buyers. That makes tracking their current locations next to impossible (a good thing) but also means we can't get to them (a bad thing).

There's an easy-ish answer to this problem. Unfortunately, it falls in an extremely gray legal area. Since the original paintings aren't available, I don't have a lot of other options.

I browse through the Studio Direct website's "fine art reproductions" (legal forgeries) catalog, jot down some names, then call a guy I know.

"Simpson Boutelle, at your service." He could fill an arena with that voice.

"Hey, Sim. It's Matt."

"Matthew, m'lad! Brilliant to hear from you again. And so soon!"

Boutelle's a huge, hairy painter from the middle of England. I think J.K. Rowling modeled Hagrid after him, minus the unhealthy habits. He does legal work for Studio Direct, semi-legal work for the gallery, and completely illegal work for me on my last project.

He dials his volume down to eleven. "Tell me, m'lad... do you need another Sargent? I've done nothing but Velasquez since the new year and I'm fit to top myself."

He's got a thing for pre-Modern portraitists going back to the Baroque, but his heart's in the late nineteenth century. "Sorry, Sim, not this time. But I do need some canvases. Do you know any artists who do Impressionist or Post-Impressionist pieces for Studio Direct?"

"Well..." He hems and haws a bit, which usually means there's a long explanation coming. "We all know one another to some extent. We're a small brotherhood, you know, toiling away, noses to the millstone—"

"'Yes' or 'no' is fine."

"Well, yes. If you must know."

"I must. Do any of them do side work, like you? In-the-style-of pieces?" In other words, do they make new Van Goghs and Monets?

"Ahhhh." I can imagine him waving a thick finger at me. "I get your meaning. You are, of course, referring to work they do for their own entertainment and development as artists?"

"Of course. Do they?"

Boutelle clears his throat dramatically. "You understand, of course, that we all do what we must to keep our work fresh for the customers. A gent can grind out only so many copies of *Las Meninas* or *Water Lilies*"—he makes both names sound like *cholera*—"before he has to clean his palate, shall we say. Do something original. All in good fun, don't you know."

I should've done this in the morning when I still had the energy to deal with Boutelle. Unfortunately, he would've still been asleep. "Nobody else is listening, Sim. You can stop dancing now."

He puts on his stage-whisper voice, which is like most people's normal speaking voice. "How can you be certain?"

"Nobody's arrested me lately." Here's where I add conspiracy to commit fraud to my growing list of sins. "I'd like to buy some of those side projects."

"Oho!" I have to jerk my phone away from my ear. "You ought to have said that first, m'lad! I'm certain we can help. What do you need?" I can hear him clearly even though my phone isn't on speaker and it's a foot away from my head.

"Bring it down, will you? Listen: I'm looking for late Impressionists, Post-Impressionists, and Fauvists. Nothing later than 1910. No marquee names. If something's a direct copy, I need the title. Every piece needs to be signed. You know what I mean, right?" I mean, signed by the dead artist whose style they're borrowing.

"Of course, of course. If I—"

"They're not going through forensic analysis; they just have to look right. The people who'll see them know art, but they're not specialists in this period or style. And Sim—this is hot. Whatever they've got, I need to know about it by tomorrow evening. Got all that?"

"Certainly, m'lad. You can rely—"

"Repeat it to me." It scares me when he says *you can rely on me.*

"Yes, yes." He pauses. "Of course. I have it here. Ehm... Impressionists?"

I work at home through Saturday until it's Sunday, then Sunday until dark. Luckily, my roommate Chloe's spending the weekend with her girlfriend-of-the-month, so I don't have to hide what I'm doing.

Which is everything.

Think about all the things in your home. Can you list them all? I need to, because we need to plant them. How many extras (people who populate the world of the con) will we need? What kind? What will they do? What will they wear? What cars does Hoskins drive? What kind of towels does he use? Does his housekeeper (shit—add her to the extras list) shop at Costco? What does *she* drive? What music does Hoskins listen to? When? Laptop or desktop? One screen or two? Where's he get his mail? Street delivery? (No, P.O. box, so nobody steals it.) Where's he put it? What's on his keychain? What's in his kitchen cabinets...?

We need a house. I can get only so far without a house.

"You *are* aware it's Sunday there?" Olivia asks me this during our fifth conversation this weekend.

I'm roaming around the pool house's front room to stay awake. Chloe sleeps in the back room; I sleep out here. She gets privacy, I get the bathroom. "Realtors work on Sundays. They do open houses. Well, not now, it's almost six. Did you get anything yet?"

"No. Patience. We've been looking for just over a day."

If she's frustrated or worried, I don't hear it. "It'd help if the clock would stop ticking."

"Agreed, but it shan't. Do stop to breathe."

If only. "Have you ever done anything like this before?"

"I have, though it's been yonks. I once had to locate and kit out a safe house in thirty-six hours. I slept for two days after, but it was a bit of fun." There's a smile in her voice.

Olivia's been dropping these little nuggets since we've been in almost constant contact. I didn't expect that we'd bond over real estate, but I'm glad for it. It keeps me from feeling too alone. "Was that for Allyson?"

"Oh, no. It was in a previous life, before I came to work with Allyson." She said *with*, not *for*. Significant?

I think about all the organizations that might need an emergency safe house and come up with a lot more reasons why I never, *ever* want to piss off Olivia. "While you're waiting, can you look for cars?"

"Certainly. Tomorrow, you and I need to start casting your extras."

"Yeah. I'm still working on that, along with everything else."

Olivia's voice turns motherly. "One-Seven-Nine?"

"Yes, ma'am."

"Don't spin yourself into a panic. It rarely helps. You and I together *shall* make this work, and you *will* get what you need, and you *will* succeed. Do you understand?"

"Yeah." I understand; I'm not sure I believe it. "Fifty-four days, Olivia."

Chapter 14

Olivia gets inquiries from fourteen different properties by Monday. All of them are bank-owned, cleared out for renovations, or have absentee owners. After we go through them, we're left with four that aren't obviously completely unusable.

I rent a car and visit three of them on Monday night and Tuesday morning, working my way west from the Hollywood Hills to Benedict Canyon. Each one's more awful than the last. Anybody who tells you photos don't lie is lying.

"They sent you all their dogs," I tell Olivia while I eat lunch at the Century City mall. "Have you gotten anything else?"

"Only if you're willing to completely re-evaluate your needs. Were the ones you saw truly so naff?" That last line's almost a plea.

"I sent you pictures. You tell me."

She sighs. "Please do try to find something nice to say about the last one."

The last one is up a narrow street on a ridgetop in Bel Air. Most people who aren't from here (like the Clampetts) think Beverly Hills is the place they ought to be. Angelenos know that the serious real-estate porn happens in Bel Air. It's a rugged area full of private roads, cul-de-sacs, and very expensive homes. You're more likely to see celebrities picking up their kids at Westland School than you are catching them shopping on Rodeo Drive. The house the Beverly Hillbillies lived in? It's on Bel Air Road.

Beth the Lawyer asks, "What sort of film are you making, Mr. Harmon?"

I'm using my Mike Harmon identity for this. He's a freelance art advisor—a male version of Savannah—who's apparently branching into production design. "It's an indie financial thriller. JC Chandor's the director, with Stanley Tucci." If she looks him up, she'll see Chandor did another financial thriller a few years ago, and Stanley Tucci's in everything.

We're standing in the core of a sprawling mid-century modern house: vaulted exposed-beam ceilings, fieldstone walls, decorative geometric iron screens, terrazzo floors, wood paneling, floor-to-ceiling fireplaces. I look out the fifteen-foot back windows, across the freeform pool, to the glass towers of Century City.

It's perfect... except it's a wreck.

It looks abandoned, not just vacant. The pool's empty if you don't count the layer of dirt and leaves in the bottom. The floors are dull and scratched. The copper vent hood over the round firepit in the living room hasn't been polished anytime this century. All the interior door hardware and most of the light fixtures are missing. Somebody did a disastrous kitchen revamp in the late '70s and never touched the place again. There's water damage on the tongue-and-groove ceiling paneling, holes in the plaster, peeling wallpaper, and at least three boarded-up windows.

But... terrazzo can polish out. The tile work in the bathrooms is original. Did I mention the semicircular wet bar in the living room? Wash these windows and the view'll be like flying low over the city. I want it real bad. "What's the deal with this place?"

Beth the Lawyer—Bethesda Van Zorn, another blonde with a city name—appears beside me with her arms folded over her open salmon blazer. She'll break bones if she falls off her heels. "The previous owners neglected the property."

"No joke. Why spend the money to buy a place up here and let it go to hell?"

She shakes her head. "You'd be amazed. Will this work for your film?"

It'll work for my *house*. I'll even do the reno work myself. "It's great. We'll just need to clean it up. Do the current owners care what we do with it?"

"Please confirm that you're insured before you burn it down."

"No worries. But... is there anything we can't do?"

Beth aims a tolerant smile my way. From a few feet away she looks Savannah's age, but up close in the light, I can see the shiny parts of an eye lift and a chin tuck. If she's going to do her face, she should do her hands, too. "My clients intend to tear it down in two weeks. You can do whatever you want."

I probably look like she slammed the eight-foot front doors on me. "They're... they're gonna *destroy* this place? That's criminal."

She shrugs. "It happens, you know. They want someplace bigger, more modern. We're on an acre-and-a-half lot, Mr. Harmon. They bought that, not this." She points at the ceiling.

Beth's right. A lot of fantastic old places like this end up in a landfill so somebody can build a white box with lots of glass.

Then something she said hits me. "Two weeks?"

"Yes. If you decide you want to shoot here, you have to be out completely by the 25th. That's when the work starts." She brushes a stray chunk of hair away from her face. "I'm prepared to conclude an agreement with you today if you'd like. Since my clients have no particular use for this house, they're willing to accept any reasonable amount for location fees."

Wow. Perfect *and* cheap. I pull my work phone from my back pocket. "Let me call the production office. I need to know what our ceiling is."

Olivia's silent after I tell her the situation. Then she whispers, "Two weeks. Good god."

My thought exactly. "I'd like three or four days in the house so I can deal with whatever the marks throw at me. If your guy starts tomorrow, that gives him seven days' prep before I have to move in. Can he do it that fast?"

"I've no idea. He built a pub for us in six days with a great deal of drama. Could you do what you're proposing in seven days?"

"I'm not a contractor." Though I probably couldn't screw it up any worse than a couple real contractors I've worked with. "The place looks structurally sound. The roof leaks, but it won't rain here for the next six months, so we don't care. I think it's all cosmetic. With enough good people working 24/7... it'll be tight, but it could happen. The problem will be furnishing and propping it out in time." I go over the to-do list I built in my head, and it gets longer every minute. "Call him. Ask."

She breathes for a while. "No. I'll tell him. If this house is ideal, we'd be daft to hope for a better one." She hesitates. "As you point out, the clock is ticking."

∎

I spend the rest of the day in the house, making lists of things to do, specing out fixtures and finishes on my phone. Beth the Lawyer left me the keys after I bargained the location fees down to $400 for each prep day and $1250 for each shooting day—and I get to define what's a "shooting day." I don't know how good that is, but it's less than her starting ask, so it's good enough.

I plod out to the back terrace, perch on a retaining wall for a dead planting bed and watch Century City turn gold in the late-afternoon sunlight. The eucalyptus and jacarandas chase the musty indoor funk out of my sinuses. The smell is so iconically SoCal that I'm surprised somebody hasn't sold it as a perfume. Somebody downslope has their outdoor grill going. (Another thing to add to another list.) I let all this wash over me until my head's in the right place, then thumb a contact on my phone.

"Rick, is that you?"

"Hi, Savannah. Hope I'm not calling too late."

"No, this is fine. So… do you love your pot?" She makes that sound like a come-on.

"It's great. I like it so much, I hope you'll pick out another one for me. Lorena's got my info, so just have her bill me."

"Oooh. You trust me to shop for you now?"

"You've earned it." As far as she needs to know. "Find me something I'll like. When you do, hold onto it. I may be up there for the day later this week."

"Really? I'd better get working. This'll be fun. When will you get here?" She sounds genuinely stoked. Either I made a bigger impression than I knew, or she's as good at faking sincerity as I am.

"I'll let you know. Say 'hi' to Jim and Lorena for me."

I want to see their reactions when I invite Bandineau and Savannah down here. I also want to make it as hard as possible for them to say no. They *have* to come. I'm staking a huge amount of money—and my job—on putting on this show.

Chapter 15

Savannah and I walk the four blocks from the St. Francis to Achara. It's 59 degrees and overcast outside, but her white above-the-knee sheath—Carolina Herrera or a good knockoff—glows like summer.

Lorena's waiting when we reach the gallery. Today she's wearing an embroidered burgundy *cheongsam*—a Chinese column dress with a standing collar—over loose black slacks. "Come right this way, Mr. Hoskins."

I zero in on a black bowl perched on a red-silk plinth on the same sideboard as last week. It's about ten inches wide by two or so deep, with a small shoulder and an indented rim. A short chunk of rim is missing, but the bowl's otherwise intact and in great shape. It shines gently in the gallery's lights. I get a surprise when I look inside: a sunburst of burnished radial lines streaks out from the center to the shoulder. It's very simple but very pretty.

I ask, "Is this mine?"

Lorena's just to my right like before. "If you want it."

"Do you love it?" Savannah appears on my left, smiling as usual.

"It's gorgeous." I look up at Lorena. "Can I touch it?"

"Let me get some gloves for you."

She brings back a pair of latex gloves. While I drag them on, I ask, "Should I always use gloves?"

"For unglazed earthenware, yes. It's porous and it can absorb any oil or grease on your hands."

"That would be bad." I hesitate for a moment, then gently cradle the bowl in both hands and raise it to eye level. It's surprisingly light, but there's still a weight to it. A highlight from an overhead spot slides across the bowl's curves as I move it.

Lorena gently presses down on the back edge. "Look just below the shoulder."

"A herringbone. That's cool." It's a single band, maybe half an inch high, circling the bowl, with burnished hashmarks forming a herringbone pattern.

Savannah says, "It's unusual on bowls. It usually appears on restricted vessels." Meaning, pots with mouths smaller than the body's width.

"Very cool." I should put the bowl down before I drop it, but I don't want to. It feels... I dunno, *right* in my hands. I eventually, reluctantly, set it on the plinth, then snap a picture with my phone. Just for the hell of it, I send it to McCarran. I have to show off to *somebody*.

While Lorena wraps the bowl, Savannah steers me into the statue gallery. "Do you really love it?"

I guess there's no such thing as stroking her too much. "It's great. You did a good job."

"Thanks." She ducks her head; *aw, gee.* "What's your schedule like today?"

I can play a little hard-to-get. "Meetings all day. I have an early dinner meeting, otherwise I'd invite you to dinner."

"Ohh, that's so sweet." A spark of mischief flares in her eyes. "But that's perfect. There's a place I'd like to show you. It's a little crazy, but I think you'll love it. It's the Tonga Room."

"Is that a club?"

"No." The way she says that, the next word should be *silly*. "It's at the Fairmont. It's like the ultimate tiki bar. It's a total throwback, but I love it. Will you go with me tonight? We can celebrate."

"What are we celebrating?"

"Your pot has a new friend. That's good. I know enough what you like to pick things out for you. That's even better."

Okay. She's basically asking Hoskins out on a date. Personally, I like to encourage this kind of behavior, but I think Hoskins might resist a little. "You work for me, you know."

She sighs. "I don't see it that way. Think of me as a friend who knows a lot about something and sometimes helps you out. Can you do that?"

"I don't pay friends to help me."

Savannah folds her arms and gives me a mildly annoyed look. "Sure you do. You buy them lunch or dinner. You buy gas for them.

Maybe you give them a present if they've done something really nice." She scrunches her cute little cheerleader nose. "It's just a little more obvious with me." She straightens the lapels on my suit coat. "Come *on*. It'll be lots of fun. And it's as San Francisco as it gets— you've *got* to see it."

I've resisted as much as it's safe. "All right, fine. I'll meet you at…" I pull a time out of the air "… eight."

If I turned a flashlight on her grin, the reflection would blind me. "Perfect! I'm looking forward to it." She points at me. "Don't wear a suit. You'll be the only one there in a tie."

"What're you going to wear?"

Another smile, sly this time. "Oh… something simple. You'll see."

I wait until I get back to my suite (I *love* saying that) and check up on the second day of construction at the house before I look at the receipt for my new bowl. The total comes to $3,562.50, including sales tax and Savannah's commission.

We're dropping what'll probably be low six figures to convince Bandineau and Lorena that Hoskins is a real, live boy. But these pots are amazingly cheap—compared to Impressionist paintings, at least, and certainly compared to the insane prices for contemporary art. With what Allyson's paying me for this project, *I* can afford to buy them.

ICE must have something juicy on the client. It makes me wonder again what exactly he's done.

And why are the feds so hot on this case? We're talking nickel-and-dime stuff here. The numbers don't add up even if Lorena's selling the Nam Ton wares for ten times what I just paid. Why are they willing to trade my freedom for what I find?

It all seems like overkill. I'm missing something.

Chapter 16

I follow a stream of happy people through the Fairmont Hotel's cream-and-gilt hallways until I turn a corner and there it is: the entry to the Tonga Room. Tiki torches, tiki gods, lava rock, a wood-plank reception stand, knots of people waiting to get in. And Savannah.

She shimmers in the dim light. Her white dress could be sprayed on. It's sleeveless, her left shoulder is bare, and her right shoulder peeks through a dart-shaped cutout. The hem ends halfway down her thighs. They're very nice thighs.

So this isn't a work-friends-going-out-for-a-drink date. This is a real *date*, the kind that ends up in somebody's bed if everybody plays their cards right. I'm not sure yet whether I'm ready for a happy ending. I *am* interested enough to see where she goes with this.

I saunter up to her like I'm used to this kind of thing. "You said 'something simple.'"

"It's all one color." She smiles up at me. "You look handsome."

I'm in a burgundy Robert Graham jacquard shirt over black Brioni slacks. It's as casual as I could manage with what I'd packed. "Thanks. You look... amazing."

Her smile says, *I know.*

A seater leads us through the bar scrum to a round four top in the corner of a fake ship's deck. There's a low exposed-beam ceiling, a mast, and an open floor reaching to another rigged mast at the room's other side. We can see most of the lagoon from here.

Yes. The lagoon. It's rectangular and maybe eighty feet long. A tiki-hut thing floats on the water at the other end. Tables line both long sides of the pool under wooden shed roofs. Nets, floats, tiki gods, ships' marker lights, and hurricane lanterns are everywhere. The crowd ranges from hipsters to boomer family groups.

Savannah leans in close so I can hear over the noise. "Isn't this great?"

"It's something else." It's a cultural relic, not a place I'd choose to drink in more than once a year.

We order from a young Asian woman in a maroon polo with a black floral pattern on the back. The house band—four middle-aged guys wearing camp shirts and Panama hats in the floating tiki hut—rolls into a Steely Dan cover.

I say, "I need to ask you something. It's work-related."

Savannah makes a face. "I'll have to charge you."

"What happened to that smart-friend-who-helps-out thing?"

"She needs to eat."

"How about if I pick up the tab?"

That brings her smile back. "Eating's overrated. What's your question?"

"At lunch last week? Jim said he needs to know who he's dealing with 'now more than ever.' What's that mean? Has something changed lately?"

Her eyebrows crunch together. Her lips purse. Maybe it's the murky light, but it seems like genuine confusion. "I have no idea. I haven't seen anything different. It's not like Jim tells me everything, though."

"Have you seen him do anything… questionable? Have any of your clients mentioned anything?"

Savannah frowns. "Why do you ask? Do you know something?"

Do you? "I'm trying to figure this out. It's like something put him on alert. Any ideas?"

"No, nothing. Sorry."

Either she's on the level or she's a damn good actress. I've seen that go both ways. It usually ends in a surprise. "If you knew, you'd tell me, right?"

"Of *course* I would. It'd be wrong to hide something like that from you." She wraps her fingers around the hand I'm resting on the table. "Rick, I want you to trust me, like I trust you. I'm here for *you*. I want to make sure *you're* happy. Will you let me do that? Please?"

My old boss at Heibrück Pacific also said *trust me*—right before he jumped bail and left me holding the bag. "Sure. I had to ask, though." I give her hand a squeeze.

She nods. She seems content to sit here holding hands, so I don't pull away. The waitress brings our drinks on a tray. Mine's a simple vodka rocks; Savannah's has a name like a Jimmy Buffett song title. It's a pinkish brew in a highball glass with a pineapple slice, a long straw, and a paper umbrella.

Savannah clinks her glass against mine. "To new friends." She sinks into her chair as she crosses her legs. The low table doesn't cover anything. Neither does the skirt hem that climbs way up her lightly tanned thigh.

It's distracting, but I won't complain. "You know, when I look at you, I don't see Asian art. Where's that from?"

She leans close. "I grew up with it."

"Did your parents collect?"

"Oh, god, no. They thought 'art' meant old European white-guy paintings. I got it from my nannies."

"Plural?"

She giggles, then sucks her straw in a way that gets my complete attention. "It's a long story. You really want to hear it?"

"I'm not going anywhere."

"Good." She sets down her glass and sweeps her hair over her shoulders. "You've probably heard of my parents. Joseph Kendicott? Sierra Pipeline? The second-largest pipeline company west of the Mississippi?"

I shake my head.

"Hmm. Gloria Stark Kendicott? She was a big deal in the old Republican Party. You know, the one before the one we've got now?" Her eyebrows become question marks.

"My folks were Democrats."

"Oh. Well, anyway, Mother was too busy to raise me, so she let nannies do it. She liked Asians because she thought they're smart and clean and cultured and hard-working and basically everything she didn't think Hispanics are."

I don't stop my wince in time to keep her from seeing it.

Savannah puts up her hands. "That's Mother. I'm not her. Thank god."

"I'm really glad to hear that."

"I'm glad you're glad." She flashes a smile. "Okay, nannies. Vu Sen—Susan—was with me until I was ten. Her father used to be pretty high in the Saigon government. She was beautiful, she had a good education, she spoke flawless English and good French…" She sighs. "I wanted to *be* Susan. Anyway, she taught me about Vietnam, about the culture, the art. I spoke good Vietnamese by the time she had to go away." Her mouth and eyes turn sad.

"Why'd she have to go? What happened?"

"Father happened." She empties her drink with a loud straw rattle, then flags down the waitress for another round. She leans in again, close enough for her warm, bare shoulder to rub against mine. "Lawan was my next nanny. You know how pretty and graceful and slender Thai women can be? That was her. She taught me the language. She'd studied archaeology in Bangkok before her family got chased out after a coup. She stayed on until I was sixteen, when she had to go away."

"Your father again?"

"Yes. Mother got her deported to Thailand. I didn't even get to say goodbye." She doesn't hide the bitterness.

That's rough, especially at that age. "What was that like for you?"

She sighs. "Lawan was my best friend. By then I'd learned to not trust the girls at school much." She grabs my hand. "I cried for days. I didn't speak to Mother for three weeks."

"I'm sorry." I really am. She may have had the silver spoon, but it had jagged edges.

We sit holding hands and listening to the music, swapping glances. New drinks appear. Savannah sucks down an inch in one draw. "Sorry to break the mood."

"No problem. So, how many languages do you speak, anyway?"

"Let's see. Vietnamese. Thai." She counts off on her fingers. "Mandarin. I learned that at Stanford. I can't read it very well, but I get by. I do okay in English."

"I noticed."

Big smile. "French, of course, though that's mostly for reading. I needed it for my major. My pronunciation's terrible. And you?"

Five languages, three different writing systems. I feel like a post-op brain donor. "English and Spanish." Right on cue, the band starts in on "Oye Como Va."

"Did you get the Spanish from the cook or the housekeeper?"

"We didn't have that kind of money. I learned from the guys working on my dad's construction jobs." Hoskins' background is a lot like mine, minus prison. "I mean, I took it in school, too, but I really learned it from them. I can't use a lot of it in polite company."

"I'll bet." She inhales another inch of her drink—it's disappearing fast—then nudges me with her shoulder. "Can you dance to this?"

"Yeah. Can you?"

"Of course." Savannah grabs my hand and pulls me out of my chair. "Come on, dance with me. It'll be fun."

I let her tow me onto the crowded deck between the masts. Most of the people sway more-or-less to the rhythm. She probably thinks I'll do that too. Her eyelids peel back when I haul her into dance frame. "On four."

I'm rusty, but she's got the beat and knows how to cha-cha. She moves like her joints are made of mercury. The last time I danced was with Carson (long story), who kept trying to lead. Savannah knows better. People make room for us to do our thing.

Savannah's grin threatens to break her face. The extra swing in her hips might be the umbrella drinks, or it could be her way to keep my attention. I concentrate extra hard on what I'm doing so my little brain doesn't think too much about what else those hips can do.

The band finishes and trickles off their raft. I try to lead Savannah to our table, but she holds back. "Stay here for a minute."

"Why?"

"Wait for it."

My arm's around her waist and her hand is on my chest. I don't remember arranging that, but it's comfortable enough. "What are we—"

"Just wait for it."

An overhead light flashes. Then thunder. Recorded thunder, but still. It starts to rain.

Not on us, luckily. (But that dress, soaking wet...) Water streams from the ceiling into the pool. Thunderclaps and lightning flashes overwhelm even the crowd noise.

Savannah laughs. "I love this place! It's so kitschy!"

We get back to the table without being rained on or struck by virtual lightning. Savannah orders another round. "Slow down," I tell her. "I'm still working on mine."

"Now you'll have a spare." She wraps both hands around my bicep. "Okay, where'd you learn to dance like that?"

"UCLA. I needed to do something to get my butt off a studio stool. I thought I'd take tennis—I played in high school—but then I saw the social dance classes. So it was like, go play outside with a pack of sweaty guys? Or be in a nice air-conditioned gym with a bunch of women who can't say 'no' when I ask them to dance?"

Savannah snorts. "You dog!"

"Woof. How'd you learn?"

"When I debbed." She points to the ceiling. "My ball was right up there."

Good lord. Another relic from a lost civilization. "You were a debutante."

"Of *course* I was." She giggles. "It's on the Poor Little Rich Girl checklist. You know how that goes, right?"

Unfortunately, yes. I've known several. "Let's see… rich parents, servants. A big, fancy house in some really white place?"

"Well, it was big. I can't say it was all that fancy. And yes, Atherton was about as white as it got back then."

"Where's that?"

"Next to Menlo Park. Walking distance to Stanford. Next."

"Daddy drank?"

"Mother drank. They both had… *adventures*, if you get my meaning."

"*Both?* That sucks. You mentioned the nannies."

She takes a big draw from her drink. "They were just the start. Father liked slumming. Waitresses, shopgirls, secretaries. My fourth-grade teacher."

"Jesus." Good thing I didn't have any vodka in my mouth. She's totally clinical about it, like she's talking about somebody on the news. "How do you know all that?"

"Mother told me. She made a point of it."

"And your mom…"

"She was more strategic about it. Sex was business. It got her what she wanted." She pokes my shoulder with a folded paper umbrella. "Father told on Mother too. Keep going."

"Okay. Private school, of course."

"You don't think they'd let me mix with the common folk, do you?"

"Straight-A student? Or did you go the other way?"

"Oh, no. Straight As. The last B I took home got me a spanking."

For a B? Harsh. "Trust fund?"

"Of course."

"Therapist?"

"Yes, but not after college."

"You scored a hundred on the Poor Little Rich Girl index."

Savannah holds up a finger. "Not yet. You forgot one."

Actually, I left out a couple because they seemed too rude to mention. "Which one?"

"Cosmetic surgery before I was eighteen." Yeah, that's one. "You know what they called me in grade school? 'Dumbo.'" She brushes back her hair, then pushes her ears forward so they look like open car doors. "From Father. I got his beak, too. And my teeth were a mess."

"So your fairy godmother made it all better?"

Savannah giggles. "This was all Mother. She decided to fix me the summer after sixth grade. I got my ears pinned and my nose done and I got braces. I didn't leave the house for almost three months, I was so embarrassed. By the time school started, the bruises were gone and my ears were where they're supposed to be, and I had my cute new nose..." She turns her head and tips up her face so I get a good shot at her profile.

"Very cute nose."

"Thanks. I still had the braces, but everyone else did, too. Oh, that's also when I turned blond. Mother said all blue-eyed white girls should be blond."

"I disagree." I pick up my glass. Is this my second or third? The pasta I had for dinner isn't soaking up enough booze. Savannah's gone a bit soft-focus on me. She's pounding those umbrella drinks like water, but it doesn't show at all. "Hey, I forgot to mention... I invited Jim to L.A. next week to see my collection and talk to my LACMA guy." Wait for it... "Would you like to come too?"

That takes a moment to sink in. Then her eyes get big. "Really? You mean it?"

"I mean it. Come down the day before, see my place, see my art. I'll show you around LACMA when Jim's in his meeting. Then you can hit the galleries. Sound good?" I want her there early because I want her invested enough to help sell Bandineau.

She gives me the look I'd hoped to see. "Yes, definitely! I want to come."

"Great. I'll take care of all your expenses. You shouldn't have to pay for this."

"Ohhh, that's so sweet." She darts forward to kiss me on the cheek before I can react. "You're the best. I can't wait!"

It rains some more. The band returns. We dance again, a rhumba to "Never My Love." We chat about nothing while Savannah demolishes her fourth drink. I've stopped nursing my third? fourth vodka? I'm as distractible as a Jack Russell terrier and my train of thought keeps crashing off the tracks.

Savannah says, "If you'll excuse me, I have to go powder my nose." She winks at me.

I watch her hips swing off toward the back of the room. So do a few other guys. It seems brighter and hazier in here than it should be. Everybody looks like they're having a great time, though.

Savannah should be completely hammered by now, but other than being more giggly than usual, she seems perfectly okay. Even as foggy as I'm getting, this feels weird. I sniff her glass. There's alcohol, but not much. After a glance toward the restrooms, I sneak a sip.

It's like fruit juice that's stayed in the fridge too long. Way more sugar than rum. Hmm…

Savannah returns a couple minutes later, drops her white Tory Burch clutch on the table, then bottoms out her semi-fermented Hi-C. "Where were we?"

I'm not sure. She orders another round. I ask the waitress for water instead. Savannah makes a face at me. Too bad. She starts in on her fourth? fifth so-called drink? The conversation wanders more than last time, but that's okay. She strokes my arm, and that's okay, too. The way she looks at me feels fine, even if she's really looking at Hoskins.

It also feels fine when her hand migrates from my arm to my thigh. My usually-right voice tells me it's time to close this down. Spoilsport. I have to concentrate to say, "I've got an early morning tomorrow, so I'm gonna have to call it a night."

Savannah's mouth bunches. "So soon? We should dance some more first."

"Maybe next time. I texted my town car to come get you. He'll drive you home."

"Are you coming with me?"

A nice thought, but… "Not tonight."

She sighs, then wraps her hands around my forearm. "Would you like to know the only useful thing Mother ever told me?"

"Sure."

"You'll like this. She said that if I want something, I need to take it. Nobody'll give it to me." Her voice is low and purry and goes straight to my little brain.

Savannah leans in for a kiss. I hesitate for an instant, which is all she needs. It's nice, light. Just a sample. She rests her forehead against mine. "You could kiss me back, you know."

That takes some effort to parse. "I could, but not tonight."

"Why not?"

"I wouldn't stop."

"That's okay."

I need to work out why she's pouring full-strength booze into me while she guzzles candy. I can't do that when we're swapping air. "Not tonight."

She pulls away a few inches. I get a full dose of big blue eyes that are stark naked and crawling into bed. "Okay. I'll let you go... this time."

Chapter 17

49 DAYS LEFT

The next five days melt into one very long one.

I work sixteen-hour days at the Bel Air house, eat pizza and empanadas, and sleep on an air mattress on the concrete slab in one of the four bedrooms.

Each day is barely controlled chaos. My desk is a dismounted door on two sawhorses in the four-car garage. I churn out an endless number of schedules on my agency laptop—doors, lighting, cabinets, floor finishes, wall finishes, fixtures, window treatments, yadda yadda yadda. I have conferences with Royce (the contractor: no idea if the name's his first, last, or only) about every thirty minutes. There's workmen everywhere, climbing on everything, chucking stuff into the battered blue dumpster in the forecourt until I wonder if there'll be any house left. It's been twenty years since I've had any regular contact with *banda* and *norteño*, but it sounds like not much has changed.

It's incredibly stressful… and a bagful of fun.

I'm still paying off the student loans I racked up to become an architect, but I haven't drawn a single plan since Kunstler Homes augered in after the 2008 crash and left us all short two weeks' pay.

Now I'm a project architect again. It's amazing how fast my brain snaps back into that mindset, and how good it feels. I've been making it up as I go along since that day I was left standing in a dirt parking lot at a dead jobsite on the edges of Santa Clarita. For once I know what I'm doing, even if it's all a fraud.

When I'm not architecting, I run to head off one disaster after another. Missing cabinets and fixtures. Subs coming late or not getting the work done. Materials delayed or unavailable. Royce (who looks like a surfer dude who decided to put on my dad's tool belt and Carhartts instead of board shorts) coming to me once every couple hours to say, "Guess what we found," which is never anything good. We have five days left to transform the house from a wreck to a showplace, but by Friday night the interior looks so hopeless that I consider jumping off the back patio.

Crates have dribbled in from Boutelle's pals ever since Tuesday. Some are usable. One joker sent me a copy of Van Gogh's *Starry Night*, which I kicked back. Not even Bandineau or Savannah will buy that Hoskins has one of the most famous paintings in the world on his wall. His collection's growing verrrrrry slooooowly. Too slowly.

The LACMA director Bandineau ~~wants to meet~~ doesn't want to meet with him. Allyson's jet is available, then not. The original cars I specified for Hoskins' garage can't be rented. On top of everything, I'm working with Olivia on casting and producing the show that happens on this set. We talk every two or three hours.

It doesn't help that I have to take off half a day on Monday for my in-person interview with Len. The office is in Inglewood: convenient to the airport, inconvenient to Bel Air. I tell him, "I'm helping a guy build a house," which is almost true. The minutes tick by extra fast.

I'd asked Royce to find me a dog. A jobsite without a dufus dog feels empty. The one he rented from one of the workers is named Feo, Spanish for "ugly," which is kinda harsh. He's what happens when a black Lab and a Rottweiler get wasted and sneak off into the bushes. When he's not flopped on my feet at my makeshift desk in the garage, he follows me around, panting. I swear I'm still alive only because Feo turns those big chocolate eyes on me now and then and lets me know that it's going to be all right.

The furniture trucks start rolling into the forecourt at nine sharp Monday morning.

I had the luxury of putting my air cushion on brand-new berber carpet last night. It felt great after a 140-mile round-trip to Riverside through rush-hour traffic to bring back something more precious than anything else I'll put in this place.

The construction's about ninety-five percent done, though the punch list I haul around on my phone has eighty-one items on it by lunchtime. The landscapers are planting the last of the new foliage all around the house. Royce tries to deconflict the work crews and the movers while I play traffic cop, pointing each piece of furniture in the right direction.

Except a third of the furniture is still missing. I get on the phone with Olivia for the third time this morning and try to straighten it out. We're both utterly exhausted; she's worked on this as much as I have, just from several thousand miles away. There are lots of gaps in the conversation as one or the other of us drifts off.

She says she'll do her best to get the rest of the furniture. I know she will. But with two days left before Savannah arrives, I can't beat the feeling that this isn't going to work.

Tuesday morning. The schedule says I'm supposed to move in today. I already pretty much moved in days ago. The brand-new washer churns a load of clothes I've worn over the past week.

I didn't sleep. I wrangled the night crew, shelved books in Hoskins' office, knocked almost thirty things off the punch list, hung a couple paintings, installed a lock on the office door, and started propping the house. Bedroom four is stuffed with bags and boxes that arrived until ten last night, dropped by five different prop houses, FedEx, UPS, a couple TaskRabbit people, and Gelson's grocery delivery. I'm in great shape to be an extra on *The Walking Dead*.

But... I make myself a latte on the brand-new Miele coffeemaker sitting on the brand-new granite countertop in Hoskins' brand-new kitchen. It tastes incredible. As I stand on the patio next to the pool—now full, slowly warming up—it feels like I might actually pull this off.

I'd better.

Savannah arrives in twenty-four hours.

Chapter 18

The white Cessna Citation's engines stop whining when the jet settles into its parking place outside Atlantic Aviation at Santa Monica Airport. A ground-crew dude in blue overalls chocks the wheels, while another one waits by the nose with a clipboard.

The front door swings down, becoming a set of four steps. Savannah ducks out the doorway a few moments later, looks around, sees me, then waves.

It's showtime.

I've got a day to sell Savannah on Hoskins' life so she'll help get Bandineau onboard. If she doesn't buy it, Bandineau may decide that Hoskins isn't worth hooking into his Nam Ton scheme. Worse yet: I could turn Savannah against me completely. Then bye-bye to that early termination Uncle Sam is waving at me.

I take Savannah's smallish roller bag from her a few paces from the plane. "I thought you only wear black or white."

"That's when I'm working." She's in a vivid aqua safari-style shirtdress that skims the tops of her knees. Button front, patch pockets, a wide matching fabric belt, short sleeves fastened with button straps. The blue sets off her eyes.

I lead her toward the car. "Was the Tonga Room work, then?" That heart-stopping white dress she wore that night fills my mental movie screen.

"Of course not. I just wanted to get your attention."

"It worked. Good flight?"

"It was fine. But I like Bombardiers better than Citations."

So much for impressing her. I heft her suitcase into the trunk, then reach for the black laptop bag slung over her shoulder. She's too zoomed in on the car to notice.

"Is this… your *car?*" Her entire face lights up. "It's so *cute!*"

It's a 1969 Alfa Romeo 1750 Spider Veloce, the big brother to the one Dustin Hoffman drove in *The Graduate*. Racing red, of course; the only acceptable color for an Alfa. The top's down. "It's one of mine. I hope you don't mind getting your hair messed up."

She pulls a hairbrush from her rainbow-striped MCM Patricia hobo bag and aims it at me with an impish smile. "Careful—I have a brush, and I know how to use it."

If I can pull it off, I'd like her to be sold on Hoskins' world before we even pull into his driveway. The weather's cooperating: a chrome-blue sky, an onshore breeze, mid-seventies at ten in the morning. Once we get above Wilshire and enter Brentwood on Bundy, the streets are lined with tall palm trees, increasingly large homes, and lush front yards.

I open up the Alfa once we enter the hills off Sunset. Not that it goes all that fast or handles all that well, but on the curvy little streets, it feels like we're clocking a hundred. Savannah buries her fingertips in the armrest and squeaks a couple times, but there's a big fat grin on her face. That's exactly what I want to see.

The garage-door opener does absolutely nothing when I roll into the forecourt. Of course; it worked when I left. I slap it against my thigh and try it again, but *nada*. I feel Savannah's eyes on me. "Forgot to change the batteries."

Her fingertips hide her smile. "It's okay. At least it's not raining."

Great start.

The eight-foot coffered front doors, now repainted Chinese red, make a big statement. The living room makes even more of one. Savannah says "Oh, geez" as she takes it all in.

The morning light streams through the back windows to glow off the now-polished pale-gray terrazzo floors. White exposed rafters stretch overhead through the glass to the vaulted roof's eaves. The reupholstered curved bar sweeps to the left toward the firepit's copper vent hood, now shiny enough to shave in.

She steps into the room and runs her fingertips along the back of one of the contemporary sofas flanking the vintage Noguchi coffee table. "I'm not sure what I was expecting, but this isn't it." Her tone's ambiguous enough to worry me. She reaches the 1960s Rocket floor lamp at the end of the couch, pauses, then fiddles with something on the frame. "What's this? I hope it's not a price tag. Not with this many numbers on it."

I park Savannah's roller bag next to the sofa and peer at what's between her thumb and forefinger: a little white tag attached to a string. *Shit.* The lamp's from a prop house; I must've missed the tag when I set up the room at two this morning. "Aw, hell. The shop must've left that on. It just came back yesterday from being refinished. Here, I'll take care of it."

She lets me pluck the thing from her fingers, then slow-walks to the back windows, taking a good look around as she goes. *What else will she find?*

Of course, the string's tangled and the tag doesn't want to come off. Ten minutes into this and already I'm paranoid and clumsy. "Is it good or bad that you didn't expect this?"

"I guess I'm surprised you're living in someone else's house." She gazes at the nearby ridge and the cityscape beyond. "Every architect I've ever known designed his own house the minute he had a few dollars in the bank."

She's right; it's an architect's rite of passage. The tag finally surrenders and lets me stuff it in my pocket. "Have you known a lot of architects?"

"A few. I dated one once." She glances at me when I pull up next to her. "Why this house? You've got enough money to live anyplace you want—"

"Not quite. See that place on the ridge? The white shoebox? That went for $26 million last year." Savannah's eyes get big and round. "A lot of it is land value, but still, that's sucker money. I don't care if it has a helipad and a twelve-car garage."

She stares at the white shoebox for a few moments, then at me. "Okay, you can live *almost* anyplace you want to. Why here? What made you want it?"

I expected her to have questions about the art, the cars, maybe the furniture. I never expected her to go off on the house. The thought of having to defend every single part of this place gives me hives. "I can't live in a new house. They have no souls."

"I get that. So…?"

When in doubt, go for the truth, or a flavor of it. "This place was a mess when I found it. The owners were going to rip it down and build one of *those.*" I wave toward the white shoebox. "I couldn't let that happen. I fought hard to buy it. It has a soul—I needed to save it."

Savannah stares out the window. Her lips do complicated things. "Like what people do with puppies and kittens from the pound?"

"Kind of. More expensive." That makes her giggle. I'm relieved that's all she does. "Come on, I'll show you around."

I point out the two canvases in the living room—a faux Johan Barthold Jongkind harborscape, and a supposed Lovis Corinth view of a sunny Alpine town—and the three in the bedroom wing's hallway. Savannah scans them carefully, arms folded, her mouth serious.

She spends some time considering the peaceful pseudo-late-Isaac Levitan landscape in the dining room. "These are nice, but I don't recognize the artists. I feel like I should."

Will she like *anything?* "No reason. This isn't your specialty. The only two Asian artists I can name are Ai Wei Wei and Hiroshige. These guys, I know."

"But why haven't I heard of them?"

"Because the brand names have sucked all the air out of the market. You have to be richer than I am to afford a Monet or a Cézanne now. But there's a lot of great Impressionists who haven't been discovered or rediscovered yet. I went for those."

She chuckles. "Aha. When they *do* get rediscovered, you can cash in."

The straight line I've been waiting for. "If I feel like it. I didn't get these because I was tired of buying stocks. I got these because I like them."

She turns back to the canvas, studies it for a while, then gives me a little smile. That feels like progress. "What smells so good?"

Fresh paint? "That's probably Gracie, making lunch. This way."

Of all the rooms in the house, I'm proudest of the kitchen, probably because it nearly killed me.

Savannah says, "I don't say this very often, but this floor is really fun."

It's sunshine yellow Marmoleum with long multicolored streaks. It sets off the flat-faced contemporary walnut cabinets and the pale-gray granite countertops. The gold, green, and red tesserae in the mosaic tile backsplash pick up the floor's colors.

We pause next to the island. "This is Gracie. She runs the place and takes care of me. Gracie?"

Graciela is a middle-aged fireplug in a black maid's dress, a salt-

and-pepper pageboy, and brutally sensible shoes. She apparently is, or was, really a housekeeper. She turns from the cooktop. "Yes, mister?"

"This is Savannah. She'll be my guest today."

Gracie gives Savannah the once-over. Her mouth puckers. "Yes, mister." She speaks perfectly good English with only a light accent, but she'd suggested that the less she says, the more people will pay attention.

Savannah tries to melt her with a smile. "Whatever that is, it smells wonderful."

"Yes, miss." It didn't work.

I stop Savannah in the office wing's hallway, where two paintings are hanging. "Can you give me a hand with this? It just came back this morning from a cleaning. All you need to do is hold it and snap the hanger on it."

It's a Charles Camoin Fauvist landscape, one of only two authentic canvases in the house. Gianna, an Italian gallery assistant from my first project, gave it to me as thanks for giving her a happy ending (not that kind).

Savannah and I pick it up from opposite ends. She takes a good look at the back, which has enough mileage to be a hundred-plus years old, because it is. It takes only a minute to click the snap-hook grippers to the hanging wire and level the canvas. With any luck, she'll now assume all the other paintings are just as old as this one.

We finally make it into Hoskins' office. A worn yellow Turkish carpet with organic red and black shapes partly covers a red-based version of the kitchen linoleum. The desk—my favorite piece—is a Jean Royere streamline rattan executive desk; it looks like something a plantation manager would use in 1930s French Indochina. Fourteen boxes' worth of my own art and architecture books fill the built-in shelves behind the desk.

Savannah says, "So *here's* where your pots went. I was worried you'd resold them."

"Man, you're a cynic." They're in a vitrine next to the door. "I spend more time in here than out front. You notice there's room for a couple more."

"I saw that. We'll have to find some for you." She drifts over to the canvas on the wall behind the conference table. "This is different. Very California. Who's Laura Hogan?"

"Mom." It's a very Californian *plein air* beach scene: a rocky cliff, a sweep of sand, tidepools, seaweed, foaming surf. It's why I went to Riverside.

Savannah stares at me. "Your *mother* is an artist?"

Laura Hogan is Mom's maiden name. If Savannah decides to look her up, she'll find a few obscure websites about this art genre and Hoskins' Wikipedia page. Mom never made it big—a couple shows, some sales—and her career mostly pre-dated the internet. If Savannah ever wants to look up Matt Friedrich's mom, she'll have to search for "Laura Friedrich." There's no reason in the world she'd do that. It's a risk, but a small one compared to the others I'm taking.

I edge beside her. "I watched her paint this. I was, I dunno, seven or eight, old enough to sit still for a while. It was fascinating, like seeing one of those old-school Polaroids develop. It's the first piece of art I fell in love with." A little catch slips into my voice. "She taught me how to look at art. How to see beauty."

I really did watch Mom paint a beach scene when I was a kid. That one sold decades ago, but this one's the same idea. And yes, Mom's art was the first I fell in love with.

Savannah's eyes survey me, then it. She finally says, "It's good. Is she still working?"

I shake my head. "She's got bad arthritis in her hands. She can't hold a brush properly anymore. It just breaks my heart that she can't do something she loves."

Savannah reaches out to squeeze my hand. "That's awful. I'm sorry."

We look into each other's eyes. Hers are big and liquid and more than a little sad.

Exactly what I wanted to see.

Gracie's a good cook. Lunch is chicken mole (my favorite) with cilantro rice and glazed plantains. Every bite makes either me or Savannah sigh.

We face each other across the vintage Kittinger teak dining table at the end closest to the back windows. I have a great view of a wall receptacle missing a trim plate. (*Grrrr…*) Savannah tells me about her travels in Asia; I tell her adventures-in-architecture stories, though some are second-hand.

When Gracie brought out the Ballast Point Sculpin IPA with lunch, Savannah skipped the glass and went straight for the bottle. This surprised the hell out of me—I didn't think she was the drink-from-the-bottle kind. Now she leans back in her chair and finishes off her second twelve-ouncer. "You have a lovely home. I'm jealous."

Whew. She might help sell Bandineau on Hoskins after all. "After you told me about your rich parents, I figured you'd be disappointed."

"No, not at all. We had this huge house, but there were only three or four rooms I wanted to be in. The rest were... I don't know, dead? Like the living room. No one went in there unless they had to. Mother had lots of parties there. Every room here is alive." She lets out a contented sigh.

"Want to see the view?"

She beams. "I'd love to."

We stroll across the pebbled concrete pool apron to the decorative ironwork railing at the top of the slope. Savannah closes her eyes, leans her head back, and takes in a deep breath. "Mmmm. It smells so good here."

Pro tip: plant rosemary. Lots of it. "And you thought everyplace smells like the freeway."

She giggles, wanders off to the pool's edge, then bends to trail her fingers through the water. The safari dress gets very tight across her butt; accidental, I'm sure. Then she turns to grin at me. "I love this place. Want a roommate?"

The good news: she's starting to flirt with me again. The bad news: I can't tell if she's serious. This is as good a time as any to let her think about everything she's seen so far... and to remind her who I'm supposed to be. "Look, I have a lot of work to do to prepare for the meeting tomorrow morning."

Savannah's mouth curves downward. "Work." She draws in a deep breath as she looks around the patio. "Okay, then. I guess you won't mind if I do some work, too."

"Knock yourself out." Though I don't know what kind of work she can do down here. I head for the patio door. "There's Gen 5 wifi throughout the house. The password's 'rysselberghe,' all lower-case." I spell it. He was a Belgian neo-Impressionist painter. "Make yourself at home. Ask Gracie if you need anything."

Just as I reach for the door handle, she calls out, "Front door keys?"

When I turn to look back, I see she's aiming an ironic eyebrow at me. "Only if you take over the payments."

She smiles. "Give me time. I'll get there."

Chapter 19

The rest of the afternoon is about building the PowerPoint slides for tomorrow morning's "meeting" and writing lines for my "staff." I also generate some agendas to leave lying around on the table. I'd wanted to get the office glass filmed so nobody could see inside, but there wasn't time. We'll have to stage the last fifteen or twenty minutes of the supposedly two-hour-long meeting in case Savannah or Bandineau goes outside and looks toward the office.

I somehow manage to get something accomplished despite spending half my time staring out the office's glass wall. It gives me the million-dollar view of the canyon and the Westside beyond. And the pool.

Savannah's propped up on a sun lounge, her top half inside a circle of shade thrown by a large burgundy patio umbrella. She works her phone and the laptop perched on a little round teak table next to her. A second table holds her beer bottle. She's hiked her skirt to her hips and knows exactly how to position her gorgeous legs so the light glistens on the sunscreen. Watching her rub that sunscreen on them was a near-religious experience.

Gracie marches in every half-hour or so to replace my empty glass of Coke with a full one. She also brings me more tags she's found on things we got from prop houses. Then she glares out the window, tsks, and marches out again trailing disapproval.

Savannah disappears around four-thirty. When she hasn't reappeared by five, I decide it's time to check whether Gracie's cooking her for dinner. Just as I push out of my desk chair, I hear the *pat-pat-pat* of bare feet on terrazzo. Savannah strolls through my office doorway, leans against the jamb and crosses her ankles. The bottom half of her safari dress is wrinkled where she'd rolled it up outside. "Still working?"

"'Fraid so. You've been busy."

"I made appointments to meet gallery owners. I thought I'd start tomorrow afternoon and go into Saturday, if that's okay with you."

"Not too late Saturday—that's when you go back home. I'll get you a car so you can go wherever you want."

"Thanks." She waves at the conference table to my right, a softly curved Heywood-Wakefield wishbone dining table. "What's all that stuff?"

"Project books. The rolls are plans. Over there's a draft request to the L.A. Planning Commission for a zoning variance. That brick on the chair"—I point to one of the six reproduction black-leather-and-aluminum Eames executive chairs—"is an EIR."

"What's that?"

"Environmental Impact Report." I borrowed all this from an old friend who still has an actual architecture job. I nod toward the plastic bag dangling from her hand. "What's that?"

"Plantain chips." She pulls one out and bites it in half to demonstrate.

"Damn, girl, you should've said something. Share."

She ambles to the desk and holds the bag out to me. "Where'd you discover these?"

"Miami." I dig out a handful. These have some kind of chili powder on them. Yum. "You?"

"There was a Puerto Rican bodega just down the street from my place in Brooklyn. When I was unhappy, I'd go through a bag of these instead of a pint of Ben & Jerry's." Savannah settles a haunch on the front edge of my desk and leans over to check out what's on my computer screen. It's a project schedule. She shrugs, then peeks inside the tumbler next to the monitor. "What's in here?"

"Coke."

She swipes a mouthful, then flashes a smile at me. That smile…

I need to think about something other than perfect teeth and that tanned thigh resting on my desktop. "Did Sotheby's make you unhappy?" She was an Asian art specialist at their Manhattan auction house.

A wistful look takes over her face as she watches the breeze ruffle the palm trees. "No. That was a great job. I loved it. I'd still be there if they let me." Big sigh. Now I get the brave smile. "But that's not the way it worked, so here I am. Glad they didn't keep me?"

Careful. "You look too healthy to be a New Yorker. You wear sunshine well."

The brave smile turns into a real one. "I'll take that as a 'yes.'" She slides off the desk and parades to the office door, holding the bag of chips high. "If you want more, you know where they'll be…"

■

Gracie cooked dinner, then left at 6:30. I'd asked her to prepare something from her home in Mexico. Savannah and I eat Michoacána *corundas* and *enchiladas morelianas* on the patio as the western sky slowly fades to mauve and the ridge crests turn gold, then black. There's lots of happy sighing.

We drift to the railing with a plate of *ate*—guava pulp cooked with sugar, then cut into cubes—and watch the lights flick on in the houses and gardens around us. Savannah stands close enough for me to feel her heat, but not quite touching. "Can I ask you a personal question?"

"You can ask."

"Are you with anyone?"

I've been wondering when she'd ask that. I've also been wondering what my answer will be. "What do you think?"

She purses her lips. "If you are, it's not serious. No woman lives here or spends any time here. I can tell."

"Don't let Gracie hear you say that."

"She doesn't get to keep things here, does she?"

"Generally not. She sets up a little *ofrenda* in the kitchen around the Day of the Dead. I add pictures of a couple people I knew who died."

Savannah scowls. "That's a lot different than having her toothbrush in your bathroom."

"True. Are *you* attached?"

"No. Not since the middle of last year." She folds her arms and squares her jaw. "Enough about me. Share."

This shouldn't be hard, right? Savannah's pretty and smart and has great legs. Yes, she's coming on awfully strong, but I get that. Hoskins is rich and straight. If he's available, he's a hot commodity in a hellishly competitive market. She'll lose if she doesn't move fast.

I used to envy the rich guys who always had beautiful women dripping off them. Turns out that gold-digger management is a big problem. I'd never heard of "pre-coital agreements" or "pre-cops" (pre-nups without the nup) until I started working at the gallery. A couple clients who were rich, single, straight guys told me stories that curled my hair. So Hoskins is probably very wary of any woman who throws herself at him.

Savannah should know this, but here she is. Why? Because of what her mom told her? Because she needs money? Or is it a test—if Hoskins goes for the gold, he can't be real because he should be more careful?

I finally say, "I see women."

Savannah looks very satisfied with herself. "I'm sure you do."

"Remind me how this is your business?"

She hands me the half-empty plate of *ate*, then takes my free hand in both of hers. Her voice gets low and velvety. "We just had a romantic, *candlelit* dinner on this lovely patio, under a pretty sunset, and had a nice conversation. I'm wondering what that means. I know what I'd *like* it to mean, but first I'd like to know if I've been sitting in someone else's chair." She leans close and whispers, "Was I?"

I'm still not ready to answer that. I need to think before I do. "It's time to take you to your hotel."

I drive Savannah and her luggage to the Peninsula Beverly Hills, a five-star sister property to Bangkok's famous Peninsula Hotel. It's a quiet drive, either because I left the Alfa's top down and it's too noisy to talk, or because she's pissed that she's staying at a hotel instead of in Hoskins' bed.

I hand her out onto the sidewalk. "A town car will come for you around 9:15 tomorrow morning. Jim should be in it. It'll take you up to the house."

"Okay." Savannah fiddles with the handle on her roller bag while the bellman stands by waiting for her to do something. "I had a nice day."

"I'm glad you did." And I am, not just because it's helpful to the project.

She passes her bag to the bellman, then spends some time watching my face. Finally she sighs, wraps her hand around the back of my neck, and stretches to kiss me. I could duck it, but I don't want to. It's like the Tonga Room kiss except longer and more intense.

After a while, she lets go and smiles. "You see? It *is* better when you kiss me back."

It is.

Chapter 20

43 DAYS LEFT

I'm out of bed before six Thursday morning—sleeping in for me. I grab a quick shower, shave, dress, and stagger toward the smell of fresh coffee. Between worrying about today and trying to figure out Savannah, I didn't sleep much last night.

Gracie's in the kitchen piling up the stuff she needs to cook breakfast for me and the extras. She shoots me a scathing look. "Is the *guera* here?" Meaning, *the blonde.*

"Not yet."

She pours coffee, then shoves the mug at me. "She wants something."

"I know. I just don't know what yet."

I race around the house, checking every prop and piece of furniture for tags or labels that I missed on Monday. I also figure the odds on what Savannah will do today. I deflected another of her passes last night; she may have written off Hoskins by now. She may not have an incentive anymore to do anything other than sell him pots. Maybe she'll try harder to land him. Or maybe she's pissed that Hoskins turned her down and she'll actively try to sabotage him with Bandineau.

With everything else going on today, I don't want to find out the hard way.

The doorbell rings a few minutes before eight. Group A of the extras isn't scheduled to show until nine, and Savannah and Bandineau won't get here until nine-thirty. A late delivery?

No, an early one. Savannah. *What the...?*

"Hiiii." She gives me her brightest smile. She's wearing a white sleeveless silk shell tucked into a white knee-length pencil skirt. Between her teeth and her clothes, she's reflecting enough light to give me a sunburn.

"You're… early."

"Uh-huh. It seemed just too sad to sit down there and eat all alone. So I thought I'd Uber up here and we could have breakfast out on the patio. I'm sure Gracie's cooking something wonderful." Her eyebrows slowly levitate. "Can I come in?"

The only thing I can think of is this morning's schedule, lying in pieces around my feet. According to the story timeline, the meeting's supposed to have started by now. Did I tell her that yesterday? "Uh, sure. I'm waiting for my staff. There's coffee in the kitchen." I should tell her *stay away from Gracie when she has knives*, but Savannah's in the kitchen before I think of it.

I step outside on the forecourt to call Olivia. "We've got an emergency. One of the marks showed up ninety minutes early. Group A needs to be here *now*."

"Oh, dear. I'll tell them presently. By the by, I had to make a substitution yesterday. She'll arrive separately."

"An associate or one of your strays?" Four of the six extras are agency associates. It's the first time I have proof that more than three people work for Allyson.

"They're not *strays*. Good lord, I'm not finding them on the pavements. They're people we've used casually in the past. The substitute is… Allyson."

"*What?*"

"Steady on. She volunteered. She's been briefed and she promised to behave."

The last damn thing I need right now. "Whatever. As long as she gets here fast."

I have to force myself to act calm when I go back inside. *Nothing to see here; move on.* I check on Savannah—nursing a mug of coffee while she waits for her laptop to boot on the patio table we used last night—then walk deliberately to the office. I want to pace in tight, fast circles to work out the anxiety and dread stuffing my brain, but Savannah might see me. (Actually, she won't. She's over twenty feet away and facing the canyon. Still.) Instead, I sit in my desk chair and pretend to work while my heart and stomach compete to see which can squeeze into the tightest ball.

I miss Feo. Now that he's gone home with his dog dad, I realize how long it's been since I've had a dog or cat to take care of, or to have take care of me. Feo kept me from blowing a gasket from stress over the past week. Patting a dog can do that. Now all I can do is check the time on my computer about every thirty seconds and strain my ears listening for the doorbell.

It rings at 8:23. A couple minutes later, five extras in business casual file into the office, two with Starbucks cups, the others clutching identical white ceramic mugs from Hoskins' kitchen. I hop out of my chair. "Please spread out around the table. We're short one, but she should be here soon. I hope you downloaded all the simulation materials yesterday. You know your roles and what we're doing here."

What are we doing here? Topanga Development's monthly project review. Our project managers (three guys sitting along the wall side of the table), the chief architect (a dude all in black), and the CFO (a woman with a thick rope of auburn hair) are here. The company counsel's missing. We look at our active projects, deal with problems, and talk about general company business. The meeting's here because we don't have an office; we all work out of our homes or at client sites. If they read the brief, they know all this.

I tell them, "We're here early because one of the marks is here way early. We need to be in here for the whole ninety minutes, but we don't need to be acting unless she comes this way."

The dude in black nods toward the window. "Is that her?"

"That's her. Questions?"

"She single?"

"Don't even. Okay, let's get started."

Laptops open; screens light up. Gracie brings in our breakfast (chilaquiles, very good). The PowerPoint I finished yesterday shows on the wall behind the table's head; the slides change automatically at different intervals. One guy reads some choice headlines from *The Onion*, getting a few laughs. The redhead shares a video of the Cutest Seal Pup Ever lumping around a diner in Santa Cruz. I check on Savannah at the top of each lap; she's tucking into her chilaquiles like she hasn't eaten in a week. Good.

The doorbell rings again about ten minutes after we start. I take a deep breath. High heels tap down the hallway toward us. Gracie opens the door and stands aside.

Allyson strides in, stops, then crosses her hands on the handle of a small black roller bag, about the right size for a laptop, some files, and maybe a clean shirt. "Pardon my tardiness. I trust I haven't missed anything important?"

Even though I knew she was coming, the reality of it takes a moment to sink in. "It's… fine. Grab that chair"—at the end of the table closest to the door—"and catch up."

I can tell which of the five other extras are associates: they're the ones with dead-pale faces and eyes the size of fifty-cent pieces. They all stare at Allyson. She notices. "I'm simply an extra, like all of you. Mr. Hoskins is in charge."

That's unusually gracious of her. "Thanks. Let's get back on track here…"

We pick up where we left off. Allyson settles in. Savannah leaves the patio. Various parts of my body unclench. *This might work…*

The dude in black sitting at the head of the table nods toward the window again. "She's back."

Savannah's at the railing, sipping from her mug. She swipes a peek in our direction, then turns back to the view down the canyon.

I say, "Okay, time to work."

Spreadsheets and Primavera project schedules fill the laptop screens. I stand at the table's head and stop the slideshow on a concept rendering of a multi-structure commercial/residential campus. "The topic of discussion is: what are you watching on TV, and why should the rest of us watch it?"

Why? So we'll look like we're talking instead of staring at computer screens—it's a meeting, not a lecture. I act like I'm refereeing the conversation, occasionally pointing or changing the slide.

Savannah drifts up the patio toward us.

Twenty minutes pass. The discussion meanders: disguises on *The Americans,* Netflix, what the Oscars got wrong. I pass behind Allyson and notice she's doing actual work on a spreadsheet that might be the agency's books. I'd love to look more closely, but she aims the Eyebrow of Doom at me.

One of the "project managers" asks, "She's getting awfully close, isn't she?"

Savannah's at the pool's deep end, maybe twenty-five feet from the office windows. Her back's to the office, but she doesn't make any secret of looking over her shoulder at us.

Allyson watches me, impassive except for her eyebrows, which are asking impertinent questions. Like I need the pressure.

I say, "Ignore her. At that distance, she's seeing more of her own reflection than she is of us. Keep at it."

Two slides later, Savannah ambles from the rail to the grill island, ten feet from the office windows. She squats in front of the little fridge and grabs a bottle of water.

One of the guys says, "Is she too close?"

The dude in black says, "Not from where I'm sitting."

The redhead growls, "Pig."

I say, "Knock it off. Look at the slide, your computer, or me, not her. She can see us, but she can't hear us." I tested it; she can't. "This is why we're putting on this show."

Savannah leans back against the tile counter next to the grill, facing us.

The next slide's the project timeline for San Salvador II, a mixed-use development next to the state university at the edge of downtown San Jose. There's a lot of red; it's in trouble. Looking in from outside, Savannah should see a head-knocking session about a project that keeps landing in the toilet. We're really debating *Deadpool* versus *Captain America: Civil War*. I like these guys; four of the six come down on *Deadpool's* side. I keep half an eye on Savannah as she nips at her water and peers straight at me.

More slides—get-well strategies, upcoming milestones, action items. Another, more successful project comes along. We move on to *Zootopia* versus *The Jungle Book* (apparently everybody except Allyson has kids). The redhead does a dead-on impression of the DMV sloth from *Zootopia* that gets a laugh out of all of us, even Allyson. My laugh dies in my throat—this is a business meeting. Should we be laughing? Did Savannah see it?

Her eyebrows are popped high. She empties her bottle, twists on the cap, then strolls back to the table and her laptop.

I sigh once she sits. "We're clear. Take ten, guys."

An Allyson-eyebrow twitch catches my eye. She inclines her head toward me just a touch. That's like a high-five from anybody else.

Allyson's the first to return to the room. She paces to the window next to my desk, where I'm massaging my knees. She's wearing a black leather bolero jacket over a fitted knee-length scarlet dress with unusual slanted black color blocks.

I ask, "Why are you here?"

"I volunteered to be your extra." A perfectly sculpted eyebrow arches. "Is that a problem?"

This is the first time I've seen or spoken to her since Vail. I'm waiting for the claws to come out. "I know you volunteered. I didn't know you do this kind of thing."

"It's good for the associates to see me do the work." Allyson's voice is carefully neutral. "This is also my chance to see what you've spent so much of the client's money on." Something tells me that's the real reason. "I'd appreciate a tour of the house if you can tear yourself away."

"Sure. This afternoon?" She nods. "You're not here just for this, are you? I mean, there's some other reason you're in L.A.?"

"Of course. I'm meeting with clients. Is four convenient?"

A guy-associate drifts into the room. I say, "Four's fine."

The next forty minutes pass slowly. Bandineau and Savannah stroll onto the patio at twenty to ten. We jump into work mode again. They spend ten minutes, then leave.

At 10:05, I say, "Okay, we're done. Remember your lines. Ignore the marks unless they engage you. You need to be out in"—I check the time on my phone—"eight minutes. Ready?"

They pack their laptops and briefcases. The dude in black scoops up the roll of plans. Their mugs and breakfast plates stay on the table. We all stream out the door, having spirited discussions about Important Business. They talk mostly to each other, but when they talk to me, they make it clear that I'm the boss. Savannah and Bandineau watch from the living room.

Five extras file into the two SUVs they came here in. I wave as they go. Allyson stands close to me on the front step, murmurs, "Acceptable work. I'll return at four," then rips away in a black Audi ragtop.

I check my phone. Group B texted 2 mins about thirty seconds ago. So far, so good.

Bandineau's in a navy-blue suit, white shirt, and sober tie. Trying to look respectable for his LACMA meeting, no doubt. He shakes my hand when I get to him. "Great to see you again, Rick. Your house is perfect. I love it."

Time to remind him who Hoskins is. "You'd say that if it was a studio apartment." I laugh once—*just kidding*. "Thanks. Savannah's showed you around?"

"I sure have." There's not a flicker in her face that shows anything unusual happened earlier. "You and your people looked like you were having fun in there."

"It was a meeting, not a death march. I see you got coffee. Need anything else?"

Savannah smiles. "Just you." A tiny bit of flirt on that.

Bandineau says, "Savannah tells me you have a very special painting in your office. I'd love to see it. Can you show us?"

I check my phone. "Not right this minute. Somebody's coming any second now, and I need to take care of him. We'll be in the office for a few minutes, then I'm all yours for the rest of the day." The driveway fills with cars. "Here they are. Excuse me."

A brown Crown Victoria with spotlights next to the side-view mirrors pulls into the forecourt. A black GMC Yukon's right behind it. The guy who exits the Crown Vic has an off-the-rack black suit, very little hair, and a curled wire coming out of his ear. The guy he lets out of the SUV is tall and slender, in a sincere blue suit, white shirt, and shiny purple tie. A middle-aged woman with a black bob and a vivid sapphire suit follows. Purple and Sapphire stride to the front door, where I am.

"Rick!" He gives me a two-handed politician handshake. He looks like a somewhat-better-looking-than-average doctor with gray at his temples. "Nice to see you again."

"Eric. Come on in." I nod to the woman, who carries a leather day planner. "Janet."

"Mr. Hoskins."

Then I introduce Savannah and Bandineau to the mayor of Los Angeles.

Well… sort of.

Tom Dykstra was a stand-up comic going nowhere until somebody told him he looks exactly like the mayor. Ever since, he's been making bank doing a routine at birthday parties and wedding receptions. Olivia says he didn't ask questions once she told him what he'd get paid.

Savannah shakes Dykstra's hand, then passes him her card. "If you need any advice about putting art in the city's buildings, please call me. I'd be happy to help."

"The Mayor" smiles. "That's a change—someone who *wants* to work for the city." He turns to Bandineau. "You're from San Francisco?"

"That's right, Your Honor."

"Welcome to California, then." He turns to me. "What do you have for me, Rick?"

"Come right this way. How long are you here?"

"Fifteen, max. I have a guest lecture at UCLA."

We disappear into the office and shut the door, letting Savannah and Bandineau absorb what they just saw. If they look outside, they'll see three cop-looking guys milling around the cars (our addition to Dykstra's act). Gracie will keep them from getting too close to the office.

Inside, "Janet" keeps track of the time while Dykstra tells about a bar mitzvah he did a few days ago in the Valley. He gets to the part where he'd started singing "I Love L.A." to the crowd when she says, "We have to go."

Back to the front doors. "It's a great project, Rick. I hope we can get it built."

"Can you lean on the Council for me?"

Dykstra holds up his hands. "I'd love to, but the Council's the Council. You know how that goes." He shakes again with Savannah and Bandineau, who look stunned. "Savannah, right? And Jim? Good to meet you. Enjoy my city."

The mini-motorcade leaves. My heart's going nuts.

Bandineau pats my shoulder. "Rick, I don't mind saying that I'm *very* impressed."

It worked. It worked. Sonovabitch, it worked!

Chapter 21

We leave the house around eleven after Bandineau has a good, long look at my paintings, my pots, and my books. Having Savannah hover around me, talking about the artists—I guess she had time to do some homework yesterday by the pool—seems to soften him up. He likes the story about my mom.

I drive them to the Miracle Mile in my Maserati Quattroporte (I *love* saying that), a low-slung, wine-red, four-door sedan that goes like a cheetah on meth. We have an early lunch at Canter's on Fairfax, an L.A. institution with some of the best comfort food in Southern California. I can use the comfort for the next play in this game.

The admin offices for the Los Angeles County Museum of Art aren't actually at the museum; they're across the street in 5900 Wilshire, a late-'60s concrete-and-glass skyscraper. I lead Savannah and Bandineau to the fourteenth floor like I go there all the time, even though I've never been in the place. The museum's offices are spare, shiny, and white, with fire-engine red public furniture and accents. The receptionist calls to announce us.

I tell Bandineau, "You're meeting the Deputy Director for Curatorial and Planning, Lars Renncroft. This really isn't in his lane, but he may bring in some other people. It's up to him. He's a good guy—just play straight with him and he'll hear you out. Okay?"

"Of course." Bandineau fiddles with the handle of his black leather briefcase. He's set a foot-square blond-wood box on the reception desk; I expect there's a Nam Ton pot inside. The way his eyes dart around the place makes me think he's nervous, which would be a first.

He's not the only one who's nervous. I'm assuming Olivia or Allyson briefed Renncroft on who I'm supposed to be. I hope he doesn't recognize who I really am, or if he does, he keeps it to himself. I hope he looks like his photo on the museum website.

He does. Renncroft's tall and gangly, wearing a medium-gray suit that doesn't quite make him look like a scarecrow. He's gray around the sides and bald on top with a gray goatee to make up for it. When he sees me, he pauses, looking a little lost. Not good.

I hold out my hand. "Afternoon, Lars. Good to see you again."

He snaps out of it, sort of. "It's been a long time, Mr. Hoskins." Saying this takes a couple swallows. "Welcome back." He has a reedy voice and the wimpy guy-in-the-arts-business handshake. His hand's trembling. What'd Allyson do to him?

"Thanks for making time."

Introductions all around. Savannah lays a business card on him, just like she did with "the Mayor." Bandineau turns on his Chamber-of-Commerce smile.

I say, "Lars, thanks again for taking this meeting. I'll leave Jim with you. I want to take Savannah across the street to see some more of my collection."

Renncroft bends a few degrees toward me, like a tiny bow. "Of course. Mr. Bandineau, please come with me."

Savannah sidles up to me. "Alone at last." A tiny smile tugs at the corners of her mouth.

"We're in public. We have to behave."

She scrunches her nose at me. "Spoilsport."

I share a dual museum membership with Chloe, so I don't have to buy tickets to get into the modernist William Pereira-designed Ahmanson Building, where the European and Southeast Asian collections live.

We go first to the European art exhibits on the third floor. We stroll through the white-walled nineteenth century galleries and talk about the paintings. She stops to smile at a Degas bronze and coo about the pyrotechnics in a Cézanne painting of trees.

"Oh. Here's one of mine." Imagine that. I point to one of Peter-Severin Krøyer's Skagen beach scenes: a diagonal sweep of golden sand with a gentle sea washing along the edges and a fishing boat under sail in the distance.

"Really?" Savannah bends to read the label. "Fontana Collection? That's you?"

Not exactly. It's somebody else's shell company. A Google search brings up exactly three valid hits, all for paintings in LACMA's collection. "It's one of the names I use."

She shakes her head.

That's when I notice a familiar face at the gallery's far end. I recognize her because (a) she's a luscious brunette I used to enjoy looking at, and (b) she was a regular at Heibrück Pacific. She was so insistent that we let her buy a Meissonier painting from the south of France. We didn't have the heart to tell her the artist's flying-M signature was considerably younger than she was. Did she ever find out?

I take Savannah's hand and pull her around so our backs are to my possibly disgruntled former client. "Come on, I'll show you another one."

She doesn't object—the holding-hands part probably helps—so I lead her into the gallery next door. The next Fontana Collection painting is a Pissarro cityscape about halfway up on the right. I try to keep an eye out for the brunette without looking like I lost something.

Savannah, of course, wants to study all the busy little people and carriages. I can't goose her along without a good reason, so I stand a bit behind her and tell her factoids about Pissarro while I watch for a possible disaster.

Which arrives after a few moments. The brunette—Candace, her name's Candace—drifts into the gallery from the direction we need to leave through.

I turn so all she'll see is my back. There's no reason Candace should recognize my back. I always wore a suit jacket or blazer in the gallery. Today I'm wearing a lapis sportshirt. Still.

Savannah finally finishes with the Pissarro and turns to me with a cute semi-mischievous smile. "So, where's the next one?"

I'm distracted enough to not pick up on her question. "Next what?"

"The next painting of yours? I mean, that's why we're here, right? So you can show off"—she holds up her thumb and forefinger a fraction of an inch apart—"just a little?"

"Not… really." A brunette with roughly the same hair passes by my right shoulder, maybe a foot away. My heart goes sideways until I notice her shirt's wrong. Which means Candace is still behind me.

"I think the third one's off display now."

Savannah's smile gets bigger. "Let's look for it. Make it a treasure hunt."

"No, that's okay. The Asian art's upstairs. Let's go take a look."

She twitches her nose. "Uh... not yet. I want to finish in here first. See something different." Now she takes my hand and pulls. "Come on."

When she pulls me around, I'm braced to go face-to-face with my former client. But Candace's over on the other side of the gallery, examining one of Monet's water-lily paintings. I can keep breathing for a few moments. With any luck, nothing will catch Savannah's eye and we can slip out while Candace is distracted.

Of course, Savannah stops two canvases up. "Ooh, a Monet. I know this one."

It's two women in the woods, one painting, the other reading, the usual loose brushwork and Monet's attention to the grass and trees. Savannah pulls her phone from her purse, leans into the label, and starts tapping her screen.

I glance over my shoulder at Candace, who's in a sky-blue sleeveless blouse tucked into very nicely-filled stretch jeans. She stands with her hip cocked and a hand holding something to her ear. I figure it's a phone until she pushes back some hair, uncovering an audioguide handset. Good—maybe it'll keep her occupied.

Savannah says, "They're both Monet's stepdaughters."

I turn to see her point at the women. "So it's a family portrait, then."

"Uh-huh. It says that she's"—she points to the painter—"the only one of the children who became interested in art. Can you imagine that? Growing up with Claude Monet and not being interested in art?"

I can, but that's not what's got my attention. I glance at the label and notice the little headphone symbol in the corner next to a number. This painting's on the audioguide tour.

Savannah says, "I remember the story now. Her father was one of Monet's patrons..."

I glance over my shoulder. Candace is turning toward me. I face forward again and try to disappear. It doesn't work.

"... and then Ernest moved to Paris..."

I try to look interested in the painting while Savannah narrates the soap opera. I sneak a peek at the canvas to my left—a landscape with a town in the distance, also by Monet—hoping to see the headphone symbol over there, too. I don't.

"...Then Monet's wife died..."

Please get to the end. Please.

Candace steps next to Savannah's other side. She thumbs in a number on the audioguide's keypad, swings her hair away from her left ear, and raises the handset. She's still as lovely as she was back then. There's no ring on her left hand anymore. Is she now the ex-Mrs. Whoever?

I snap my head forward so I don't stare. I'm told I helped convict nineteen gallery owners, dealers, and collectors with my testimony, and caused at least three divorces and two suicides. I'm not proud of that (especially the suicides); I did it to save my own skin. Was Candace one of those divorces? She did the buying—her husband just gave her the checkbook. She didn't know a lot about art. It was easy to rook her... like fishing for koi with depth charges.

Why did we do that? She didn't offend us, like some of our clients did. We did it because we could. A shitty reason, looking back.

This is the first time I've seen one of my ex-clients since I got out. If she confronts me, she'll blow my cover. But more than that... what do I say? *Sorry? Nothing personal?*

Is there anything I *can* say?

Fucking stop.

"... and that's how they got to be Monet's stepdaughters."

It takes a moment to notice that Savannah's stopped talking. I don't dare look her way; Candace's over there. "How do you remember that?"

"I don't know. The prof told us stories about the artists so they'd be more real to us, and a few stuck in my head. Some of the artists had amazing private lives."

"Shhh." Candace holds up the handset, then glares at Savannah.

"Oh! Sorry. Sorry." Savannah puts up her hands like she's surrendering, takes a step back toward me.

Candace glances straight at me. Her beautiful green eyes narrow a bit.

Tick. Tick. Tick.

Shit.

She returns to the painting and puts the audioguide to her ear again.

She doesn't remember me, or I've changed. For the better? I need to restart my heart either way.

I grab Savannah's hand. "Let's go."

Chapter 22

Savannah comes home at just past six, stoked after an afternoon of successful gallery schmoozing. She gives me the lowdown over beers next to the pool.

Bandineau shows up at the house at five to seven. He pulls up in a white Camry that screams *rental!* from every angle. Either he didn't get the "casual dress" memo or didn't read it; he's still wearing his suit shirt and slacks. At least he's rolled up the sleeves. He has the wooden box cradled in the crook of his left arm.

After we shake and get through the usual pleasantries, I say, "Savannah's made dinner plans for us. Asian-Latino fusion." Savannah's nowhere to be seen. Hmm. "Interested?"

"Of course."

I grab a beer for him while he sets the box carefully on the dining-room table. "Are you going to show me what's in there, or do I have to guess?"

Bandineau shakes a finger at me. "I *thought* you'd be interested." He slides open the lid, pulls on the latex gloves on top of the packing peanuts, then starts excavating.

The unmistakable sound of heels on cement announces Savannah's appearance in the living room. She's wearing a bright teal square-necked tank, a fitted white high-low mini, and strappy white dress sandals. *Where'd that come from?* Her hair is down. I say, "Well, look at you."

Bandineau twists to see her. His eyes go circular. "Savannah! I've never seen you wear anything like that. Is this the L.A. version of you?"

"No, it's the it's-warm-and-I'm-not-working version of me. Rick?"

"You look great."

She joins us, grinning. Bandineau gently pulls the pot from the box and sets it on a napkin he folded on the table. He removes the top layer of bubble wrap, then the second layer.

It's a petite, white, round-bodied Nam Ton bottle with a slender, flared cylindrical neck. The neck is a vivid cobalt blue; the footring is unglazed. A ring of loose blue brushstrokes around the bottle's equator (the body's widest part) suggests a garland of leaves.

I sink into the chair opposite the pot to take a close look. This is the first time I've seen one of these not behind glass. It's a lovely little thing, and I say so.

"Isn't it?" Bandineau stands there looking like the proud father of twins. "It would fit perfectly here. Now I see why you're so taken by these."

He made the connection. Good. I glance at Savannah. "What do you think?"

She leans her elbows on the back of the chair she's standing behind to scope out the pot. Incidentally, I get a great view down her top. I'm sure that's unintentional. "What can I say? It's gorgeous. Do you like it?"

"I do, a lot."

"You should buy it, then."

I give Bandineau a significant look. "I'm working on it. How's that going, Jim?"

He flashes a fast, empty smile. "I still need to talk to Lorena. She handles the sales."

Sure. "What would this one go for?"

He rests his palms on the back of his chair and switches to his careful smile. "This one isn't for sale—it's part of the museum's collection."

"If it *was* for sale?"

He studies the pot for a while. "I can't speak for Lorena, of course, but I'd venture… twelve to fifteen thousand."

"Three to four times what the Phimai blackware sells for."

"In that area. Nam Ton is much scarcer here than Phimai, so it makes sense."

I look toward Savannah. "Is that what you've seen?"

Savannah stands straight and folds her arms. "Jim's the expert." She shoots me a cryptic look. "We'll talk later."

Twelve-to-fifteen grand's still not much compared to what the client and Uncle Sam are pouring into investigations. Savannah knows something. It's time to see if being potential boyfriend material is enough to get her to spill it.

The 1000 block of Abbot Kinney Boulevard in Venice is a jumble: an elementary school, cafés that use the words *organic* and *free-range* a lot, an auto shop, repurposed light-industrial space. On the third Thursday evening of each month, it turns into a food-truck hotspot.

"There it is!" Savannah practically bounces. "The blue one."

The electric blue one—first in a line of ten—with big white lettering on the side: *Oh! Oh! Oh!* Yeah, like that. Maybe fifty people are waiting in line to get to it.

Bandineau looks puzzled. "Wait a minute. We're eating at a food truck?"

Savannah grabs one of each of our arms and marches us across the street to fall in line. "It's not just *any* food truck. It's Norris Oh. He's the hottest thing in Asian-Latino fusion right now. He's got half a million Twitter followers."

The line inchworms along. The bright LED streetlights give the area a football-stadium vibe. I watch the hipster street theater. I know I'm not that much older than some of these people, but I feel like I'm an ancient creature from another planet.

Bandineau says, "Savannah, thank you for trying, but I'd like to eat sometime this evening. I'll just go down there and see what I can find. I'll meet you at the car in an hour."

I say, "If you leave, I can't buy you dinner."

He chuckles. "It's a food truck. How expensive can it be?"

Savannah and I watch him go. I say, "He's got no idea."

"None." She hugs my arm against her side. "Alone at last."

"We're still in public."

She tsks. "That keeps happening." Before I know it, she's captured my hand. I don't mind, and surprisingly, neither does Hoskins.

I say, "You said we'd talk later. It's later."

Sigh. "Okay. When you asked about the pot's value? Jim didn't need to think about it—that was just a show. He appraises ceramics."

The only thing that shocks me about this is that nobody's mentioned it before. "Including Nam Ton?"

"Of course. How do you think Lorena sets her prices?"

I try a stab in the dark. "By asking her *supplier?*"

She squints at me. "How'd you know Jim's her supplier?"

"It wasn't hard to work out." It's a cozy arrangement. Does the Norris know?

"True." She shrugs. "It's not like there's much of a market for it that you can get to yet. You've looked, right?"

"Yeah. I haven't found any for sale. Makes you wonder how Jim does his valuations."

"It does, doesn't it."

There's something in her tone I can't quite figure out. "Do you know of any other suppliers?"

Savannah stares into the near distance. The warm wind kicks her hair around. Random tangles of cooking smells waft by. "Not back home."

"Somewhere else?"

"In China."

"So you know what it goes for in China?"

"I do, but that's not useful." She brushes a rogue chunk of hair away from her face. "The Chinese art market's even crazier than ours. There's a ton of money sloshing around, looking for something nice to buy. A lot of it's about buying things to send offshore to get around currency controls. Their prices don't apply here."

I think about my next question. It's something I need to know, but it's pretty blunt. Savannah seems to be in a sharing mood, though, so I should take advantage while it lasts. "Do you think Jim's fronting for the supplier, or is *he* the supplier?"

She frowns. It's a thinking frown, not an angry one. "It could go either way. My 'female intuition'"—air quotes—"says he's it."

"For everything, or for Nam Ton?"

"I'm pretty sure it's only for the Nam Ton wares."

"How'd Jim get involved in Nam Ton, anyway? Did he ever tell you?"

"No. I know he read the journal article. I think someone gave him his first piece. Why?"

"I'm wondering whether he looked for it or it looked for him. Just how well do you know him, anyway?"

Savannah pulls her hair into a ponytail. "He's a friend. We've talked a lot, mostly about art." She cocks an eyebrow at me. "If you're really asking if I've slept with him, then no. He's not my type. He's a nice guy, but… well, you've noticed. He's not a lot of fun. Besides, when I met him, he and Lorena were a thing."

No surprise. "They're not now?"

"I can't tell for sure. Not a regular thing, at least." She checks our place in line—we'll eat something this spring—then hugs my arm again. "Look, I want to take good care of you. I'll make sure you get a pot you like for a price you're happy with. We trust each other now, right?"

I remember her spying on Hoskins' meeting. "Sure."

We get back to the house by nine-thirty. Bandineau says his goodbyes a few minutes later. Savannah and I end up at the patio rail with a glass of white wine each, watching the Westside lights twinkle like grounded stars. Blue pool light dances on the walls and plants.

She says, "Today was fun."

I think about a guy I knew who did skydiving. He told me that the first time he jumped he was scared shitless until he landed, then he thought, "This is fun!" and wanted to go up again right away.

Today was like that. There was a huge pucker factor until we left LACMA, but looking back on it, it *was* fun. Exciting. And somehow, having Savannah in the middle of it made it more exciting.

She asks, "Done with your glass?"

"Yeah."

Savannah takes both glasses to the grill island, kicks off her shoes, then saunters back to me. She slides an arm around my waist and cuddles against my side. She fits well.

Hoskins doesn't object, so I wrap an arm around her shoulders and give her a squeeze. The rosemary mixes with the jasmine and eucalyptus and jacaranda and leftover wood smoke from the neighbor's outdoor grill. The result reminds me of so many happy summers in L.A.

She says, "That was a big sigh."

"Yeah. This is why I love this place."

"I get that." She kisses my shoulder, then my cheek. Her fingers on my jaw turn my head so she can kiss my mouth. She tastes like

Riesling and bibimbap. I flash back to us pulling bits off each other's food boats after we finally got dinner. Laughing.

She slips away and drifts off. I hear her fingers swish through the pool water a few moments later. Then nothing. I peek over my shoulder to see where she went.

Savannah drops her top on a nearby sun lounge. Her mini's already off. Her lacy white lingerie looks just about perfect on her.

Somewhere along the way, I forget to breathe.

She skims off her thong in one fluid motion, drops it on her skirt. The bra follows. Her all-over tan probably came from a store, but it's lovely anyway.

Savannah half-turns and holds out a hand. "Swim with me."

Chapter 23

42 DAYS LEFT

Friday morning. I'm sitting at the other round glass-topped table, this one set back from the pool's shallow end. Another large burgundy umbrella throws shade but can't do anything about the early heat. Fixing the air conditioning was the smartest move I made here.

Savannah sits next to me wrapped in a towel, plowing through her breakfast of muesli and yogurt, cubed fruit, and a big tumbler of something green. Her hair's still wet and dead straight from her forty-minute swim workout. I should think about what I'm going to say to Bandineau, who's due at nine, but watching Savannah's lips wrap around her fork is fascinating.

I think about last night. Sex is play for Savannah. She even calls it that. She has a lot of energy, she doesn't mind being silly, and she has zero body hangups. We laughed a lot. In some ways it reminded me of when I first got together with Janine, my ex-wife. It was fun, but exhausting. If she's not on my side now...

Gracie appears at the door. "A man is here for you, mister."

"Thanks, Gracie." She leaves. I check my phone. "Five minutes early. Staying or going?"

Savannah's fork doesn't even hesitate. "Staying."

"Remember how Jim looked at you last night when you showed up in a miniskirt? Imagine what'll happen if he sees you in a towel. The poor man'll have a heart attack."

She covers her mouth with her hand until she swallows. "It's good for him. Besides, I don't really care if he knows we're together. Are you ashamed of me?"

"What? No. Why would you think that?"

"Just checking." She takes a big swig of green slime. "I'm not ashamed of you. So why hide it?"

This is a debate I won't win. I kiss her. "I'll talk to him inside."

Bandineau finally figured out a definition of "casual": he's in a green-striped golf shirt tucked into khakis. He pumps my hand with his usual enthusiasm. "It's good of you to see me on such short notice. I just need a few minutes of your time."

"No problem, Jim. Have a seat." I gesture to the sofas. We chat about the local museums. I tell him about Koreatown and the huge surplus of Asian restaurants in Monterey Park and Alhambra. It seems to interest him way more than the food trucks did.

Gracie appears with a coffee mug after a couple minutes. Apparently she remembers what he'd asked for yesterday. I need a Gracie in real life.

"What do you have for me, Jim?"

"Yes, of course." He sets down his coffee more carefully than he needs to. "I spoke to Lorena last night. The long and short of it is, we'd be delighted to have you join our group of collectors."

Yes! My reaction.

"That took long enough." Hoskins' reaction.

He puts up a hand. "I understand perfectly. I'm sure it seems like there were hoops to jump through, and I apologize. We simply need to make certain our collectors are legitimate."

"'Now more than ever.' You said that at lunch the other day. I've been wondering—what's changed? Why's it more important now than it... Jim?"

I've lost him. He's staring out the back windows. "Is that...?"

I twist to confirm he's seeing what I think he is. He is: Savannah stands at the pool's edge, pressing her phone to her ear with her left hand, holding her half-empty glass of green slime in her right. At least she's still wearing the towel. "It is. Now—"

Bandineau sighs. "You're a lucky man, Rick." I hear *you bastard* at the end.

"Luck had nothing to do with it. Back to my question. What's changed?"

He fiddles with his mug. "All I meant was, now that we're gaining more collectors and getting Nam Ton into more museums, we need to know that our collectors are respectable, influential members of their communities." He emphasizes his words by tapping the tabletop with all five fingertips. "We want people who can represent Nam Ton to other potential collectors."

Sure. "Has that been a problem?"

"Of course not, and we'd like to keep it that way."

Would he know yet? Maybe not if the feds haven't started raining indictments. "What happens next? Where do we go with this?"

"It couldn't be simpler. Let Lorena know the next time you're available. She and I will put our heads together and bring a selection of wares to the gallery for you to look at."

"No passwords or secret handshakes?"

Bandineau chuckles. "No, no, nothing like that. You're a member of the club now."

"You'll be there?"

"Certainly. You could say I'm part of the bargain."

I nod. "Good. I plan to be up there for the day on Wednesday. I'll let her know my schedule." Now it's time to work on the next part of Hoskins' story—why Bandineau will profit by having him involved. "What do you get out of this?"

His eyebrows try to knock together. His mouth grows serious. After some thought, he says, "I suppose you could call me an evangelist for Nam Ton. It's extraordinary work and I want people to have a chance to see it before the looters and smugglers make it disappear. That's a huge problem, and it's not getting better."

"That's not exactly what I'm asking. What do you *personally* get out of this? I mean, you're doing all this work. It's a lot of effort, probably a lot of expense. Where's it leading you? What's your goal?"

"I'm… not sure I understand." He looks it, too.

I pretend to weigh my next words. "Can I be frank?"

"Of course."

"I've seen how you look at this house. How you look at my collection, my business, the mayor's visit. How you just looked at Savannah. I—"

He has both hands up. "Rick, I'm sorry if I crossed a line—"

I wave that away. "It's okay. Her in a towel… if you *didn't* look, I'd wonder. Remember how I said that being with Savannah isn't luck? None of this is. I built this life. I didn't have all this planned when I was a junior architect figuring out where I wanted to go, but I knew what I wanted. I'm trying to work out how being a 'Nam Ton evangelist' gets *you* to the house and the woman, because I'm not seeing it."

Bandineau stares at the table for a few seconds, sighing occasionally. I can't tell if I broke him, he's trying to think of an answer, or he's pissed that I'd get so personal.

I say, "If it's too soon to talk like this—"

"No, not at all. Besides, I pried into your life; I suppose it's fair that you get to ask about mine." He leans back into the loveseat. "You're right. I do have ambitions. I'd like to live in a house like this with a beautiful woman. Any man would. That's… not attainable in the Bay Area. Property is much too expensive, for one thing, and there are far more successful men there than successful women of any age."

"So you're looking to move?"

"Not actively, but I always have feelers out. What I'm doing now puts my name out in the regional and national arenas. Being known is a step."

"Museum director? You're practically doing it now, if I'm reading the museum's YouTube channel right."

He nods. "I'd certainly find that interesting, yes."

How looped would Bandineau have to be to stop talking like he's being interviewed? "Are there museum groupies?"

That jolts a smile out of him. "There… *are*. They tend to have interesting eyewear and sensible shoes."

I've seen them. "We need to get you to branch out, then." I stand and hold out my hand. "Jim, I have to get to work. Thanks for coming by. I'll see you Wednesday."

As he drives away, I wonder if anything I said got to him. I have to remind myself that this is just the first shot. I'll have more opportunities to set myself up as a life coach or mentor or whatever so we can bond. There won't be too many, though; the clock's still ticking.

But there's progress. Step two's only five days away.

Chapter 24

Savannah kisses me goodbye at 9:45 on her way to the day's first gallery appointment. She says, "Miss me terribly." She wears the Escada from the first time I saw her, white pumps, subdued makeup, and an asymmetrical French twist. Except for color choices, her style sense is remarkably similar to Allyson's. She roars off in the azure BMW Z4 convertible I rented for her yesterday afternoon.

I boot my computer and bring up the program that lets me look at the security camera feeds. The cameras are wireless, upload through wifi to the cloud, and shift automatically to night vision when it gets dark enough. They're also so small that if you don't look for them, you won't see them.

I rewind to around 12:30, when Savannah finally let me fall asleep, and start the camera playback in slow fast-forward.

At 1:42 a.m., the camera in the bedroom wing's hall shows the master suite's door creep open. Savannah slips out. The night-vision picture is green, grainy, and low-contrast, but she's clearly naked and her hair's a sexy jumble.

I watch her on one feed or another as she spends the next twenty minutes going through every scrap of storage in the house. Sometimes she'll pull out something, light it up with her phone, then put it back. What's she looking for?

Maybe she's not all about being a rich man's girlfriend. My good mood runs down the drain. Being taken advantage of isn't fun. Then again, that's what I've been trying to do to her. Maybe she saw the lie behind Hoskins. Maybe she's looking for the truth.

She ends up at the office door. A sudden flash of panic: *did I remember to lock it?* Apparently, I did; she tries to open it, can't, then stands there with her fists on her hips. She finally returns to the kitchen, pours a glass of water from the spigot in the fridge door, then drinks while she looks out the back windows. The droop in her shoulders tells me she's not satisfied with whatever she found.

Is that good or bad?

I spend the rest of the day studying in the office.

For $25, I buy from ScienceDirect the article that described Nam Ton for the first time. "Ceramics from the Nam Ton Culture: A Preliminary Investigation," by Dr. Pensri Udomprecha of Silpakorn University, appeared in the Winter 2010 issue of the *Journal of Asia-Pacific Archaeological Research.*

Yeah. It's as exciting as the title. I have to look up every fifth word.

The short version: in 2008, Dr. Udomprecha dug up what was left of a settlement dating from the late thirteenth century that doesn't seem to be linked to any other cultures in the area. He found kiln sites and more than three hundred intact or reconstructible wares of a style nobody had seen before. The map in the paper shows a box drawn around northern Thailand and a chunk of Myanmar along the border. The name "Nam Ton" comes from the stream that runs by the site.

Here's where it gets messy. If you Google "Nam Ton," you get 138,000 hits. This includes pages about the pottery as well as a singer, a doctor, and a news photographer. It's also the Thai name for a type of unglazed ceramic bottle made in the sixteenth century. The hits attached to geography mostly point to (a) a river in Laos, or (b) a suburb of Chiang Mai in Thailand.

It wouldn't be any fun if it was easy. Right?

When I can't stand archaeology-speak anymore, I check in with Len, then look up Savannah's parents. I haven't had a chance to since our Tonga Room date. They both have Wikipedia pages.

Joseph Kendicott inherited his dad's small pipeline company in Oklahoma and West Texas. He turned it into a giant through the sheer force of asshattery. He sabotaged competing pipelines, sued competitors into the ground, broke two separate unions, and rammed new pipe through ecologically sensitive areas before anybody knew what was happening. In other words, he was the poster boy for twentieth-century American capitalism.

Gloria Stark was an heiress with nothing to inherit; the Great Depression ruined her grandparents. She ran away to be a two-bit Hollywood actress in the late '60s and early '70s. A 1973 head shot shows a more spectacular, more Nordic version of Savannah, a platinum blonde with high cheekbones and a swan neck. No wonder Joseph married her—he was a total troll, so she gave his future children a fighting chance of not looking like the Alien. She had two miscarriages before she "delivered a daughter, Savannah Abigail, in 1980."

Between Gloria's beauty and talent as a hostess, and the trainloads of cash Joseph poured into the state and national election committees, Savannah's folks had the ear of two generations of California Republican politicians. Now I understand what she meant when she mentioned her mom's "political parties."

The fairy tale passed its sell-by date in the late 1980s and spiraled into pathos in the 2000s. Savannah's childhood and young adulthood weren't all sunshine and unicorns. Poor little rich girl, indeed.

The weekend is two bookmatched, postcard-perfect Southern California days: clear, sunny, high seventies, an onshore breeze. The marine layer burns off by ten, just in time for me to wake Savannah (it's an elaborate and lengthy procedure), for her to finish her morning swim workout, and for us to eat breakfast, share a shower, dress, and head off for the day's adventures.

Savannah was supposed to be on the jet Saturday morning, heading north with Bandineau. But Friday night after we got home from listening to soul and blues music at The Mint on Pico (her idea), she asked if she could stay the whole weekend. I said yes. We were in the middle of having sex on a patio lounge; I'd've said yes if she'd asked to roast and eat me.

On Saturday, she asks to see what I consider to be "my L.A." These days that's pretty small: the pool house in Palms, the Starbucks in Santa Monica. I have to think back to before the 2008 crash, when I was still an architect with a steady paycheck and Janine hadn't gone completely off the deep end yet.

We go to Frank Lloyd Wright's Hollyhock House in Barnsdall

Park. She asks me a lot of good questions and seems to bond with the art glass and bas reliefs. Afterwards, lunch at the Farmer's Market at Fairfax and Third. We're eating at the counter of Loteria Grill (her choice) when I say, "I've got a question about Achara."

Savannah puts down her taco *al pastor* and shoots me a look. "Do we *have* to talk about work? This is our first weekend together. Can't we just be us?"

"Sorry. It's been bugging me for a while."

Heavy sigh. "Okay. One." She holds up an index finger. "I charge for the next one."

"I'll keep that in mind. The first time you took me to Achara, there wasn't any Phimai ware there. But—"

"There was, but it had a buff slip. You wouldn't recognize it."

"Okay. No Phimai blackware. But after that lunch, there were three pieces. I never saw any Nam Ton there, but when I went to get the second pot, McCarran was getting a Nam Ton bowl. I haven't seen any doors or a hall to get to a storage room. So where does Lorena keep her off-display stock?"

She finishes her taco, wipes her hands, takes a mouthful from her Negro Modelo bottle. "She doesn't have a storage room. Not like you mean—she's got a little closet for boxes and paper and stuff. I've noticed the same thing, but I really don't know where she keeps it. I ask, but all she does is this." Savannah's hand closes a zipper on her lips. "That's it for work questions... unless you don't want to play later."

I definitely want to play later. Her answer gives me an idea, though. When she goes off to powder her nose, I ask Olivia to put Bandineau and Lorena under 24/7 surveillance. I need to know if either of them goes somewhere that can plausibly be used for storage.

After the La Brea Tar Pits, we twist up Laurel Canyon to Mulholland—the perfect road for the Alfa—then roar west along the crest to get home. We pass a movie shoot at the Narrows Overlook. It's a very L.A. day.

I ask her, "Have you thought about where you'd like to go for dinner?"

Her mischievous smile comes out. "Take me someplace you liked to go when you were a kid."

Dr. Hogly Wogly's Tyler Texas Bar-B-Que is sandwiched between a liquor store and a barber shop on Sepulveda in Van Nuys.

It's not much bigger than two double-wides stuck together, but the 'que is great. Savannah laughs and eats messy and licks sauce off her fingers. Seeing that becomes my new favorite memory of this place.

I drive the Alfa back to the house through the warm night with the top down. Savannah's hair streams out behind her in the wind. All that's missing is stars; you just can't see them here. Then the house, the pool, the bed.

The security video.

It's like living an Eagles song.

Chapter 25

"Harmon?"

I look up from the menu. "George?"

He's Asian, probably Chinese, short, built like a wrestler. A medium-blue tee with Magritte's *The Treachery of Images* (the one with the pipe) on the front, black jeans and a shapeless gray windbreaker. You'd pass right by and never notice him. He slides into the banquette on the other side of the table. Jazz trumpet leaks out the earbud dangling from his neck. "Your number?"

"One-Seven-Nine. Yours?"

"Ninety-Nine." Too bad he doesn't look like Barbara Feldon. "Where are you staying?"

"The Marriott on Second until Tuesday night."

We're in what looks like a diner: lots of Naugahide, Formica, and linoleum, with fluorescent lights blazing in the kitchen on the far side of the counter. If you look closer, you see the shallow barrel-vaulted ceiling, the bar with beer on draft, and flatscreens here and there showing ESPN or cable news. Oh, and Indian food on all the pictures. It's called Chaat Corner.

We don't say anything until we order from the grumpy Indian woman who's built like George. I pour some water from a fluted glass bottle and watch the going-home traffic pile up on Third Street. "Has anything interesting happened?"

"Not a thing." George pours and chugs some water. "He goes to work, goes to lunch, goes back to work, goes home. Boring, boring man. The only thing that changes is *when* he goes home. Same-same with Montford. She went grocery shopping last night. It was very exciting for that team."

We don't have to worry about anybody overhearing us; the group of ten tech bros at the tables between us and the counter—most bearded, most wearing black tees with a company logo I don't recognize, all various degrees of geek—make enough noise to cover a jet flyby.

"Well, we keep watching until ten on Wednesday. If they don't do something before then, it doesn't matter." I try to say this with all the confidence I can dig up, which isn't much. It's all a hunch. I feel bad for wasting the time of four associates on the most boring assignment ever based on what could be indigestion. "When's your next shift?"

"Eight." He checks his watch. "You're sitting in?" I nod. "Hope you like jazz."

Bandineau lives in a two-story, late-Victorian townhouse on 18th Street on the Mission District's western fringe. It's neatly kept, pear with cream and rust trim, bay windows stacked over the single flip-up garage door. George says Bandineau lives downstairs; there's light behind the double-hung windows on the ground floor.

George and I have been parked three doors down since we took over from the other watcher at eight. KCSM-FM plays jazz softly on the car radio. We were talked out in the first hour. That's okay. There's plenty going on in my head to keep me occupied.

I'm still absorbing four days and nights with Savannah. When she hooked up with Hoskins, I expected her to want to go to $200-a-plate restaurants and $1000-a-booth clubs. To go shopping with his credit cards. To drop hints about wanting to keep the BMW. But she seems to be just as comfortable wrapped in a towel as she is wearing Escada. I never saw a bigger smile in Mélisse (a high-end French restaurant I ate in once on the gallery's dime) than I did on Savannah's face at Hogly Wogly's. She could've asked Hoskins to spend a mortgage payment for tickets to see Beyoncé at the Rose Bowl, but she wanted to go to a semi-dive to hear blues instead. My kind of woman, even if she's a blonde.

Hoskins has to act like he's into her, but it's surprisingly easy to do that. I'm getting hooked on her smile. It's been a long time since I had this much fun while spending so little money and seeing so much joy on a woman's face. If she's auditioning for Lead Mistress, she's got the part. The little brain is very happy.

The big brain remembers the security video and wonders when she'll drop the Big Ask... and what it'll be.

Bandineau shuts off his lights at ten-thirty. George and I take turns napping. Our relief comes at two a.m.

A wasted night.

I'm on solo starting at eight a.m. Tuesday morning. At nine I follow Bandineau's black Tesla in my silver Prius from his townhouse to the Norris Museum. There are so many Priuses on the street, mine's essentially invisible. Now I'm half a block from the entrance to the Norris Museum's underground parking garage, waiting for something to happen.

Someone calls my work phone at around ten-thirty. It's a 323 area code—West Los Angeles—but I don't recognize the number. "Hello?"

"Mr. Harmon? It's Beth Van Zorn. How are you this morning?"

Beth the Lawyer. "Just fine. Did your clients make a decision?"

The longer I'd stayed in the house, the more I thought tearing it down was a crime that needed preventing. So when I got back from dropping Savannah at the airport on Sunday morning, I called Beth and invited her over to look at the place.

She was amazed. I led her around the house and grounds, showing her what we'd accomplished. She kept saying, "You did all this in seven days?"

I got her to agree to postpone the demolition until her clients could see for themselves. They came Monday morning. They were maybe in their forties, white, glossy, looking like they stepped out of an ad in *Forbes* or *Architectural Digest*, with two junior high-age boys. They, too, were amazed. He goggled at the office; she loved the kitchen; the kids zeroed in on the pool. How cliché.

When the tour was done, I gathered everybody in the living room, poured what was left in one of Hoskins' wine bottles, and gave them the sales pitch of my life. A beautiful house, solidly built, (almost) everything working. You can move in tonight. Keep the house, you get twenty-five grand in top-end appliances and twenty-plus grand in new mechanicals for free. Whatever you build here, you'll never be able to beat this view.

I thought I had them. If I could've given them something to sign—if Beth hadn't been there being a lawyer—I'd've hooked them. As it was, Beth thanked me for the offer and said she'd be in touch.

And now she is.

Beth says, "They're astonished by the work you and your company did. They took into account your very generous offer."

"And...?"

"And they accept. They want to keep the house."

Yes! Yes! I saved that gorgeous house from being murdered. If I wasn't in the car, I'd do a happy dance. Oh, to hell with it—I do a happy chair dance.

Beth blah-blah-blahs about an inventory and transfer agreement and so on. But it's all formalities. Some good came of all this.

Wait, inventory? Good thing that the microwave behind the bar, the Miele coffee machine, the brand-new knife set, the food, and the new towels and bedlinens (all of which we had to buy) have already made it to my real home.

George pulls in behind me at two p.m. in a white Ford Focus. There won't be any high-speed chases in this operation. He asks, "Anything happen?"

"Nothing. Either he ate in the museum café, or he went out the back door and walked to lunch."

"Very boring man. See you at eight."

I drop the Prius at the appointed place, take a nap to catch up on lost sleep from last night, eat an early dinner, then check into the St. Francis. If I wasn't about to spend the night sitting outside Bandineau's house, I'd call Savannah and ask her if she wants to come out to play. Duty first, damn it.

George rolls down his window when I finally get to his spot down the street from Bandineau's place at eight-ish. A jazz combo on the radio provides background music. "You're late."

"Sorry. The one-way streets are killing me."

He waves me into the Focus' passenger's seat. "Mr. Boring isn't so boring after all. He left the museum at five-forty and drove to Potrero Hill."

"Where's that?"

"South of here, between the Bayshore and the Embarcadero Freeway."

They name their freeways up here instead of using numbers like civilized people. "Doesn't help. What's there?"

He smiles. It's the first time I've seen his expression change. "Safe Spot Storage."

It's all light industrial east of the 101, a.k.a. the Bayshore Freeway. Light industrial always looks scary at night. We park out back of a buzzing electrical substation between a couple RVs that don't look like they've gone anywhere for a while. The self-storage place's white, eight-foot-tall back gate is across the street. I ask, "Which unit is he in?"

"Don't know exactly. See the second aisle past the gate? He's in there. Half a dozen units at most." He looks my way. "Do we go in?"

Why do I have to make that decision? Oh, yeah, because I'm project lead. "What about the cameras?" I point toward the warning sign on the gate.

George shrugs. "We can take them down. They'll know something happened, just not what."

"How?"

"I call Olivia, she calls her hacker."

It's weird to hear somebody I don't know talking about Olivia. "Guards?"

"Don't know. Website says they do a security check at closing time. Doesn't say what happens after."

Fun. "Locks?"

"They require keyed locks."

"You can pick those?"

"I get by."

So here's where I get to decide if we're going to commit burglary. This is why ICE wanted the client to fund a black-bag operation: so a couple idiots like us can do the illegal shit the feds don't want to, then admit to it in writing. I'm starting to wonder if another year with my PO is such a bad thing.

The storage units look like white cargo containers shoved together. Each block of containers has two small roof-mounted floodlights pointing into the aisles between the blocks, one on each side. The doors I can see are painted purple. At least everything's clean.

I look around at the RVs and campers surrounding us. No lights, but that doesn't mean nobody's home. I've read there are hundreds, maybe thousands of people living in cars in the Bay Area. Even people making six figures.

George asks, "What are we looking for?"

A pile of pots? A pile of money? A pile of old *National Geographics?* "If I knew, we wouldn't have to look."

"Fair enough. Do we go?"

It's only two to three years of my life. No biggie. "We go."

Chapter 26

George says, "The hacker's trying to find the place."

"Okay. How do we get over the gate?" It's gotten taller since I started staring at it.

"Climb." He swivels his phone mic to his mouth. "What was that? Right." He presses his phone against his chest. It's the same kind as my work phone, but he's added a translucent lime-green case. "He found it."

"You have Olivia there?" He nods. "Tell her 'hi' for me."

He does. "She says you haven't rung in donkey's years, whatever that means."

It's been two days. "Tell her I still love her, but I need my space."

"Not telling her that."

A couple minutes of silence pass. The gate gets taller. The butterflies in my stomach turn into giant bats that swoop up and down in time with the percussion solo jangling out of the radio.

George says, "Thanks." He thumbs off his phone. "Cameras are down. The hacker went through the fax machine. Let's go."

Hacking a fax machine? Whatever. I snap on the yellow latex gloves he tosses to me, then follow him out of the Focus. A cold, sharp little breeze knifes down the street. When we get to the gate, George gets down on one knee and interlaces his fingers to make a step. I put my foot into the step; he practically throws me over the gate. He pulls himself up and over while I'm recovering from my flying lesson.

While it's twilight on the road circling the ranks of containers, it's noontime in the aisles between them. If there are guards or dogs here, they won't have any trouble seeing us as they go by.

There are four violet rollup doors to my right in Bandineau's aisle, one to my left. George brushes past me, heads for the singleton, plugs in his earbuds, then gets busy with his set of lockpicks. I've learned from Carson that the best thing I can do in this situation is to stay out of the way. After what seems like an hour (probably only fifteen or twenty seconds), the padlock comes off the hasp.

George pops an earbud. "This what you're looking for?"

I smell the antique furniture packed in the forty-foot container before my phone lights it up. It's a blend of old wood, dust, and baked varnish. Most of it's from Europe, mostly the nineteenth century, and not a pot in sight. "Nope."

While George starts pulling the locks off the other four doors, I peek around the corner down the road leading to the front gate.

There's a guy at the end walking our way. A dark nylon bomber jacket, dark baseball cap, flashlight. As he paces past an aisle to his right, he slows to look toward it.

The *Star Trek* battle-stations klaxon goes off in my head. I hustle toward George, who's opening the third of the three small storage cubes at the end of the aisle. I stage-whisper, "Guard. Coming this way." No reaction. I yank the nearest earbud out of his ear, making him jump. "Guard."

"How far?"

"A couple hundred feet, maybe. Stay off your soundtrack."

He stands back, then points to each of the small cubes in turn, starting from his left. "House junk, empty, kid stuff." He means a cradle, playpen, and open boxes of tiny clothes.

"Nope."

"Close them up."

I do, then scurry to the edge of the drive. The guard's closer: three aisles— maybe a hundred feet—away. I ask George, "How's it going?"

"Somebody got a good lock."

Great. "We've got maybe two minutes." I'll regret saying this... "Let's get in the empty one."

We duck into the unused storage cube after George pops the padlock in about two seconds. It's six feet square, plywood floor, and white ribbed steel walls. George carefully pulls down the metal roll-up door partway (I'm sure they can hear the scraping and rattling in the Financial District), ducks underneath, then eases it closed. It gets very dark. It's still cold, but at least the breeze is gone.

Faint, hard-edged jazz squeaks nearby. It takes a moment to figure out why. I hiss, "George. Kill the tunes." He grumbles, but the music stops. "This one had a lock."

"Yeah, a cheap-shit one."

"Why do you lock an empty locker?"

"Keeps the homeless out."

With housing prices the way they are here, I get that. "He'll notice it's gone."

After a few beats, George mutters, "We'll see."

I concentrate on the thin glowing line at the bottom of the door where the floodlights leak into the cube. It reminds me there's an outside. I've always been mildly claustrophobic, but prison made it way worse. Of course, I end up hiding in a closet at least once every project.

My ears strain to hear footsteps outside, but all that comes through is the wind rattling things around. Well, not all—there's a scratching sound I can't place. I hiss, "George! Stop it!"

"What?"

"That scratching."

"Not me."

Great. Rats, maybe. Squeakless rats. Giant, genetically-engineered silent rats. One of Google's secret science projects escaped from the lab. They eat stray dogs and cats and people hiding in storage cubes... "How long?"

"Two minutes."

That's all? I gotta get a watch; using my phone as a clock just isn't cutting it anymore. My eyes have adjusted to the not-quite-complete darkness. George is a dark shadow against a slightly less-dark wall across from me. It doesn't help.

More wind, more scratching.

Footsteps. Outside.

George and I try to squeeze into the eighteen inches of wall on either side of the door.

The door clatters up about three feet. A flashlight beam stabs into the back corners, sweeps along the base of the back wall and halfway up the side walls. The sudden light burns my eyes. I stop breathing. I stop thinking. If I could stop my heart, I would.

If that circle of light gets a few inches closer, I'll end up in a place like this for years.

The guard mutters. The door slams down.

We wait five minutes after the footsteps fade away. By then, I'm ready to chew my way through the door. "I'll check."

George says, "Careful."

We inch the door up far enough for me to stick my head out. No guard. George lifts the door higher so I can crawl out. Good thing I wore jeans. It's dead outside by the time I get to the corner.

George gets back to work on the last door while I watch for guards or dogs or drones or rodents of unusual size. For all the trouble George's having with that lock, there better be something good inside. After enough time passes for the San Andreas Fault to move L.A. several inches closer to San Francisco, I hear the click of a lock opening and George's whispered "finally."

We enter together, close the door. He flips on the strip lights.

It's a twenty-foot cargo container. The door's about ten feet from the far end. Half the wall opposite the door is covered by two black, five-shelf steel commercial shelving units. They hold pots.

Dozens and dozens of Nam Ton pots.

George says, "This is what you're looking for. I can tell."

"Yeah." I'm sure there's a huge blinking sign on top of my head saying *Eureka!* "Look for paperwork."

The pots are like magnets dragging me to the shelves. There's almost a hundred Nam Ton pieces arranged in neat rows on the lower four tiers. Each one has a yellow sticky note plastered to the shelf in front of it; each note holds a numeric code that looks like an inventory number. Bandineau's a museum guy, all right.

I check "15-0131," an elegant, foot-tall, tapered vase right in front of me. It's clean: no dust, no dirt, ready for a display case. Because I don't see duplicates of the last four digits following the "15," I assume it's the 131st pot brought over in 2015. What's really disturbing: there's enough room in the numbering scheme to support ten thousand pots smuggled in one year.

Ten thousand pots a year. Is Bandineau delusional, or is that really the volume he's moving? Could there possibly be that much Nam Ton ware in the world? I was expecting maybe a few dozen a year sneaking into the country, stuffed in the back corners of shipping containers. Even at a thousand a year, it wouldn't take long to empty whatever archaeological site they're in.

Which is plunder, not collecting.

I use my phone to shoot overall photos of each shelf and close-ups of groups of three to four pots. It takes more time than I like, but I need complete documentation when I send it to ICE. I ask George, "Find anything?"

George's been rummaging on and under the workbench behind me, trailing a whisper of jazz behind him. "The only paper here is butcher paper."

"His records must be on his phone or laptop." Bandineau's gotta have records; there's no point to inventory numbers if nothing tracks them. "What's with the—"

Bangbangbang.

After I scrape myself off the ceiling, I realize the noise came from the door. A guy's voice yells, "Open up in there!"

George and I swap stares. His eyes are as round as mine feel.

Bangbangbang.

My brain reboots. When in doubt, brazen it out. I grab a Nam Ton water bottle off a shelf, place it on a large green beanbag on the workbench, then jam on the nearby magnifying visor. "Hold on, in a minute."

Georges scowls at me. I motion to him to take off his gloves and go to the cube's far end. Then I clomp across the wooden floor to roll up the door. "What?"

It's the guard I saw earlier, a pale, youngish guy with a scrubby ginger beard. "What are you doing here?" He swings his flashlight beam into my face.

My first instinct is to be nice—try to get on the guy's good side. After losing his cameras, though, he may not be looking for a friend; he may be looking for somebody to blame. What would Carson do?

Go on the attack.

I growl, "Get that goddamn thing away from me." My heart sounds like a diesel engine at top rev. I hope he can't hear it. When the light slides away, I puff myself up as big as I can and try to work up an attitude out of thin air. "Twenty-four-hour access, right? What's the problem?"

"I didn't see you come in." The guard tries to peek around the doorjamb.

I block his view. "Not my fault. You weren't there. Aren't you supposed to be guarding the place?"

"I was on patrol." He waves to his left, toward the three small cubes. "See anyone else around? Someone swiped the lock off onea those."

"Just got here. I'm working."

"Late for that, isn't it?" The guard squints at me. "I don't remember you around here before. What'd you say your name is?"

"None of your fucking business. With two esses." *Don't push it too hard.* But he's getting too nosey and I'm starting to channel my inner Carson, who's all about pushing too hard. "Look, you got a problem with us being here? Call Mr. Bandineau. He'll be pissed if you wake him up, though. He'll want to know why you didn't see us on your cameras."

"Well, I—"

"Whatever." Good thing he can't see the back of my long-sleeved black work shirt—it's plastered to me with sweat. "It's the middle of the night and we've got work to do. Either call him or let us finish. Decide now."

The guard's jaw bunches. Did I go too far? He reaches for a jacket pocket. Hesitates. Shines the flashlight in my eyes again. "Make sure you go out the front."

"Make sure you're there to see me." I slam shut the door, then gulp air to shove the bile down my throat. It takes a few moments to breathe semi-normally again.

George whispers, "Brazen. I like it." We bump fists.

I pull off the magnifying goggles and wipe my forehead on my sleeve. "What's with the crates over there?"

"I'll check."

I scan the bench for anything that looks like a clue. Everything's freakishly neat. Then I look in the black metal trash can under the bench. It's empty... well, not quite. I drop it on the bench and shine the articulated lamp in it. There's a dusty half-round something plastered to the inside, about halfway down from the rim. After I poke at it some with a dental pick, I get it to unfold into a round sticker, about an inch across.

The center is a series of parallel red, white, and blue stripes that mimic the Thai flag. The dark-blue outer band holds white sans-serif lettering that says, "Made in Thailand." It's like something you'd see on a flowerpot at Cost Plus.

"George? You find anything over there?"

He's been rattling around, moving things. "Nothing so far."

"Look for anything about Thailand."

He doesn't ask why. I manage to pry the sticker off the trash can and attach it to a square yellow Post-It. Then I start (carefully) turning over pots to look for stickers. There aren't any, of course. No rolls of stickers anywhere.

My phone says we've been in here just shy of fifteen minutes. That may be too long. What if the guard decides to call Bandineau? SFPD could be lining up outside to blast through the door. "We should—"

"Got something."

George's hunched over a loose top from a wooden crate, about two feet square. He shines his flashlight on a sturdier version of those plastic sleeves you put on the outside of FedEx packages. Ghost text from the shipping document that used to be inside transferred to the plastic. Some of it uses standard Roman characters, while the rest is in Thai. I point. "What's it say?"

"Do I look Thai to you?"

I shoot a couple pictures with my phone, then use a metal putty knife from the bench to scrape the sleeve off the wood. I'll figure it out later. "We've been here too long. Let's go."

Are the cameras online? I try not to worry about it on the way out. We walk in the street's darkest part, keeping our heads down. The front gate doesn't open when we reach it.

My heart starts doing aerobatics. I count to ten, then look toward the office's glowing windows. The guard's standing in one of them, watching.

We stare at each other for forever. He doesn't look happy. He finally aims a remote at the gate, which starts to squeak and rattle open. George and I walk toward the growing gap. We'll be out in a minute.

The door screeches to a halt, then starts to close. I glance at the office; the guard's sneering at me. Little men with little power. I make a dash through the opening, George a couple steps behind me. We don't stop running until the floodlights can't reach us anymore.

Chapter 27

37 DAYS LEFT

Savannah's waiting for me at Achara's door when I get there at just before ten on an overcast, cold Wednesday morning. The wind bashes through my steel-gray Canali suit coat.

I say, "Well, if it isn't Savannah Abigail."

She rolls her eyes. "You've been reading Mother's Wiki page."

"Is it accurate?"

"As far as it goes. They're way too easy on her." She steps up to give me a lingering kiss. "Hiiiii."

"Hi. This' a different look for you. I'm used to you in a dress."

"It's too cold for that. You like it?" She turns a full circle to show off a cropped black suit coat with a standing collar and a low-cut white shell tucked into high-waisted, tapered-leg black slacks.

"I do. It's very sophisticated." I touch the necklace of cylindrical, earth-toned stoneware beads. "What's this?"

"It's Khmer." She takes my hand. Her skin's warm. "Ready to buy your first Nam Ton piece?"

"Yeah. Ready to protect me from the wolves?"

"Uh-huh." She pulls my hand around her back until we're in a clinch. The rest of her is warm, too. Her voice goes purry. "You're spending the night, right?"

"Just for you. Should we be doing this in front of the gallery?"

"I keep telling you." Kiss. "I don't care if they know." Kiss. "Let's go in before we freeze."

I shake with Bandineau (navy blazer, gray sweater-vest, windowpane plaid white button-down) and Lorena (sunflower-yellow *ao dai* over white slacks). Lorena offers us tea. While she pours, I act like I'm checking emails on my phone. I'm really turning on the audio recorder.

Teacups in hand, we gather around the usual sideboard.

Four Nam Ton wares rest on red-silk plinths at even intervals on the tabletop: two small bowls, a smallish tripod incense burner, and a voluptuous foot-tall vase with a graceful neck and trumpet mouth. They're all pretty, but the big piece is gorgeous. I'd be mighty impressed if I hadn't been inside a metal box last night with eighty-one of its cousins.

What would Savannah make of Bandineau's stockpile of pots? Would she see it as a travesty? The sacking of a culture? The best toy box ever? Or (I hope not) a business opportunity? I wish I knew.

Bandineau stands at the sideboard's corner. "Rick, this is why you've been on this journey with us. I know you've been unhappy with the delays, but it all pays off today." He swivels an open hand toward the pots. "These will be yours soon."

"All four?"

"Yes. I'll explain why in a few minutes. Now, Savannah tells me you've been studying Nam Ton. Are you comfortable with what you know about these pieces and the culture? Is there anything you'd like me to tell you about them?"

I guess pillow talk is fair game. Good to know. "Where do they come from?"

He laughs. "That's the million-dollar question, isn't it? Actually, Savannah's been looking into it."

I'm less than shocked, though it would've been nice if she'd mentioned it.

Bandineau holds a hand out toward her. "Can you share anything new with us?"

Savannah gives him a smile that looks like a sunny day at the North Pole. "I'll let you know."

Bandineau swivels to me. "The map at the museum is still the best idea we have. Is there anything *else* you'd like to know?"

I've been rethinking how to play this since last night. I don't want to slam Bandineau with the pictures yet; that needs to happen in a one-on-one. After playing hardball with them at lunch a couple weeks ago, I can't suddenly turn into a mushball. At the same time, I need this buy to happen so I get some product into my own hands and show Allyson some progress.

"What's the provenance?"

Lorena—who's been standing by the sideboard's other corner—smiles not quite enough for it to reach her eyes. "These pieces are from a collection assembled by a U.S. Air Force officer in the late 1950s. I'll provide you with the documentation once we finish the sale."

No surprise. "David Johnson again? Like the Phimai wares you sold me?"

"No, another man. A Colonel Spenser."

I glance at Savannah. She's watching me, her eyes and eyebrows curious.

Let's see how she reacts to this. "You know, I looked this up after I bought the first Phimai pot. The Air Force didn't go into Thailand until April of 1961. So, who are these guys? How'd they have enough free time to build these collections?"

Savannah's mouth twists. Amusement or shock? Bandineau shuffles his feet.

Lorena's face hasn't changed a bit. I wouldn't want to play poker with her. "I understand he was with the embassy. An attaché or some such."

Nice save. "Why's he selling now?"

"The colonel's widow died last year. His children are selling the collection through my gallery. Does that give you the information you need, Mr. Hoskins?"

Savannah hides a smile behind her teacup.

"Just as long as the provenance holds up when it's pushed." I hope they'll read that as moral flexibility. "Jim, how is it that people in the '50s could collect these wares when Nam Ton wasn't discovered until 2008?"

It's a reasonable newbie question, but it's a softball. Bandineau smiles as he fields it. "It wasn't studied scientifically until 2008, but pieces have been appearing in markets for decades. I'm sure that's how the colonel came by them." He points his hand toward the sideboard. "You're concerned that these aren't here legally?"

The edge in his voice suggests this might worry him. Good. "I'm concerned there's not enough of a story to answer basic questions about how they got here, and when. When ICE knocks on my door, I want them to go away happy."

Bandineau's smile freezes. Just for a second, but I catch it. Lorena barely blinks.

I feel Savannah's lips brush against my ear. "You know that saying about gift horses? This is that." When she pulls back, she ticks up her eyebrows just enough for me to see.

She knows. I don't know how, but I know she knows. I'll have to ask her later, after I break some customs laws.

Bandineau says, "Don't worry about that, Rick. The provenance has held up to scrutiny perfectly well so far. Feel free to call on us if there are any problems. Do you have any other concerns? Do you need any more information?"

I slowly scan the four wares. How long did they sit in that storage locker? How did Bandineau select these for me when there were so many to choose from? Did he take the dirt off them at that workbench, or did they come already cleaned and conserved? So many questions he'll need to answer soon, when I have his nuts in a vise. "How much?"

Relief washes over Bandineau's face. Even Lorena cracks what looks like a real smile. She says, "Before we get to the actual price, there's something we'd like to discuss with you."

Here it comes. "Well, let's get on with it. I have a meeting to go to."

Lorena throws Bandineau an *after you* glance. Bandineau says, "Of course. You asked about why there are four pieces. Only this one"—he points to the vase—"is for you to keep. Rick, do you remember how I mentioned that one of our goals is to have our collectors donate Nam Ton wares to museums?"

"I remember something like that." And I hope he's about to do what I think he is.

"Excellent. First: do you understand why we want to place Nam Ton wares in museums?"

"It makes the wares respectable. Safe for collectors. That boosts the value and broadens the market." It works for other kinds of art, too. Collectors are generally conservative even if they buy crazy *avant garde* work; you don't want to be a pioneer when you're writing an eight-figure check. That's why they take cues from big-name collectors or branded museums or buy from branded galleries or auction houses.

"Exactly. Nam Ton still isn't well-known in the U.S. The Norris put on an exhibition four years ago, but it didn't get the notice I thought it deserved. We still live in the shadow of our big brother in the Civic Center." He means the Asian Art Museum.

Savannah says, "It got Chad's and Brandon's attention."

Chad? Brandon? Two more of her clients? I'll need to look that up.

Bandineau smiles at her. "Yes, it did. Two of its few successes." He turns to me. "You and I already talked about how cautious accession committees can be. That's why we need potential patrons—like you—to donate pieces to museums to kick-start their collections. This is how we do it." He holds his hands on either side of the vase without touching it. "This is a beautiful piece, and I hope you like it as much as I do." He spreads his hands across the other three. "These are also nice, but not as spectacular. Still, any museum wanting to start a Nam Ton collection would be happy to have these. We propose that you buy all four, then donate these three to one of our partner institutions. The Museum of Asia-Pacific Cultures in Portland is interested in adding them to their Southeast Asian collection."

I focus on the pots, waiting for the other shoe to drop. It doesn't. "I don't want all four of them. The three small pieces don't speak to me." A polite way to say *meh*.

Lorena volleys. "That's understandable. We can offer you a special price for the lot. And you'll have the satisfaction of helping a small, regional museum that's trying to become an important institution in the Northwest."

Bandineau says, "I'm sure MAPC"—he pronounces it *map-see*— "will be happy to recognize your generosity."

Savannah snickers. I say to her, "Tell him how I'm recognized at LACMA."

She says, "The Fontana Collection" with a big smile.

"I'm not in this to get my name on a label. Lorena, tell me about that special price."

Another glance between Lorena and Bandineau, this one edgier. Lorena's back to her poker face. "It's $31,000 for the lot. A very reasonable price, I assure you."

Bandineau smiles again. He's going to wear out his teeth. "Two or three years from now, you'll call this a huge bargain."

"Maybe." I turn to Lorena. "How's this price 'special'?"

"I'll explain. When you purchase all four pieces, Jim will provide you with appraisals for each. The appraisal for the vase"—the tall one I'm coveting—"will be...?" She throws a look toward Bandineau.

"Twenty-seven to thirty thousand," he says without hesitation.

"A very fair price, in line with the market." Without mentioning that *they're* the market. "The other three will appraise for…?"

"Nine thousand each for the bowls." Bandineau waves toward the incense burner. "Ten to twelve thousand for the censer."

That doesn't make any sense. Either those prices are way inflated, or they have one hell of a margin on the sales. "Let me get this straight—I buy one and get three almost free? What's the catch?"

Bandineau says, "Why does there have to be a catch?"

"You're offering me a free lunch. Every time that happens, I wonder how I'm gonna pay for it down the road. I'm still trying to figure your angle."

Lorena says, "Our 'angle,' if you want to call it that, is this: you have an incentive to donate more pieces to museums. That brings in new buyers. Prices will go up. Also, you won't be satisfied with one piece. None of my other clients have been."

"This is like the dope dealer on the corner giving me a dime bag to get me hooked."

Lorena makes a face like her breakfast is eating her. "That's a rather… *sensational* comparison, but it's apt. Nam Ton is addictive. Savannah dear, how many Nam Ton pieces have Mr. Mellin and Mr. Cort purchased so far?"

Cort and Mellin. Last names for Brandon and Chad? I'll find out soon.

Savannah says, "That they've kept? Four dozen or so between them." She winks at me. "You've got some catching up to do."

"It's a race?" I swivel to Bandineau. "You'll give me written appraisals?"

"Of course."

"So I could donate the three little pieces to Portland and use those appraisals to claim an inflated tax writeoff. Is that a bug or a feature of this deal?"

We worked this scam at my old gallery. There was a regular client, a fund manager for Chase, who'd come by in November or December to buy some cheap canvas. He'd throw down a strap of hundreds and ask us to write up the sale for ten times the actual price. He'd donate the piece to some charity and claim the juiced valuation. He was proud of this. We did it because only part of that cash ever went on the gallery's books. We finally paid for it; I don't think he ever did.

Bandineau and Lorena exchange knowing looks. Bandineau says, "We certainly couldn't encourage you to do that."

Lorena: "It would be illegal."

Bandineau: "It's between you and your tax accountant."

Lorena: "It's not unheard of, of course. But we can't advise you on the matter."

Shit. It's obvious what they're doing here, but they're smart enough not to say it out loud. My recording's useless. They won this round.

I get a full dose of Savannah's perfume when I lean in to whisper in her ear. "What do you think?"

She props her right elbow on her wrist and holds her chin in her hand. After pondering a few moments, she asks Lorena, "How much for just the vase?"

Lorena smiles. "Twenty-nine thousand dollars."

Savannah bumps an eyebrow at me.

I say to Lorena, "At the top end of the market. In other words, it doesn't make sense for me to not take your deal."

Lorena nods once.

I know I have to buy the pots. I know it's not worth Hoskins' time to dicker over the price. What I have to do now is theater. "I need to talk to my advisor for a minute." Then I grab Savannah's arm and steer her into the statue gallery. She doesn't seem to mind when I get all up-close-and-personal with her. I murmur, "When I asked you whether you'd seen Jim do anything sketchy, you didn't think to mention this?"

She scowls at me. "It's an art gallery. Everyone does it." Not everyone, but enough do. "Don't feel special—they've done it to all my clients."

Aha. "Do any of your clients push back?"

"They tried. Ohlmeyer succeeded, but that was early on."

Ohlmeyer? Our Client's name? I can't ask her. Too bad Allyson didn't tell me. "What I need to know is, will Jim stand by his appraisals even if the feds put the screws to him? I don't intend to be the only one twisting in the wind if it goes bad."

Savannah pulls away, her eyebrows stretching. "Does that include me?"

The real answer is *yes*, but it's not the one she needs to hear now.

I take her hands and kiss her forehead. "You're my favorite art advisor in the whole wide world."

She peers into my eyes for a few moments, then squeezes my hands and smiles a little. Either she didn't notice I didn't answer her question, or she did and figures it's as good as she's going to get. "What do you want to do?"

"What can I do? I either take the pieces they're dumping on me, or I get nothing."

Savannah glances toward the ceramics gallery, then grabs my hand and tows me almost to the front door. "Remember what I said about the Chinese market?" Her voice is low, but not so low that my phone won't pick it up. Yes, I feel a little like a jerk.

"Yeah."

"I have a friend there." That's convenient. "I send the wares to him. He sells them, takes his commission, then sends the rest to me. I take my commission and give you what's left. Since your basis is $2,000, you'll definitely make money on them." She pulls back enough to show me her smile. "It's part of my services."

Services for clients, or services for boyfriends? "If I do this, what'll Jim and Lorena do?"

"Who says you have to tell them?"

"He'll ask when he doesn't hear from Portland."

"He didn't say to do it tomorrow." She cozies up again. "What do you want to do?"

I try not to look into those big blue eyes so I can think straight. I need to get those written appraisals so the IRS can work out a tax-fraud charge. I'm also curious how Savannah's scheme will turn out. And after all, I'd have to file Hoskins' tax return to be guilty, right? "Let's go buy some pots."

Chapter 28

I text Olivia the moment I get back to the suite: I have nam ton pots.

Congratulations.

I'd expected more enthusiasm, but whatever. Next, I email the photo I took at Achara to McCarran. He'd emailed on Monday to say he'd be in San Francisco today through Friday if I want to meet. I do; maybe he has more info for me, or maybe he got sucked into the donation racket too.

Finally, I pull my personal phone, scroll through the contacts, think for a moment, then punch one I haven't touched since before I went to prison. I half-expect the tones and "sorry, Charlie" recording, but it actually rings.

"Hello?" Very careful, like she expects her phone to explode.

"Toni? It's Matt Friedrich."

Long silence. "Matt? Are you out of jail?"

"Yeah, have been for a while. How's it going?"

"Uh... okay?" At least she's talking. Some people just hang up.

"Toni" is Antonia Torricelli, a nice Pennsylvania girl now living in Lotusland. She works (worked?) in the Getty Museum's conservation lab. Other than an annoying verbal tic (everything she says sounds like a question), she was a pretty normal person. My boss Gar and I bailed her out of a situation with her student loans (long story), and to repay us she'd do the odd checkup on canvases that came through our gallery's back door. If we were going to get stuck with a fake, we wanted to know about it.

"Say, do you still work for the Getty?"

"Uh... yes?"

"Great. I need some ceramics dated. Can you help me out?"

"I don't do ceramics? That's another lab?"

"Know anybody in that lab who'd help for some extra income?"

Another long pause. I hear rubbing against cloth. "Matt?" She's whispering. "Look, I really appreciate that you didn't tell anybody about me, but... well, I can't do that stuff anymore? I've been promoted? I've got a really good job with the Trust? I'm *married?* Please don't ruin it for me? Please?"

Toni always reminded me of the timid shop clerk in old movies who'd take off her Coke-bottle glasses and the hero would say, *Miss Baxter, you're beautiful!* Except with Toni, the glasses actually help. I put on my calming-the-spooked-horse voice. "Don't worry. This is legit. I just need a pot dated, fast. I'll pay with clean money. Do you know anybody who can help? Up there, out in the world...?" No answer, just hyperventilating. "You know you still owe me money, right?" Actually, I can't remember if she does or not; I hope she won't either.

Toni squeaks. "Okay, okay, okay, okay, I'll find someone. Please don't come here, okay? Please? People still know you?"

While I wait for my lunch at the Tadich Grill (the oldest continuously-run restaurant in California, apparently with some of the original staff), I look up "Chad Brandon Cort Mellon."

The top hit is for Brandon Cort, which leads to Chad Mellin (strange spelling). Tech bros, mid-forties, made their first fortunes at Yahoo. They co-founded BizBang five years ago. The *Wall Street Journal* called BizBang "eBay for the Fortune 1000" before its IPO last year. Cort's CEO; Mellin is COO. *Fast Company* says they had a falling-out over a bid Oracle made to buy them out about two years ago (Mellin was pro, Cort was anti; Cort won). All is supposedly forgiven (sure).

Artnet News ran a profile on Silicon Valley art collectors around the time of the BizBang IPO. Both Mellin and Cort showed up in it. They share a taste for Asian art: Cort buys both contemporary and antique pieces while Mellin is strictly old-school.

They also share an art advisor.

Bourbon and Branch hasn't changed in the three weeks since I was here last. The millennials are different, but they're dressed the same. I'm in the same booth as before. The password changed: tonight's is "Glenfiddich." The only thing missing is McCarran.

He'd emailed me at lunch to say he'd meet me at six. It's now six-fifteen. I'm starting to get peeved—I told Savannah I'd take her to dinner at seven.

Trey ambles in at six-twenty and shakes my hand as he sits. Same leather bomber jacket, different work shirt. "Beg pardon for bein' late. Once them Google boys get talking, they plain don't stop. Glad to see you ordered."

I drown my irritation with a pull from my Clase Azul Plata tequila, the same kind I got last time. "I'm sorry, too. I can't stay very long—I have a date at seven."

"Well, ain't you the lucky one." He gives me his crooked smile, then waves down a waiter and asks for a flight of bourbon. "Whatcha been up to lately?"

We chat for a few minutes about work without actually saying much. Part of it is from being dudes, but I know I'm trying to keep my work details from being traceable and I suspect he may be doing the same. Or maybe that's me being paranoid, appropriately or inappropriately.

McCarran's wooden platter of drinks appears. He samples from one of the snifters. "Those were some fine-looking Nam Ton pieces you got. I 'specially like the tall one."

"Me, too. The others were part of the package deal."

He nods. "Them the ones you're s'posed to donate?"

"Yeah. He got you on that too?"

"Yup. Which museum?"

"The one in Portland. You?"

"Someplace in San Diego. I told that ol' boy, 'Find me a museum in Texas I can donate to. Least then I got a reason.'" He rolls a sip of bourbon around his mouth for a few moments. "Gonna do it?"

"Do what?"

"Give 'em them pots?"

Something in his tone makes that a not-simple question to answer. "Did you?"

"Yup." McCarran leans back into his seat. "Lorena makes it real easy. She writes the letter for you—all you gotta do is sign it. She'll pack up everything and send it herself. You ain't even got to touch 'em if'n you don't want."

This sounds like something I'd expect to hear from Bandineau. "I don't know. It seems like a lot of trouble for not much upside."

He nods again, slower. "Yup, I reckoned the same 'til I started thinkin' on it. You do it a few times and it starts to add up."

"Sounds like you think I ought to do it." He shrugs. "It's tax fraud, you know."

He gives me a chuckle that sounds like it's coming out of the subway. "Rick, you know as well as I do that when you get to where we are, the whole damn tax code's a fraud. Think on all them things you ain't gotta pay taxes on or you can write off that regular folk can't. The way I see it? I'm givin' these here pots to museums that probably can't afford to buy 'em 'cause people like me and you holler so much about payin' the taxes that fund their grants."

"Just giving back."

"Yup."

This sales job is so comprehensive that I wonder if McCarran's part of the scheme. Is he Bandineau's way of following up, making sure I behave? If so, Jim's got more on the ball than I'd thought. What happens if I say no? What happens if I say yes?

I pretend to think about it as I finish my tequila. There's probably more of a downside to "no"; the supply of pots could suddenly dry up. "I've gotta say, you've got a point. I plan to buy more this year. Do you have any wares lined up to donate?"

He sets down his almost-empty snifter and thinks about it. "As it happens, I do. Why?"

"Want to swap? I send mine to San Diego, you send yours to Portland. At least I've got a better reason to give to a San Diego museum than you do."

McCarran finishes off the last swallow from his first snifter, then nods. "I reckon that'd work just fine." He taps the tabletop. "Beg pardon, but I gotta see a man about a horse." He pronounces it *hoss*. "Be back in two shakes."

While he's gone, I try to figure out why this conversation feels a little off. I didn't expect a hard sell from McCarran on anything, far less on the donation scam. But I have a hard time seeing McCarran as Bandineau's shill. If he's legit, what would he get from it? If he's a poseur like me, how can Bandineau afford him and still make money on this deal?

I'm frowning into my empty glass so hard that I don't notice

McCarran return until he thumps into the bench across the table from me. Only, it's not McCarran: it's a big, thick-featured, heavy-shouldered guy with a brownish crew cut gone too long between trims. Huh?

I say, "That seat's taken."

His mouth twitches into what he probably thinks is a smile. "Yeah. By me."

My meerkat brain's trying to tell me to dig a burrow and jump in. I don't listen to it. "Friend, you're not getting it. You're sitting somewhere else. I—"

"Nah, you're"—pronounced *youah*—"not getting this... Mr. Friedrich."

An iceberg forms in my stomach. He knows my real name.

The guy reaches for the black lanyard I didn't see around his neck until his hand went there. He pulls a black vinyl pouch from his black tee and lets it clank on the table. I stare at a gold eagle, a big "U.S." in the middle.

I say, "DEA." He nods. "I haven't touched anything stronger than weed since college."

"Not about that."

My meerkat brain's burrow is about ten feet deep now, and he's backfilling. I feel like the sentinel meerkat... the one the raptors take while the rest of the pack disappears. "This is a bar. Shouldn't you be ATF?"

"Not about that, ethah." His voice is from New England somewhere.

It finally dawns on me: McCarran's DEA. Tonight was a setup. I walked right into it. "What's it about?"

The DEA guy folds his arms on the table and leans in. "It's about me and you having a long talk. At my place. *Now.*"

Chapter 29

When the FBI finally took down our gallery, they weren't very nice about it. Gar tried to run, the stupid asshole. I'm sure that riled them up. I couldn't do anything; I was stunned. They said they told me several times to raise my hands. I don't remember hearing it. Actually, I don't remember much of what happened at all. They took complete paralysis for resistance and, as the report said, "compelled the suspect's compliance to direction." Let's just say I was glad I'd mopped the floor two days before.

DEA Special Agent Bruce Carruthers is a little more civilized. He doesn't cuff me in public; he lets me lead him out of the bar. Two of his buddies meet us outside and escort me to a black Taurus, which zig-zags us to the Phillip Burton Federal Building a few blocks away. Some tiny part of my brain works enough to do what I'm told; the rest is trying to force itself into that meerkat burrow before the hawks eat me.

They lead me to an interview room that looks exactly like every other federal interview room I've ever been in: eight by ten, beige walls, a steel door with a small reinforced-glass window on the latch side. I sit on a narrow wood-frame chair at the standard Formica-top table with its aluminum legs bolted to the linoleum floor. I'm still not cuffed, but they left shackles attached to the pipe across the tabletop to remind me how fast that could change. I'm facing a two-way mirror on the opposite wall. It shows me a pale, scared-looking bonehead who didn't see this coming. Good thing I talked to Len this morning; otherwise my probation would be breaking along with the rest of my world.

I was terrified by the time I hit the sidewalk outside the bar. A five-year-old could've led me here. Now that I've had however long to get my brain working again—there's no clock, and they took my phone once they got me in the car—I'm able to think more clearly about my situation.

I'm not under arrest. They didn't Mirandize me; they didn't restrain me. Of course, Carruthers said *yet*, so they think they have something on me. What worries me the most is that they have my real name. How'd they do that? I didn't tell McCarran. If they search my suite, the only name they'll find is "Hoskins." Yes, my fingerprints and DNA are probably in a bunch of government databases, but how would they have known to look? It's good I didn't have dinner; I'd probably have lost it by now.

Shit. Dinner. I've stood up Savannah. Not my biggest problem now, just another one.

The door's electric bolt sounds like a starter's pistol when it throws. Carruthers lumbers in, trailing another guy from the car, and sighs into the wooden chair across the table from me. The other guy leans against the wall next to some kind of control panel. Is that the one that gives me electric shocks?

Carruthers tosses two files on the table. I recognize the top one: it's my federal jacket, or at least one of them. A sharp pain sears my stomach. Is it the FBI's file? The Bureau of Prisons? The Probation Office? If it's the last one, I'm screwed; they'd get that from Len. The last thing I want is for Len to know I'm in this jam.

He waves over his shoulder at the other guy, who looks like an extra from the movie *Sicario*. That guy pushes some buttons on the control panel. Carruthers recites, "The time is 1937 hours"—*owas*—"Pacific Daylight Time on Wednesday, May 25th, 2016, in the U.S. Drug Enforcement Agency district office in San Francisco, California." He points to me. "Tell 'em who you ah." His voice grates like a rusty hacksaw on old pipe. His accent's way down my list of favorites.

"Matt Friedrich."

"Full name."

"Matthew Benjamin Friedrich."

Carruthers applauds silently. "Also present are DEA Special Agent Carruthahs and DEA Special Agent Medina. This is an informational interview only. The subject has been informed that he is here"—*heah*—"voluntarily and is free to go when he chooses. The subject will acknowledge this." He waits for me to figure out it's my cue. When I don't, he points to me again.

"So informed." It's the first I've heard about it, but I'm not in a position to complain.

First we go on a forced march through my criminal history. I had to do one of these for every single deposition I gave for all the other people I took down with me. It's like, can't you guys cut-and-paste? I think they do this so I'll feel like a skunk, which I do by the time we're done.

When we finally get to this year, I signal him to stop the recording. He scowls, then says, "Special Agent Carruthahs pausing the interview at 2041 hours." When Medina gives him thumbs-up, Carruthers growls "what?" at me.

"I can save you guys a lot of time. Talk to ICE. I'm their CI." CI = confidential informant. Hopeful Me thinks this is a typical interagency fuckup that they can settle among themselves with a phone call. Hopeful Me isn't right very often, but it never hurts to try.

He stares at me for a while. His eyes are gray and bloodshot. "Which office?"

"Here. San Francisco."

"Who's the case agent?"

"I don't know. It's part of the investigation into Chad Mellin and Brandon Cort." I spell it for him.

"How do you not know who the case agent is?"

"I've never met him. Look, this is a hands-off thing. There's a cutout between us. But they're getting reports." Or they're supposed to be.

Carruthers sighs. He gestures to Medina, who pulls his phone and starts a murmured conversation while he faces the wall by the two-way mirror. Medina's shoulders look like they'll bust out of his black DEA polo any minute.

Carruthers says, "This bettah not be bullshit."

I shake my head. "Look, I know how this works. Their people didn't tell your people, and now things are all balled up. I've been there before. This interagency stuff just never seems to work right, does it?"

He snorts and leans back in his chair.

"How'd you get my name so fast?"

"Last time you were in that bah? We got your glass."

Note to self: wipe the glassware. "So McCarran's one of yours."

"Neither confirm nor deny."

Medina stows his phone. When Carruthers looks back, Medina

shakes his head. Carruthers' face is several shades darker when he glares at me.

I hold up my hands. "Wait wait wait. What do you mean, 'no'?"

"I mean, they don't know you." Medina folds his arms, which makes his biceps look huge. "Tried both names."

Shit. The fear seeps back in. I shouldn't be surprised something fell in a hole, but Hopeful Me was so sure it wouldn't this time. My brain throws up a straw, so I grasp at it. "Walter J. Harrison. He's a federal judge here. The order for my early termination was drafted for his signature. Call him—he should be able to tell you."

Carruthers leans in over the table. "Not rousting a federal judge at nine at night to check your bullshit story. So, thanks loads for wasting twenty minutes of my life. Now we get back to—"

"Wait." My fear's strong enough now that I'm more afraid to not do something than I am to piss them off. "If you won't call the judge, then I want my phone call and I want my lawyer."

"You're not under arrest, remembah?"

"Maybe not now, but if I walk out of here, I will be by the time I hit the front door. I want to help you guys out, but I don't want to get screwed doing it. So."

Carruthers' face darkens a couple more shades. He twists to look at Medina. "Recording's good?"

"Yes, sir."

"Fuck it." He stands and glares at me. "Matthew Friedrich, you're under arrest for conspiracy to commit tax fraud. Please stand. You have the right to remain silent…"

A holding cell.

The upside: I'm by myself. No tatted-up gang neck-breakers, no meth barons, no biker thugs.

The downside: I'm alone in a tiny cell. The walls closed in about fifteen minutes after the door slammed behind me. Two hours later, I feel like I'm in an Altoids tin.

I called Olivia before they tossed me in here. It's lucky I memorized her number because they wouldn't give me back my phone. She promised a lawyer would be here "as soon as possible." But it's the middle of the night; who's going to come here now?

Since I'm scared wide awake, all I can do is stay curled up in the corner of my steel bed and let my brain bounce from one random thought to another.

Why the DEA? How do pots tie in with dope?

I have no way of telling Savannah what happened—even if I knew what to tell her.

Will they notify Len right away that they arrested me, or wait until morning? Either way, I just violated my probation.

I won't get bail. A felon facing a second felony charge? It's pretrial detention for me.

This is the first day of another really shitty part of my life.

As my thoughts circle the drain, I appreciate what a good idea it was for them to take my belt and tie.

The worst part in a whole sea of bad parts: there's no day, no night. Only humming fluorescent lights. The coldest, nastiest artificial interior lighting there is except arc light.

Appropriate for the coldest, nastiest night I've spent since I left prison.

Chapter 30

A contractor in a khaki uniform leads me to a dowdy conference room in the DEA office suite in the Federal Building. It's shocking to see daylight out the windows. The digital clock on the wall says it's 7:48. I got maybe an hour's worth of sleep in five- or ten-minute increments during a night that lasted an eternity.

I wonder why I'm in a conference room and not an interview room. The guard didn't say. I could try to walk out, but the roomful of cops outside makes that seem like a bad bet even as poorly as my brain's working now.

At ten after eight, an admin ushers in an elegant, silver-haired black man wearing a navy three-piece pinstripe suit that looks like it grew on him. He says, "Are you Friedrich?"

"Yes, sir."

He extends his hand. "Lemuel Samson, Esquire. Lazarett, Holt and Singleton. I'll be representing you." His mellow baritone feels like a warm blanket. Just what I needed.

"Thanks. Olivia sent you?"

"Ms. DeWitt sent me. Let's get down to business, shall we?"

"Why are we here and not downstairs?" Meaning, in the holding area.

"I have a meeting here with the DEA at nine." Samson slips on his readers and starts hauling files out of his Maxwell Scott briefcase. "All this splendor is for us until then."

"This is splendor?"

"All the lights work and all the ceiling tiles are in place. For a federal building, that's splendor." Samson speaks calmly and deliberately, like he's talking me off a ledge. He slides a multi-page document in front of me. "Our standard representation letter. Please initial each page and sign at the end. Until you sign it, I can put anything you tell me on Facebook."

It's the familiar eye-watering legalese. I start skimming. "Your firm doesn't have a Facebook account, and your website's useless."

"Son, we don't get our clients from the internet. Simon Lazarett—the name on that letterhead—was a justice on the Ninth Circuit. The other partners call him 'the underachiever.' When my firm calls someone in the middle of the night, they tend to get their calls answered. That's how we found your ICE case agent so quickly. Are you actually going to read all that?"

Hearing they found the ICE guy takes a couple tons off my chest. "Habit. Is there a part in here about how I pay you?"

"No. There *is* a part about how the DeWitt Agency will pay my firm *unless* we discover you've acted counter to the agency's interests." He peers at me over his readers. "Did you?"

"I haven't gotten a good handle on what the agency's interests are."

"Understandable. Sign the form, son." When I'm done, he says, "Ms. DeWitt sent a summary of what you've been doing for the past thirty days. What I need to know is: why were you discussing committing tax fraud with a federal agent?"

"He started it." I tell him about McCarran from the time I met the man until he left the table last night. Samson takes notes on a yellow legal pad using a walnut-burl Montblanc. Once I finish, I ask, "It's entrapment, isn't it?"

"That may be beside the point." He flips through his notes and makes checkmarks next to several lines. "Did you ever suspect McCarran was a federal agent?"

"I didn't know what to make of him. He had a really good cover—better than Hoskins'—but I couldn't get comfortable with it."

"But you stayed in contact with him hoping he'd give you more information."

"Yes."

"Which you would've included in your report to ICE."

"Um… sure. Have you heard the recording yet?"

"Not yet. I hope to at the meeting." Samson sets his readers on the notepad and swivels to face me. "What do you know about Chad Mellin?"

My guess: he's the client. "I did some research on him after his name came up." I give him a rundown of what I found. "Why?"

He rocks his chair for a few moments, considering me. "I suspect most of what I'm about to tell you is available in public if you dig hard enough, so that's where you found it in case anyone asks. My firm represents Mr. Mellin. ICE has been looking at him since they started their investigation two years ago."

"Why's it taking so long?"

"It hasn't been a priority. I'm sure you've seen that the numbers involved aren't large. But now it's a *big* priority."

"Why now?"

"You haven't watched television since New Year's?"

"I get my TV streaming."

"You're leading a truly blessed life, son. There happens to be an election going on. The administration wants to clean up before the new people come in. Also, nailing the scalps of a few privileged white men to the wall would make certain parts of the electorate happy enough to leave their La-Z-Boys and vote."

That makes more sense than what little Allyson told me. "Is Mellin the type who'd pay six figures for information to get on ICE's good side?"

He chuckles. "A man as rich as Mr. Mellin wouldn't even stop to think about it if it keeps him out of handcuffs or out of jail." Samson leans back with a smile. "That's the beauty of being rich, or so I'm told."

"Where's the DEA fit?"

Samson shakes his head. "That, I can't tell you. I hope that subject will come up in the meeting."

"What's this meeting about, anyway?"

He rocks out of his chair. "This is when they'll decide if you're going to be a DEA asset..." he claps me on the shoulder "...or a suspect."

Chapter 31

They stick me in a small, windowless room with a smaller oval table before the nine o'clock meeting starts. It reminds me of an interview room, except not as homey. I'm not supposed to exist, so I guess I don't get invited to the party.

Twenty or so minutes later, another contractor appears, has me sign forms, then hands me a sealed, clear-plastic bag with my phone, cash, wallet, tie, and belt in it. I don't ask what happened. I don't care right now. They're letting me out.

Savannah called my phone three times last night and sent a dozen texts. They begin with `Running late?` and escalate to `Where are you? Are you ok? Please call I'm worried` ☹.

When I call back, her phone rings twice, then rolls to voicemail. What do I tell a machine? I send a text (`I'm ok something came up I'll try to call again`) instead.

A frosty text rolls in a few minutes later (`You're still alive`). I've been in the doghouse enough to know when I'm in the doghouse. I can't afford to have her pissed off at me—I don't know what she'll do with it.

I try to call again and finally reach her. After a chilly conversation, we settle on dinner, where I promise to tell her everything—at least, everything I need her to know. I say, "I promise I'll be there."

"You'd better be. If you're not, don't call me again." Click.

I get almost ninety minutes to stew about that, and McCarran, and whatever else jumps up to torture me. I call Bandineau to set up lunch so I can hit him with the storage cube. Somewhere along the way I fall asleep for fifteen minutes. It isn't restful.

Finally, Samson walks in. "Son, you're off the hook. They've dropped the charges."

Thank god. Something finally went right.

He gives me the *TV Guide* version of the meeting. After a lot of interagency head-butting, they came to a typically bureaucratic decision: DEA will continue its investigation separately, but they'll meet weekly with the Task Force (HSI and the IRS) to "discuss" information their operations uncover.

He says, "Both case agents are on their way to talk to you. Cooperate with them, answer their questions, make them feel good. They're just looking to catch up, not to trap you."

"Will you be here?"

"No. You don't need me for this." He must see the panic in my eyes because he pats me on the shoulder. "You'll be fine, son. If you get nervous, call me."

Carruthers and another guy appear five minutes after Samson leaves. Carruthers looks like his suit and tie are smothering him. The other guy gives me the once-over. "Friedrich?"

"Yes, sir."

He sticks out his hand. "Vern Talbot, ICE HSI. Good to meet you finally." He's in his late forties, balding, a profile off a Roman coin. He seems more comfortable in a suit than Carruthers does.

We settle around the table. Carruthers stares at me like I give him indigestion. "Whadda I do with you? I already got a UC working this line." He flops his arm on the table with the hand stretching out to Talbot. "Don't get why you need him neithah. You got agents—I know you do."

Talbot leans back, all smiles. "Sure. I've got UCs all over." I assume *UC* means undercover agents. "But I'll tell you—Friedrich here's about as far along as my UCs, but he did it in thirty days instead of a year, *and* he's not burned yet. I'm happy as a clam"—he flicks a glance at me—"so far."

That gives me a few seconds of warm fuzzies until I notice they're both staring at me. I guess it's my turn. "Thank you, Agent Talbot. I'm glad you're happy with my work."

"So far."

"Right." Warm fuzzies—gone. I watch Carruthers drill holes in my teeth with his eyes. "Agent Carruthers, I've got one big question right now: what do pots have to do with drugs?"

He makes a sour face and scratches the back of his head. The look he gives Talbot is almost a plea—*help me out here, will you?*

Talbot says, "Go ahead, Bruce. I'd love to hear this."

Carruthers sighs. "Fine. Back 2011, early 2012, Oakland PD starts finding dead junkies. They got some kinda super heroin. Real pure"—*puah*—"real strong. Not cut with fentanyl or any of that shit. Number Four, except better, you know? OPD calls for help. We figah the Mexicans for it. They own heroin on the coast, right? So we spend two years trying to work out which cartel's shipping in the dope, and how. By then, we got dead junkies all up and down the East Bay, and it's in Frisco. Thing that gets everyone spun up? Techies are getting it—and they're dyin'."

My brain tilts. "Wait a minute—techies are taking heroin?"

Talbot chuckles. "It's not just for skanks anymore."

Even Carruthers laughs a little. "True that. Look. This place's fulla people working eighty, hundred hours a week, week in, week out, to hit these crazy deadlines. How d'you think they do that? They start out on Red Bull when they're kids. Time they get here, they've moved up to Adderall, Provigil. When that don't give the bump no moah, it's coke or meth. They go to parties, drop Molly. Then they're all cranked up, can't sleep. So they take oxy or hydrocodone. When that don't work no moah, they move to heroin. God knows they got the money for it, not that it costs so much anyway."

Talbot smirks. "Score another one for the War on Drugs."

"Hey, watch that shit. We bust illegals all the time, but I don't ride you for it."

I put up a hand to each of them. "Guys, seriously? I'm losing my faith in federal law enforcement here."

Carruthers nods toward me and says to Talbot, "Smartah than he looks." He turns to me. "Right, I was sayin'. Couple years back, we get stupid lucky. TSA grabs a couriah with half a kilo of this shit in his checked bags. He flew Bangkok to Honolulu to Oakland. So now we know we're looking for Thais…"

Oh, god. Cops and their stories. They're worse than fishermen. Because I don't want to sit through the next half-hour of this, my brain's already running through the possibilities until I get to the one that makes most sense. "Are they smuggling heroin in the pots?"

Carruthers looks like I stole his best punchline. "Uh… yeah."

Oh, shit. Heroin.

My undergrad studies in pharmacology convinced me of one thing: I don't like other people stoned, and I really don't like me stoned. So other than the very occasional joint in social situations, I take my mind-altering chemicals out of a glass.

But the art world and drugs go together like hot dogs and nitrites. I saw... well, a *lot* of eye-opening things at gallery parties. And the big takeaway there (and at school) was that the people who sell hard drugs—like heroin—aren't at all nice.

I say, "How does that work? Why don't you guys find them coming in, like you do at the border?"

Carruthers leans back, nodding. "Yeah. We were wondering that, too. Then we busted a load on a containah ship in Port of Oakland. Out of Singapore, caught a storm"—*stoam*—"knocked around some containers. Sniffah dog alerted on a twenty-footah. We cracked it open, found crushed boxes, broken pots, and horse. So, lab guys tested it. It's the clay."

I swap a confused look with Talbot. He says, "What's the clay?"

"There's something in the clay." Carruthers points to his nose. "Confuses the dogs. They can't smell the junk."

Talbot laughs. "For real?"

"For reals."

I ask, "White slip, vivid blue underglaze?"

"Squiggles on the outside? Yeah, some of 'em. Some just painted, you know, red, tan, stuff on the outside. Mean something to you?"

Someone's mixing the Nam Ton wares with other styles of ceramics, all made from the same clay. "Got pictures?"

"Yeah. We shot everything."

Talbot makes a choking sound. "*Now* we find out. Can we get those?"

Carruthers shrugs. "I'll talk to the ASAC."

My brain's busy working out the next step. "You think they're moving the heroin around in the pots here?"

"Maybe. That's the angle McCarran's working. Not his real name, by the way."

"Yeah, I figured." I stop to think carefully about my next question. If the DEA already knows all about the drugs, they may also know where the ceramics come from and they're sitting on the info. If that's how it is, ICE doesn't need me anymore. Bad news for my early termination. So the last thing I want is to ask if they know where the drugs come from.

Talbot rocks his chair for a few moments. "Know where the H is coming from?"

Shit.

Carruthers says, "You mean before it hits Khlong Toei? No. We—"

I ask, "What's Khlong Toei?"

"Main seaport for Bangkok. We've run samples against all our comparators. Nothing. New product. We're getting shit cooperation from the Thais. Probably means whoever's doing this is hooked up with the army or the government. We're stuck going over containahs originating in Thailand manifested for handicrafts or souvenirs. Which is a—"

"Wait." I hold up a finger to put him on "pause" while I think about this. "Why those?"

"That shipment we busted? Bills of lading said 'handicrafts' and 'folk aht' and 'souvenirs'."

"Those pots you found. Did they have 'Made in Thailand' stickers on the bottom?"

"Yeah. Why?"

"I found one in Bandineau's storage cube. It was in the trash." I also still have that document sleeve but haven't had time to do anything with it yet.

"Yeah?" For once, Carruthers looks interested in something I said. "Tell me about this cube."

Talbot wrestles some papers out of his black leather portfolio and shoves them across the table. "His report. Merry Christmas."

Carruthers leafs through the report. "You talk about the stickahs in here?"

"Yeah. Toward the end."

"Pitchas?"

Talbot slides a thumb drive toward him. "Happy New Year."

"What else you got in there?"

"Ask. We'll see."

I ask, "Did you look at Bandineau or Montford?"

Carruthers is reading my report now. "Yeah. Staked out the gallery—what is it, Achama?—intercepted a couple packages. Nothin'. They're moving the pots, though, so we're still looking. Bandineau's up to his neck in it, but we got nothing on a narco connection yet."

I hesitate to ask this, but I need to know. "How about the art advisor? Kendicott?"

"Oh yeah, her. Yeah, we looked at her a lot." Carruthers winks. "A real lookah, that one. She's a busy girl, but we didn't see nothing that'd get us a warrant."

Phew. At least Savannah's not their prime suspect. "What do you want me to look for?"

Carruthers drops the report on the table, rocks back, and folds his hands behind his head. "Just stay outta my way. Don't fuck with my people, just—"

"For chrissake, Bruce." Talbot squints at Carruthers like he's aiming at him. "He's going to be out there anyway. He doesn't know who your people are. While he's asking questions for us, he can ask for you. Don't be a dick."

"You should talk." Carruthers swivels toward me. "You know what drugs look like, Mistah I've-Only-Done-Pot-Since-College?"

"I've got a good idea."

"Good. You see any, let us know. Otherwise, stay out of our shit."

After more jousting and more stories, Carruthers leaves to talk to his higher-ups. Talbot and I sit side-by-side, sighing and staring at the table.

Talbot says, "Good work."

"Thanks."

"How'd you get in so fast?"

I'm sleeping with one of the suspects? "Just talented, I guess."

"Well, keep it up."

I never expected to get a shot at the guy who officially doesn't know me. Since I have one, I might as well take it. "I know the deal with Mellin was for sixty days. If I'm close to something on Day 59, are you really gonna pull the plug on it?"

"We'll see. Something for you to remember—you're useful only if you're developing intel for us that we can't get. If we develop the intel ourselves, we'll run with that instead of yours. It's cleaner for us. You hear me?"

In other words, I'm racing against his people to get to the end. "Yes, sir."

"Something else. You noticed nobody was taking notes in here, right?" I nod. "This meeting didn't happen. You're still off-books. We had to read Bruce in on you so he'll stop arresting you. So even though you've seen me, nothing changes. Everything goes through your normal channels—nothing comes straight to me. You hear that, too?"

Translation: if anything happens, we don't know you. "Yes, sir. One more question. How far do you want me to take this?"

He considers this. "To the source."

The worst possible answer. "The *ultimate* source? Where the pots come from? Or just to who's importing them?"

"Where they come from. We want this stopped. The only way to do that is to keep people from digging up the pots. We can't do that until we know where they are."

And here I was starting to feel good about this. "Nobody knows where they are."

"Somebody does." Talbot zips his portfolio and stands to go. "Find that somebody. You've got plenty of time." He checks his watch "Thirty-six days. Better get to it."

Chapter 32

The Tabletop Tap House on Fourth Street in the Metreon mall's ground floor is full of a mixed bag of geeks: the local ones who work around here and the visiting ones from the IEEE convention across the street in the Moscone Center.

Bandineau and I grab two seats at the end of the long tufted-leather banquette that stretches along one wall of the hangar-like dining room. Between the groups of tech bros using their outdoor voices and the sound bounce from all the hard surfaces, there's no chance we'll be overheard.

We make polite chat until the food arrives. I don't want to hit him right away; I want to lull him into a false sense of security first. I'm halfway into my grilled chicken-bacon-red-leaf-lettuce-tomato sandwich before I reach into my coat pocket and drop a four-by-six manila envelope on his side of the table.

He gives it the confused-dog look, then opens the envelope and starts sorting through the printouts of the photos I took Tuesday night. His face slowly bleaches. His left hand—the one holding the stack—starts to shake. "Where did you get these?"

"Due diligence."

I've never blackmailed—actually, extorted—anybody before. It's not something I ever thought I'd do. I'd tried to figure out how to do this without actually threatening the man but could never make it work. I finally had to decide this morning which way I'd go: keep one of my few remaining scruples or grab for my freedom. Being sleep-deprived and grouchy from last night made the decision easier, if not better.

He carefully sets down the photos, then props his elbows on the table, folds his hands, and rests his mouth against them. He breathes so deeply, it makes his shoulders rise and fall. "Why do you have them?"

"I want to know who I'm doing business with." I'm letting

Hoskins handle this...

"I can explain."

"Then start." ...and Hoskins can be such a prick. I hope he's not really me.

Bandineau stares at the table for a while. "What do you want?"

"Well, you can start with that explanation."

He nods. "Ehm... the wares come in batches. Every quarter. It... takes a while to sell them. We're being careful, as you already know."

"Even quarterly deliveries don't explain the backlog. You've got pots there that came in last year."

"The high-quality ones sell first." He still hasn't made eye contact since he opened the envelope. "Then we go through the... middling ones, if you will. They're often the ones we pick for donations."

"'We' is you and who else? Lorena?"

"No, not her." He objects fast enough to make me believe him. "She knows I can supply the wares, but she doesn't know anything more. No, it's... it's just me."

Watching Bandineau slowly droop makes me feel like a heel. As far as I can tell, he's not exactly a bad person. But I still hear Talbot saying *better get to it* and know I can't start feeling sorry for him. "Do you get only Nam Ton wares, or do you get other types, too?"

He sits straighter. "I'm not sure I'm comfortable telling you anything more. I've said too much already."

Figures. Well, if I'm not already destined to burn in hell, I will be after I finish this. "Did you know there's a DEA investigation going on right now?"

The small amount of color that had crept into Bandineau's face runs right out. "DEA? Why?"

"Why do you think? The people who're importing those pots are importing drugs, too. Did you know that?"

If there's something paler than white, that's the shade he turns. "I had... I had no idea. I'd..."

Time to finish crushing him. "They're looking at you, you know."

A little broken sound leaks out of his throat. "Oh, god." He breathes hard into his steepled hands. "Why...?"

Good thing I don't always need a mirror to shave. "Well, you made yourself a public advocate for Nam Ton. Or was it an evangelist? I can't remember which word you used." I force myself to keep watching him panic. "Look, I get it. You don't want to answer any more of my questions. I'm just some guy, right? But... I'm sure the DEA would be interested in those photos. You can explain it all to them."

"Please. That's not necessary."

"No, it isn't, not as long as you keep answering my questions. But it's gonna be a problem if you try to grow a spine."

His hands move randomly, like they've decided to ignore his brain. It's the first time I've seen him make gestures that don't seem programmed. I once accidentally broke one of my sister Diane's Barbies and I felt then like I do now—like a skunk.

He gets his breathing under control after a while. "Who *are* you?"

"I'm a dissatisfied customer. Here I thought I could grow my collection quickly, but you throw this bullshit 'donation' thing at me like it's something I have to do. You don't know your customers. That kills so many businesses."

Bandineau sits there blinking at me. "I... I don't understand."

I fold my arms on the table and lean forward, giving him my most sincere look. "Jim, I don't want you to fail. I want you to *succeed*. But you're screwing up, and we can't have that. So you're going to do what I tell you, and we're both going to win, and you'll get the job and the house and the woman. Got it?"

He looks bewildered, but he seems to be slowly getting it together. "Yes. I think."

I have an ask in here. If I come right out with it, he'll probably push back, and then I have to threaten him some more, and he'll hyperventilate again. But I can layer it with so much bullshit that he'll want to do it. I hope.

I point to his plate. "Eat. Your brain needs food. Now, you're a nice guy. I'm sure you're very good at your day job. But you're not a businessman. We need you to start thinking like a businessman. Okay?"

Bandineau nods in mid-chew.

"Good. First thing: know what business you're in. What business are you in, Jim?"

"Well... ehm... there's a philanthropic part, and there's—"

"Stop. Charity isn't a business unless you're the charity. You're in the luxury goods business. Nobody *needs* a five-million-dollar painting. Nobody *needs* a half-million-dollar car. And nobody *needs* an antique pot. People buy them because they *want* them. And preferably, they want it so nobody else can have it, but everybody else can see it. With me so far?"

He's stopped eating and is just watching me. "I think so, yes."

"Good. Next: know your customer. Who he is, what appeals to him. What appeals? They want to buy something their friends don't have. And they want the best. Nothing 'middling.' What doesn't appeal? Your donation scam. Your customers don't give a damn about a five-grand tax write-off, so just knock that shit off and leave the IRS out of it.

"That takes us to three: you can't covet something you can't see. Why isn't there Nam Ton ware in Achara?"

"Ehm… we don't want it to look as if there's a lot of it around. I'm sure you know about the Ban Chiang scandal. We're trying to learn from that."

I'm glad he brought it up. "Good. The people running the Ban Chiang thing were idiots. They flooded the market with product. They brought in so much, there was no way they could come up with credible provenance for it. It was obvious they were looting. I like what you're saying, but you learned the wrong lesson from that. Don't make Nam Ton invisible, which—"

"It's in museums. That's why we're trying to—"

"Jim. Nobody gives a shit about a small regional museum in Portland, or the number-two Asian museum in San Francisco. Your customers don't care. They'll care when Nam Ton shows up in the Met or the Kimbell or your competitor in the Civic Center." Bandineau raises his hand to object, but I beat him to it. "Yes, I know, that's why you went to LACMA. You won't get a Nam Ton placement there until a trustee marches into the director's office with one under her arm and says, 'Here, this is for you.' Trustees need to see it in a place where they can *buy* it."

Bandineau's recovered enough to manage a little laugh. "I feel like I should take notes."

"If you need to, do it. By the way: Lorena's great. She's a lovely woman. But she owns one gallery in a not-very-important art market. You need at least two more galleries selling Nam Ton—one in L.A., one in Manhattan. Maybe one in Vancouver—it's hip-deep in Chinese flight capital. They all need really primo display pieces with really primo prices."

"But we don't want to get the prices ahead of the market, do we?"

He doesn't get it—he owns the market now. "The pricing *makes* the market. Remember, you're selling luxury goods, not socks. The more expensive they are, the more luxurious your customers think they are." Gar pounded all this into my head when I started working at the gallery. I came in with my Econ 101 ideas of how markets work. He taught me that the art market is like quantum physics: all the normal rules don't apply.

He stares off into the middle distance while he thinks this over. "This will be quite a change in the way we do things."

"That's the point. You said your shipments are quarterly. How big are they?"

Bandineau spends some time examining his salad.

"Don't stop now. You know what happens when you stop."

Sigh. "It varies, but usually eighty to a hundred pieces."

"All Nam Ton?"

"Now, yes. They tried to sell some others to me, but they were all modern reproductions. Souvenir-shop stuff." There's that word again: *souvenir*.

"Of those eighty to a hundred, how many are good pieces? I mean, like that vase you sold me."

"Half or less. The rest are fine, but they're nothing special."

Forty or fifty high-quality pots every quarter. Two hundred a year. "How long before they run out?"

"No one's mentioned running out. I have no idea how big the site is. I'm afraid to ask."

I sit back and watch him study the table, trying to figure him out. "That takes care of the scarcity angle. There's got to be a bottom to the supply. You're still buying all of them, though. You need to stop that—you're just throwing money away. Tell your source you're only taking the good stuff, the ones you pick. He can keep the rest."

This makes him sit up straight. "The others are still eight hundred years old! I can't just leave them to… this person. What if he throws them away?"

"Why would he do that? Why wouldn't he sell them to

somebody else?"

"Then they'll be competition."

"Selling the cheap stuff. It'll make yours look better. Remember, Jim: *luxury goods*. You don't sell the factory seconds. What's your margin?"

"I'm sorry, I don't understand."

"Your profit margin. Two digits?" His face doesn't change. "Three?"

He gives me a weak little smile. "It's healthy."

Damn, I'll say. "Is your source here or in Thailand?"

"Why do you ask?"

"C'mon, Jim. It's a basic question. If he's local, you can pick the pieces in person. If he's overseas, you have another link in the chain to get them from there to here. Another middleman; more lost profit. Is he local or long-distance?"

He folds his arms and watches his food get cold for what turns into a long while.

This looks like resistance, which I can't afford. "Do I need to remind you what happens when you stop answering questions?"

His eyes squeeze closed. "Local."

"Good." Now I try for what I wanted in the first place. "I need to talk to him soon."

Bandineau's head snaps up. "Why? He's *my* contact. It's *my* deal. Why do you need to get involved in it?"

Dammit, I was afraid he'd say that. I lean forward and aim a loaded finger at him. "Because DEA somehow made the connection between whoever's moving the drugs, to you, then to me. Maybe it was your lack of security, or maybe it was your source's. We can fix yours; we can't fix his. But it sounds like it's time somebody else took a look at this guy to see how untrustworthy he is."

"How are you qualified to do that?"

"There are a lot of weasels in construction supply. I've gotten pretty good at smelling them. I also skated close to the edge with a couple canvases I bought. Art weasels smell like building-supply weasels, just with nicer clothes." I pause for effect. "I thought you wanted to know who you're doing business with."

He's been shaking his head a lot today. "I don't know if he'll even agree to meet with—"

"Tell him it's not optional. If he doesn't, I drop a bridge on you.

While you're going down, you'll tell the feds all about him. Then he gets to meet with the DEA. They won't be friendly, and they have guns. Understand?"

Swallow. "Yes."

I can stop beating on him now. I may be as happy about that as he'll be. "Good. When's your next shipment due? I can't wait to see the new pots."

His smile looks tired rather than happy. "Two weeks or so. It left Bangkok on the tenth, and it takes four weeks or so to get across the Pacific if there aren't any weather or port problems. My source brings me the new inventory about a week after it arrives."

"Let's get things straightened out before that happens." He nods. "Once we get this enterprise of yours tightened up, with your margins, you'll be raking it in. Then you can go after your dream house and the woman that goes with it."

Bandineau aims a weary look at me. "If I don't get arrested first."

That goes for both of us.

Chapter 33

I was too busy to think about it this morning, but the address Savannah texted me sounded familiar. I understand why when we stop on 18ᵗʰ Street half a block west of Guerrero. A two-story, late-Victorian townhouse, pear with cream-and-rust trim, with bay windows stacked over a flip-up garage door.

Bandineau's duplex.

Okay.

Savannah comes out of the right-hand door, the one to the upstairs flat. I hold open the limo's back passenger-side door. I need her inside before Hoskins starts beating on her.

A curtain twitches open in the upstairs bay window. A cute young Asian woman and a slightly less-cute young blonde peer down at me. They giggle, point, nudge each other, then start taking pictures with their phones as Savannah gets in range.

I point to the window. "You have fans."

She glances up, rolls her eyes, then gives them the get-outta-here wave. Her fans just giggle and take more pictures.

I hand her into the back seat. "Friends of yours?"

"Sometimes." She's wearing a vee-necked little black dress, cap sleeves with a standing collar. It slips nicely up her thighs as she settles into the seat. Her hair's done in a low-hanging French twist. She leans forward to tell the driver, "974 Valencia. It's between Liberty and 21ˢᵗ."

Once we leave the curb and the junior paparazzi, she crosses her legs, folds her hands in her lap, and watches the streetscape roll by. I expect frost to form on her window.

If I was being me, I'd try to apologize my way back onto her good side. But Savannah knows rich men—grew up with them—and knows how they act. To her I'm Hoskins, and after the night he'd had, she'd know he wouldn't give a damn about her hurt feelings. He doesn't, but I do, and I hate what I have to do now.

She'd told me when she visited the Bel Air house that she wears black or white when she's working. Hoskins says, "Black dress. So this is work?"

Her jaw flexes. "What's her name?"

"Whose name?"

Savannah takes in a breath that inflates her whole upper body, then lets it out slow. "You stand me up and you don't answer your phone." Every word snaps. "Then you send me a text that doesn't explain a thing. I know what makes a man act that way. So please tell me her name so when we argue about her, I can call her something other than 'your bitch'."

Shit. I'm in a deeper hole than I thought. I need to fix this. I need her, and I like her. I've had time to decide how much of what to tell her—I hope I can give it to her the way Hoskins would instead of trying to be nice.

I wait the better part of a minute. "Bruce."

Her eyebrows make a run for her hairline. She finally stares at me. "Bruce?" I nod. Her jaw slowly sags open. "Uh… okay. I wasn't expecting that. You seem so… straight."

It's all I can do to keep from laughing. When I first met Carson, she thought I was gay.

"I can be open-minded. I just…"

"Special Agent Bruce Carruthers. Drug Enforcement Agency."

"DEA?" Now she looks bewildered. "What did you do?"

"I bought a pot from Achara." I throw the words at her. "They got it from somebody who's been smuggling heroin into the Bay Area. My good friend Bruce took my phone, interrogated me, arrested me, and threw me into a holding cell. It took until this morning for my lawyer to get me out. I texted as soon as I got my phone back. I was too tired to figure out how to put all that in a text. Not sorry."

Savannah stares at me. There's lots going on behind her eyes. She finally shakes her head hard. "That's crazy. That's just… I'm sorry, are you serious?"

That would piss me off even if I was being me. Hoskins pins her with a stare until she shifts in her seat and swallows. "Let's get something straight. You and me? We're not married. There's no paperwork between us. I've made no promises. So if there *was* another woman, I wouldn't bother to lie to you about it." *I hate talking to her this way…* "Now, I can guarantee that the last twenty-four hours have been way shittier for me than they have for you. So when I give you an explanation, have the courtesy to believe me." I tell the driver to pull over. "Or you can get out right here. Pick one."

Savannah's expression is like I flogged her with a bag of wet fish. Her mouth opens and closes a couple times without any sound coming out. She stares out her window. I can tell she's scoping the neighborhood, figuring whether she can get out of a limo in an expensive dress and survive here long enough to get a ride home. Whether she can do without the commissions she thinks she can get from Hoskins.

I throw her a bone. "I was having a drink with Trey when they came for me. In your Uber back home? Call him; he'll tell you."

I called McCarran earlier this afternoon. He didn't pick up—big surprise—so I left a voicemail along the lines of *no hard feelings, but if Savannah calls, tell her what happened, okay?* He may not have many reasons to tell the truth. Maybe it'll blow his cover or something. I'm hoping he'll do the right thing, using my definition of "right" instead of his.

Savannah finally forces out some words. "Trey was with you?"

"He saw them take me."

More stewing. She inspects her manicure, which is flawless. She watches a dog walker trot by behind enough dogs for a sled team. She gets out, then slams the door behind her.

I don't want to go this way. I can't tell her that without turning off Hoskins.

Savannah stands on the curb with her back to me, her shoulders stiff. Then she turns to stare at the window she used to be on the inside of. After a few moments, she raps on the glass.

I wait a beat, then open the window.

She glowers at me, though her chin isn't as strong as it was. "Aren't you going to ask me to get back in?"

"You led me into a trap. Ever wear handcuffs? It's fucking humiliating. You want back in? Climb in. But I'm not begging you for anything."

She swallows. Hesitates. Gets in, slams the door. Leans forward to tell the driver, "Keep going." Then sits bolt upright, her chin turned up. "Bastard."

"Say that after you've spent the night in a holding cell."

We pull to the curb on Valencia, one of the Mission District's main commercial streets. It's a lot of two- and three-story Victorian townhouses with commercial on the ground floor. The streetlights glow and the sidewalks bustle in the twilight. I remember how scruffy this area was when we came to see Mission Dolores when I was a kid. Not anymore.

Lolo is crowded and noisy, with a lot of action near the front door around a bar with a photomural of palm trees and sunsets behind it. The seater walks us to a table underneath a collection of car doors hung on the back wall.

I ask, "What *is* this place?"

"California Jaliscan." She bites off the ends of the words.

We order drinks and dinner. Savannah folds her hands on the edge of the table and watches me for a moment. "There's something you should know about me."

"What's that?"

She works her mouth for a few moments. "My ex-husband used to disappear overnight. Wouldn't call or answer his phone. He'd come back the next day and give me a story about how he'd worked late, then went out drinking with his work friends and he didn't want to come home drunk, or whatever. He'd bring me a 'sorry' present. I bought it the first few times. I was young and…"

"Naïve?"

She sniffs. "Stupid. Being in love lowers your IQ by about forty points. I figured it out, though. I didn't want to believe it—denial's a big part of being in love, too, I think—until he caught the clap from one of his playmates and gave it to me."

"Ouch." Wait. "You're better now, right?"

She snaps, "Nine years ago. Yes, I'm better."

The waitress brings our drinks. Savannah takes a hit from a tumbler with an orange slice floating in a sea of brown. "I cried a lot, got insanely mad and confronted him at his office in front of all his work friends, then filed for divorce."

"Good for you." I mean it, too. Giving your steady an STD is just plain rude.

"Thanks. Now you know why I reacted the way I did." Savannah sets down her glass, then folds her hands again. "You know, you're right. We're not married. You haven't proposed. I'm just some girl who sleeps with you sometimes." Her jaw stiffens. "You said you expected courtesy from me? Well, I expect it from you, too. If you ever talk to me again the way you did on the way here? I'll walk away and disappear. Is that clear?"

I admire her sticking up for herself and telling off Hoskins. He's not so wild about it. "If you ever talk to me again the way *you* did in the car? You won't have that decision to make. Is *that* clear?" I wait for her lips to finish disappearing. "Now what the hell have you gotten me into?"

I give her a highly sanitized version of last evening's festivities, mixed with some nuggets I learned this morning. We chip away at the house-made tortilla chips and chunky fresh salsa more for form than out of hunger. She asks a lot of questions. Sometimes Hoskins even answers them.

Savannah looks and sounds lost by the end. "I have no clue about any of this. Jim and Lorena moving drugs around? It's crazy. If I saw anything like that, I'd go to the police." She shakes her head. "Where did all this come from?"

"My good buddy Bruce. Your competition. He's been watching them... and *you*."

Her eyes go circular. "Me? He's watching *me?* Why?"

"Maybe because you're friends with these people you hooked me up with. The ones with the DEA on their backs? Thanks for that."

"I didn't know!"

"You're supposed to know. That's why I pay you."

Ever since Tuesday night, I've been trying to figure whether it's worth dumping the photos of Bandineau's storage cube on Savannah. It is. I slap them on her placemat.

She gets through the first two before she asks, "What *is* this?"

The waitress interrupts with the first part of our food: small, Instagram-ready dishes, a kind of Mexican tapas. I scoop up a spicy beef *albondiga* (meatball with tomato sauce) before I answer. "Jim's storage locker. It's in Potrero Hill, if you know where that is."

"How did you *get* these?" Her volume's about doubled.

"Keep it down. I have ways."

Savannah sorts through the pictures, glancing at me now and then. She stops at a shot of the two shelf units. "Wow." She doesn't sound shocked, only mildly surprised.

Wow? That's it? When she starts to count the Nam Ton wares, I say, "Eighty-one."

She works her way through a meatball and a *tlacoyo* (basically, a Mexican vegetarian pita pocket) while she reviews the photos again. Then she flags down the waitress to order something called a Mezcal Mule.

"Well?"

She stacks the photos, slides them into their envelope, then gives it to me with a slightly trembling hand. "I never thought he'd stockpile them like this. Not at this scale."

"Any idea who his supplier is?"

"They're not coming from the markets—not this many." She bolts the remaining half of the last *albondiga*. "They're not that common. I know; I've looked."

"Where, then?"

"I'd be guessing."

"So guess."

Savannah's Mezcal Mule appears, an amber drink with a lime peel on top of the ice. The way she disappears the top inch says she's more rattled than she lets on. "Maybe he has some kind of pipeline to northern Thailand? Someone with resources?"

"Like a drug trafficker?"

Savannah sags as the fight goes out of her. She drops her face into her hands and pleads, "What do you want me to say?"

"You can start with 'I'm sorry.'"

Sniff. "I'm sorry." She pushes out of her chair and swipes her purse strap off the back. "I have to go to the bathroom." There's no swing to her step when she leaves.

It's amazing what Hoskins can get away with. Having that kind of power would be awesome. I'd never be able to look in a mirror again, though.

Our empty plates are replaced by two more full ones while Savannah's gone. My appetite's gone, too, but Hoskins needs to eat. I pick at the new food, watch the ice melt in Savannah's drink, and hope that she'll come back.

She does after fifteen minutes or so, drops her purse on her chair, then stands next to me. When I look up, she bends, takes my face in her hands, then gives me a long, lingering kiss. She whispers, "I'm so sorry. Last night must've been horrible for you. I should've believed you."

"You talked to Trey?"

After a while, she nods a fraction of an inch. "Forgive me?"

Hoskins takes a shot before I can stop him. "You believe him, but you don't believe me?"

She works her mouth a few times without making any sound. "I...I thought you told me so I could call him and he can back you up." She tosses her hands. "Sorry. Forgive me?"

Hoskins wants me to say *not yet; maybe never.* I tell him to shut the fuck up—I'm tired of abusing Savannah and I won't kick her anymore. I stand and wrap my arms around her. "Forgiven."

We stay locked together for a few moments with the waitstaff brushing past us until she kisses me again, then sits and starts attacking the food. "I guess we both said some things—"

"Shhh." I watch Savannah eat for a while, then consider the wall behind her—painted mango, half-covered with origami boats. "How're you and Jim living in the same house?"

Her glass skids to a stop halfway to her mouth. After a deer-in-the-headlights moment, she slowly sets down her drink. "How do you know where Jim lives?"

"He and Lorena aren't the only people who can pry into other people's lives."

She sighs. "Promise you won't repeat what I'm about to tell you. *Especially* not to Jim."

"I promise." Until I need to.

She takes a bit more liquid courage. "It's mine."

"You own it? That must be some trust fund you've got."

"It was. When I finally got control of it, about six years ago? I had a lot of losses to make up for. The Leech did a—"

"'The Leech'?"

"My stepfather. You read Mother's Wiki page, right? Stanley Wilkes?"

"The hedge-fund guy."

"Get it right—the hedge-fund '*genius.*'" She says *genius* like it's a disease. "He's been bleeding her dry since they met. My trust fund, too. I needed to invest in something that never loses value, and the only thing I know of like that is San Francisco real estate. The house's worth about three times what I paid for it. I'm a millionaire again—not like you, but I'll take it."

"And Jim doesn't know you're the landlord."

"No. I dropped a hint that my building had a vacancy and he

moved in."

An idea explodes in my brain. I hate myself for thinking of it. But it's a pure Hoskins play to separate Savannah from her friends and have her totally commit to his goal.

I finish my beer while I roll the idea around and knock off the rough edges. "Ever hear of forfeiture?"

Her eyebrows try to meet in the middle. "What's that?"

"Once you're indicted, the DA will move to seize any assets that may have been bought with the proceeds of a crime. It's how they clean out drug dealers' accounts so they can't pay for fancy lawyers with dirty money. If you're convicted, you forfeit the seized assets to the government. It's a profit center for a lot of big-city PDs and the DOJ."

"Okay." She looks puzzled. She hasn't connected the dots yet.

"Your friend Jim—your tenant—is part of a criminal conspiracy. Whether it's about customs laws or drug smuggling, who knows. Doesn't matter. Knowing Jim, he'll flip on you the moment they cuff him."

The light dawns. Savannah's mouth sags open. "They wouldn't."

"Sure they would. A nice house in central San Francisco would pay for a lot of new toys for the DEA. Even if you're not convicted, you'll probably have to sell it to pay the lawyers."

Her face starts to dissolve. "No. Not my house."

Hoskins, you're such a bastard. "We're both in this, now. The DEA knows about you. They know about me."

She cups her hands around her nose and mouth and starts to breathe noisily. She whimpers, "I haven't *done* anything."

"Sometimes it doesn't matter." I hold out my hand to her, sweep my fingers as a prompt. She grabs it like she'll fall into the bay if she doesn't. "I don't want that to happen to you. I like you. The way we stop it is to make sure that if Jim goes down, he doesn't take you with him."

"H-how do we…?"

"We find out where he's getting the pots and who's giving them to him. Then we hand it to the feds." I squeeze her hand. "He sinks like a rock and we don't get splashed. You keep your house; I keep mine."

The pain in her eyes almost breaks my heart. She whispers, "He's my friend."

"Somebody looking at a stretch in the federal pen? He's got no friends." *Ask me—I know.* "I'm doing this with or without you. I'd rather do it with you."

I expect tears. They're there, shimmering in the candlelight. But she holds it together, wipes her nose with her napkin, blots her eyes, then sniffs. "What do you want me to do?"

Chapter 34

Southwest drops me at LAX at 11:35. I wait seemingly forever for my checked bag to pop out the chute. The Nam Ton vase is in my carry-on; I left the three sacrificial pots with Savannah to dump on the Chinese. We'd kissed (and other things) and made up last night.

I flog my rental car straight up the 405 to Getty Center Drive. I hand over the pot to Toni in the parking lot of the Leo Baeck Temple, the synagogue across the street from the entrance to the Getty Center. She's jumpier than a cat in a room full of vacuum cleaners. She promises she'll have it for me in a week, then slams the door and flees.

I sigh. It's hard to believe I still have this effect on people here. What happened to forgiveness?

After I finish my report and send it to Olivia, I go for a run to shake the stiffness out of my body, bake the Bay Area chill out of my bones, and think about what's next.

Two things need to happen to finish the project. One depends on Bandineau: he needs to get me a meeting with his supplier. That'll tell me if the supplier gets the pots direct from Thailand or from somebody on this side of the ocean. I hope it's the former—if the supplier has a domestic connection, then I have to do all this again, which will eat up more time I don't have.

The other depends on... well, somebody: I need to know where Nam Ton comes from. Hopeful Me hopes that Bandineau's connection pulls the stuff directly out of the ground in Thailand and ships it here. It would save a whole lot of time, but not even Hopeful

Me believes it'll work out that easily. Realistic Me has already decided Bandineau's supplier won't solve my problems and may add some more.

Maybe I should look for the source myself.

This is not only the kind of resourceful, success-oriented behavior Allyson expects from her associates, but also gives me an excuse to keep billing the project. That hasn't been a problem up to now, but I no longer have a house to build and I doubt Allyson will keep paying me €1500 a day to read books.

Savannah hasn't had any luck at this. But she's not as motivated as I am. I can do this.

I can do this. I keep telling myself this as Friday afternoon turns into Friday evening. I manage to find the places Savannah said she'd rejected, and the places I'd found last time I did this. The problem I keep running into is that I don't know how Thailand is set up, I can't read Thai, and I can't recognize when the same place has multiple names. None of that's going to change this weekend even if it is three days long (it's Memorial Day).

I grab a Stone Ruination IPA from the fridge—I've used my agency money to step up our beer game—and plunk into a plastic lawn chair on the patch of mostly-dead grass that used to be a pool. It's warm with a gentle onshore breeze that helps clear my head. This leads to thinking, then plotting, then some internet research on my work phone, then a call to Olivia.

She says, "At last, you ring. I've been pining."

"It's been five days."

"Time does tend to stretch when one is pining. How may I help?"

"Our mutual friend Rick"—Hoskins—"needs a weekend getaway to San Francisco."

Savannah says, "Oh, this is pretty. I love it already."

"This" is a city-view executive suite on the sixteenth floor of the Four Seasons San Francisco. Lots of cool grays and taupes, contemporary furniture, and an all-marble bathroom big enough for a party. Why not the St. Francis? The Four Seasons has a spa; the St. Francis doesn't. I figured Savannah would appreciate that.

I made a simple deal with her: she'd get the run of the place, including the spa, but when she wasn't being pampered, she'd help me look for the place where Dr. Udomprecha found Nam Ton. It's the name of a river, after all; it's got to be on a map someplace.

But after hours of searching spread over Saturday and Sunday, we come up with nothing. All I learn is that Dr. Udomprecha is female. "Pensri's a woman's name," Savannah tells me. "It means 'beauty of the moon.'" I've now got more digital maps of northern Thailand than I ever knew existed, but no better idea of where Nam Ton wares come from.

We don't work nonstop. It's fun letting Savannah haul me around, showing me her favorite places in the city. She also wants to play a lot. The things I do for the agency...

Using Savannah's phone to take a picture of her gets me a look at her call log. There's a lot of numbers with an "86" country code going back for weeks. Country code "86" is China. Her friend there? She was calling way before I got the wares for them to sell. Hmm.

On the flight home on Monday, I can't shake the feeling that the entire weekend was lost.

Then while I wait outside Terminal 1 at LAX for an Uber to take me home, I notice my work phone has a voicemail.

It's Bandineau. We're going to meet his supplier on Thursday.

Chapter 35

29 DAYS LEFT

Bandineau and I sit in the silver Chrysler 200 I rented at Oakland International Airport a few hours ago. We're parked in a long, narrow lot at the very northern tip of Alameda Island, across the street from what used to be Alameda Naval Air Station. It's now a collection of empty buildings and whatever businesses decided to hide out here. *Mythbusters* used to film their experiments on the runway a couple hundred yards west of us. Across the channel, Godzilla-sized cranes threaten two city-sized container ships in the floodlights' artificial sunshine.

The clock on the dash says it's 9:36 p.m. and it's 58 degrees outside. Bandineau's contact is late.

Bandineau hasn't had much to say since I picked him up at BART's 12th Street Station in downtown Oakland an hour ago. I can't tell if he's pissed at me, if he's talked out from his day, or if he's scared. Maybe all three.

I finally say, "How long do we wait for this guy?"

"He's usually late. Not *this* late, but late."

"How long have you known him?"

"Almost five years." His voice is like the air leaked out of him.

Around the time when the super-heroin problem flared up. "You sold Nam Ton before that, though."

"Yes, in small numbers."

I glance his way. Bandineau's dressed for work—a white suit shirt, russet tie, tan sweater vest, coffee-heather sportcoat. There was no handshake, and he hasn't looked at me since he got in the car. I up my estimate to mostly scared and pissed. "How'd you find him?"

"He found me. He said someone had given him my name as a dealer in Nam Ton. He said his company had taken over the supply line and there'd be more regular product for me. I didn't ask how all this happened or why." He finally looks me in the eye, then deflates a bit more. "I hope you appreciate he didn't want this meeting. I had to be very forceful with him."

"I do appreciate it, Jim. I think ultimately you will, too."

He turns to look out his window. There's nothing but empty, cracked asphalt between us and the next car fifty yards away. The streetlights look lonely.

The past three days have given me nonstop heartburn. Nothing more from Bandineau on the meeting, nothing from Allyson. The only new thing I actually finished was translating the document pouch from the crate in Bandineau's storage cube. Actually, another associate did, giving me an address in Thailand and one in Oakland. I'll send that in with my report from this meeting.

The days ticked down one by one. Yesterday was hard: it was Day 30 of the project, and I had to let it crawl by without accomplishing anything. Then Bandineau called first thing with the time for tonight's meeting. I guess he figured I could just hop in Hoskins' jet. If only. Because it's so late, I'm stuck here overnight.

"How'd you get involved with Nam Ton?"

He doesn't answer for a while. Then he chuckles. "She didn't tell you?"

"She who?"

"Savannah." He glances at me, maybe to check my reaction, then back to the parking lot. "She brought it to me. She gave me a printout of the journal article and asked me what I thought."

Not exactly what she'd told me. Although when I think back, she said *I know he read the journal article*, which isn't lying. Why not just tell me she'd given it to him? Unless she didn't and Bandineau's throwing shade.

When he doesn't continue, I say, "What *did* you think?"

"Well, of course, it's special when someone discovers a new culture. The photos were... extraordinary. I told her I thought it was very interesting and asked her to bring me any other information she came by."

"How come you hadn't seen it already?"

"She brought me a peer-review copy. It hadn't been published yet."

"That's not strange?"

He shakes his head. "I assume she still has connections at

Columbia. I'm familiar with one of her old professors—his work, at least; I've never met him. Anyway, a few months later, she returned from a trip to Thailand and brought me a lovely Nam Ton ewer. She said she'd bought it at a market. It was the first Nam Ton piece in our collection."

Savannah: *I think someone gave him his first piece.* A fudge, or the truth? I'll have to sort it out later.

"You mean, even though you knew it was exported in violation of Thai cultural heritage laws and the UNESCO treaty."

Bandineau throws up his hands. "If she'd bought it at a market, the damage was already done. It was already out of its context and for sale. At least if the Norris has it, it won't disappear into some collector's basement." He shrugs. "Sometimes we have to make these judgment calls. It's not black-and-white."

I wonder if ICE will see it that way.

A black Camaro swings into a space three over from ours on my side. There's one guy in it, but I can't see much of him. He turns on a phone—the inside of his car lights up—then holds it to his ear.

Bandineau's phone starts buzzing. "Yes?" He leans forward to look past me. "I see you... all right." He hangs up. "That's him. He wants to meet outside, between the cars."

"Let's get to it, then."

There's a sharp wind off the bay that rattles trash across the lot and ruffles the channel. I'm dressed like Carson out for a skulk: black jeans, black turtleneck, black windbreaker, black leather gloves. I figured Bandineau's source will take me more seriously if I look like one of him.

The guy who meets us is a shade shorter than me, blocky, square-faced. He's draped in a dark squall jacket (the lights screw with colors out here), dark Dockers, and what look like khaki lace-up boots. His hands are in his jacket pockets; I hope there's not a gun in there, too.

Bandineau says, "Thank you for coming. Rick, this is—"

The man says, "Dan."

I say, "Rick." So much for the formal introductions.

Dan jerks his head toward Bandineau and demands, "What are you to him?"

"Let's say that I'm a customer who's taken a close interest in Jim's success... and security."

Dan nods slowly. "He told me about that. Thought I had a tail on my way here—that's why I'm late." He has a normal-good voice: baritone, no accent, no *Goodfellas* tics.

Whoever followed him probably wasn't the DEA or ICE; as far as I know, they don't know about him, though they will after I file my report. I edge my back toward the bay. It gets the wind out of my face and out of my phone's microphone, which has been recording since Bandineau got in my car.

Still, I need to act pissed. "Christ. Did you bring them here? Are they out there?"

"No, no. I lost 'em before the tunnel. We're good."

"You better hope so. They know. They know about the heroin; they know about the pots. Tell me how that happened."

He waves his left hand. Is there a gun in his right? "I got nothing to do with drugs. I'm a legit importer. I—"

"A legit importer who handles trafficked antiquities. What else do you leave off—"

"Look. I don't know from trafficked." He's starting to sound irritated. I hope it'll make him talkative rather than homicidal. "I specialize. Toys, trinkets, souvenirs, folk art, handicrafts. These guys offered me a deal. Folk art, straight from—"

"Asian guys?"

There's just enough light on his face to let me see his eyes narrow. "Who told you that?"

"Seriously? This shit's coming from Thailand. Who else's gonna handle it? Are these the guys with the heroin?"

"How would I know?" Dan's voice gets louder. He steps toward me. "How do you know all this? How do we know *you're* not DEA?"

Suddenly, there's a gun in my face.

Bandineau finally wakes up. "Dan! No! Put that away, we don't need—"

Dan snaps, "How do you know he's not a narc? You bring him here, he says all this shit…"

I don't move. I can't; I'm paralyzed. Sweat runs down my flanks. I try to stay focused on Dan's eyes so I don't focus on the gun barrel about an inch from my forehead. I hope he reads this as stone-cold attitude rather than sheer terror.

"…Did they get to you? Is that why we're meeting? Jim, I—"

"I've been to his *house*." Bandineau sounds almost as panicked as

I feel. "I've seen his collection, his cars. His *housekeeper*. He knows the *mayor of Los Angeles*. For God's sake, put the gun down!"

Dan swivels his eyes to me. "Is that true? You know the mayor of L.A.?"

I hope the turtleneck hides the big gulp I need to get my voice going. "I gave Eric a bunch of money for his campaigns. We talk." I stick my hands in my windbreaker's pockets so he can't see them shake.

"I *saw* him." Bandineau's almost pleading. "He came to the *house*."

"Look, asshole." That must be Hoskins—or maybe Carson—talking because I can't think of a thing to say. "They arrested me. Probably because they know about *you*. They got talkative. I pulled a lot out of the questions they asked."

Dan stares at me for way too long. I try to stare back. The gun's muzzle moves in a tiny circle, like it can't decide which part of my brain to remove. Bandineau keeps pleading over and over with Dan to put the gun away, to the point where *I* want to tell him to shut up.

Finally, the gun disappears as quickly as it appeared.

My knees want to turn into Silly Putty, but I convince them to hold off. Breathing's another story, though. After a while, that restarts and I can talk again. "Can we get back to business now?"

Dan growls, "What do you want?"

"Your buddies on the other end of this have caused me a huge problem. They may cause a bigger problem for Jim. We need to know all you know about them so we can protect ourselves. You better start thinking about that too. Got that?" Dan nods once. He doesn't look happy, not that I especially care. "Okay. These Thai guys—are they the ones bringing the pots into the country, or are they just a cutout for whoever's the real importer?"

"Far as I know, they're the guys. But I was gonna tell you before, they're not Thai."

"They're not? The pots are coming from Thailand."

Dan sighs and shakes his head. "They ship from Bangkok, but they're not Thai. They're from Myanmar."

Holy. Shit.

No wonder I couldn't find Nam Ton in Thailand: it's not there.

No wonder the Thais aren't cooperating with the DEA: it's not their party.

Nobody says anything. I break the pregnant pause. "Jim, you got something to say?"

"I... I had no idea. I saw the Thai shipping documents and just assumed... Why didn't you mention this before?"

Dan says, "You never asked. I never got that you wanted to know much about where they came from."

Time to get back on track. "Okay, whatever. What ties you to these guys? Do you talk to them on the phone? Email? When you meet, is it always in the same place? Is it the same guys all—"

"Wait, wait." Dan holds up his hands. "Jesus, you ask a lot of questions. What's it to you?"

"We went over this right up front. Jim and I have a DEA problem." I bite off each sentence to make a show of being impatient. "We probably caught it from you. What we need to know is, are you protecting yourself? If you're not, I'm gonna assume your car is bugged or has a tracker and we're both out of here and you never hear from either of us again." I ignore the choking sound that comes from Jim's direction. "So answer the fucking questions or you get to look for another buyer."

I suppose I should be more careful talking to a guy who was holding a gun to my head a few minutes ago. I tell myself that if he wanted to shoot me, he'd have done it by now. It doesn't help.

Dan mutters something I don't try to decipher. "Jim, are you onboard with this? We had a deal."

Bandineau doesn't answer. I hope it doesn't mean he's rethinking our arrangement. I realize how close we are to the water, and how easy it would be for a body to go into it.

"Yes." Bandineau's voice cracks. "Yes, I am. Rick apparently knows how to do this better than I do. He's asking for both of us."

"Whatever." Dan shakes his head. "Different phone number every time. Same meeting place. One guy's there a lot, but he's always got someone different with him. Plain-wrap white panel trucks. Good enough for you?"

"You got a burner?"

"Of *course* I got a fucking burner. I've been doing this for years. *Never* had a cop problem 'til now."

"You've hooked up with heroin traffickers before?"

He doesn't answer.

We may be done here. I know better than to try for names or places; he'd know those make no difference to Hoskins. I've already found out more than I expected. I hold out my hand. "Give me your card."

Dan laughs. "So you can give it to the cops?"

"Get real. If I was a cop or worked for them, they'd already have about a thousand pictures of you and your car and have this whole thing on tape. They don't need your damn card to find you. This is so I can contact you without having Jim in the middle of it. Unless you want us as a package deal?"

He hurls a sharp look Bandineau's way, then hauls out his wallet and slaps a card on my palm. "If you never call, I won't be disappointed. Jim, watch your ass." He stalks away without another word.

Bandineau and I stand in the wind for a good minute after the Camaro growls off into the night. I hold the card to face the nearest light. *Manresa Imports, Daniel Coulson, President.* A West Oakland address. If the feds didn't know about him already, they will now.

Bandineau asks, "Should I be worried?"

"You should've been worried a long time ago."

Chapter 36

As soon as I get back to my motel room—I'm in the Holiday Inn Express just outside Oakland Airport, and no, I don't feel any smarter for it—I bring up Dr. Udomprecha's map on my laptop. The chunk of Myanmar in the box is what Savannah called "Shan State." Told me to forget about it. "The Bamar didn't have the skills back then to make anything like the Nam Ton wares," she said. I believed her.

It was too specific a diversion to be a mistake. She lied to me.

I wake up my laptop, go to English Google, and type "'Nam Ton' + 'Shan State'." Two hundred fourteen hits.

That sounds promising. The top two go to a site called travelingluck.com, and they look the same. I click on the first one. Once I scroll past the time zone and sunrise/sunset times, I get a slice of Google Maps with a green pin in the middle of a green patch of landscape. I zoom out until I can see borders. The green pin is north of Mandalay, in the northern part of Myanmar. Way outside the box on the paper's map.

I close that tab and go back to the search. I'm about to blow off the second link until I notice that the URL is slightly different from the first one. *Oh, what the hell.* I click.

What... the... hell...

The green pin's next to the yellow line of a road, apparently Highway 45. When I switch to satellite view, I see there's a river there. Promising, but of course, it's not labeled. I zoom out until I find the Thai border, then look in the box on the report's map for a border that matches. It's a hump that wraps around Doi Pha Hom Pok National Park in Thailand. Then I follow Highway 45 north until I find a town: Mongton.

I know I have a digitized map that covers this area. Finding it is another thing.

Where I end up is with a very busy topographic map drawn by

the U.S. Army Mapping Service in 1960. Of course, the Thai border doesn't show up, but I can tell it should be beyond the east edge and that the area I'm looking for should be in the lower right-hand corner. The town names are in small black type set against dense brown elevation contours, so it takes a lot of squinting and panning to make them all out.

I find Mongton. I slide south along the black squiggle of a road.

"Ohhhh, *there* you are, you little bastard."

Tiny blue letters on top of a brown contour line, next to a thin blue line: "Nam Ton."

Chapter 37

28 DAYS LEFT

Back in L.A. and unpacked early Friday morning, I set up my laptop and hunt the two companies I know are tangled up in smuggling Nam Ton: Manresa Imports and WCZ Trading Ltd., the originator on the shipping document pouch from Bandineau's storage cube.

"Manresa" gives me 16,900,000 hits. Among other things, it's a town in Spain, a beach and surf break near Watsonville in northern California, and a three-Michelin-star restaurant with a fire problem in Los Gatos in the Bay Area. "Manresa Imports" gives me a couple hundred hits, nearly all from directory sites that list the same address and phone number on Coulson's card. The company has no website or social media presence. For $122 of the client's money, I get a Dun & Bradstreet report that says Manresa Imports LLC is a branch of Manresa Investments. It has several lines of credit it doesn't use very often, judging from how spotty its credit history is. Lots of cash transactions? That would make sense given who it does business with. "Manresa Investments" turns up a history so sparse, it can only be a shell company. "Manresa Thailand" and "Manresa Myanmar" both come up empty.

That data aggregator I use gets another $49 from the client to give me a report on Daniel R. Coulson, who lives in a P.O. box at the Fruitvale post office in southern Oakland. He has a decent credit rating, the usual credit cards with moderate balances, and no mortgage or car loan—which means he rents his crib and owns the car, has the loans under Manresa or another company, or pays cash for a lot of things. Manresa isn't listed under his assets. That last bit's interesting, but not immediately useful.

WCZ Trading doesn't exist.

Its address exists—a shitty corrugated-iron warehouse on Ninth

Street in West Oakland with a panoramic view of the Nimitz Freeway—but a search for the company name gives me no valid hits. D&B's never heard of them. Staying on the down-low is one thing, but this is nuts.

Then I wonder: what would happen if I searched for the company name in Thai or Burmese? Not that I know how to do that. I know someone who probably does, though.

Olivia says, "You brought me a puzzle. How sweet of you."

"Anything for you."

"I'll have a go at it straight away. Unsolved puzzles are the work of the devil, you know. I'll let you know what I find about your mystery company. While I have you… is there a reason I need to pay hire for a dog? Did you need a dog for your cover?"

"The contractor's billing you?"

"Yes. Are you aware of it?"

Feo. "Um… every construction site needs a dog. It's a union thing."

Long silence. Olivia clears her throat. "Of course."

I don't think she believes me.

I've been in the parking lot for the Skirball Center—a Jewish cultural center and museum at the top of the Sepulveda Pass off the 405—long enough to report to Len before Toni's mint-green Fiat 500 rolls up next to me. It looks like an overgrown gumdrop on wheels.

Toni's an owl-eyed woman in her early thirties with a stereotypically Italian nose and obsidian hair cut in a not-too-unattractive pageboy. She's hiding behind a baseball cap and huge tortoise-shell-rimmed sunglasses. She ducks through my rental's passenger door quickly enough to catch me snickering. "What's so funny?"

"I love your disguise. How old is my pot?"

She shoves a Macy's shopping bag at me like it's hot. "The TL results were inconclusive?" TL = thermoluminescence, a method of dating pottery.

"What's that mean?" The pot's in the bag, swaddled in bubble wrap. I pinch open the clasp on a manila envelope and pull out half a dozen pages full of text and graphs and tables.

"It means there wasn't enough data to assign an age? It's all in the report?" Toni shoves open the door and bails out.

Last I checked, I don't have leprosy. "Toni?"

She stops, stands with her back to me for a moment, then slowly turns and collapses in on herself. Her shades are full of my car's reflection.

"Thank you. I really appreciate this."

After some lip-chewing, she says, "I checked? I don't owe you any more money? So please don't call me again, okay? I like my job?"

I wait until the gumdrop whirs away before I skim the report. Thermoluminescence dating depends on how many loose electrons have built up in ceramics since they were fired. You heat a piece of fired clay to free the trapped electrons and pick up the resulting flash of light on a photomultiplier tube. The more light, the older the ceramic.

The lab did this, but they ran into two problems. The first problem is that they didn't have a soil sample from the discovery site to compare readings to the finished ceramic. The lab needs to know roughly how fast the electrons pile up over time so it can figure out how many years the pot's been in the ground, and also what the local soil is made of so the lab can do radioactivity tests. The other problem is the material itself: the report says the ware's body is made of "white kaolinate clay" that has "very low TL sensitivity and radioactivity." In other words, not many loose electrons end up lurking in the minerals. There's nothing to measure.

Inconclusive = the pot could've been fired yesterday—or a thousand years ago.

But somebody must've dated these things once, right? How else would they know how old they're supposed to be?

Let's see what Savannah has to say about it… and how she reacts to me testing the pot.

When she picks up, I say, "I have a question for you."

"Yes, I'd love to go to St. Barts with you for the weekend." She giggles.

Cute. "That wasn't what I was going to ask, but I'll keep it in mind. My Nam Ton pot? I just had it tested, and the lab can't figure out how old it is. Should I be worried?"

Things stay quiet on the other end of the line for a few beats.

208 • LANCE CHARNES

"You tested it? Why?" A little bit puzzled, a little bit guarded.

"I wanted to make sure I got what I paid for." I let that hang for a moment. "Did I?"

"Of course you did." She sounds more confident now. "It's been a problem with the Nam Ton wares since Pensri found them. She used stratigraphic dating to estimate an age for them. You know what that is?"

"Carbon-date something organic in the same dirt layer as the pot."

"Close enough. What lab did you use?"

"The Getty."

"Oh. Wow." Surprised. "Really? *The* Getty?"

"As in, the richest private museum in the world? Yeah, that one. You keep calling Dr. Udomprecha 'Pensri,' like you know her. Do you?"

"It's a lot easier than saying 'Dr. Udomprecha' over and over, right?"

"Nice sidestep."

She growls. "You know, Nam Ton isn't the only Thai pottery that doesn't play well with TL. Sukhothai-period wares from Si Satchanalai have the same problem, maybe for the same reason. Trust me—it's nothing to worry about."

I worry when people tell me *trust me* or *don't worry*. But *both*...?

Crawling through traffic to get home gives me more than enough time to take stock.

I've recorded Bandineau and Lorena not-really conspiring to commit tax fraud and more-or-less admitting to trafficking in looted antiquities.

I've recorded Savannah encouraging me to go along with Bandineau's scheme, and admitting to sending probably trafficked antiquities to China for sale.

I've located Bandineau's stash of looted and trafficked antiquities.

I've recorded Coulson talking about the connection through him between Bandineau and unnamed Burmese, probably fronting for an apparently nonexistent company that's probably involved in heroin smuggling between Myanmar and the U.S.

I've narrowed down the source of the ceramics to a few miles along a small river in Myanmar next to the Thai border.

All this should be in ICE's hands by now.

Am I done yet?

Chapter 38

24 DAYS LEFT

The weekend passes pretty quietly other than nursing Chloe through yet another breakup. Either there's a lot of clueless lesbians in L.A. who can't see what a gem Chloe is, or she turns into some kind of monster around the women she sleeps with. Whatever it is, it takes a lot of wine, hugs, Kleenex, and bad fantasy films to get her off the metaphorical ledge.

My email to Olivia on Friday (Does the client need anything more from me?) seems to disappear into the bit bucket. That is, until my work phone blasts me awake at 5:18 on Monday morning. I fumble it off the coffee table, check the number—not one I've seen before—and mumble, "Hello?"

"Who have you been talking to?" It's Allyson's voice, and it's not happy.

I wake up real fast. "What do you mean?"

She draws in her version of a deep, cleansing breath so loudly, it sounds like she's in the room with me. "The client contacted me last night your time. *Very* early this morning my time. He told me that when he presented your reports to ICE yesterday, they told him they already had the information from another source. He believes he knows who did it. Would you care to guess?"

If it's Savannah, Allyson would rub my nose in it right off the top. I think about the situation until another suspect pops up. "Brandon Cort?" He and Ohlmeyer are the only two other clients she's mentioned.

Allyson hesitates for a moment. Surprise, or winding up to take my head off? "Yes. The client has reason to believe that Mr. Cort is also under investigation and may also have made the same arrangement with—"

"It's a competition? Seriously? Why didn't anybody say anything before now?"

"I asked the client the same question. He didn't provide a satisfactory answer. Who have you been talking to about your inquiry?"

Sigh. "Savannah. But you already know that—it's the whole reason I kept her around."

"The *whole* reason?"

Shit. Shit shit shit. "How is it you didn't know somebody else is in the race?" The best defense, yadda yadda. "Isn't that part of what you're supposed to do? What—"

"You had no idea she'd try to help another of her clients?" Her voice is slowly turning into concrete. "This is a huge surprise to you?"

"I had no idea somebody else had done the same deal with ICE. She never mentioned it. Samson didn't mention it. The ICE dude, Talbot, never said anything. Usually when they run two CIs after the same target, the feds play them off each other, not hide them. What, I'm supposed to be clairvoyant?"

"It might have occurred to you had you been thinking with a clear mind."

I give myself a ten-count so I don't say the first thing that comes into my head. I say the second thing. "Okay, fine, I've been sleeping with her. What's *your* excuse?"

A low growling sound ekes into her end of the line. "If you want to fight with me, I'll indulge you, but I'd rather not. We have a problem to solve. Does she know everything?"

I go over what I've put into the reports and try to remember what, if anything, I've told Savannah about it. "Maybe eighty percent. She doesn't know I've been reporting on her. I doubt she's told Cort everything she's been up to. I didn't tell her anything about Coulson or Manresa, but she may have known about them before. I also didn't tell her about WCZ. Whatever's she told Cort has holes in it."

"As you said, unless she already knew."

"Yeah." I'd figured Savannah had an agenda for Hoskins, but this wasn't it. "I can try to find out if she's involved with Cort."

"I can only imagine how *that* conversation will play out." At least Allyson's voice has loosened a skosh. "You sent an email to Olivia. The answer is: you are *not* finished yet. I had to persuade the client to not cancel the project."

Oh, shit, no no no…

"I spoke to the ICE agent in charge of—"

"Talbot?"

"Yes. You have yet to prove a link between WCZ and Manresa in a way that's useful to him. He has his own resources trying to establish that link. If they do, he won't need your information. I expect you understand the consequences of that."

No early termination—freedom—for me. "Is that all he needs?"

"No. You've also not yet discovered the link between WCZ and the source of the pottery. He mentioned that he'd told you he needs this."

"Yeah." It feels like I had a forkful of prime rib in front of me, and a dog just licked it. "For the first thing: do you have any crooked customs guys you can strong-arm into opening a shipping container in a bonded warehouse?"

"Unfortunately not."

"You don't? I thought that would be your kind of thing."

"Civil servants can't afford us."

Of course not. "As for the second—the only way I can do that is to go to Thailand and Myanmar. Will the client pay for that?"

"I'll ask." Her voice stiffens again. "Be warned, though—if Mr. Cort manages to present ICE with information before the client does one more time, the client will end this project. Act quickly and be very careful what you share with Miss Kendicott other than your bed. Do you understand?"

Chapter 39

Olivia says, "That's rather more difficult than you may think."

"Come on. Everything's online now."

"Perhaps so, but not everything online is accessible."

I'd called Olivia immediately after Allyson hung up on me to ask what I thought was a simple question: does WCZ have any cargoes on any container ships coming to Oakland? "Okay. Can you at least tell me if any ships coming from Thailand are arriving at Oakland in the next few days?"

"That, I can do. It so happens we have a subscription to a service that tracks such things. Please bear with me." A keyboard chatters in my ear. "I've yet to solve the last puzzle you gave to me."

"Thanks for trying." While she types, I stare at the wall calendar in what passes for the pool house's kitchen. Today's June sixth. Last Thursday, Bandineau said it took a week after the ship pulled into port for Manresa to get the pots, and that his next shipment was due in two weeks. That means the ship must be arriving this week or could already be here.

Olivia clears her throat. "Right. Are you ready?"

"Sure."

"The last ship with a port-of-call in PAT Bangkok to arrive in the Port of Oakland did so on third June. The next arrives tomorrow, eighth June. The *M/V Panay Voyager*, should you be interested. After that is the *MSC Lucinda* on Sunday next, twelfth June. Do you need more?"

"No, that's fine for now." If Bandineau was right, his pots should be on one of those two ships. We can't get access to the terminals, but we can check the WCZ address. If it's anything more than a candidate for redevelopment, there might be something useful there. "Is Ninety-Nine still available?"

After a few moments and more keyboard action, Olivia says, "Yes. Do you need him?"

"Yes, please. And I need to fly to SFO. Today."

When I tell Savannah I'm passing through on my way to business in Seattle and ask if she'd like to have dinner, her squeal nearly takes out my eardrum.

Savannah turns on her searchlight smile the moment she spots me in the St. Francis' lobby. I haven't seen her since Memorial Day—a week—but I realize I've missed her. The way she keeps squeezing my hand as we eat dinner in the hotel's Oak Room Restaurant makes me think she missed me—Hoskins—too.

We skip dessert in the restaurant so we can have dessert in bed. She's *very* glad to see me. So much so that I don't have a chance to ask her about Cort even if I remembered to (which I don't). By the time she's curled up next to me asleep, I hate the thought of questioning her. If she's talking to Cort, it's out of loyalty to a client and not to undermine Hoskins; after all, she doesn't know Cort and Hoskins are competing. I sleep better than I have for a week.

We kiss goodbye after a room-service breakfast early the next morning. I hate to see her go. I'm not thinking straight about her… and I'm not sure I care.

George edges our clapped-out 1998 Ford Econoline panel van—easily the shittiest rental vehicle I've ever seen—into a gap between an RV with flat tires and a gutted pickup truck, both on the north side of the street across from WCZ's public address. He props a reflective sun visor across the windshield while I set up the folding camp chairs in the back. We grab Cokes from a big, high-mileage Igloo ice chest and settle in for a long Tuesday evening of watching through the blacked-out back windows.

WCZ's cozy little nest at 1835 Ninth Street in West Oakland looks like the "before" picture in a Rustoleum ad. I'm not sure if it's still standing because of the rust's structural integrity, the multiple coats of graffiti, or some combination of the two. It slumps on a half-empty concrete slab and is completely dark in the twilight. Some buildings seem to have life even when they're empty; this isn't one of them.

I ask, "Find out anything more about this place?"

George shakes his head. "No more than what Olivia knows. A shell company owns it. Used to be a pipe warehouse twenty-some years ago. No history of police calls in the past ten years." He plugs in earbuds and brings up Spotify on his agency phone.

Four hours crawl by. Twilight turns into a mercury-vapor-orange night. Traffic noise from the freeway fades from a roar to a buzz. The last decent-looking cars on the street—they probably belong to students at the trapeze school next door to us—skitter off into the dark. Feral things (dogs, cats, children) prowl by.

By midnight, the ragged people living in the two vans across the street from us throw dirt on their oil-drum fire and turn in. An hour later, there's no sign of life on the block unless you count the herds of rats grazing in the weeds. I nudge George awake. "It's time."

We go out the front doors, ease them closed so we don't make noise, then pick our way through ruined cars toward the skate park at the end of the street, next to the freeway sound wall. The gravel's compacted enough that it doesn't crackle anymore. I watch for movement or lights both at WCZ's warehouse and in the five vehicles parked outside it. I also try not to step in dog shit or tear my legs open on rusted metal.

The skate park gives us a platform to get over the chain-link fence into WCZ's domain. George hands me a black ski mask and drags on his own. The front door's completely coated with graffiti, but surprise! It's solid, heavy-gauge steel with a serious deadbolt on it. George waves me to follow him around back.

We find the front door's twin set into the warehouse's back wall. There are no windows. George pulls on latex gloves, then starts annoying the deadbolt with lockpicks. I ask, "Shouldn't you check for alarms or cameras?"

"If we don't see them now, we won't see them until it's too late."

I glance around for night creatures taking an interest in us. The cracked, weedy slab we're on reaches seventy feet or so to the back fence. Oil stains, spray paint, and at least one sizable burn mark decorate it. A loading dock squats about thirty feet down the wall from us. No wolves, mobs of giant rats, or zombies... yet.

A click, then the grating of a deadbolt against a strike plate. George stows his pick set and draws a pistol from behind his back.

"If an alarm sounds, go back to the skate park. If someone starts shooting, go back to the skate park. If there's a dog—"

"Skate park. I get it."

No alarms, dogs, or zombies come after us when we slip through the door. George runs the supernova beam of his tiny flashlight around the doorway. "No alarm contacts." He pads away.

I lock the door, twist on my red Mini Maglite, and follow. Several ranks of empty industrial shelving reach front-to-back across the warehouse's floor. A boxy office enclosure about the size of a single-wide trailer is attached to the wall about where the front door should be. There's a pallet jack in one corner, unrusty enough to still be usable, and a couple appliance dollies. Somebody swept the concrete floor recently; the one trash barrel I find is empty. Somebody—WCZ?— still uses this place.

I've been pretty chill about this so far, mostly because there's nowhere to hide anything in here. The bad news: there's nowhere to hide us, either. I eye the office, waiting for the door to fly open. That's what happened in Milan on my first project. It wasn't fun.

George says, "Office?"

Should we? It's not like drug smugglers or antique smugglers keep paper records anymore, if they ever did. All we're likely to find is an old pinup calendar and a coffee mug with "My pusher went to Bangkok and all I got was this crummy cup." There won't even be a phone to bug. Still, somebody might've gotten sloppy. "Yeah. Let's—"

Something that sounds very much like a car door slamming thumps behind the back wall.

George and I swap startled glances. He bolts for the office door.

Who's out there? A security guard? A cartel heavy? Why are they here? Did they plan to be here anyway, or did we trip an alarm?

A key scrapes into the back door's deadbolt. Yes, I can hear it from yards away. "Quickly…"

"Quiet." The lock clicks. "Inside, now."

The office is long and narrow, with fake knotty-pine paneling. Three massive steel-gray desks—probably refugees from some government-surplus auction—jut out from the back wall. There's a door at the far end, probably for a toilet, and old chalkboards line the front wall. It's hard to get a real picture of the room because I can see only a small circle of it at a time.

"Turn off your light." George has his ear to the door. "They're inside."

I turn off my flashlight. The room gets very dark. I whisper, "They?"

"He. It."

I stand still for a few moments, not wanting to breathe or even blink hard. But then I think, *wait a minute.* "Gonna look for the front door."

"Don't use your light."

Okay. I walk backwards until I bump into a desk. Now I know where the back wall is. I skim my foot forward an inch above the linoleum tiles, slowly transferring my weight. After four paces, my outstretched hand hits the front wall. Now all I have to do is sidestep to my right to reach the door.

My foot nudges something soft. First thought: a dead body. My stomach rolls up into a ball. But another nudge tells me that whatever it is, it's not solid enough to be meat. I slowly squat, reach down, and grab a handful of something that squishes, like a cushion. The thing is roughly oval. WTF? I twist my Maglite's head so the barest glimmer of light comes out.

It's a dog bed. A *big* dog bed. "Um, George?"

The growl at the room's other end sounds big enough to fill the bed.

George's eyes snap from me to the growl. I open my light a bit more and aim it at the far end of the office.

There in the shadows, a large, square-bodied, square-headed dog is aimed right at us. Probably a pit bull/Clydesdale mix. His fangs reflect the light. His eyes glow orange.

George hisses, "Turn off your light. Find the door. *Now.*"

A bright light in the warehouse bay sweeps past the gap under the office door.

The moment I twist off my flashlight, I hear the galumphing of big paws carrying a bigger dog straight at me. No way I can get out of the way in time. All my insides join my stomach in a ball, hoping they can avoid becoming dinner. I grab the dog bed, wrap the ends around my hands, and hold it like a net in front of me.

A sack of cement covered in hair slams into me. I slide a few feet on my back. Stars from my head bouncing off the floor. A thousand pounds of pooch stands on my chest, his head wrapped in the dog bed sandwiched between my hands. His teeth tear at the cloth that's keeping his bellowing from bursting my eardrums.

I don't wanna be eaten. Please don't eat me.

A burst of bullets punches through the hollow-core office door and thuds into the drywall above my head. Gypsum dust cascades into my eyes. I feel George's feet swing past my head as he lunges for the front door. Even if we get out, the guy in the warehouse will be right behind us.

Unless…

The dog jerks back, almost tears the bed out of my hands. I manage to kick him off me. He barks louder. I push myself against the office door, untangle my left hand. Reach up to flip open the deadbolt just in time for Cujo to crash into my chest again. My free hand manages to grab his leather collar, as wide as a man's belt. The side of his muzzle slams my arm into the wall. Dog spit and dog breath smother me.

George's voice, just audible: "Door's open! Come on!"

With what little strength I have left in my arms, I shove Cujo off me. He yelps, then roars. Claws scrabble on the linoleum.

Wait for it. Wait for it…

A paw stomps my calf. I twist the doorknob, then roll to my left.

The dog slams into the door, ripping the knob out of my hand. He sails through into the warehouse.

A man screams louder than the barks.

Chapter 40

I say, "Did I mention how much I hate warehouses?"

George yanks out an earbud. Mournful jazz piano dribbles out. "What was that?"

"I hate warehouses."

We're in the Shooting Star Café at the northern edge of Oakland's Chinatown. It normally closes at 1:30, but George knows somebody who knows somebody, and they let us slide in just shy of two while the night crew cleans up. It's not the kind of dive you'd expect to be open this late—it's clean and orderly, royal-blue walls, plush high-back chairs with tufted magenta upholstery, and LEDs as twinkling stars in the deep blue ceiling.

George chews his garlic fries thoughtfully. "I don't mind warehouses. Can't say I'm fond of the dogs that live in them, though. Now what?"

I wolf down another spring roll. Being terrified makes me hungry. "Did we just burn that place?"

"I thought so when we left." He sips something from a tall glass. It's the consistency of iced tea except it's hazy pink. Since he ordered in Chinese, I have no idea what it is. "Now I think, maybe not. He never saw us. I didn't return fire. For all he knows, we were some punks who broke in to steal something and the wolf spoiled our plans."

"Unless they had cameras."

"Don't think so. If they did, they'd have seen two of us. They'd have seen my weapon. They'd send more than one man."

"You're sure there was only one?"

"Unless the others were flying, yes."

Levitation doesn't seem worth considering now. "You think they'll use the place again?"

George shrugs. "I wouldn't be surprised. If they do, they'll step up security. Better locks. Maybe give the dog a vacation. Put a man in the office."

"So what you're saying is, we'll never get inside again."

"Yes."

Great. I've gotta figure out how to make the WCZ-Manresa connection. That warehouse is all I've got. It's frustrating to get this close and then blow it. "We can stake it out, I guess. See if there's any activity."

"We can do that. If there is, then what?"

Stake out = sit and do nothing while the clock ticks down. The last thing I want to do. "I'll have plenty of time to think about that."

We watch the activity around WCZ's warehouse.

Nicer cars than the neighborhood calls for drive around back every six hours. A guy goes inside the warehouse; some other guy comes out, drives off.

On Thursday, a dude in a green Transit van replaces the back door's original deadbolt and installs what looks like a magnetic lock along the header.

I see all this from a swaybacked 1980s Winnebago parked on the west side of Pine Street, across a large vacant lot from the warehouse. It's one of a line of apartments-on-wheels on this block. George set up a Nikon DSLR with a bazillion-millimeter lens on a tripod on the kitchen table; all I have to do is aim and shoot whenever something happens. That, and ignore the mildew smell from the ratty harvest-gold carpet.

George and I swap out every eight hours. I can't decide which is worse: sitting on my butt in the motorhome watching paint dry, or sitting on my butt in my hotel room doing the same. I read and do more internet research. I run a lot to burn off all the crap I eat in the motorhome. Savannah keeps calling; she's lonely and wants me to visit. I have to make up a string of out-of-town meetings to duck her, which I hate doing. Olivia finally gives in to my whining and moves me to the Hyatt House Emeryville. It's just up the freeway from West Oakland and has a wider variety of available food than I had next to the airport.

Still, I'm climbing the walls by Saturday morning. It marks forty days since I started this project, twenty days to the end. I need to do *something* to move this along. But what?

An email from Olivia helps wake me up.

```
WCZ Ltd. owns a facility on
Highway 1340 outside the village
of Arunothai, Mueang Na Sub-
District, Chiang Dao District,
Chiang Mai Province, Thailand. I
cannot guarantee this is the same
WCZ as the one you are seeking.
```

The satellite shots in Google Maps show Arunothai as a jumble of houses and businesses hugging the Thai-Myanmar border. StreetView gives me paved roads and small single-story houses, not huts or shanties. Highway 1340 leads south from what I think is the center of town (at least, it has a gas station and grocery store). If I follow it far enough, it connects with highways that eventually hit Chiang Mai, the big city in northwest Thailand. A road big enough to be marked with a yellow line heads north from the end of Highway 1340, skirts the border, then crosses it a couple miles outside town. It becomes Highway 45 inside Myanmar.

Highway 45 leads to the Nam Ton river.

If this isn't the right WCZ, it's a helluva coincidence.

Monday morning. Eighteen days left.

George says, "Got a plan yet?" He's here at eight to relieve me after a dead night at the warehouse except for the guard changes.

"I'm waiting for a phone call."

"Don't wait too long." He lays his breakfast burrito and coffee on the table next to the camera. "Their timeline isn't our friend."

That follows me back to the hotel and through breakfast.

Len calls me before I can call him. "Starbucks says they haven't seen you in weeks. What the fuck, Friedrich?" I have to remind him about the freelance job and helping build the house. He reminds me that the employment audit is coming soon and he hopes all my work records are squared away. They aren't. I can't be done with this shit soon enough.

I crawl into bed, exhausted, but can't sleep right away. Worrying about going back to prison is part of it; the other is the steady ticking of the project clock. I don't know what Plan B is if Allyson doesn't come through.

Pounding blasts me awake at noon, the middle of my night. I pull on some boxers and yell "What?" through the door.

A sharp-faced, crew-cut guy in a dark suit holds his ID up to the peephole. "Special Agent Montooth, ICE HSI. Open up."

Either Allyson came through or things are going to get unpleasant. "Hold on." I throw on some jeans and a polo, then open the door. Montooth pushes past me, checks the room. "Why don't you come in?"

He looks in the bathroom. "You're Friedrich?"

"Yeah."

He stands in the bathroom doorway and folds his arms. "Talbot sent me. You wanted to talk."

Talbot was supposed to come himself. "And I believe you why?"

He sighs, pulls his phone, stabs his screen. "Yeah, boss, he wants to know I'm legit... Okay." Montooth pushes the phone at me.

I expect it to shock me when I touch it. "Agent Talbot?"

"Yes, it's me. I sent my man there to talk to you. I can't be seen anywhere near you. He's briefed in, at least enough. Understand?"

"He speaks for you?"

"He knows my number."

Well, duh. This doesn't make me happy, but I don't get a say in it. "Okay, we'll play it your way. Thanks."

Montooth stays on the line for a minute of "uh-huh" and "yes, sir," then pockets his phone and nods to the desk chair. I wave him to it; I need to stand so I don't fall asleep.

Once he settles, he says, "You wanted to talk to us. So talk."

I bring him up-to-date on what George and I have been doing with the warehouse. "We should see a handoff from WCZ to Manresa sometime in the next couple days. That's the link you guys need, right?"

"Yeah, if that's what's happening." His tightly-crossed arms say he's not convinced. "What do you want?"

I've had some time to work out what I'm about to say. I need them to buy off on this on my terms. "We'll keep watching. We're part of the landscape now. I'll send you several dozen photos of the cars and people who've gone in and out of the place so you can ID them. When the meet goes down, I call you, and you crash the party. That gives you the players and the pots. You get a nice big break in your investigation with very little effort on your part. Sound good so far?"

Montooth's face hasn't changed. "I'm listening."

A little encouragement would be nice, but no. "I'm passing this directly to you because I don't want it getting out to anybody else, like your other CI. I want Talbot to know that *I* got this for *him* on behalf of *my* client. Understand?"

"Why aren't you going through your back channel anymore?"

"Because I don't feel trusting right now. I think I know where the other CI's getting his intel from, but I need to cover myself in case I'm wrong. But make no mistake—the other CI's swiping my intel. I want to make sure that stops. Do we have a deal?"

Montooth gives me Mt. Rushmore for a few beats, then rocks out of the desk chair. "Stay here." He disappears into the bathroom and closes the door.

I sag into the chair and put my head in my hands. My body clock is totally screwed up. I've become more convinced each day that I've wasted a week I can't afford to lose. Allyson still hasn't gotten the client to pop for a field trip to Thailand, which is the only way I can finish this and still get my golden ticket to the chocolate factory. And now my head hurts and all I want to do is sleep.

Montooth marches out of the bathroom to the nightstand, writes on the notepad, tears off a sheet. "Put your photos someplace we can get to. Text the address to this number. We'll take a look. We'll be in touch if it's worth anything." He folds his arms. "No promises. You got our attention. The rest's on you."

Tuesday night. Seventeen days left.

I was supposed to be off from four to midnight, but George called me in a couple hours early. "Something's happening," he said, without saying what exactly.

I peer through the camera. Three cars are lined up just west of the warehouse on the concrete slab. That's more action than we've seen in almost a week. A wiry dude's standing outside the back door with some kind of assault rifle slung over his shoulder. "What's up out front? I don't see the campers."

"Our friends paid them off about two hours ago. All five cars left. The big surprise is that they could all still move."

That's the big hint something's going down. We exchange meaningful looks.

Unfortunately, I haven't heard from ICE. Olivia tells me they grabbed the photos from the Dropbox she set up yesterday morning, but it's been radio silence since then. Does that mean they're not playing?

I still have Montooth's note. Does the number still work? There's only one way to find out. `Warehouse prepping 4 action. 3 cars outside 1 armed guard. Ready?`

We watch a dark SUV roll through the warehouse's double-gated east entrance. It backs into place beside the other cars. Three guys get out and walk in formation to the back door. George shoots pictures. The three stop at the door; the guard lets them in.

George says, "Two knocks, then one, then two more."

During the minute that bit of action happened, I checked my phone three times for a reply from ICE. Nothing. I text the door signal to Montooth's number in case somebody's paying attention. For all I know, they're in some bar watching baseball.

Just shy of eleven, a weathered white panel truck turns right onto Ninth from southbound Pine Street. It trundles toward the warehouse, stops, then carefully turns into the driveway. The driver backs it into the loading dock like he knows what he's doing. The dock's roll-up door opens, throwing a rectangle of light over the truck's cargo box. A guy wheels out an appliance dolly while another guy opens the cargo doors. A minute later, the dolly has a crate on it and is headed inside.

I text, `Delivery happening now. R u there?`

Another crate comes out. Then another.

My phone pings. It's a text from Montooth: `Hold`. Does that mean "stay there" or "hold, please"? Do I get Muzak next?

George says, "Well?"

"I'm on hold, or 'ignore.' It's like I'm calling the cable company."

The loading-dock door slides down, cutting off the lightspill.

Then, nothing. The guard outside the back door sparks up a

cigarette.

Thirty minutes. "Come on, guys," I mutter for the eleventy-seventh time. "Don't fucking blow this."

An hour. I've paced the Winnebago's aisle almost enough to wear out the carpet. The loading-dock door opens. The same dude with a dolly loads two crates into the truck.

Are they leaving? Did ICE just punt this? I ask George, "Can we block them if they leave?"

"Are you bulletproof?"

"No."

"Then no."

The truck leaves the loading dock, pulls into Ninth Street, then parks in front of the warehouse. I try to telepathically short out his fuel pump. What's he doing?

Ninety minutes. The loading dock closes. The light outside the warehouse's back door dies. A yellow Ryder panel truck chugs past us toward Ninth. It swerves right, then backs down Ninth to the white truck. It stops a few feet away.

Coulson? Are Bandineau's new pots in the white truck?

The two drivers meet on the sidewalk—just two dark shapes in the orange streetlight wash. After a few minutes, they crack open their cargo boxes.

Something moves in front of the broken-down junkyard across the street from them. At first, I can't make it out. Then it hits the edge of the streetlights: a line of federal ninjas spreading out around the two trucks.

Out back of the warehouse, another ninja has the guard flipped on his front and trussed up like a turkey. More ninjas melt out of the dark.

A block north, a conga line of cars and vans with flashing blue-and-white lights roars south.

The cavalry's here.

Chapter 41

> Immigration and Customs
> Enforcement agents got more than
> they bargained for last night when
> a raid on a West Oakland warehouse
> uncovered nearly fifty kilos of
> pure heroin...

Even though I'm seriously sleep-deprived, I'm pretty stoked about the raid. It's on all the local morning news shows and even made it to KNX, L.A.'s all-news radio station. Along with the heroin, Talbot's guys got Coulson and ten members of what ICE describes as an "international narcotics-smuggling syndicate," plus the usual cash, guns, and fast cars.

Better yet? Montooth texted me somewhere around two a.m.: Is this it? and an attached close-up of a Nam Ton pitcher.

I texted, Thats it. R we good?

Were good.

Yes! I slept better than I have since last Monday's visit with Savannah.

Now all I have to do is get Allyson to get the client to send me to Thailand so I can draw the line between WCZ in Arunothai and some archaeological dig in Myanmar.

No problem. Right?

Except it doesn't happen.

All that happens Wednesday is that I go home. My work phone never gets more than a foot away from me, even in the bathroom, not that it helps. I'm grumpy with Chloe and I can't eat. When I started this, I didn't think I'd come this close to the end and get stuck. Now I have to imagine it, and it's frustrating as hell.

The Thursday morning call I get isn't the one I've been

expecting and hoping for. It's from Savannah. "Have you heard?" She sounds worried.

"Heard what?"

"They arrested Jim and Lorena and raided the gallery."

Holy. Shit. If she reached through the phone and slapped me with a badger, I wouldn't be as surprised. It takes a few moments to find where I dropped my voice. "Um… who arrested them? ICE?"

"No, the DEA." She takes a shuddery breath. "I was *there*. Or I was almost there. I was walking down the street to meet with Lorena and I saw what looked like every DEA agent in the world go in there. I just stood there. I… I couldn't think. They were in *handcuffs*. I… what if they come for me?"

It didn't sound like Carruthers was interested in Savannah as anything other than a pinup. I wish I could tell her that. "Have a lawyer?"

"Of course I… uh, no, not this kind." She sounds more lost than I've ever heard her. "Maybe someone in his firm. This is *awful!* It isn't about that thing in Oakland, is it?"

She really sounds rattled. I feel for her; I know what it's like to see people you know get carted away in cuffs. "I'm sure it is. They've got a straight line from the heroin to Achara. I guess the DEA wanted to grab them before they tried to get away."

"Get away? To where?"

"Southeast Asia, for one. They've both been there. They probably know people. Lorena's already got the wardrobe. We've got no extradition treaty with Vietnam, Cambodia, or Myanmar." Yes, I was looking. It's always good to know your options.

"But that's crazy! They wouldn't…" Long pause. "Oh, god. Should I go bail them out?"

"You can't yet. They have to go to initial arraignment and have bail set. The U.S. Attorney will claim they're flight risks, so they may not get bail."

"How do you know all this?"

You spend time in the system, you learn. "A banker once tried to skip the country with a wad of my money. Look, you can't do anything for them right now. There's a process they have to go through." I get a bright idea. "DEA's probably not very interested in them. The USA will probably corner them into talking; see who they tie into this." Probably not what she wants to hear. "Just go to work, or go home, or whatever will take your mind off it. Making yourself sick won't help them."

She breathes hard into the phone for a few seconds. "Can I come see you? I don't want to be alone right now." Her voice is barely above a whisper.

I gentle my voice as much as I can. "I'll be home in a couple days. Until then, call if you want to talk. I'm sorry you had to see all that."

Sniff. "I am too. See you soon."

There's nothing on the news yet about the DEA bust at Achara. It doesn't make a lot of sense as an operation unless the feds can prove intent to distribute. As a bureaucratic play? *Look at us, we're busy too!* That I can understand.

I call Olivia to tell her what happened and to suggest that Allyson should warn the client. It might shake loose the go-ahead to send me to Thailand so I can close the project. I hope.

My work phone doesn't ring again until I'm in the middle of dinner with Chloe (Healthy Choice entrees—it's hard to do better when all you have is a hot plate and a microwave). "Can you talk?" It's Allyson.

I trot into the back yard. This could be either very good or very bad. "What's up?"

Allyson clears her throat. "The DEA took the client into custody this afternoon."

Shit.

I collapse into a plastic lawn chair and stare at the ratty cypress trees lining the cinder-block wall. Can this possibly get worse? "Have you talked to him?"

"No, but I have spoken to his solicitor. The client has terminated the project."

Nooooooooooooooooooooooooo...

"The solicitor told me that the client said, 'If this is how they treat me, then to hell with them.' I'm not certain when, or even if, I'll have a chance to intercede with him." She waits for me to say something, but I'm too stunned. "I'm really very sorry, Matt. I know what this meant to you. I'm personally quite put out by this—the client has several thousand euros of our billings in his hands and I've no idea if he intends to pay them."

"Not the same."

"I understand that."

My lemon-pepper fish starts fighting to get out. I hang my head between my knees and breathe deep. This wasn't supposed to happen. I was supposed to finish the project and get my early termination and become an independent adult again. Being so close to getting off probation in the next couple months, then suddenly having it stretch out a year again...

"Mr. Friedrich?"

"Yeah. Have you talked to Talbot?"

"He's neither taking nor returning my calls." Allyson sounds peeved. "I imagine he's occupied just now."

Or he's cleaning up loose ends. "Give me his number."

"Why would he talk to you directly? He wants the insulation the client and I provide."

"He *owes* me. I handed him that bust. He didn't have to do a fucking thing except show up." I haven't thought through a word of this. I probably should, but *damnit...* "He told me he needs to know where the source is. I can still do that as his CI."

"How? If you work for him directly, you won't have the agency's resources to draw on. I sincerely doubt the government will finance your trip to Thailand."

So do I. "Maybe he can pay you to run me. Cut Mellin out of it. You've worked for governments before, right?"

"Of course. It's not my favorite arrangement. It exposes the agency to more scrutiny than I care for." Pause. "I have an idea. It may not lead to a solution, but it's a different avenue of approach. Wait for my call."

As I rip out a text to Montooth—Get yr boss 2 talk 2 my boss SOS—I wonder how often agency clients cancel their projects, and whether they survive the experience. Not that I care much about Mellin's survival right now.

I wish I had a plan for this.

I don't.

Chapter 42

14 DAYS LEFT

My work phone rings at 4:18 a.m. Olivia says, "A car will be at your home at 5:30. Be ready for it."

She hangs up before she hears me say, "What the fuck?"

The town car takes me to Allyson's jet at Santa Monica Airport. It drops me at Oakland International's Kaiser Air in the middle of a flock of other business jets. A Latino guy in a black suit leads me through the cold, breezy morning (glad I wore the hip-length Barbour Bedale field jacket I bought for my last project) to a black Audi Q7 SUV idling in the parking lot. He opens the rear driver's-side door for me.

Allyson's in the back seat. "Please get in. We have a schedule."

The SUV sweeps out of the lot as soon as I climb in. I ask, "Where are we going?"

"It's not far."

"That's not what I was asking. Why am I here? What's happening?"

She considers me for a moment. She's wearing what looks like a black, long-sleeved Armani knit sheath, except the wide color-block stripe running down the full length of the front is scarlet rather than the standard aquamarine. Does Armani do custom? "I'm meeting with Agent Talbot in twelve minutes. I need you here in case he wants to talk to you directly."

Talbot? That sounds mildly encouraging. "Is he gonna sponsor the rest of the project?"

"I haven't asked yet." She watches the airport's rental-car lot roll by. "I've proposed another solution—that he rescue the client from the DEA's clutches with the understanding that the client continues the project to its conclusion."

Not an entirely crazy idea. The feds swap witnesses and suspects like a bad cold. I testified in cases investigated by ICE, the IRS, ATF, and the DEA back when I was trying hard to stay away from prisons full of knuckle-draggers. Talbot will have to duke it out with Carruthers, but when we were together in the conference room three weeks ago it seemed like he was used to that.

"Does he sound interested?"

"He didn't dismiss it out of hand."

We're on a busy frontage road sandwiched between the airport's outer fringes and a choppy inlet. We turn right at the entrance to the Bill Osborne Model Airplane Field, pass through a gate I suspect isn't supposed to be open, then stop behind what looks like the fenced-in remains of an old incinerator. Nobody will see us from the road. Not a bad place for an execution if you need that kind of thing.

I ask, "How long will I be up here?"

She doesn't even look at me. "Have you something better to do?"

"I need to meet my PO at three. You don't want me to miss that."

Allyson swivels toward me. "You're right, I don't." Her lips purse. "If this works as planned, it will be much easier for me to assign projects to you. You'll be able to move about more freely. I hope that idea doesn't distress you."

It doesn't. More work = more money = my debts go away faster. Another excellent reason to keep at this.

A midnight-blue Crown Victoria with tinted windows and federal plates backs past us a few minutes later and parks facing us behind the incinerator. Allyson sighs, loops her purse strap over her shoulder, then pushes open her door. "Stay here. I'll signal if I need you. If I do draw you into the discussion, I need you to bring Mr. Hoskins' attitude with you. Is that clear?"

I'm not sure that's the best approach, but I'll deal with that when I get a chance to read the situation. "I get it."

She marches to Talbot's car and ducks through the passenger's door. People dressed like her probably don't sit in that seat often. The SUV driver's already busy with his phone, so I have nothing better to do than watch Allyson and Talbot talk and wish I had some coffee.

Even if Allyson can get Talbot to buy off on her idea, there may not be enough time to make it happen. He'll have to get Carruthers onboard, then the USA. That'll take time even if they don't put up a fight, which is unlikely. Will Mellin go for it? It wouldn't be the first time a bruised ego makes an exec do dumb things, like refusing to cooperate when he's ninety percent of the way to fulfilling his immunity deal with the feds.

I check my phone. Mellin's arrest is all over the news this morning, along with a truly unflattering picture of him sandwiched between two linebacker-sized DEA agents. They also picked up Cort and three other semi-well-known collectors. The DEA spokesman says the agency will make an announcement later today.

Allyson and Talbot are still in the Crown Vic and aren't trying to strangle each other yet. That's a good sign, right?

But what happens if Talbot doesn't buy it, or can't do it?

I try not to think about that.

"Hey." The driver nudges my shoulder. "She wants you."

Allyson stands behind the Crown Vic's passenger's door, waving in short, sharp movements.

She meets me halfway between the cars. She's looked happier. "Agent Medina says the DEA won't let the client go before arraignment, which is scheduled for next Tuesday."

If I was close enough to a tire, I'd kick it. "So much for the easy way." Then I pick up on the name. "Wait. Medina?" The dark DEA agent who sat in on my interrogation. "What's he doing here?"

"I gather he's representing his agency on behalf of his supervisor."

I wonder if Carruthers is in the doghouse. "Did you ask Talbot about hiring the agency?"

Her jaw sets. "Yes. He's... shall we say, *highly* skeptical. He wants you to tell him exactly what you intend to do and how long you expect it to take. You *do* have a plan, I assume?"

"Yes, I do." No, I don't.

She points to the car. "Tell him. Be persuasive."

"Sure. Um, Ms. DeWitt?" She stops in mid-turn. "Can I sit in front? I get flashbacks when I sit in the back of a Crown Vic."

She glares at me but stalks past the open front door.

Talbot's got a navy tie under his black ICE windbreaker. Medina's slumped in the back seat, swaddled in a DEA windbreaker and a long-sleeved black tee. Both men do a double-take as Allyson climbs into the back seat.

Talbot thumbs over his shoulder. "You've met Medina."

The DEA agent nods. I say, "We go way back."

Talbot snorts. "I take it you know what's happening?"

"DEA's being difficult." I ask Medina, "What're you guys looking to charge the collectors with?"

Medina growls, "Not your problem."

Talbot: "The narcs are torqued off that we got the fifty-kilo heroin bust and they didn't. Now they're stomping on our dicks to look like they're not asleep."

Medina: "Hey, watch that shit."

"If you've got a better explanation, I'm all ears. No?" Talbot shrugs. "Okay. Friedrich, tell me how you're going to find the source for the Nam Ton pots."

I take a moment to try to herd my stray thoughts together. I need to get this right. This is like the ultimate sales job. I can do this. *I can do this.*

"Okay. First I need to visit the WCZ warehouse in Arunothai to see if there's anything useful there. You still need to connect them with that end of the pipeline, right?"

"Right."

"Next, I enter Myanmar wherever I can in that area. The closest official border crossing may or may not be open. Did you get my report about the Nam Ton River?" He nods. "Good. Now, looking at the terrain, I'm focusing on a ten-mile stretch of the lower Nam Ton that starts about twenty-two miles north of the border and goes to just past Wan Mè-kin. It's forest and mountains above that, so there's nowhere to plant crops. I follow the river over those ten miles until I find the excavations. They should be hard to miss given the volume of wares coming out of there. Once I find it, I shoot the GPS coordinates and make a run for the border."

Talbot's lack of pickle face tells me he didn't hear anything that scared him. "How long?"

This part, I have no clue. But I can tapdance. "A lot depends on local conditions. It's monsoon season, though it looks like the rains are late. Also, all bets are off once I enter Myanmar. It's a mess in there."

Medina says, "Everyplace we work is a shithole. You get used to it."

Talbot rolls his eyes, then stares at me for a few beats. "How long?"

Shit. I glance toward Allyson. She says, "It's very difficult to estimate with any accuracy when there are so many unknowns. I always give my clients a range—"

"I—*we*—won't sign up for some open-ended sightseeing trip." Talbot actually shakes his finger at Allyson. Her lips get thin, but she doesn't explode. "If we're"—he points to himself and Medina— "supposed to stick our necks out on this, we need to know what it'll cost. *How long?*"

Allyson swings her steel stare in my direction.

"Okay. It takes two days to get to Bangkok, one in flight and the one you lose crossing the International Date Line. Another day to get to Arunothai if I fly to Chiang Mai and drive from there. Let's say two days to check out the WCZ place. A day to get to the Nam Ton's south end—that gives me time to get around the border crossing if it's closed. Four or five days to check the river. Another day to get back to Thailand so I can send the results. Call it two weeks."

Medina twists to face Allyson. "How much do you pay him?"

"I can provide you with our billing rates, if you'd like."

"I'd like you to tell me."

She gives him a sharp look. "We bill Mr. Friedrich's time at €3750 per twenty-four-hour period."

Allyson gets 150% overhead on my daily rate. She doesn't pay benefits, sick time, holidays, paid time off, retirement, or payroll taxes. Now I know how she can afford such a great wardrobe.

Talbot pokes at his phone. "That's over four grand a day. Even split, we'll never get that approved."

She gives him a chilly smile. "Think about how much the Department of Homeland Security pays for consultants and private security contractors. The Department of Justice too, Agent Medina. Also, Mr. Friedrich won't be able to do this alone. He'll need support from an associate with in-country experience and language skills."

Talbot shakes his head. "Twice as much that won't get approved. You're not helping yourselves here."

This doesn't make any sense to me. "This is like beer money to you guys. Two federal agencies dickering over a few grand? What, did you spend it all on weed and hookers?"

Molina growls, "We're not the Secret Service."

Talbot makes a strangling sound. "This comes out of the black budget." Meaning, how they fund all their black-ops capers. "It's all allocated. We'll have to take it out of someone else's hide, and that's a huge pain in the ass."

I shrug. "Do it yourself then. Though, something tells me the reason you agreed to this setup in the first place is that you can't."

Talbot rounds on me. "Damn straight. It was hard enough when it was Thailand. It's impossible in Myanmar. They'll never let us send in a chopper and an SRT to poke around unsupervised. If we're supervised, they won't let us see anything."

Medina asks me, "You know what's in there, right?"

"The Shan State Army?" One of the bazillion ethnic militias infesting northern Myanmar.

He gives me an empty smile. "We can deal with the Shan. That area you're talking about is the United Wa State Army's turf. They fund themselves selling heroin and meth. They don't want us there. Plenty of people in the government on *both* sides of the line make money off that. *They* don't want us there."

I guess I should've spent less time on geography and more on the political situation around Nam Ton. The only thing scarier than a mafia running drugs is a rebel army running drugs. This is normally when I'd bow out, but I keep seeing that letter with the magic words *early termination*. Rock, meet hard place.

I say, "If that's how it is, then both of you need us—*if* you want to close your cases." I get into a short staring contest with Medina. "I know what Talbot wants. Why are you here?"

Medina flicks a glance at Allyson, then shifts to glare straight at me. "We want the asshole behind the super-smack. We've gotta stop it coming here. Find the pots, maybe you find him too."

I'm not so sure about that—if there's an actual guy behind this, he probably has minions to handle chores like packing and shipping. Besides, I'm not too anxious to meet a Burmese Scarface. "Got it."

Talbot stares out the windshield. His fingertips drum an angry rhythm on the steering wheel. Medina crosses his arms and glooms at me.

Allyson says, "Mr. Friedrich, if you could wait in the—"

I hold up a hand. I've got an idea. "Talbot, I've come through for you, right?" He nods. "Have I ever fed you bad intel?" He shakes his head. "Okay. You know I'm on the level. You know I'll do what I say I'll do. Right?" After a while, a nod. "Medina. Talbot's guys got the big stack of smack and all you people got are a couple art geeks and some totally pissed-off millionaires. Why isn't Carruthers here? Somebody chew his ass off?" Medina snarls at me. "All we need is a little money here and I can finish this off for both of you. Talbot, how much cash did you seize Tuesday night?"

He sighs. "A hundred forty grand and some change."

"Think about how you got that money." I lean in. "You got hundreds of thousands of dollars' worth of investigative services for free." I switch to Medina. "How much of what you busted Bandineau and Montford for did you get from me? Did you have *anything* on them before you tripped over me?" Of course, he doesn't answer. "Guys. For a few thousand more, you get your case wrapped up. The cost won't be as much as what you seized the other day. Think of this as an *investment*. In this case." Push harder? Sure. "In your *career*."

Talbot's eyes close. After a long ten-count, he blows out a lungful of air. "It's too damn early in the morning to deal with this." He sags into his seat. "Talk to me."

I throw a glance at Allyson: *your turn.* She thrusts a finger toward the Audi.

I pace in circles for a while before I get back in the SUV. It's still cold, but the activity helps clear out my head and gets my circulation going. Once inside, I get a good view of the negotiations through our windshield and Talbot's. There's a lot of intense discussion, hand gestures, shaking heads, nodding heads, pointing fingers. At one point, I get a text from Allyson: Miss Kendicott's daily rate?

Why does she need to know that? Good thing I asked about it the first day we met. $150/hr $800/day. Yes, she gets less than I do. Crime *does* pay.

Allyson steps out of the Crown Vic after what seems like half of forever. She gestures to me to come out. I meet her in the same spot as before.

She says, "I believe we've come to an agreement. You may not like it, but it's the best we can expect."

Oh, Allyson, what did you do? "What is it?"

"They'll approve your expedition to Thailand. The agents are still arguing over how to share the cost. You're to leave on the nineteenth." That's Sunday, two days from now. "I insisted that you fly business class unless they want to send you on a government aircraft. They resisted, so we'll split the airfare between us. To finance that, I'll need to rescind your pay for the six days you weren't actively working on the project since 27th May."

"*What?*" Okay, I wasn't working very hard, but I was getting heartburn every day.

"It's either that, or you spend fifteen hours in a coach seat in the rear of the aircraft. I wouldn't wish that on a war criminal. You'll still get your usual €100 retainer for those days."

I'll be a little ahead of where I'd be if I was selling coffee. Still, it pisses me off. I bet she won't give back her cut. "What else?"

She glances toward the Crown Vic. Talbot's watching us like we're the Super Bowl; Medina's a dark shape behind him. Her jaw hardens for a moment. "They won't approve a local associate, even at a reduced rate. It's something about paying for a third-party non-citizen that, frankly, sounds suspicious to me, but they wouldn't—"

"Wait, wait, wait." This is worse than the pay clawback. "You can't seriously be considering sending me into the jungle by myself. I can't—"

"Let. Me. Finish." The steel in her voice cuts through my vocal cords. "I know you can't operate there independently. Agent Talbot will approve sending another U.S. citizen with you for support. It so happens you're already acquainted with someone qualified to help." Her left eyebrow arches.

"Savannah."

Her icecap smile flashes by. "Yes. As you were so quick to inform me, she's familiar with the area and knows the language. She also costs far less than an associate, which both men find gratifying. And I doubt you'll find it unpleasant to spend time with her in the tropics."

Maybe if we were on the beach in Phuket. "Have you forgotten the part about her leaking information to Cort and almost sinking the project?"

"Of course not. Mr. Cort is now in a holding cell. By the time he's released, you and Miss Kendicott will be in Thailand. Do whatever you must to keep her away from her phone. I'm certain that by now you know several ways to distract her." She says all this completely deadpan, so I can't tell if she's turning my crank.

"Let's hope she doesn't have an international roaming plan.

Talbot needs to square things with my PO so I don't have to try to report while I'm gone."

"I mentioned that to him already. Do you object to anything you've heard so far?"

"I object to a lot of it, but it probably doesn't matter much. How long do I have?"

Allyson stares at me coolly for several seconds that get longer as they go by. "The original deadline is in place. Your last day is the first of July. Do you agree to proceed under these conditions?"

Fourteen days from now. Tomorrow's wasted. Three days in transit. And I have to trust Savannah to lead me through a jungle full of meth-cooking militias.

But: freedom.

Rock, meet hard place. Again.

"I'm in."

Chapter 43

I wake at 2:18, groggy and not entirely certain where I am. The ceiling fan makes a sound like sandpaper on metal. There's just enough light leaking through the curtains to show me the ghost of our hotel room: spotless, surprisingly large, no A/C, warm, stuffy.

Savannah and I fell asleep holding hands on top of the low double bed's sky-blue sheets. It was too hot to touch more than that, far less do anything more strenuous. She's now flipped almost onto her stomach, her face pushed into the pillow, her leg cocked, her knee pressed into my thigh. The light glows on her skin.

Go to sleep. You need the sleep.

It doesn't work. I try to concentrate on the soft whir of Savannah's breathing, but all I can hear is the fan and the sounds of dripping water outside. It's lunchtime, Matt Daylight Time. I eventually edge carefully off the bed so I don't wake Savannah. The tile floor is cool under my feet as I pad to the window.

We spent twenty hours in transit from LAX to Bangkok, including a short layover in Hong Kong. No matter how nice Cathay Pacific's business class is, that's a long damn time to be trapped in an aluminum tube. We crashed (metaphorically) at the Bangkok Airport Novotel, made the hour-plus flight to Chiang Mai just after lunch yesterday, then the three-hour drive from Chiang Mai to Arunothai, bribing half-a-dozen cops at checkpoints along the way. It's a fifteen-hour time difference between here and home. I think I know what month it is, but that's as close as I can guess the time.

"Been awake long?" Savannah's voice, small and slow.

"Did I wake you?"

"Uh-uh. I was faking. Hoped if I act like I'm asleep, I'll fall asleep. Sometimes it works. What's out there?"

"It's raining. Not very hard—more like a drizzle."

"Huh. It'll be cooler out there." She sits up, pushing hair off her face.

"Wanna take a walk?"

She gives me her sleepy smile, which is both cute and sexy. "Okay."

I pull on yesterday's board shorts and grab a couple Phuket lagers; she ties on a short white-satin robe.

Our hotel's a smallish place, with a front office and common room, three bungalows, and two long buildings with multiple rooms. We're in the long building at the far end. It's around eighty outside and humid, but the tile walkway in the arcade outside our room is cool and damp. The only lights are little lanterns attached to the outside faces of the posts supporting the arcade's shed roof. They shimmer in the water beading on our pewter right-hand-drive Toyota Hilux (a.k.a. Tacoma pickup back home) parked outside the room.

We circle the gravel-and-dirt parking lot until we reach the front office. Off to one side are two benches on a metal platform facing each other across a glass-topped table, covered with a peaked awning. We each claim a bench. Savannah unties her robe and lets it fall open. It's not a come-on; the breeze feels great.

She watches me as she nurses her beer. "I've wanted to ask you something for... a while. Now's probably as good a time as any."

This wouldn't sound promising at any time of day. It sounds ominous at two-something in the morning. "What's that?"

She takes another mouthful, then sets down her bottle. "Who are you really?"

I'm dopey from a lack of sleep, so it takes me a moment to process that. "Say what?"

"I can believe your name is Rick Hoskins. I'm pretty sure you're not who you say you are, or who you want me to think you are. So that makes me wonder... who are you really?"

Shit. Suddenly I'm wide awake. "Where did this come from?"

She lounges against her bench and stretches her arms along the back. It may be coincidental that this opens her robe even more, but I wouldn't bet on it. "I've been thinking about it since you showed me around your house—or, *that* house. I'm not convinced it's yours." Her voice is calm, matter-of-fact. "It just felt... off. There were no pictures, for one thing."

"There's pictures all over the walls." I know that's not what she means, but she's right and I need to push back before she gets any momentum going.

"Paintings. I mean photos. There's not a single photo of you or your family. Okay, I get that you don't like having your picture taken. But your *whole family?*" She holds up her hand when I start to say something. "Then I thought, well, maybe he doesn't like his family. It happens. I don't have a single photo of Mother or Father. But I've never met a rich man who didn't have an I-love-me wall in his office or his home. You know, where he has all those awards and pictures of him with other rich people or famous people. *Never*... until you."

I'd thought of it, but it would've taken a lot more time to pull off than we had. Stupid me—I figured she wouldn't notice. "I'm not a trophy hunter."

"But you are." She points her bottle at me, then takes a pull. "Your paintings are trophies. Now your ceramics are. But that's not the only thing. The appliances? There weren't any scratches or dings. They looked brand new."

She noticed that too? I totally underestimated her. "I replaced them a few months ago."

"*All* of them? At the same time? Also, the stuff in the drawers. Not the pots and pans; the little stuff, like spatulas and measuring cups and whisks. They were all brand new, too, like you bought them all at the same time."

"So that's what you were looking for." Blank look. "I saw you going through my cabinets and drawers." Now confusion. "Cameras."

Savannah frowns. "I didn't see any cameras."

"That's kinda the point to hidden cameras. I'd wondered what you were doing. Why didn't you ask me about it then?"

She sets down her bottle, crosses her arms. "I wasn't absolutely certain what I was seeing. Maybe you were just different. Rich people can be, you know. I wanted to see where things went." She shrugs. "They went to bed, so I thought, in for a penny, right?"

"If I remember right, you engineered that."

Big smile. "Uh-huh. What better way to find out more about you? Plus, you're cute, and you're nice. *Usually*. And that chicken mole was wonderful. And I thought it'd be fun. And it was. *Is*." She scrunches her nose. "This makes me sound all cheap and slutty, doesn't it?"

"Yes, but it also makes you sound devious."

"Hmm. That's two of us, then. After we got together, it just got stranger. Your obsession with finding where Nam Ton comes from. You getting those pictures of Jim's storage locker. You asked questions that no other client ever has before, things that aren't your business. Then this." Savannah holds her arms out, taking in the world around us. "You're too busy to see me for two weeks, then you drop everything to run off to Thailand with me. Not to Phuket or someplace normal, but *here*." She folds her arms on the table. "So, who are you really? I like you, but I'd like to know who I'm sleeping with."

She's got me. I've been in such a rush, I've been sloppy. That's the problem with rushing. But she said *I like you*. I've gotten to like her. Maybe I can still pull this out.

Don't. Admit. Anything. "I could ask you the same question."

"This is about you, not me." That sounds semi-irritated.

I ignore her. I need to buy a few minutes to figure out how much she knows. I can clam up or go on the attack. Hoskins would charge. "You're not like any heiress I've ever met, and I've met a few. The Tonga Room? Food trucks? The Mint? Loteria Grill? *You* picked those places. Beer from a bottle? Ghirardelli chocolate?"

"I like Godiva too, if that helps."

"I'll keep that in mind. I'm not complaining—I liked all that, too. But if I picked you up in a bar and we spent the weekend together, I'd never guess you came from money."

"Good. That's the way I like it. I absolutely know what you're talking about, though." She smiles absently at what's become heavy mist. "I had a little black dress when I was eight."

Huh? "Did you rock it?"

"I owned it. I don't think you can 'rock' anything when you're eight. Mother and Father would let me wander through their cocktail parties with my little wine glass of milk and listen to the grown-ups talk about politics and business and whatever. I was a great prop for them. They could use me to make people think they were human. A lot of people made that mistake."

"How long was it before you were debating with Pete Wilson?" The Republican governor of California in the '90s.

She laughs. "I actually met him when he was still a senator. I wasn't really supposed to talk to anyone unless they talked to me first. But, you know? *Everyone* wanted to talk to the little girl with the milk. It turns out that those people didn't really like my parents very much. They were willing to fake it for the money and the connections. I started noticing things—what people wore, who they talked to, what they said, how much they drank. I was like Harriet the Spy. Of course, Mother would interrogate me at bedtime so she could find out what I'd seen."

"You do know how weird that is, right?"

"Absolutely. I figured that out by the time I was ten or so. But by then I'd started noticing things about Mother and Father, too. Things like how Father touched my nanny or the cook in places I'd only ever seen husbands touch their wives. How Mother drove off every friend I was ever stupid enough to bring home. How each of them told me to lie to the other one. How they'd do really evil things to hurt people who'd made them mad—start rumors, mess with their businesses, that kind of thing."

I can't help feeling sorry for Little Savannah. Nobody should have to live with that crap. "How old were you?"

"I had a pretty clear picture by junior high."

By junior high, I'd figured out my parents had some problems, but no details. I can't imagine being this aware of their failings that young. "Did you have anybody you could talk to?"

"Lawan, until Mother threw her away. After that?" She shrugs. "I could trust the other girls at school if our interests aligned, but I didn't have any friends-forever kind of friends. We were too competitive for that. We all needed to get into Stanford or Harvard."

I'd wanted to be one of the rich kids in high school. Maybe I dodged a bullet. "You know, the biggest political issue I had in high school was who to take to the dance."

"That sounds so nice." Wistful. Savannah shakes her head. "You know, I'd learned all this, but I missed the big thing. Mother and Father didn't really love each other, and they didn't love me. I was a *project*. Mother would've stopped after the first miscarriage, but Father insisted they have at least one child because *that's what people did*. You know how I know that?" I shake my head; it's my job as an audience. "Mother told me right before I went to Stanford. I was pretty proud of getting in there. She put me in my place. She *always* put me in my place."

"Jesus." A thought comes to me: with that kind of upbringing and that kind of emotional abuse, is she a psychopath now? Is this when she cuts my throat?

"Nice, huh? But it's okay. I badgered them into letting me live in a sorority. I learned. So. Much. I learned that it's okay to go to dinner in your bathrobe. I learned that food doesn't have to be prepared by a chef to taste good. I learned that I could have fun with food, and booze, and sex, and drugs, and music, and it was okay. I learned that places like the Tonga Room are fun—it's just a bonus that Mother and Father thought they're common and stupid. And I learned who my parents really were." She leans in, takes my hand in both of hers. "They were evil. They were hypocrites. They were racists. They were cheats. They were thieves. So many people thought my parents were some 'golden couple.' They weren't. I was raised by con artists." She aims an adoring look at me. Her voice goes sticky-sweet. "That's how I can recognize one now."

Aw, hell. She knows.

She strokes my cheek, wearing a saccharine smile. "So you're right. I don't act like other heiresses. You know why?" The smile dissolves as she sits up. Her voice turns hard. "I woke up. I joined the real world. But I am what I am. You?" An eyebrow arches. "I'm not so sure."

My first reaction: she seems so happy and well-adjusted. How did that part of her survive this mess? How is she not broken?

My second reaction: good for her. Other women I've met who grew up like this threw their lives away on nose candy or cosmetic surgery or multiple bad marriages. Savannah washed her hands of it and made something of herself.

I so wanted to trust her once I got to know her. Apparently, I was thinking with the wrong brain. "If you're so sure I'm a fraud, why did you come with me?"

She polishes off her beer and falls back into her bench. "I said I don't think you're who you say you are; I didn't say you're not worth knowing." She's back to being casual Savannah. "You've clearly got resources, though I'm not sure if they're yours or someone else's. You must've spent a fortune setting up that house. And, last-minute business-class tickets to Bangkok? That's got style. Did I mention you're cute? And you're fun to play with?" She grins. "I'll stick around for a while longer. See what you turn into." She holds her hand out into the drizzle, then splashes a palmful of water on her face to sluice off the sweat. "You don't think I forgot my question, do you? Let's try this again: who are you?"

I have to be careful here. The less I admit, the more of Hoskins that survives, but the less she believes. My gut tells me she hasn't yet told me everything she knows or suspects; maybe she's trying to catch me in an obvious lie. I let her watch me for a good long time. "Did you like the house?"

"I *loved* the house."

"The inside was all me. I designed it. I made it happen."

"You did a good job, then. That painting you said your mother did? Was that real?"

"Yes, she really painted it. You looked her up?" Savannah nods. "Did you like the car?"

"The little red one? I loved it."

"I picked it. I've always wanted one. Any gripes about my wardrobe?"

"No, none. You look handsome in a nice Italian suit."

"Thanks. Those are *my* clothes, not costumes." I hold my hand out across the table, palm up. After some thought, she sets her hand on it. "All these things you loved were real. They were really me, and I really loved sharing them with you. So maybe I'm not as different from what I told you as you think."

"Was that your house?"

"Does it really matter?"

She traces the lines on my palm with her thumb. "Well, I'd like to go back there, so, yes."

"I get it. You only want me for my swimming pool." I get back a sour look. "We're here now, together. There's a couple little things I need to do, then we can do whatever you want. Within reason."

"I know one of those 'little things' is finding where Nam Ton comes from, which isn't little at all. What's the other one?"

"Don't worry about it. It's here; I'll take care of it."

She wraps her hand around my middle, ring and little fingers and squeezes. Hard. *Ouch.* "Don't do that." Her voice is low and hard. "Don't you dare. If we're here together, then we're here *together.* You don't get to keep secrets from me anymore. You—"

"That cuts both ways."

"Fine. It so happens there are a couple of things *I* need to do, and I need you to help me. This mystery thing you have to do here? Let's do it together. We can bond as a couple through shared experiences." She's got her determined face on.

I can't slip out in the dead of night to do this without her knowing, especially since neither of us can sleep. I have maybe ten seconds to decide whether I drag Savannah into this... or I piss her off enough that she strands me out here in the sticks.

How do I explain this without blowing Hoskins' character?

Maybe the truth... or something like it.

"You know the drug gang ICE busted in Oakland? They have an office or warehouse here. I need to take a look inside it."

Both of Savannah's eyebrows shoot skyward. "Are you a cop?"

"I'm *so* not a cop."

"But you work for them."

"Not voluntarily."

Her eyes narrow. "What's that mean?"

I hesitate for effect. "The DEA didn't just let me off. Thanks to you, I'm a 'known associate' of your friends, the ones who're in bed with heroin traffickers. That house you love so much? The feds showed me the written motion to seize it if I don't play ball. I'm useful to them. They want me to go places they can't and report what I see. If I do, DEA puts my file through a shredder. If I don't..." I turn up my free hand.

Savannah stares into my eyes, maybe trying to find the lie. After a few seconds-like-hours, she leans forward, not breaking lock on my eyes. It's almost as intense as Allyson's death stare. "Where's this supposed place?"

"We probably passed it on the way in. It's off that main road from Chiang Dao, about two miles south of downtown, wherever that is."

More staring. "You'd better not be lying to me. I'll make you regret it."

"Same here."

She ties her robe closed. "Let's get dressed and go find it."

Chapter 44

Arunothai is asleep as we trundle down its main road. No windows are lit; all the roll-down steel shop doors are firmly shut. A very occasional streetlight washes the ground pale orange. It's a big difference from twelve hours ago, when the place was full of shoppers and people walking or biking home from work. The only living creature I see other than Savannah, who's driving, is a gray tiger-stripe cat on the hunt for an early-morning snack.

Then we're past the sky-blue, Chinese-style arch across the road and into more-or-less open countryside. The only scenery is an occasional tree or plant or road sign clipped by the headlights' aura as we pass. "Are the cops out this early?" I ask.

The dashboard lights throw a faint blue glow on Savannah's face. Her eyes shuttle from the windshield to the rear-view mirror to me. "Not usually. They might run into criminals, and that would mean work. Is there any landmark for this place?"

"The highway cuts through a dirt road right at two miles from that intersection back there."

She nods. She's wearing a loose olive button-up blouse with the sleeves rolled up, a mid-calf tan cotton skirt, and hiking sandals. When she dresses down, she goes for it.

"I've noticed lots of olives and browns in your outfits here. I've never seen those colors on you before."

"I'm usually in the countryside when I come here. Every place I go is dirty. I cover up so I won't be the clueless *farang* girl flashing lots of skin at the farmers."

It's an echo of what Carson told me about her wardrobe, which is mostly jeans and long-sleeved tees or polos: "I go to the kind of places where rape's a sport." If nothing else, I've learned a lot in this job about appropriate female dress for Third World travel.

The truck slows after a few minutes. "Two miles is up there."

We stop next to some bamboo frameworks that look like skeletal roadside stands. The headlights pool on a patch of paved road interrupting red-dirt tracks on either side.

I point to my left. "Google Earth shows two buildings about a hundred yards that way. I'd say that road's big enough for a truck, judging from the ruts."

Savannah's mouth bunches. "If we're trying to be sneaky, we shouldn't drive there."

Good point. We park on some gravel and hike down the track, staying on the grassy verge as much as possible. Leaving the truck's air-conditioned cab was like stepping into a hot, wet blanket. My Mini Maglite doesn't light much, but it's stronger than the moonlight the clouds are still blocking. Branches appear from nowhere to smack us in the face. It smells like a compost heap. "Are there poisonous snakes in Thailand?"

"Pit vipers, kraits, monocled cobras. One of those spit at me about five years ago. It didn't hit me, but it was scary."

I had to ask.

I switch off my flashlight when we get near the edge of the scrubby woods. We fumble through the last few yards until we reach a wide, plowed space. The dark shape of a wood-plank monitor barn with gable and shed roofs nestles into a small stand of darker trees about twenty yards away. It looks big enough to hold a forty-foot shipping container with some room to spare. Next door is a gable-roofed shed about the size of a two-car garage. A tractor with a flat tire hunches next to it.

Savannah whispers, "This looks like a farm. You're sure this is it?"

"No, but it's the only thing in the right place."

"What's so special about it?"

"It's supposed to belong to WCZ Trading. That's the company shipping the pots with the heroin in them. If this really is it, then it's the start of the pipeline."

The road curves around to the farmhouse. There's a thin coat of gravel scattered over what acts like a forecourt; we skirt it to avoid stepping on anything crunchy. Two big wood-plank doors face the forecourt, locked with a heavy chain and a padlock that looks sturdy as a safe.

The door on the east side is a different story. It's a well-weathered solid wood slab that's about the size of the front door to a suburban American house. The knob is rusty and pitted in my hand, but it turns. The door opens only an inch, though. I run my hand up the jamb and hit a metal chain guard.

Savannah whispers, "What is it?"

I peek through the gap into the building. A single bulb hanging from a wire barely lights the open-bay interior and exposed rafters. The windows have been boarded over from the inside. I can't see much, but I can see three wooden crates lined up against the far wall.

I ease the door shut and whisper to Savannah, "The door's unlocked, but it's chained from the inside. Somebody's in there."

Even in the dark, I can see she's startled. "What? We need to go."

"We can't. I saw crates in there. They look a lot like the ones in Jim's storage cube."

"But if someone's in there—"

"It's three in the morning. They're probably not as jetlagged as we are. I'll go in, shoot pictures of the crates, then leave."

"Alone? You're crazy."

"I'll be fine." No I won't, but I need to be brave for her benefit. "Go back to the truck."

She frowns. "No. I'm staying."

"Why?"

"To help."

Okay. It takes a moment to think of something she can do. "First thing? Get us inside. Your hand's smaller than mine."

She cracks open the door and slips most of her hand behind it. The chain makes little scratching noises as she fiddles with it. Then it stops. "Somebody's coming."

We duck behind the spindly trees on the other side of the path. It's not much protection, but it's something. Savannah crouches behind me and slips her hands onto my shoulders. Nighttime in L.A. sounds like crickets and police helicopters; here, it's just the crickets and an occasional comment from a bird or a frog. I assume the kraits and pit vipers don't say much.

A minute or so later, a guard pushes out the side door followed by a patch of weak light. At least, the gun stuffed into the back waistband of his cutoff camo shorts makes me assume he's a guard. He's stocky and bandy-legged, wearing sliders and a ratty orange tee with some kind of white-and-black shield on the chest. How does a security guard get away with wearing sandals? He plods halfway down the long end of the barn with his nose buried in his phone, then unzips and pees on the wall.

Savannah mutters, "Geez, really?"

"Now we know there's no outhouse."

The guard shambles around the barn's front corner, unlocks the front doors, then drags them open with much scraping of gravel. He disappears inside. A minute later, bluish fluorescent light blasts out the front and side doors.

Savannah's breath blows hot on my ear. "In case you care, he's a Chiangrai United fan."

"Great. We can bond over soccer."

"*Fuutbaan.*" She draws out the last syllable.

"Whatever. He's open for business. Somebody or something must be coming. You'd better move the truck. We don't want the guests to see it."

Sigh. "Okay." She melts into the darkness.

I wait for an unquantifiable while. I don't dare turn on my phone to see the time. The clouds thin a bit, leaking moonlight. Leaves drip warm water on me. The bugs have found me now that I'm not moving. Do I taste different than the locals? The crickets occasionally drop out, then start their concert again. I nearly freak out the first time it happens, thinking it means somebody or something is moving around, but it's a regular thing.

Savannah scares the crap out of me (not literally) when she creeps up behind me some while later. "All parked," she whispers. "Anything happening?"

"Nothing. I can't even see Soccer Fan anymore." That doesn't mean he's not there. We didn't see anything alive at the WCZ warehouse in Oakland until Cujo tried to eat my throat. "I'd love to get a shot at those crates."

"If you try, I'll leave you here."

We shift to our left to get a straighter view into the barn. The dirt floor looks dry and firmly packed. Two ranks of three six-foot strip lights give the place that homey airport-apron look. Other than four oil drums to the right, the crates to the left, and some wooden folding screens in the back, the place is empty.

I settle against a tree trunk. "If somebody's coming, it must be soon. It wouldn't make sense to leave that dude here for days.

When's the local border crossing open?"

"Kew Pha Wok? It depends. It may not open at all depending on how things are between the Thais and the Burmese today. If it's Wa coming here, they may get through even if it's closed. It's not hard to cross."

Excellent. It could be anytime between right now and hours from now. Or maybe not at all, and the owners keep someone in the barn to stop the local kids from having raves here.

Still… three brand-new, empty crates just sitting there. They must have a use for them; they'd make great firewood otherwise.

The air's still heavy and damp but not as stifling as it was a few hours ago. The bugs are out in force, though, and I wish I'd worn something that covers me better than a black tee and khaki walking shorts. I didn't expect to be staking out the barn outside.

Savannah rolls down her sleeves, curls her legs underneath her, then slathers bug spray on her exposed parts. I can barely smell it above the general wet-rotting-vegetation stink. "You sure know how to show a girl a good time."

"Michelin-star dinners and Broadway tickets are so overdone."

At least she chuckles. "I swear, once we're done here, I'm taking you to Koh Mook."

"What's that?"

"An island in the Andaman Sea. Some of the most beautiful beaches you've ever seen. All the tourists go to Phuket, so it's quiet and cozy and the water's amazing."

"It's monsoon season."

"So? You're living in the water anyway. You can't get more wet." She passes me her bug juice. "You'll need this."

Time passes. The bugs get as tired of us as we do scratching their bites. Traffic noise whines by on the highway every once in a great while; none of it comes here. Savannah dozes with her back against a tree, her chin almost on her chest, her hands stuffed between her thighs to keep them away from biting things. I'm getting stiff and dopey, too, but the worry and the residual adrenaline from sneaking around keep me awake if not alert. I feel like I'm back in the RV in West Oakland, watching the WCZ warehouse hour after hour, waiting for something to happen. The RV was a pit, but it was way more comfortable than this.

The eastern sky's shifting from charcoal to violet when a truck rumbles toward us along the drive. It's an old, white stakebed with lots of miles on it. The engine whines on each downshift. When it backs toward the open barn doors, I see two guys in baseball hats in the cab and a load of what looks like cabbage in the back. The baseball-cap dudes step out, drop the tailgate with a *wham*, then saunter inside.

Savannah yawns, stretches, and tries to massage her own neck. "What do we do now?"

"See what they're up to. Take pictures if anything happens."

Soccer Fan shuffles from the screens to the barn doors with the baseball-cap dudes behind him. He stands back as the other two haul themselves onto the flatbed and start tossing cabbage toward the cab end. I snap lots of pictures with my work phone.

A baseball-cap dude—older, with a moustache—pulls a well-filled plastic bag from under the produce. It's about the size of a five-gallon freezer bag, but instead of turkey parts, it's full of something bright red. I zoom up the last photo I took—the thirteen-megapixel camera gives me lots of room for magnification—and discover the red is actually a mass of smallish round pills. Old Cap hands it down to Soccer Fan, who carries it inside the barn. Young Cap brings up the next bag, and pretty soon half a dozen sacks of pills have disappeared into the barn before the baseball caps take a break.

Savannah presses against my back. She's very warm. She whispers, "*Ya ba.*"

"What's that?"

"Pills made of meth mixed with caffeine."

"That's redundant." I feel her shrug. "We're looking for heroin."

"Poppies are a fall and winter crop. Meth you can make anytime."

Right. "Does it smell like anything?"

"Chocolate. Why?"

"How do you know that?"

"Well, first, Thais call it '*chocalee.*' Second, I tried it once. You can get it anyplace. I hated it, but I still remember what it smells like."

"Do they need the pots to move it around?"

"How should I know?" Her whisper turns sharp. "I'm not a drug cop. The junta's talking about legalizing it, so I doubt the police spend a lot of time on it except to get their bribes."

The baseball caps come outside with bottles of water and gather around the truck's back end to shoot the breeze with Soccer Fan for a couple minutes. The caps climb back onto the flatbed after they finish their break, then commit more produce abuse. More bags of happy pills surface and shuttle into the barn. After the tenth one, Old Cap shouts something at Soccer Fan, who gives him a dismissive wave.

Savannah warms my back again. "They're done."

The caps rearrange the cabbage. Soccer Fan shambles out of the barn and tosses a bulging plastic grocery bag to Old Cap. I've seen enough bundles of cash to know what they look like wrapped in plastic. The men throw jibes back and forth, then the caps climb into the truck's cab and drive off.

Soccer Fan lounges against the right-hand barn door while his phone entertains him. So much for us moving.

His phone rings a few minutes later. The ringtone is something in a minor key with a heavy backbeat. He has a grunting conversation with whoever called, shoves the phone in his thigh pocket, then trudges into the barn.

He doesn't close the doors.

Soccer Fan wanders to the pile of red-filled plastic bags by the crates. He flips the lids off all three crates, then turns one lid forty-five degrees and sets it on top of the closest crate to us to make a table. Then he dredges something out of the middle crate, dumps a bunch of straw out of it, and sets it on the makeshift table.

It's a cylinder, maybe six inches tall and six wide, a deep terracotta red with black bands around it. Soccer Fan starts filling it with small bags of red pills, then puts a familiar red-and-blue sticker on the bottom.

Savannah whispers, "That's Shan. It's a ceramic box with a brown slip. But why put the pills in it? They could've left it in the produce."

"The clay in the pots masks the smell from drug dogs. That's why these people use the Nam Ton wares to move heroin."

"You're kidding."

"Nope. DEA told me, and they've got no sense of humor."

I check both ways on the road and then, without thinking too long about it, step out of the bushes and scurry to the right-hand barn door. I have a good-but-not-great view of Soccer Fan's work...

but if he turns around, he'll have a great view of me watching.

A flapping noise makes me glance over my shoulder. Savannah's pounding the pad of her index finger into her palm, making the sound of a small bird flapping its wings. She looks half-scared and half-pissed. She mouths, *What are you doing?*

I point to my phone, then Soccer Fan, then point to her and then toward the highway. That seems to piss her off more.

My phone's camera has a pretty good built-in zoom, so I can get decent pictures of the setup and of what Soccer Fan's doing in the barn. At least, I can when he gets out of the way. The view from the other door would be much better. I wait for him to have his back square to me, then dash across the open doorway.

My foot lands hard on some gravel. *Crunch.*

The flapping noise gets my attention again. Savannah's crouched behind a tree, holding up her hand palm-out: *stop.*

I plaster myself against the door. It's at least ten yards from here to the treeline and the only cover nearby.

Nothing happens for a thirty count except for my heart trying to hide behind my stomach. Then I hear it: the scratch of rubber soles on dirt. Noisy breathing. I can smell him—he needs a shower even worse than I do. Can he smell me? Savannah's disappeared into the thicket, so at least she's safe unless she does something dumb, like I did.

B.O., breathing. I start a silent count. He's standing just inside the doorway, close enough to touch. What's he doing? I mean, other than looking for me?

When the count reaches twenty-two, the breathing and B.O. cut off. The sound of his sandals trails off into nothing.

You can't get good help these days. Thank god.

I get some decent-ish pictures. *Gotcha, assholes.* Just as I wonder what else to do, a bright light catches the corner of my eye off to my left, toward the highway.

Headlights. Coming this way.

To hell with the gravel. I bound across the forecourt and duck between a couple saplings with seconds to spare before the front of the barn lights up. A late-model white Toyota Hilux skids to a stop, then jerks backwards to present its tailgate to the barn. Two guys bail out of the cab and march inside. A few very fast heartbeats later, a second pickup, this one black, barrels into the forecourt, backs up next to the first truck, and spills another load of guys.

I meet with Savannah at our blind across from the barn doors. The trucks block our view inside, which means they also block the bad guys' view outside. I shoot a couple more photos: trucks, license plates.

Savannah hisses, "Let's go! I'm done with this!" She grabs my collar and hauls me away.

Chapter 45

There's a metal stool and a small wooden table in the arcade outside the sliding glass door to our room. That's where I watch sunset paint the clouds gold as they sweep across a lavender sky. It's still hot, but the breeze moves the air around better than the fan in the room. It's actually nice out here.

A few other guests—mostly Thais, another pair of westerners—lounge in the arcade or on the bungalow porches. A couple cute Asian kids, maybe eight or nine years old, are playing on the benches outside the front office. A black rooster scratches around the parking lot.

I just woke up. I've been asleep for over ten hours. My brain feels like day-old cotton candy. At least I'm not running into walls anymore. My arms and legs are spotted with calamine lotion so I don't go crazy scratching the bug bites.

The door slides open behind me. Savannah leans a shoulder against the jamb, I think more for support than to look casual. She's wrapped in that short, thin white robe from last night. Her eyes are at half-mast and her hair's messed up. "Hi."

"Hi." I go back to watching the sunset.

A few moments later, she slides her hands over my shoulders and down my chest. On my way out here, I pulled on a clean pair of board shorts but didn't bother with a shirt. This is more contact than we had in bed. She kisses the back of my head.

I ask, "Are we speaking again?"

She was angry-quiet on the way back from the barn. Once we got here, she slammed the bathroom door in my face, then went from the shower directly to bed without bothering to dry off or to say a word to me. I took the opportunity to go through her luggage.

"Sorry I've been such a bitch." Her voice is low and sleepy.

"I understand. I put you in danger. You didn't sign up for this."

"Actually, I did. This is me exhausted and jet-lagged. Like it?"

"Not much."

"I don't either. I usually don't leave my room the first day I get here. I'm not fit for human company."

I stroke the soft hair on her arm. Her skin's very warm. "Is this the first time you've come here with somebody?"

"Uh-huh. Sorry you're the guinea pig." Savannah kneels by my stool and sits on her heels, close enough to be warm but not touch.

"What are you doing down there?"

"The Thais don't like public affection. This also covers me up."

"These are the same people who have that crazy red-light district in Bangkok?"

"That's for the *farang*. We're not there." She pulls my hand next to her, holding it so nobody can see. The clouds and a few sighs go by. "Get what you needed at the farm?"

"Yeah. I wrote the report for the feds after you went to bed. They emailed me a couple hours ago saying they liked what they got." All this went through Allyson, of course, but I'm impressed by the turnaround.

"So are you done with the DEA?"

"Afraid not. The barn's only the Thai end of the pipeline. They want to know where the heroin originates. And I still need to find where Nam Ton comes from." I avoid mentioning ICE because it makes the story too complicated.

"That's too bad. By the way, you should wear a shirt out here. Thais think it's tacky to show too much skin in public."

Oh, well. I'd like to simply sit here and watch the sun go down, but I hear the countdown clock ticking in the back of my brain. "We need to get ready to go into Myanmar."

"Not right now."

"Soon. Today."

"There's not much of today left."

"I know. There must be something we can do. Buy water or something."

She squeezes my hand. "We need to sleep more. Today's a good day for that. We won't get to relax once we go over the border."

How do I tell her we're on a deadline? The thought of losing another day may be enough to keep me awake. "The State Department website says we need visas to get in."

"Uh-uh. Pay the border guard, like, five thousand kyat." She pronounces it *chat*. "He'll wave you through."

"How much is that?"

"Uh… four dollars. They call it 'tea money'."

There's another phrase I'll never be able to hear the same way again. "What do we need to take in with us?"

"I'll make a list." She stands, stretches. "I'm starving."

"Put some clothes on and I'll feed you."

"Okay. I want to shower first." She holds out her hand. "Come scrub my back. I'll make it up to you for being a bitch."

Bedhead, soft eyes, a dreamy smile—she's adorable. I feel like such a schmuck for playing her. "Deal."

We eat dinner at the Tayoung Yunnan Noodle Restaurant downtown; an open stall with pictures of food lining all three walls. It's apparently famous among western tourists who come to places like this. Savannah orders—in Mandarin—for both of us. The fried dumplings would be good even if I hadn't gone almost a full day eating only energy bars. Then we raid the So Good Super Mart (an ambitious 7-Eleven by any other name) across the street for a dozen flats of water, canned food, first-aid kits, mosquito netting, bug spray, and some things I didn't realize we need. "Diapers?"

"Gifts."

Now it's nighttime.

Thousands of stars glimmer between the scattered clouds. A more-than-half-moon hovers above the hills to the east. A few lights glow amber behind curtains at the hotel.

I stand at the hotel parking lot's far edge, hoping the rooster won't attack me. The cell reception is best out here and I'm as far away from eavesdroppers as I can get and still be on-property. My thumb punches a contact on my work phone.

"Yeah?"

At least she sounds awake. "It's Matt. Where are you?"

Carson says, "You called, and you don't know where I am? Coulda been sleeping."

"I checked the time in Kiev and Toronto, and it's daytime in both places."

"Huh. Toronto. You?"

"Thailand."

"The fuck're you doing there?"

"Working. I need some advice. Got a few minutes?"

She sighs. "Yeah, okay. What?"

"I'm going into Myanmar tomorrow—"

"The fuck're you doing that for?"

"Work. From what I've read, it's your basic corrupt Third World basket case. I know you have experience with those. What should I watch out for? Lonely Planet goes only so far."

"Jesus. You there alone?"

"Somebody's with me."

"Who is she?"

"What makes you think it's a she?"

"I know you. Tell me it's not that art bitch."

I told her about Savannah weeks ago. My lack of an answer is my answer.

"Really? The one you can't trust? Good going, you dart."

"I think we have that worked out. Savannah's got an agenda and she needs me for it, so she has an incentive to play nice."

"And you're fucking her."

"What makes you think that?"

"I know you. Tell me she's useful for more than blow jobs."

"She knows the area and speaks Thai and Mandarin."

"Oh." Surprise. "Okay, listen hard. Know who to bribe and how much. Don't overtip."

"Overtip?"

"That line on the expense report? 'Gratuities'? That's for bribes. Pay 'em too much, they figure you have more. Next. Bring gifts when you deal with the local movers. They like western shit—booze, cigs, watches, runners. Anything branded."

Probably not diapers, though it explains the four cartons of Marlboros Savannah made me buy. "I assume the more senior they are, the better the gift?"

"Yeah. Next. Don't be an asshole unless you need to. They're used to asshole Americans. They know you people are usually hot air. Don't be a pussy, either.

"Next. They come on hard, you come back harder. You show fear, you're done. They respect strength. They threaten to kill you or rape your girl? You threaten to burn their village."

"That actually works?"

"Yeah. Done it. Sell a good line of bullshit, you can make it work."

There are depths to Carson I haven't even started to explore. "Anything else?"

"Yeah. Listen good to this one. Don't fuck with the local women unless the men invite you to. Nothing gets you dead faster than getting caught with the warlord's girlfriend. Hear me?"

"Yeah."

"Repeat it."

"Don't fuck with the local women."

"Good. Keep telling yourself that. Finally: they like you more if you're useful. You're a businessman; so are they. Show them how they win by helping you. They'll love you... this time. You're only as good—"

"—as your last deal. That one, I know." Is she telling me how to work with the mafia or the finance industry? "How do they feel about horse heads in beds?"

"Depends on how they feel about horses. I know places that works. Myanmar probably isn't one. That help?"

I'm afraid to think that it really could. "Yeah. Thanks. How'd your project work out?"

"I'm alive." Pause. "Watch your ass. Where you're going is my world, not yours."

"I know. I wish you were here."

She doesn't answer right away. "Glad I'm not."

Chapter 46

8 DAYS LEFT

I wake up to the sliding glass door clicking shut. Savannah's not on the bed anymore. Her robe isn't draped over the back of the desk chair, either.

My phone says it's 5:18 a.m. I knuckle the crud out of my eyes, then shuffle to the door and peek around the drapes. The coming sunrise paints everything a soft pearl gray. Savannah's marching across the parking lot toward the place I called Carson from last night. When she gets there, she puts her phone to her ear and paces back and forth, pushing her fingers through her hair.

Who's she calling at this hour? Somebody back home? She already knows I told the feds about the barn; she gets nothing from telling them again.

Her Chinese friend?

She hasn't told me yet what she needs me to do for her. Is she setting that up?

Is she setting *me* up?

The Burmese immigration officer frowns at our passports.

Getting through the Thai border post at Kew Pha Wok wasn't nearly as hard as I'd thought it would be. Savannah talked to the head soldier in Thai and gave him her prettiest smile while two of his buddies nosed around the truck. She'd told me they don't really care much who leaves, just who comes in. She didn't even have to bribe them.

The Burmese checkpoint a few dozen yards away is a whole different matter.

It's less developed than its Thai counterpart: a shack, a barricade, a sandbagged emplacement next to the red-dirt road. Three guys in the kind of lizard-green fatigues you see in Vietnam War movies are digging under the truck's hood and seats. One taps the door panels and fenders, probably looking for hidden compartments. They're Myanmar Army, apparently almost universally called Tatmadaw.

The immigration dude strokes his chin. The chevrons under the blue "Immigration" patch on his short-sleeved olive uniform shirt say he's a sergeant, if their ranks work like ours. I'm sweating like a horse and even Savannah's long button-up olive dress shows some dark spots, but the sergeant doesn't seem to notice the humidity.

He peers into Savannah's eyes, then says something slowly in Thai. Until just now, I didn't know it's possible to speak Thai in less than fast-forward. He and Savannah had to start their discussion by asking each other about languages until they found one they could both understand.

Since I'm completely out of the conversational loop, I can look around without being disrespectful. The mountains of Myanmar look like what you get if you tell a child to draw hills—an abrupt rise, rolling rounded tops, green to the crests. They form a wall to the east, stretching north into the morning haze. The sun pushes shadows across the farmland toward Highway 45, the road we'll take north to the Nam Ton if we ever get past here.

Savannah says "Co-lum-bi-a U-ni-vers-i-ty." It's the first thing she's said over the past ten minutes that I've understood. She holds a business card so the sergeant can see. Then another long string of Thai while she somehow keeps smiling.

The three soldiers have managed to get the truck's front driver's seat to lean forward. One shimmies next to the bench that serves as a vestigial back seat and pulls on the seat cushions. He'll have to work smarter, not harder; there's a way to get the pads off, but it involves screwdrivers. Still, it's worth watching him, because under the seat pads is a space big enough to hide the "gifts" (cigarettes, booze, diapers) we bought in Arunothai. I don't know if this is standard equipment on a Hilux or a special deal through Olivia's preferred car-rental agency.

The sergeant and Savannah have started debating. It's not angry—Savannah says that people here don't respond to public anger—but there's a lively back-and-forth. He keeps tapping the passports with his fingertips and she keeps waving her right hand toward the north.

The soldiers haven't made any progress with the back bench and are now peering under the truck. For a nation that's a prime exporter of heroin and meth, what kind of import is so threatening that it's worth this much trouble to find?

Now Savannah points toward the shack, then makes the "you and me" hand gesture between her and the sergeant. This one I get: she's saying, "Let's take this inside." Where the bribery happens.

The sergeant nods, then throws a command in what I'll assume is Burmese at the soldiers. The youngest trots to the guard post, grabs his assault rifle, then jogs to stand in front of me with his gun held across his chest.

Savannah says, "Stay there. I'll be back soon." She disappears into the shack with the sergeant.

Like I'm going anywhere. The kid soldier guarding me—he looks like he's about fifteen—has a round face and broad nose, very different from the Chinese in Arunothai or the fine-boned Thais on the airplane and in the airports. His bush hat (basically a green fabric cowboy hat) is a tad too large. Luckily, so are his ears.

I say, "English?"

He scowls, adjusts his grip on his gun. So much for conversation.

His buddies are still trying to deconstruct the truck. One dude has the bright idea to look under the floor mats. It reminds me that I never checked those to see if the last driver left behind any Shan independence propaganda or satirical cartoons involving the Buddha (both extreme no-nos). The other still futzes with the back bench.

He worries me. If he keeps at it, he'll eventually figure out how to get past the cushions. I'm not sure if smuggling is a capital crime in Myanmar and I don't want to find out.

Savannah's still gone. I don't know for sure how long she's been in there, but I know it's longer than it takes to make a payoff. It would be just our luck to run across the only honest immigration officer in the whole country.

I smile at my guard. He looks confused.

Savannah marches out of the shack with the sergeant trailing along behind her. She's clutching the passports to her chest. That looks like potential good news, but I don't get too excited until she flashes me a big grin as she passes. "Got it."

The sergeant barks at the three soldiers, who scurry like the werewolf from Oakland is after them. They have the barrier swung out of the way by the time Savannah and I have strapped in and the truck is ready to go.

We're in Myanmar. In an area we're not supposed to be in, with no legal visas and no intention of following the rules for foreign tourists. I can't say this is the stupidest thing I've ever done, but it's definitely in the top five.

"How much did the good sergeant cost us back there?"

Savannah concentrates on the road, which looks and drives more like a riverbed than a highway with a number. "About seven hundred baht."

"That's Thai money."

"That's what he wanted. It gives him options. He can go into Arunothai to shop, or he can change it into kyat at Ponparkyin, where he's based."

I do the math: thirty-five baht to the dollar. "Twenty bucks? That's all?"

"That's what he makes in a month."

Seriously? No wonder they're on the pad.

We stop after half a mile. Savannah pins up her hair, then covers it with a slate-blue kerchief. She also buttons her dress all the way up and down.

"What are you doing?"

"Getting ready for the Wa checkpoint about half a mile up."

"Are they Muslim?"

"No, they're Christian or Buddhist, but I'm awfully blond for around here. I already stand out—I don't need to make it worse. Can you dig some cigarettes out of the back?"

When I hear "ethnic rebel militia," I think of skinny people in ragged clothes hauling cast-off weapons through the jungle. The United Wa State Army looks as organized as the Tatmadaw—the same green uniforms, the kind of flat-topped fatigue caps you see in Korean War pictures, even a red tape reading "U.W.S. ARMY" over their left chest pockets. Their patches are more colorful.

Compared to the prolonged negotiation at the government checkpoint, this is like checking out at Walmart—fast and impersonal. The head guy (I assume; he's the oldest) strolls to Savannah's window and asks in English where we're going; Savannah tells him, "Mongton"; he names his price; she forks over four thousand kyat ($3.42) and a pack of Marlboros; he smiles and waves away the guy standing in front of the truck with his rifle aimed at us; and we're off. The twelve-year-old behind the sandbags doesn't even shoot us with his machine gun.

Once the checkpoint's disappeared into the distance, I ask, "Should we be glad or sorry that those guys seemed more together than the government?"

"Around here, they *are* the government more-or-less." Savannah unbuttons her dress to mid-thigh and mid-sternum. There must not be any more roadblocks coming soon. "Being more organized than the Naypyidaw government is a pretty low bar."

We're not in Kansas anymore. "Well, the good news is we're only thirty-five kilometers or so from Wān Namhawng. We should make it by lunchtime." Wān Namhawng is a village near the confluence of two rivers that create the Nam Hang, the closest I can find to an end to the Nam Ton.

Savannah peers at me over the top of her sunglasses. "Don't count on it."

Not surprisingly, both our cellphones lost signal once we crossed into Myanmar. I knew we'd need a GPS here—it's not like AAA stocks maps of this place. While I chowed down on free food in the Oneworld Business Class Lounge at LAX, I searched for "use gps on cell phone without signal" and ended up on the Adventure Alan website. It's doable so long as you download the maps ahead of time. I installed ViewRanger, a GPS app, on my phone and proceeded to scam off the lounge's wifi to download every single street and topo map I could find for northern Thailand and eastern Myanmar. It works fine.

That's how we know the names of the villages we pass through. It's not like the local Kiwanis put up "Welcome to Wān Longhpakhpit" signs at the city limits. It's also how we know where the Anti-Destination League does its best to stop us from making any progress.

First it's the washout just south of Wān Namyūm, about five and a half kilometers from the border. Some UWSA soldiers watch a bunch of skinny civilians try to reassemble a short bridge across a stream that became a river in the past few days. We have to pay a $2 toll and creep across a rough wooden pontoon bridge at walking speed to get to the north bank.

Next it's the flatbed truck overloaded with huge logs that forces us off the road above a nameless village about two and a half klicks past the washout. It took a while for us to get out of the ditch we ended up in.

As we approach the southern fringes of Wān Nam-hu, three klicks north of the Logging Truck Incident, a military convoy shoves us off the road again, this time into a farmer's boggy field. Savannah grumbles "Tatmadaw" as the cargo trucks roar past us.

"How can you tell?"

"The soldiers have helmets."

There's a UWSA roadblock as we enter Ponparkyin, a village big enough to be considered a town. A mixed herd of trucks and motorbikes waits to get through. Young UWSA troops pace up and down the line, trying their best to look fierce.

I'm driving this time. "It's taken us over an hour and a half to go fifteen kilometers."

She nods. "That's about right."

"And we've almost gotten killed twice."

"That's about right, too."

Great. The truck drivers mill around on the road, smoking, talking. A few look twitchy, pacing too fast, making abrupt gestures. I see one guy dig something out of a plastic bag and pop it like a pill. "Those guys are using?"

"A lot of truck drivers use meth to go long distances. I think now you see why."

Forty minutes later, Savannah handles the checkpoint negotiations from the passenger's side of the truck. We grab lunch at a makeshift grill in an open stall (Wa spicy fried fish for me), then crawl through midday foot and scooter traffic to get on our way. I almost flatten three bikers as we go. They don't seem to notice.

The good news: the highway's paved (after a fashion) once we leave Ponparkyin. The bad news: it's a little over one lane wide. I'm constantly swerving onto the crumbling shoulder to let trucks or military vehicles pass.

Savannah taps my thigh, then points out my window. "See those terraces over there?"

I glance out the driver's window long enough to see the stairsteps climbing the nearby hillsides. Each one has a tall fringe of green on top. "Yeah. What's that they're growing?"

"Corn now. Usually poppies."

"Like... *opium* poppies?"

"Uh-huh. The farmers grow corn between April and August to recondition the soil." She sweeps her hand across the valley ahead of us. "This is poppy country. It's their whole economy."

I'm not sure what to do with that information. I've always thought of pot and opium growing in jungles or under camouflaged nets so the narcs can't see it from the air. Maybe I watch too many movies. "Just right out in the open like this?"

"Uh-huh. It seems strange, doesn't it? But everything's about heroin and meth here."

I think about that until my brain makes a random connection. "Everything? Even pottery?"

"*Everything.*"

"So you already knew there was a connection between Nam Ton wares and drugs."

"Uh-huh. It's not much of a secret."

"It was to me." Something else she kept from me until the DEA blindsided me. "How do you know all this?"

"I got some of it at Stanford and Columbia; the rest I've had to learn for work. There's a contemporary art community in Myanmar now. It's small but it's growing. Artists are getting more exposure to the outside world since the country started opening up."

"That's probably not happening here."

"No, mostly in Yangon and Mandalay."

"You seem pretty comfortable up here, though."

She shrugs.

I should pursue that, but not now. I'm already painfully aware that I'm almost completely dependent on her. Pushing too hard might end up with me walking back to Thailand.

■

We creep into Wān Namhawng ninety minutes and twenty kilometers later behind a pair of overloaded motorbikes. My hands shake when I pry them loose from the wheel. I'll never complain about L.A. rush-hour traffic again.

Now it's time to do what we came here to do.

Chapter 47

5 DAYS LEFT

It looks so easy on a map.

We're searching for anything that looks like an archaeological dig, even a dormant one. Somebody's getting Nam Ton wares out of the ground. But where?

It must be somewhere along the eighteen kilometers (about ten miles) of river between Wān Namhawng and a bit north of Wan Mè-kin. Some of it closely parallels the highway; other parts have roads nearby.

No problem. We'll head north, drive the parts of the river we can, walk the rest.

Sure.

If you take your eyes off the highway, you die. The driver can't see shit on either side. All the passenger can see are buildings or trees, sometimes a field.

The roads near the river? All dirt. It rains almost every night: sometimes a sprinkle, sometimes buckets. The dirt roads are now long, thin mudholes, something we discovered two days ago when it took us two hours, a passing water buffalo, and three thousand kyat to get the truck out of one. So, driving the river? Not happening.

I thought we could ask people in the villages if any outsiders are digging big holes around town. Savannah said, "We need to limit our contact with the locals."

We're left with walking. One of us hikes a couple klicks; the other drives to the nearest passable road to pick up the walker.

It should work, except for one other glitch: the river mostly flows through a tree-canopy tunnel. If you're on one bank, you may not be able to see past the other bank. This is a problem since what we're looking for may not be larger than a couple typical suburban house lots.

I haven't even mentioned the rain, the heat, the humidity, and the bugs.

This is all stuff you can't get on maps or satellite pictures. There isn't much documentation about this area that isn't about drugs. There aren't many photos that aren't about the guerrilla wars. If there'd been a way to figure out whether this plan would work, we'd probably have come up with a different plan.

After the first day, four klicks a day seems impossibly ambitious. But we walk. Because we have to. *I* have to.

It hasn't rained yet today, though the gathering clouds look like they want to. It doesn't matter much because I'm already drenched with sweat. I quickly understood why Savannah insisted that I get a pair of hiking sandals when we arrived in Chiang Mai. "You don't want mud in your regular shoes," she'd said. "You'll never get it out. And when the rain turns the streets into rivers? You'll still have to walk through it. Sandals dry out; gym shoes won't."

It's pretty out here. The mountains on either side of the river are carpeted with dark blue-green trees. The fields I walk through are vivid green mixed with the rust of wet dirt. The river—more a creek here—flows fast and brown with earth washed down from the hills by the rain. Birds dart everywhere, singing and squabbling.

The farmers aren't so pleased. Each one I pass stops to watch me. I try to be pleasant, saying "*mengalaba*" (hello) as I reach them. They stand silent as scarecrows in their wide-brimmed straw hats, long-sleeved shirts, and *pasus* (a kind of Burmese sarong), holding their hoes like weapons at the ready.

Yesterday we covered a whopping three kilometers. The river disappeared into wilderness; not even a track to follow. We ended up backtracking several klicks to get to a passable road that crossed the river. The locals weren't any more welcoming on the rebound.

Savannah's been a surprisingly good sport about all this. She doesn't complain more than I do and she puts in her end of the slogging. Her legs may be pretty but they're strong, too, and she walks like somebody used to doing it a lot. "It's the other way I get my exercise," she told me two days ago. "You should see me climb Nob Hill in heels."

I'm a kilometer and some change into my second hike of the day and I'm ready to hang it up. The segments we've covered have gotten shorter as we get more tired and sore. I eat naproxen like M&Ms.

After three days of *nada*, I have to think: what happens if we don't find anything?

Two possibilities, neither good.

One is that the site is on the upper Nam Ton in the trackless forests and mountains north of Mongton. Maybe there was arable land up there eight hundred years ago. Maybe the reason nobody excavated the site until 2008 is because nobody could get to it. We could spend weeks slogging through the bush, trying to find a little patch of dirt that grows pottery. Well, *I* could—Savannah'll bug out if she's even half as smart as she seems to be.

The other possibility? Dr. Udomprecha's notion of "near the Nam Ton" is more expansive than mine. We may have already walked past the site, except we were thinking "near" means dozens of yards and the good doctor thinks it means hundreds of yards. The net result is the same: me bushwhacking for weeks through virgin forest while Savannah checks into the Peninsula Hotel in Bangkok on the government's dime.

Another klick later, I leave the river and head east along the edge of a swampy dirt track. I've just finished my fourth bottle of water since I started walking this afternoon and wouldn't mind a fifth. Here I thought twelve flats of water was overkill; now I wonder if it's enough.

I turn a corner and see our Hilux parked on a dirt-and-gravel road a hundred feet ahead. Savannah stands by the truck in a long, demure slate-blue dress and straw safari hat.

The soldier facing her wears a UWSA uniform.

Oh, shit. I duck behind some shrubs to scope out the situation.

Savannah's having a spirited conversation with the soldier. I can't hear any of it—the wind's behind me—but it looks like she's doing most of the talking.

A tan-and-olive-drab camo Hilux with a roll bar across the cargo bed's back end blocks the road behind our truck. The satellite shot pops up in my head: there's no other way out.

A soldier in his mid-teens steps out of the passenger's side of the camo Hilux. He peers into our truck's cargo bed, pushes something around. Other than the water and a tarp, I can't remember what's back there anymore.

Should I join the party? I can't decide if I'd make things better or worse. Having a pretty, western blonde drop from the sky may be a cute anecdote; two westerners is an invasion. Then again, having me around may make it harder for them to turn her into a sex toy… though, admittedly, not much harder. What's my best move?

Savannah pulls some cash from a pocket. She offers it with both hands and a big smile to her soldier.

He snaps handcuffs on her.

Holy. Shit. I try to not freak out. It's hard. I need Savannah. She speaks the language, knows her way around, knows who to bribe when. Not to mention what they might do to her.

She puts up a fight. She doesn't hit either of the soldiers, but she does her best greased-pig imitation to try to get away. But there's two of them and she's not a boxer, so she ends up pinned to the side of our truck with a bloody nose, squawking loud enough for me to hear from almost thirty yards away. Each soldier grabs an arm and marches her toward the camo truck.

Think fast.

I can stay under cover, let them haul her off, then come out when it's clear. I'll never find her; I wouldn't know where to start, and I stand out like crazy here.

Or I can rush the trucks. Not to attack the soldiers—that decision would be worse than most I've made in my life—but to somehow hide in a truck so I go where Savannah goes. I have no idea what I'll do there. In the meantime, they could catch me almost instantly.

Despite her wriggling like a cat about to go into a bath, the soldiers are forcing her into the back of the camo truck's cab.

Think faster. Or, stop thinking.

I channel my inner Carson, stop thinking, and *do.*

I launch across the road, then sprint as best I can while bent over. Can they see past our truck? *Don't think.* Savannah's yelps and the soldiers' growls get louder with each step. It feels like I'm making a whole parade's worth of noise, but I keep scurrying along, trying to stay out of both the mud and the soldiers' eyeshot.

Twenty yards. Ten.

A door thumps closed. Savannah's voice disappears. Time's up.

I risk a prairie-dog popup to see the two soldiers' heads bobbing above the camo truck's cargo bed, talking. A few seconds later, I reach our truck's tailgate and hunker down for a beat to catch my breath. Now what?

The rental truck's driver's door clicks open. The truck shifts a smidge. I can feel the door slam before I hear it. The engine roars awake.

Now or never.

I slither over the tailgate and flatten myself on the steel floor just as the truck jerks forward. I'm directly behind the driver; there's no reason he should turn around and look down, right? The tarp's big enough to cover me and still have a mind of its own. That means it'll make its own landscape that'll help camouflage the human-sized lump over me.

They drive seemingly for days. The ridged floor absorbs exactly zero of the bumps and heaves as we jounce. Every few minutes, the truck lurches dramatically and my head whacks against metal, sprinkling stars in front of my eyes. The tarp doesn't breathe and it's sweltering under here. I peek out to see the sun to the truck's left. We're heading north. But to where?

We finally stop in a town that announced itself with an increase in noise and a decrease in speed. The driver climbs out, slams the door again, then helps his bud haul Savannah out of the camo truck. (I can hear and feel all this, not see it.) I listen to the ambient traffic buzz for some time before I dare stick my head out in the open.

Both trucks fill most of a small dirt lot behind a tiny flat-roofed, cinder-block building. The sky-blue paint's been trying to peel off the walls for years. The parking lot's rimmed with other squat cinder-block boxes. All the visible windows are papered over with ads or newsprint. Nobody's around to see me.

Yet.

Chapter 48

I finally crawl out from behind a stack of rotting wooden pallets when the sky goes fully dark at 8:30. "Crawl" because I've been curled in a tight ball for over five hours, terrified to move and risk being seen or heard. The smell's going to be stuck in my sinuses for hours.

Despite being temporarily crippled, I'm glad I escaped when I did. The teen soldier spent a lot of time supposedly searching our truck earlier in the afternoon. Some of it involved thoroughly testing the radio and air conditioning, but he also looked under the hood and under the chassis (where I'd considered hiding). As far as I can tell, he didn't work out how to get under the back bench.

The traffic noise has faded to a whisper. Nobody's come in or out of the blue building's back door for at least two hours. This may be my best chance to figure out where I am and what to do.

The blue building is on a dirt side road maybe twenty yards away from what looks like a main street bustling with scooters and walkers. Nobody's coming this way. Two royal-blue metal signs are screwed to the cinder block on the building's front. On top, under Burmese script and something blanked out by two strips of duct tape, white English text says "MONG TON TOWNSHIP WAN MÉ-KIN POLICE OUTPOST." Below is a smaller sign that says in Burmese and English, "MAY I HELP YOU." At least, I assume the Burmese says the same thing; given the reputations of the Myanmar Police Force and the UWSA, it could say "GO AWAY" or "ABANDON HOPE, ALL YE WHO ENTER HERE."

The sign's next to a pair of open wood-panel doors, their formerly-white paint about as far gone as the blue on the walls. A trapezoid of cold fluorescent light spills out on the crumbling concrete front step and the dirt. Pop music grates out of a tinny speaker inside.

I trot across the road to get a view of what's in the police station. The teen soldier is lounging behind a battered metal desk in a bile-green office, smoking. There's a filing cabinet behind him, some flyers and official-looking paper tacked to the wall, and a little swiveling metal fan trying to move the heavy air around. I edge sideways toward the main street. Just before the left-hand doorjamb cuts off the view, I see a door of old-fashioned iron bars set into the room's right-hand wall.

That must be where they're keeping Savannah... if she's still there.

It occurred to me while I hid behind the pallets that somebody from Mongton (the big city around here) may have collected the western spy anytime this afternoon. The only way to know is to go in the police station and look. And the only way to do *that* is...

Well, we'll see.

I prowl the side roads, slipping through gaps between homes, skirting lit windows and the voices of people sitting on their front stoops or back yards. This walking is easier than what I've been doing for the past few days; the ground's level and mostly isn't a mud pit. But it's harder, too. I can't afford to be seen. Any noise I make could trigger someone to peek out a door or window and see a westerner wander by. That would probably be big news here.

After about ninety minutes, I have a plan. I don't like it. It's a shitty thing to do. But I need to get the kid soldier out of the police station so I can either rescue Savannah or find out she's not there. That means giving the soldier something urgent to do.

A quarter mile north of the station, I find a cinder-block box masquerading as a house. The front door was open when I came by half an hour or so ago; now the door's closed and the light's out. A beaten-up motor scooter leans against a beheaded tree trunk outside.

I pluck two men's black socks off a clothesline next door. I creep back to the scooter, tie the toe of one sock to the leg of the other, then stuff the free toe into the scooter's gas tank.

During my walk, I'd found a cheap plastic cigarette lighter. Now, as my thumb hovers over the spark wheel, I stop to think. This scooter may be a piece of shit—rust and duct tape are all that's holding it together—but it belongs to somebody who probably can't afford to buy a new one. He hasn't done anything to me. I'm about to ruin his week.

If I don't, Savannah will rot in a Burmese jail cell because I got her into this mess.

This scooter's the only one I saw parked far enough from a building to be safely exploded without burning down the house. If not here, where?

Shit. What a time to develop a conscience.

A pair of drunk-sounding dudes trudge down the road past me. I fade into a shadow until they're long gone.

I can't stay out here forever debating the ethics of what I need to do. I can't leave Savannah with the cops. (*Would she leave you?* Of course I wonder that now.) Besides what they might do to her legally, there's a whole list of things they might do illegally. Whatever she's up to, she doesn't deserve that.

I flick the lighter.

The socks are mostly polyester, so they flame right up. It'll still take a minute or two to hit the gas tank. I need to be well on my way back to the station before they do.

Moving quickly and silently isn't anything I usually need to do, so I'm not very good at it. Dogs bark; a cat yowls; a door squeaks open behind me. But whatever noise I make stops being a problem a minute and eighteen seconds after I lit the socks.

Foom.

I glance back in time to see an orange glow above the rooftops behind me. People spill out of their homes to gawp at the light and the uplit thread of smoke and chatter about *what was that, anyway?* They don't notice me edge through the shadows.

Half a dozen people crowd the doorway into the police station by the time I slip behind a tree across the street. I can't translate what they're shouting, but I understand it: *What was that? What are you doing about it? Protect us!*

The kid soldier's standing in front of the crowd, his palms out toward them, trying to yell over them in a reedy voice that doesn't carry far. It sounds like the usual *don't worry, be happy* speech that usually means *head for the hills.*

Come on, dude. Do your job. Go find the terrorists.

The crowd's not buying his act. They eventually badger the kid into strapping on his gun and following them to the disaster site. He closes the station doors on his way out.

Did he lock them? We'll see.

Once the street goes back to sleep, I trot to the station and twist the rusty doorknobs. They turn but the doors don't open. There's a deadbolt, though judging from the few inches of play in the doors, it's not much of one. I scour the neighborhood for people being too interested in me, then yank on the knob. The doors rattle and give a bit but stay shut.

Well, I've already committed arson. What's a little B&E on a police station?

I start yanking on the knob in time with "We Will Rock You." Each time I pull, the doors bow out a little more. The deadbolt soon starts making crunching sounds. Finally, the bolt gives way with a loud *crrrack* and I nearly clock myself with the door.

The lights are still buzzing loudly. I rush to the barred door. "Savannah?"

She spins, stares my way for a few moments, shakes her head hard, then whispers, "Rick?"

"Yeah. Are you okay?"

"No." She shuffles toward me.

"Where's the key?"

"I don't know."

I rifle the desk—our truck keys are in the middle drawer—and a metal credenza before I discover an old-school skeleton key in the top drawer of the filing cabinet. The cell lock needs WD-40, but it still works. The hinges shriek like they're being flayed.

Savannah staggers out of the cell, shaking. Dried blood coats her lips and chin. Her dress is caked with dirt and her nosebleed blood, and the right-hand sleeve droops from a torn shoulder seam. "You came back for me." She sounds like she doesn't believe it. "My hero." I don't think she's kidding. When I step in for a hug, she stiff-arms me. "Don't touch me! I'm filthy. This place is disgusting."

I'm more worried about her face than the cell, but whatever. "You said you're not okay. Can you walk?"

She nods way too fast. "I can walk. I need to get clean. Get me out of here."

I close and lock the cell, put the key back, then fit the front doors together so they look unmolested. Savannah climbs into the cargo bed. I say, "What are you doing?"

"Don't wanna get this mess on the seats. Go south. Hurry!"

I pull through the alley. The kid soldier's standing in the middle of the road.

We stare at each other for a beat. He scrabbles at his holster. I stomp the gas and fishtail down the road with my heart beating as fast as hummingbird wings. A hole appears in the back window about a foot to my left. There's a *clang* behind me.

Highway 45 isn't busy at this time of night, but there's still traffic and it's all going slower than I like. I start driving like the Thais do— creating my own lanes, swerving into oncoming traffic, passing in the slow lane. Closed shops flash by on both sides. None of the other drivers seem to think this is strange.

We need to get out into the open countryside. We have options out there. We're too easy to bottle up in town.

I finally let off the gas when we pass the man-made ponds at the southern edge of town. Savannah knocks on my window. She yells, "Keep going! He's probably after us."

"Probably not yet." I fish something out of my pants pocket and heave it into the river we cross just past the ponds.

"What was that?"

"His truck keys. They were next to ours in the desk."

"He still has a phone."

"I know. Where are we going?"

"Keep going straight. Turn right in about half a kilometer. There's a road."

I don't bother to ask how she knows this.

"Road" is a generous description for the rutted path we turn onto. The forest crowds both sides and blots out the cloudy sky. Twigs scrape the side-view mirrors. I stop when the trees close in behind us and climb out onto the dirt. My hands ache from my death grip on the wheel.

Savannah pops up in the back. "Why did you stop?"

"To catch my breath and find out where we're headed. Are you okay?"

She sighs, settles back on her heels. "I'm better than when you found me. I went to some pretty dark places in that cell." Her voice is fast and shaky. "Keep driving to the river. I gotta wash, I gotta get clean. I peed myself in there. My skin's crawling. I can't tell if it's bugs or just... just a reaction, but I have to wash *now*. Okay?"

The road breaks out of the trees after a couple hundred yards and takes us almost due west across planted fields. Low hills make dark shapes against the sky ahead of us. I pull the truck into a stand of trees to hide it from anyone looking for us. When I get out, the tumble of rushing water fills the air.

Savannah bustles past me toward the river's sound and smell. I step-slide down the embankment in time to watch her literally rip off her dress and panties, then wad them in a ball and heave them into the river. She plunges into the water.

There's barely any light. I turn on my phone's flashlight and sweep it around. We're at the edge of a slow pool sheltered from the rest of the river by rocks and a tree trunk. The light splashes on Savannah as she dunks her head. "Sure you want to swim in that?"

"Get my bag. Please? There's antiseptic soap and lice shampoo."

When I hand her the squeeze bottles, she scrubs at herself so hard I expect to see blood. I'm not sure what kind of reaction I expected from her, but this wasn't it. "Did they hurt you?"

"They roughed me up some. I fought them."

"I know." I add up her cleaning frenzy and the shell-shocked look in her eyes when I let her out. "Did they do… anything else?"

"Like rape me?" She splashes water on herself, then starts scrubbing again. "No. The younger one wanted to—I could tell. They groped me pretty hard when they were searching me." Suddenly she stops washing and stares at me, her face dissolving. "They didn't get a chance. I was lucky. Lucky." She starts to cry.

I wade into the water—it's on the edge between cool and cold—wrap my arms around Savannah and let her bawl into my shoulder. Her skin's solid goosebumps. The water or her experience? Doesn't matter. I rock her gently, whisper "Shhhh" and "You're safe now" and pat her back. All the things I used to do with Janine when she came undone.

Her sobs eventually settle into hiccups. She draws back enough to look up at me. "Sorry."

"Don't be. If you didn't freak out, I'd worry." I kiss her forehead and give her a long, tight hug. "Sorry I took so long. I had to wait 'til nighttime."

Savannah holds my face in both hands. "I almost gave up on you."

I take her hands in mine. Her knuckles are raw. "Sorry I wasn't there in time to keep them from arresting you."

She shakes her head. "I'm glad you weren't. If you were, they'd have got you too, and we'd both be in that nasty cell." She squeezes my hand. "Let me finish washing."

"Okay." She's a faint glow in the darkness as she steps back into the pool. "Is that safe to be in?"

"With all the rain, it's cleaner than most of the tap water here."

I sit on a log and listen to Savannah splash in the river. I never expected to see her cry. *Vulnerable* isn't a word I associate with her. But I know first-hand how shattering it is to have that door clang shut behind you and not know when—or if—it'll open again. She's going to dream about today for a long time.

She finally perches on a rock and runs a fine-toothed metal comb through her hair. "You should take a bath, too, while we're here."

"It's cold."

"It's not that bad. You'll feel better. You'll smell better, too."

I take the hint and plunge in after hauling my bag down from the truck. Savannah's right—getting clean feels great even at the cost of head-to-toe goosebumps. She lets me share her rock while I towel off. Her hip is warm against mine. I ask, "Where are we?"

"Well, this is the Nam Ton. We're less than a mile below Wan Mé-Kin." Her voice is back to near-normal.

"That's not helpful."

"Sorry." She pats my thigh. "They're going to be looking for us. We need to stay off the road for a while. We can stay here tonight and decide what to do tomorrow."

"Why not drive out now, in the dark?"

"It's not safe to travel at night."

"With them after us, it's not safe to travel in daytime, either."

"For different reasons. Besides, you haven't found the source for Nam Ton yet." She pecks my cheek. "We can sleep another night in the truck. It's cozy, and they won't think to look for us here. And tomorrow…" she kisses the corner of my mouth "…well, who knows what we'll find?"

Chapter 49

4 DAYS LEFT

I stumble out of the truck's cab and stretch several different ways to get all the kinks and stiff spots worked out. We've been sleeping in the truck since we crossed into Myanmar. That's a big no-no—foreigners are allowed to overnight only in certain places, and then only in registered inns or guest houses. There aren't any of those in the villages we've passed through. Nobody's rousted us yet, but we keep a rotating watch in case our luck runs out. I was on duty when the sun peeked over the mountains to the east.

The pool looks more inviting in daylight than it did last night. I rinse off my face and run water through my hair to flatten it out. As I look around, I notice some tree trunks a few yards downstream that span the Nam Ton without being obvious about it. Nobody builds those for the hell of it; there must be something worth the hike on the other side.

I end up on an oblong patch of scrubland surrounded by three abrupt hills on the south, west and north. It's maybe a hundred yards to a side, hard-packed dirt with spotty grass and scattered stubby bushes. No rocks worth mentioning. Based on what I've seen here, it's certainly big enough to plant. Why isn't it?

That's when I notice the village in the saddle between the south and west hills.

It's a narrow line of houses on pilings on either side of the path. It climbs a low rise and disappears around the south hill's cliff-like slope. A couple smoke plumes from kitchen fires thread their way up from the corrugated iron rooftops. Figures trace the path. A dog barks; he's either small or a long way away.

I step off the path and poke around on the scrubland. It's uneven and pockmarked with slumps and bulges eroded by rain. Something about this feels familiar, like I've seen it somewhere before, but not recently.

Somebody shouts.

A guy stands about thirty yards from me at the base of the rise leading into the village. A mop of darkish hair, an open long-sleeved check shirt over an undershirt, a dark blue *pasu* at mid-calf. It's the rifle slung across his chest that gets my attention, though.

I raise my right hand. Not quite a wave, but what I hope is a friendly gesture around here and not some obscure blood insult.

Then I trip and fall flat on my face.

Not quite: my chest hits the edge of one of those slumps, leaving me staring into a foot-deep hole. The bottom's still wet from last night's rain. I'm not looking at that, though. I'm looking at the tip of something hard and white sticking out from the side of the hole, probably washed out (and washed clean) by the rain.

It's a potsherd. White with a sliver of cobalt blue.

The old guy with the rifle—his hair is more salt-and-pepper than mine, so I can call him old—herds me into the village's edge and deposits me in front of the first house we come to. He barks something at a boy in baggy blue shorts and a worse-for-wear yellow SpongeBob tee; the boy pelts away down Main Street. Then the old guy turns to watch me, cradling his rifle. I get the message: stay put or become target practice.

I'm not sure yet how concerned I should be about this. If the guy wanted to kill me, he could've done it by the river and not risk getting blood on his nice, clean dirt road. On the other hand, maybe he needs the village chief's permission to feed me to his pigs. For what it's worth, I'm not getting an immediate-deadly-intent vibe off him. He's got that rifle, though.

Ever since he captured me, I've been saying the same thing to him: *Pensri Udomprecha.* Maybe that's why he hasn't killed me yet. But what if this isn't the right village? What if she's on the road or back in Thailand?

That idea doesn't help my insides unwind.

My guard keeps glancing up the path. I start doing the same. People stroll around up there in that leisurely way I've seen before in the tropics. They don't come close to me or the guard.

The houses I can see are all variations on a theme: wood pilings six to eight feet tall, weathered wood-plank walls, unglazed windows, pitched corrugated-iron roofs crusted with rust and moss. Each one has a small yard area surrounded by a fence made of stripped branches. It looks like people live upstairs and black chickens and smallish dark-gray pigs live downstairs. The general smell is wood smoke, semi-decomposing vegetation, wet dirt, wet livestock, and people in touch with their natural essence. In other words, mostly what I've smelled for the past few days.

How likely is it that Savannah would know about that road but not about this village? *Not very* is how I see it. What did she say last night? *Who knows what we'll find?* I found this, whether or not I was meant to. If I wasn't supposed to, why bring us here?

I don't have to worry about keeping myself occupied with all this running through my head. The hard part is to not freak out about it. I'm completely at the villagers' mercy, the area's crawling with guys with guns, and I very clearly don't belong here. There are places in America where this wouldn't end well.

My guard's attention stays on the visible end of the path. A woman and two men slowly pace toward us. They take their time getting here, giving me a chance to make up worst-case scenarios.

They finally stop next to the guard and look at me like I'm in the ape exhibit at a zoo. The way the guard defers to them makes me think they're important.

The woman's the tallest of the three, though not by much. She wears a seafoam-green, long-sleeved tee over a navy *longyi* checked with a red-and-white geometric pattern. I can't tell how old she is; she's obviously not a kid, but what I can see of her hair is completely black, and I can't tell if the lines in her face are from age or mileage.

An old man—his thin hair's completely gray—hangs onto the woman's left arm. His midnight-blue *pasu* is tied around his ankles, looking like breeches. The man on the woman's right is maybe middle-aged, with a well-developed black moustache, a green-and-gray-striped polo, and a black *pasu* overlaid with a tight gold windowpane plaid. He looks sort of like the older guy minus twenty years or so.

We stare at each other for a while. I can't tell if they're going to invite me to the village feast or make me the main course at it. Looking calm is hard when everything inside you says it's time to run and see whether the guard really can hit a moving target. I avoid doing that. I probably don't look like I'm enjoying this.

I finally say, "Do you speak English?"

The woman adjusts the ocean-blue scarf she has wrapped like a turban around her head. She pats the old man's hand, gently pulls her arm away so she can step closer to me, then bends slightly to peer down at me. "Yes, I do. They don't. What's your name?" Only a slight accent, otherwise American English.

It takes me a moment to remember which name I came here under. "Rick Hoskins. Can I stand? I'd like to stretch my legs."

"Of course. Move slowly, though." She points her chin at the guard. "Sai Mai may worry if you stand suddenly."

I'll avoid that.

After having been trapped in the truck cab overnight, the enforced inactivity here didn't do me any favors. The woman watches calmly as I carefully get vertical. Once I straighten up, I see that she's almost as tall as Savannah. That's unusual around here.

She says, "You've been asking for me."

"You're Dr. Udomprecha?"

"Yes. If it's easier, you may call me Nan Pensri."

This can't be a coincidence. Savannah *had* to know about this. She *had* to.

Pensri's straight-faced and utterly calm. Her hands haven't moved since she folded them in front of her hips. I pull the blue-and-white ceramic fragment from my pocket and hand it to her. "You lost something."

Pensri turns the sherd over in her palm, then lets out the ghost of a smile. "Thank you. The rains always uncover more of these."

"So this is where Nam Ton wares come from?"

The smile gets thinner. "It was once."

My quick flash of triumph—*finally!*—melts away like ice cream would in this weather. *Was?* "It isn't anymore?"

Pensri ducks her head. "I apologize. I've been very rude. I haven't introduced you to my companions." She points her chin at the old man. "He is Saya Kham, our village chief." She says a few words to the old man, ending with "Sai Hoskins." Then she aims her chin at the middle-aged guy. "This is my husband, Sai Htun."

I say *"mengalaba"* to each man. Then I wonder: is this one of those words where if you pronounce it one way, it's a greeting, but it's a curse if you pronounce it another way?

Pensri and the two men pull away for a sidebar, leaving me with the guard. Sai Mai looks like he's getting bored with this. A small knot of women and children has gathered up the path from us to watch the action. I'll bet they don't get many westerners here.

Where exactly is Savannah now? I may need rescuing.

After a short conference, Pensri returns and says to me, "Please, come with me." She says something to the guard that must mean "stay here," because he doesn't follow as she leads me away.

We stop at the edge of the oblong tract by the river. "This is where I found the Nam Ton wares." Pensri waves across the scrubland. "There were more on the other side of the river, but most of those sites had already been disturbed. Because you're here, should I assume you've read my paper?"

"You should. Both of them."

She turns to me, eyes wide and eyebrows high. "Both? Including the one I never published?"

"Yeah. Why didn't you publish the second one?"

"Things... changed." She steps off the path, heading for the center of the flat area. "The two kiln sites were there and there. Both had sherd piles and shared a single mound of wasters. As best as I can determine, the old village was where the new village is. The river has changed its course several times over the past eight hundred years. It's hard to determine what's been lost." She stops, faces me. "Why are you here?"

I'd wondered how long it would take her to ask that. "I wasn't satisfied with the mystery. Where Nam Ton comes from. You were pretty vague in your papers."

"Deliberately so." Her mouth turns more severe. "The people here have been looting the site for decades. It's a small miracle there was anything left to discover. I'd wanted to protect the site as much as I could. Obviously, I failed. People like you were able to find it and empty it. Are you alone, or with someone?"

What's the right answer? If I say I'm alone, the locals may drag me into the forest and shoot me to keep their secret. If I say I'm with somebody, she'll want to know who, and where they are. It feels like Door Number Two is a better choice. "There are others."

Now her mouth gets really grim. "You came here to take wares home with you? Perhaps sell them?"

"No. Pure curiosity. I'm one of those people who can't stand to see a puzzle go unsolved. I can buy all the Nam Ton I want at home—I don't need to come here to do it." This seems like a good time to try an experiment. "Does the name 'James Bandineau' mean anything to you?"

"No. Should it?"

"I dunno. He's trying to turn Nam Ton into the next big thing in America. Maybe he's the one you should be mad at." Try it? Sure. "How about Savannah Kendicott?"

Was that blink a tell, or something in her eye? "I'm sorry. I can't help you."

"Right." *Liar.* I nod toward the village. "Do you make pottery here?"

"Yes, of course. The people work on it during the dry season between planting and harvest. It brings in extra money for the village." She crosses her arms. "The Nam Ton culture came from a different heritage. These people aren't its heirs, if that's what you think. They're Shan. The Shan have been here since the first century BCE."

"I thought the Wa chased the Shan out of this area."

"They tried. This village managed to stay. It's out of the way and not very wealthy, so I suppose the Wa had no reason to bother with it." Pensri looks me over coolly, like I'm a worm she found crawling over an artifact she's just dug up. "You've solved your mystery, Mr. Hoskins. I'm afraid you're too late if you want more than a set of coordinates. The Nam Ton culture is gone from here. If you leave now, you and your travel companions should reach the Thai border before dark. It's not safe to travel at night." She passes me the sherd. "Take this as a souvenir. It would be a shame to go home empty-handed. Goodbye, Mr. Hoskins."

Chapter 50

Savannah's on her rock, dangling her feet in the pool, by the time I get back to our camp. Her long cotton dress is the color of dusty green olives and is wrinkled from having been rinsed out in the rain a couple times. Only four of its twelve buttons are fastened. She says, "Where'd you go?"

I've had enough time to get mad about her conning me about Pensri's village, so I don't answer right away. "Across the river."

"Find anything?"

You know damn well. "A village." Pause. "Dr. Udomprecha."

She continues brushing out her hair. She's using a brush instead of her nit comb; I guess she's not infested. "How is she?"

"Chilly."

"I don't doubt it. She doesn't know you."

"I'll bet she knows you." That comes out like an accusation, just as I intended.

"Of course she does." Savannah lobs her brush into her open duffle, stretches, yawns. "I don't remember you leaving the truck."

"You were still asleep." I cross my arms and give her what I hope reads as a stern look. "You knew all the time where she is. Ever since we started this."

"Uh-huh."

"And you didn't bother to tell me."

"I promised her I wouldn't tell anyone." She slides off the rock and pads toward me barefoot. I push her away when she stretches to kiss me. "Are you mad at me?"

"What do you think?" That sounds just as hard as I meant it to. "You wasted my time. We could've come here on the first day, but no—you have me running around here for three days, *knowing* we weren't anywhere near this place."

She backs up a step and hugs herself. "I knew you'd work it out eventually. You'd be proud of yourself—which you should be—and

I'd've kept my promise. Everyone wins."

"Everyone. Wins." I have to count to thirty to keep from saying the first four things that rumble into my head. "This your idea of a game?"

"What? No." Sigh. "Darling… I'm sorry I've made you mad, but… well, I've known Pensri a lot longer than I've known you, and I made her a promise, and I don't like to break those if I can help–"

"But it's okay to lie to me and everybody else, right?"

She drops back another step. "It's for a good cause."

"For fuck's sake!" I pace a small circle to let the steam leak out my ears. My better nature's holding on by its hangnails.

Savannah watches me finish a couple orbits before she starts undoing the last of her buttons. "Come on, let's go for a swim. You'll feel bet—"

"No. Holding your head underwater would make me feel better."

She winces, then refastens the buttons she'd undone plus a couple extras. "What happens now?" Her tone is cautious. "Are you going to spank me? Make me walk home? Fire me? Break up with me? You found the village. You won. Now we can go back to Thailand and have a lot nicer time than we've been having here."

"Not so fast." I give her the condensed version of what Pensri told me.

"Do you believe her?"

"No. If Nam Ton wares aren't coming from here, where's Jim getting his? You said they're not like anything else here."

"True." She takes a wary step toward me and pauses, like she wants to see if I'll try to drown her. "Maybe they're not as unique as we thought. Why would she lie to you?"

"Easy—to make me go away. She thinks I'm gonna go home and tell the world I found this place. If I think the well's dry, I might be her last uninvited guest."

"You may be right." She chews on her lower lip while she watches me closely. "Darling… will you hurt me if I come closer?"

Will I? That head of steam I'd built up has mostly vented by now. Talking rationally made me remember that I've never been physically violent with a woman. "No."

"Good." She steps to me and gentles her palm onto my chest. "We can't leave. The Was'll still be looking for us. So we should go to the village together. Pensri will protect us. She owes me."

"She... why? Who is she to you?"

Savannah stares at the second button on my camp shirt for a long time. "Remember Lawan? My Thai nanny?"

Huh? "Um... yeah."

"I tried to find her as soon as Mother got her deported. I finally did a year later, at her university. The coup was over and Thailand had a civilian government again. All was forgiven. I started sending Lawan money from my allowance so she could afford books and things to finish her degrees. We've been in touch ever since."

Must've been some allowance. "I'm glad you found her, but how's this important now?"

"Thais change their given names a lot. Sometimes they do it because they've had bad luck and they want to escape it. That's why Lawan changed her name when she got back to Thailand. It's also why it took so long for me to find her."

I rummage through my brain to find the things she'd told me at the Tonga Room. "Did she happen to change her name to 'Pensri'?"

She smiles. "You remembered. She was an archaeology student."

"That's how you got the early copies of her papers."

"Right again. And that Nom Ton ewer I gave Jim."

Of course. It makes perfect sense now. It also explains Pensri's reaction when I mentioned Savannah's name. "Another thing you didn't tell me."

"You didn't need to know until now."

Another flash of anger. I count to eighteen before I come up with something civil to say. "I decide that, not you."

"You're wrong. I decided." She tries a smile that doesn't quite work. "We should go to the village now, before any of the farmers see us here. Help me carry in the presents, okay?"

"What happens when we get there?"

Savannah pats my chest and starts out for the truck. "You'll see. Trust me?"

"Absolutely not."

Chapter 51

It's mid-morning by the time we trudge across the scrublands where the Nam Ton culture made its pottery. I'm lugging two cases of cloth diapers. Savannah has her duffels slung over her shoulder; our clothes and survival gear's in them, along with several bottles of good booze and the surviving unopened cartons of Marlboros.

My favorite Shan guard stops us at the foot of the rise leading to the village. Savannah greets him with a big smile and a flood of friendly-sounding Thai (or at least, what I think is Thai). I guess pretty-woman magic works worldwide: he wanders off with a smile on his face, leaving us to loiter around the house where I'd spent part of this morning.

Pensri appears much faster this time. The two women crash together, hugging and kissing cheeks and swooning in mixed Thai and English. Savannah finally turns Pensri toward me. "You've already met my boyfriend, Rick."

Pensri's smile dims a few watts. "Mr. Hoskins. Welcome."

"Am I?"

She considers me for a moment. "You're with Savannah. Of course you are." Meaning, *don't get too far from her.*

A couple villagers haul the gifts behind us while Pensri leads us up the rise. Savannah tells her a simplified version of yesterday's events. Pensri tsks and shakes her head. "I taught you better than that," she says at one point.

"I know. Sorry. Can we stay here a little while until it's safe to go back south?"

Stay? Four days until the project dies and she wants to *stay?*

"Of course. We have two empty houses at the end of the village. You can stay in the less-ruined one." Pensri shoots a glance at me. "I'll have to ask you to *stay* there, though. I'll have someone trustworthy bring you food. Please don't mix with the villagers—it's hard to predict what they might tell outsiders."

I guess that's why we're being paraded down the village's main street. It sounds like a form of house arrest to me. Then again, there won't be any freedom on the road today, either.

The Shan house tilts slightly on its eight-foot pilings. Two rooms. Lots of cobwebs and mold. We left our sandals on the open porch before we went inside.

The room I'm pacing in takes up half the structure. The missing wall on the side nearest the porch and the windows on the two exterior walls let in the only light this place is going to get. Not much furniture: a couple stools, a handmade table holding a metal water basin, a battered wooden cabinet that might be the pantry. A rough wood post shoots up from the middle of the floor to the ridge beam. A framed drawing of the Buddha fills much of a rough wooden box set into the east wall. The sleeping room is on the other side of an open doorway with a foot-tall threshold.

A random collection of mats and rugs covers the wood-plank floor, everything from striped plastic ground pads you might use on a picnic to fraying woven Chinese rugs. I may wear out my feet, but at least I won't get splinters.

Savannah says, "Would you please stop? You're driving me crazy."

She's perched on a stool near the north window, wearing a loose pink crew-neck blouse with three-quarter sleeves over pale-yellow panties, with a trade paperback of *The Nightingale* in her lap. She doesn't *look* almost crazy, but maybe she hides it well.

The air's heavy and still. I smear the sweat off my forehead with my sleeve. "We're supposed to just sit here?"

"Uh-huh."

"For how long?"

"Until Pensri tells us it's safe to go."

In the meantime, the clock ticks down. We have three full days left before Talbot's deadline. "If the Nam Ton wares aren't coming from that place out front of the village, where else might they be?"

Savannah sighs. "*As I said before*, it could be anyplace. Pensri may not know about it."

"How likely do you think that is? That she wouldn't know?"

"Not very. I just wanted to bring it up."

Sure. "Around here?"

"She thinks the old village is under this one. They could be digging up people's yards."

"I didn't see anything like that on our death march here."

Her eyebrow arches like a Halloween cat. "Death march? Really?" She shakes her head. "I don't know if she knows how far back the old village goes. The dig could be out there someplace." She points out the open end of the room and the porch.

That sounds as likely as anything. "Let's go look."

"*No.*" Savannah bolts off the stool. "Pensri told us to stay here. That's for their protection more than ours. I promised her we would. She's still my best friend—I won't betray her trust."

"You mean, like you betrayed mine?"

Her throat gargles a disgusted sound. "I won't apologize for what I did. I had good reasons for it. And we already talked about how you lied to me, so you're not exactly innocent here."

She's got me there. I pace to the south window and watch not very much happen on the main—and only—street. "Look. I have to tell the DEA where Nam Ton comes from. If they come to check, Pensri'll tell them she's fresh out. That could go seriously bad for me. *Us.*"

Savannah appears next to me with her arms crossed tight. She doesn't look happy. "Do what you have to do. I don't need to be there with you. If you're going to go someplace, at least do it after dark. It'd be dumb to do it now, and I don't think you're dumb."

Gullible, maybe. "Okay. I flew eight thousand miles to find this place. I can wait until dark to make sure I've found it."

Htun brings dinner—a pot of roasted chicken and rice, same as lunch—as sunset turns the gathering clouds coral.

It's completely dark before nine. The clouds snuff the moon and stars. Htun brought the stub of a candle on a tin dish along with dinner; it's now flickering on the table, throwing wavering shadows on the walls.

Savannah appears from the sleeping room wearing a new addition to her costume: a *longyi* (sarong) with a salmon lower half and maroon upper half. She ties a yellow headscarf over her hair. "I'm going to talk to Pensri."

Other than her height, you could believe she's one of the lighter-skinned local women if you squint enough. "You just happened to bring that with you?"

"I thought it might be useful."

She knew she was coming here. I can't decide if I should be mad or in awe of her planning. "How long will you be gone?"

She stops halfway to the porch and frowns at me over her shoulder. "How long should I be?" There's an edge to that. "We have plenty to talk about."

I'll bet. "Stay out as long as you can."

The sound of her sandals on the stairs disappears into the night.

I wait fifteen minutes, then step to ground level and edge out to the side of the road. To the east, the windows in the nearby houses flicker orange with fires, candles, or the occasional lantern. There are the hints of voices in the wind and someone singing in a minor key. To the west: dark.

I head west.

The road quickly turns into a path a few feet wide winding through the trees. Apparently enough people use it to hack away the underbrush. That worries me: who am I likely to meet out here? Villagers? Wa soldiers? Meth labs? Poachers? (Pangolins—a kind of mutant jungle armadillo—live here, and the Chinese think they're funny-looking walking Viagra. You do the math.)

The red gel in my Mini Maglite casts a dim glow on the ground, hardly enough for me to avoid the tree roots and occasional rocks. I stumble over invisible things.

Then the gunfire starts. First single pops, like firecrackers, then short bursts, then the jackhammer sound of something heavy. It's northwest of me, though I can't tell how far. My rational mind tells me I don't have to worry about it. I'm not in touch with my rational mind right now.

It's easy to lose track of time in the forest. The scenery doesn't change in the dark: black tree trunks, black bushes, a few square feet of trail. Little forest noises compete with the gunfire: bird squawks, frog belches, bat squeaks, the *plumf* sounds of things falling from the canopy, the rustle of things pushing past leaves.

Something like thunder rumbles in the distance. It's not

thunder, though—it's short, flat thumps with echoes, not that prolonged rocks-rolling-downhill sound. I've heard it in war movies: distant artillery. Welcome to the neighborhood.

Up ahead, I see what I think are flickering yellow lights moving around randomly. They grow as I approach. Then I hear murmurs of words I don't understand. Other sounds I can't figure out.

I almost stumble into a clearing. I catch myself before I take those extra couple steps, push myself into the trees, then thump down hard on my butt.

The clearing's ends fade into the dark in both directions. The lights—torches—show it's maybe ten or fifteen yards wide. I remember this from the satellite shots; it looked like a dry riverbed. Maybe it was once upon a time. But that's not what interests me.

A dozen or more men are digging a neat, square-edged hole across the clearing's far width, maybe twenty feet long, two feet wide. Ground level comes to just above the knees on the men digging inside the hole. Not enough for a grave. That's not what interests me either.

What does interest me? Pensri's directing the work. She barks at the men, shining a flashlight on places where she wants the hole cleaned up or extended. Other than her outfit, she's the very picture of an archaeologist running a dig.

The other interesting thing is on a tarp a couple feet from the hole's long edge. The torchlight flickers gold on a dozen or so white-bodied wares. The green parts puzzle me until I realize it's yellow light on blue.

Nam Ton wares.

It's hard to tell from over here, but they look awfully clean for having just been dug up. Were they left out in the rain?

Is this where the Nam Ton wares are coming from? Is this whole clearing an archaeological site? There's room for hundreds of pots under the dirt. Thousands. Bandineau could keep selling Nam Ton until he retires. Does he know?

A soft noise behind me. I twist to look. A guy's there, staring at me. That's all I see before he clocks me with his rifle butt and I dive into my own personal night.

Chapter 52

3 DAYS LEFT

I wake in this afternoon's Shan house. The candle's still burning on the table, though it's significantly shorter.

I'm sitting on the floor with my wrists tied with woven cotton clothesline on the other side of the post. They're nearly dead. My ankles are also tied, so I can't stand, which I'm desperate to do. Despite the pads and rugs on the floor, my butt's officially lead. Every part of me either hurts—starting with my head—or is stiff from not moving much for however long. The only good news would be bad news under any other circumstances: they took all my clothes except for my boxers. At least I'm not simmering in the heat and humidity. Much.

Who jumped me? He wasn't in uniform, which means he probably wasn't the Wa State Army. Villager? Maybe. He seemed to know what he was doing with that rifle, though that may not be unusual given the area's history.

If he wanted me dead, he'd've shot me in the forest and left my body for whatever eats dead meat around here. Somebody's got a plan for me. I can't think well enough yet to figure out who.

A thought I don't need creeps into my head: did they decide to nab Savannah too? I don't know how well Pensri can protect her. A pretty western blonde's gotta be worth something to somebody around here. Is she in the village, or is she in the back of a truck on its way to some warlord's hideout? I've read about what happens to trafficked women, and it's not pretty.

Voices outside.

I turn up the gain on my ears. The first voice I hear is a woman's speaking rapid-fire something. Then a man's voice, lower and slower. They go back-and-forth for a while. Because the tones are completely different from any languages I'm used to, I can't tell what's going on, which makes me even more nervous. Is this the cavalry… or the firing squad?

Finally, I hear heavy steps stomp down the stairs. I twist as much as I can to catch a glimpse of the porch in the corner of my left eye.

Savannah walks in. She's barefoot, wearing her Burmese costume minus the headscarf.

Thank god. She's safe.

Now that I'm done being relieved she's not some mobster's sex doll, I wonder, *did she have anything to do with this? What did she tell Pensri?*

"There you are." Her smile's bright enough to reflect the candlelight. "Stay there. I'll untie you."

"Like I'm going anywhere." That comes out hoarse; my throat's dry and I haven't said a word to anybody for hours.

She kneels behind me. I can just about feel her hand on my wrist. "Promise you won't try to run away."

Promise what? "You kidding? We're outta here once you cut me loose. We can't stay here. We'll—"

"*Promise.*"

Something in her voice tells me I'd better obey if I want to feel my hands again. "Okay, whatever. I won't get far dressed like this. Neither will you."

"Don't worry about that." She jostles my hands and arms around, making my shoulders whimper. "There. I'll get your ankles."

For a few moments I can't feel any difference with the rope off. Then it's like my hands have been dipped in a vat of fire ants. I drag my arms out in front of me and almost scream at the pain in my shoulders. The fire ants discover my feet next. I look their way to see Savannah massaging my now-untied ankles.

It takes a few minutes before I can move my arms and legs without nausea-inducing pain and I can actually work my fingers again. Savannah opens a bottle of water and holds it to my lips. "Drink. You need the water."

I finally rasp, "Are you okay?"

"I'm fine. How's your head?"

"Hurts like a sonovabitch. Who did this?"

She stands, holds out her hand. "Let's get you on your feet."

Standing keeps me busy for the better part of a minute, but not enough so I forget she ducked my question. Once I can shuffle around without help, I say, "Let's try this again. Who hit me? Why?"

"Villagers. You saw things you shouldn't have."

"Like... the secret stash of Nam Ton wares?"

"That's what we need to talk about." She joins me as I slowly hobble around the room, trying not to trip on things I can't see. She wraps her hand around my bicep after a few laps. "Can we stop walking for a minute? Maybe over by that window?"

The window faces the forest. The sky looks like tapioca made from coal dust, and there's not a whisper of wind in the trees. The air weighs a ton; it wants to rain real bad.

Savannah settles a haunch on the windowsill and gazes out into the dark. "Pensri came here for her thesis project. She spent two whole dry seasons here. Long story short: she fell in love with the place and the people... and with a local man, Htun. He happens to be the headman's son. They eventually got married and they have a little boy."

"She gave up her Ph.D. and a university position to live *here?*"

"Don't judge. I'm glad she's happy. This place has a lot of problems, and she's doing what she can to help work them out."

If my head didn't already hurt, it would've started by now. "That thing I wasn't supposed to see... that was Pensri looting her own dig, wasn't it."

She suddenly finds the forest fascinating. "Well... it's complicated."

"'Yes' or 'no' isn't complicated."

"Well... yes."

Of course. I drag a red plastic stool to the window and sit facing Savannah. All my body parts have circulation again, I'm tired of pacing, and I'm just generally tired, physically and mentally. "Why would she do that?"

Savannah sighs and shakes her head. "Like I said, it's complicated. These poor people"—she waves out the window—"are in the middle of all kinds of trouble. They're Shan in an area the government tried to turn into a Wa enclave in the '90s. The Tatmadaw burned villages, they killed thousands of people, raped hundreds of women... all the things they do so well. These people hung on; God knows how."

"Pensri told me it's because they were too poor to bother with."

"Maybe. That didn't save other villages. You saw the corn

growing on the hillsides around here, right? This village is surrounded by poppies. Both the government and the Wa are hip-deep in drugs. The Tatmadaw's on one side, the UWSA's on another, and the SSA-South's on a third, all fighting each other. The Wa and the Tatmadaw grab people for forced labor, like at that bridge at Wān Namyūm. They charge households two to eight thousand kyat each to buy materials for fixing roads and bridges. They also draft young men who don't run away fast enough. It's…"

"A shitshow?"

"Uh-huh. So the local Wa 'commander'"—she uses air quotes—"drug lord—found out the ceramics made here hide the scent of heroin from drug dogs. The village started paying off the Wa in pottery ten years ago."

I'm starting to see how all this goes together. "Let me guess—when Pensri found the Nam Ton wares, they started using that as part of the payoff."

Savannah scrunches her nose. "It's… more complicated than that."

"Complicated how?"

She wipes her forehead on her sleeve. "Pensri sent me pictures. This was not too long after I got laid off from Sotheby's and went back to the Bay Area. I'd just started advising. I looked at these beautiful things and… well, I told her, 'You know, you can get a lot of money for those over here.' And she said 'science,' 'cultural heritage,' all that. So I said, 'Send me a piece and let me see what I can do with it.' She did. I took it to Lorena—we'd gotten pretty friendly by then—and I asked her if any of her clients would be interested. She found someone right away. I sent Pensri almost $7,000 in cash. That's a lot of money up here. It paid off the Tatmadaw for a *year*."

"That's all it takes?"

"The village has forty houses. Eight thousand kyat per is 320,000 kyat."

"That's like… less than three hundred bucks."

"In a place where they're doing great if they make twenty or thirty dollars a month. That's *one* project for *one* of the three sides. And they have to pay, especially the army. The army can shell their village if they don't. Anyway, I told Pensri to send me three good pieces a year and the village could pay off the Tatmadaw and the

SSA. That's how it all started. I was trying to do something good."

"You and Lorena did all this for free, right?"

She makes a face. "Of course not. I took my commission, and so did she. It was work, and quite honestly, I needed the money. The Leech had almost wiped me out. But most of what we got for the wares came back here. That's the way it ought to be, isn't it?"

Okay, I know this breaches scientific ethics and breaks the UNESCO convention against looting antiquities and all that, but… look at it. Three pots a year. They'd end up in a university's warehouse or on some tourist's mantle otherwise. The village gets most of the money from the sales. They use it to keep from becoming refugees or being on the wrong end of a pogrom.

Then I think of Bandineau's storage cube. "It's not just three pots a year anymore."

"I know." Savannah nods sadly. "Once they learned how much the wares are worth, they started turning them into extra cash. They sold them to antique stores in Chiang Mai. The Wa agreed to give them more credit for the Nam Ton pieces because they can sell them on the other end for more money."

This is the part I dislike. I'm sure the Wa and those antique stores aren't giving the villagers anything near what the wares are worth. Three pots a year is a noble sacrifice for the common good; the rest is just plain looting, and the people who should benefit from it aren't.

I'm dying to ask where I come into this, but since she's sharing, I need to encourage her to keep going. Talbot and Carruthers may want to know some of this. "Where'd it go wrong?"

"I showed it to Jim. He got really excited about it. You know he has bigger ambitions than the Norris, right?"

"I got that impression."

"Well, the next thing I knew, he was talking about collectors and museums and donations and how that would help me get more money for the village, and…" She stops sing-songing and sighs. "I knew it was all about him. This was how he was going to be chief curator at the Met or something. I tried to keep control of the wares coming over, but…" she looks toward the forest again "…*Coulson* snaked that out from under me."

Finally, something that surprises me. "You know Coulson?"

"Yes, I know him." She doesn't have to say *I'd rather not*. "Then my clients heard about Nam Ton and wanted in on it. Ohlmeyer was first and got the good prices, like I told you. By then my friend in Shanghai was also interested. Ohlmeyer let me sell some pieces to him. That's how the Chinese market started."

Savannah skipped over an important detail: how the Chinese friend found out about Nam Ton. I suspect she told him so she could develop a market without Bandineau's interference.

"Ohlmeyer's pretty accommodating." I take a moment to add up all the bits and pieces I've learned about him over the past two months. I think I finally see the puzzle's picture. "*You're* Ohlmeyer."

There's a flash in her eyes. I recognize it: it's that rush of shit to the heart when you realize somebody's figured you out. It's gone in a moment. She deadpans, "You say that *why?*"

"A reclusive collector with an obscure name who just happens to get in first on Jim's scheme. He's able to negotiate the prices down, then he lets you take pieces from his collection to sell to this guy in China. I'm pretty sure your friend would mean zero to a real Ohlmeyer. He sounds like the kind of character you make up when you're laundering money or ducking customs or avoiding currency controls." Our gallery had several clients who existed only in Gar's head and some receipts and bank records. It's a great way to clean dirty cash.

She gives me a tight-lipped, closed-mouth smile. "Believe what you want."

Believe what you want is what you say when you don't want to say *neither confirm nor deny*, which is what you say when giving a straight answer will drop you in the shit.

"Are you still selling pieces for the village?"

"Three a year, through my friend in China. The village gets more money that way."

"But you sell more than that, don't you? Someone's keeping the Chinese market supplied. Does Ohlmeyer have any Nam Ton left in his—her?—collection, or is it all in China?"

Savannah folds her arms and stares out the window for a while. "It's all in China." It's a confession, not an argument.

That's probably as close as she'll get to admitting she's Ohlmeyer. "When'd you find out about the heroin?"

"I knew about that from the start." She's beginning to sound irritated. "Pensri told me, remember? That's why the Wa wanted ceramics."

"And that was okay with you?"

"The wares Pensri sent me were clean."

"The ones Ohlmeyer bought weren't."

She snaps, "I know. I didn't have any control over that. That was Coulson's deal, remember? Him and the Wa." Savannah lunges off the windowsill and stalks away. "I blame Jim for that. If he didn't get so greedy, if he didn't make that deal, it would've been okay."

I wonder what Bandineau's telling the DEA right now. Does any of his storyline up with Savannah's? He says he's the victim; she says she is. Maybe they both are, or neither.

Savannah pivots toward me. "This system I built? I never designed it—it was all a reaction. Now the DEA and Homeland Security and whoever else want to tear it down. It's time to change." She squats in front of me, folds her arms on my thighs, then turns those big blue eyes on me. Her voice goes soft. "I'd been trying to work out how to get here since last year, ever since I found out about the DEA."

Another bomb goes off in my head. "Wait—you already knew about the DEA?"

"Uh-huh. Brandon told me." Her face says she's not a bit sorry about the lie.

She'd seemed so surprised when I told her. "If the art-advisor thing doesn't work out? You totally need to try acting."

"Thanks for the suggestion." She gives me a chilly smile. "You solved a big problem for me. I knew I needed to do something about the wares, but I didn't have enough money to fly over, get a car, get here. Then you called and invited me along. That was a huge help."

"Glad I was useful for something. What happened to you being a millionaire?"

"I'm a real estate millionaire. All the money's in the house. Cash-wise, I'm mostly broke. You don't make a lot of money doing what I do unless you have a crazy-good resume and lots of contacts. What I got from selling Ohlmeyer's ceramics dried up when they ran out. I still need to pay for food, Uber, new shoes. I needed to get over here to fix my income, but I didn't have enough income left to get over here. Until you brought me." She squeezes my knee. "Thanks."

I already knew this; I just didn't know I knew. I'd seen the wear on her dresses, how many are from two or three years ago, the mid-market lingerie. I didn't understand why until now. "What's this thing you need me to do?"

"It's pretty simple. The U.S. market's gone now. Between ICE and the DEA, Nam Ton will be toxic to legitimate collectors. It's still hot in China, though. I need the wares to go straight to my Shanghai friend. It'll cut out a lot of middlemen and the village will get more of the profits. It's another one of those win-win situations."

"I bet you'll get a bigger cut, too."

She shrugs.

I don't have to think too long or hard to see the obvious flaw in the plan. "To change where the pots are going, won't you also have to change where the heroin's going?"

"Uh-huh. Now that the Wa lost their U.S. operation, I'm sure they'll want to switch up."

I sit there, stunned. She's proposing sending a stream of ultra-pure heroin to China like it's a new brand of lipstick. There's no doubt or guilt in her eyes. "This doesn't bother you... even a little?"

She makes a face. "The Wa already ship heroin into China. All I'll do is hand them a new connection, farther north. At least it won't be going to America anymore." She moves to the window, leans against the frame. "If you're not interested in helping..."

Good god. I didn't see this coming from her.

Our gallery had some truly sketchy clients. I'm sure at least a couple used drug money to buy art or maybe used the art they bought to move drug money. I already mentioned how hard it is to throw a gallery party without dope. The concept is nasty, but it's not shocking.

Except... it's coming from Savannah. Pretty, smart, fun Savannah.

It's hard to keep my voice calm, but I manage. "What do you want me to do?"

Savannah smiles. "I'd hoped you see it that way. That Wa commander I mentioned? He'll be here later this morning. I need you to be Hoskins for him. A different version of Hoskins."

Aha. Medina wants the asshole behind the super-smack... and he's coming *here*. I can satisfy both my sponsors at the same time. "Meaning?"

"I need to get him to agree to this deal. The problem is, I'm a woman."

"I've noticed."

She smiles. "The way it works around here, he wouldn't bother talking to a mere woman. He certainly wouldn't discuss business with one unless she's a prostitute. So I need you to make the deal with him."

"Do *what?*"

"You heard me. I'll be the interpreter. He doesn't speak English. Don't worry; I'll tell you everything you need to know to say more-or-less the right words. When I translate, I can fix whatever you say so it's right."

"I'm a beard."

"That's an old-fashioned way to put it, but, yes."

My first thought is, *seriously?* But it makes a certain kind of sense... especially when I consider that the risk is all on my head, not hers. As far as anybody else will know, it's *my* deal.

So *this* is what she wanted Hoskins for. I totally underestimated her.

Savannah kneels in front of me and cups her hands around my knees. "What do you think? Can you do it?"

I know I *can.* The real question is, *should I?* "If I say no?"

Her face crinkles in pain. "I hope you won't. If you do... well, the villagers will probably just give you to the Wa. You made them look bad in town—"

"You mean, when I rescued you?"

"Uh-huh. They'll want to make an example out of you. They'll probably kill you after a while."

"You're welcome, by the way."

"I didn't say I'd like it. There won't be a lot I can do about it, though." She gives me a sad smile. "Come on. You sold that house to me. I *know* you can do this. Once you do, we can leave and I can show you around Thailand and we can have a lot more fun than we've had this past week. Maybe we can have a good conversation about us. What 'us' is. I'd like that a lot. Would you?"

Negotiate a major narcotics deal that will lead to hundreds, maybe thousands of deaths.

Or die.

I've done some bad things. Worse than the fraud and tax evasion and money laundering at the gallery. Something I helped do drove a woman to kill herself. My partner killed somebody right in front of me and I did nothing to stop it. I didn't intend for either of those things to happen, but, well, *intentions*...

There aren't a lot of lines I won't cross. Those there are, I stay well away from.

Mass murder is one of them.

But the project turns to dust in three days. If I say "no," my expiration date will come sooner. Savannah will still get the deal done, and I'll be fertilizing the forest.

Gulp. "Yeah. I'd like that, too."

Chapter 53

The Wa commander arrives around ten in the morning with an entourage of a dozen soldiers. They all look like the UWSA troops we've seen before, except cleaner and with better tailoring. None of them wear anything I can identify as rank insignia, which seems weird. The only way I can tell which one is the head honcho is that he's the only one without a red scarf tied around his neck, and he's packing what looks like a Rolex.

I'm standing in front of what Savannah tells me is the village chief's house. She's next to me in her Burmese outfit with her hair covered by a yellow kerchief. The chief is next to her, then his son, then Pensri. They gave me back my duffel earlier, so for the first time in days, I'm showered (last night in the rain, with Savannah), shaved, and wearing relatively clean clothes.

The rain also washed some of the humidity out of the air. It's damp but not sweltering (yet). Ironically, this is the nicest morning we've had since we entered Myanmar.

Ironically, because my stomach's turned into a pretzel.

The soldiers set up a cordon between us and the rest of the village. The village guards flank us outside the ring of Wa. A few villagers watch the show from outside the screen of guards. I can't tell if the security is to keep the villagers out or to stop us from escaping.

The chief and the Wa honcho have a long exchange that sounds like telling each other how wonderful each other are. Savannah moves her mouth next to my ear. "He's Colonel Kyon." Pronounced *chon*. "He's in charge of the Wa troops around here and runs the local poppy grow."

"So the Rolex is real?"

"Probably."

"Met him before?"

"No. Pensri's always kept me away from him. He didn't need to know about western visitors until now."

Colonel Kyon is round-faced and stout, but I don't get that he's soft. His eyes are dark, sharp, almost piercing. He stands straight with his shoulders square, but it's not a pose; it looks natural on him. "You're sure he doesn't speak English?"

"That's what Pensri says."

"We'll need to test that."

Two teenage girls bring out stools for the six of us. The chief and Kyon get the nice, shiny white plastic ones, while the rest of us get handmade wooden ones that have been around the block a few times.

The chief hands Kyon the booze and cigarettes we brought, then finally gets around to introducing me. Kyon lights a Marlboro and shifts his stare to me.

I doubt this is what the DEA expected, but I'm about to cross off the last item on my checklist. "*Nin hao ma?*" Savannah told me this is Mandarin for *how are you?* This is where we shift from Burmese to a language Savannah can speak... and cut out everybody else.

Kyon bobs his head and says something short. His voice is semi-tenor, not quite what I expect for someone his shape or position.

Savannah says, "He says he's very well, thank you."

"My name is Richard Hoskins." Since pointing is considered rude, I nod toward Savannah. "This is my interpreter."

She translates. He answers. "He asks if you're American."

I had to do this a few times at the gallery. One rule I remember is to always speak to the person I'm talking to, not the interpreter. "Yes, I am. So is she. She works for me. I like to have control over my interpreters. Is Mandarin acceptable to you?"

"He says he understands, and Mandarin is fine."

I nod once to him. "The soldier standing behind you is about to shoot you in the head." I say it like I'm commenting on last night's game.

Not a flicker. Kyon switches his focus to Savannah, expectant. I guess Pensri was right.

Savannah says, "I told him that you appreciate the opportunity to discuss business with him. He said he's willing to discuss business with anyone serious about it. He asks if you had a pleasant journey here."

Ah. We have to chat first. So we chat through Savannah, who keeps a perfectly blank face through the whole exchange. I finally notice that her stool is shorter than mine. That probably isn't accidental.

The two teenagers bring out ceramic cups for all of us and pour tea from a scorched metal pot. I lean in to Savannah and whisper, "Is it safe to drink this?"

"It's hot. You probably won't catch anything too serious."

Great. I don't drink tea—it tastes like dirty water to me—but I can play the game.

We chat some more. I look more closely at the cup. A slender cone, white thin-bodied ceramic, vibrant underglaze cobalt blue on the lower half, a cloud-like blue figure on the white ground above. It could be Nam Ton work.

Is it? If so, it's perfect—no chips, no fading, no crazing on the glaze, no stains from being underground for hundreds of years. Pristine. Hmm.

More chat straggles by. Savannah says, "He says he doesn't recall you mentioning who you represent."

"Does this mean we can start talking business now?" She nods. "Tell him that I understand his partners in America were just taken off the table."

She gives me a slow blink. "This isn't the approach we discussed." Her face is still carefully neutral.

"I thought about it. The approach you fed me doesn't give me any leverage. This one will. Tell him." It's not that I have so much experience making international drug deals—I don't—but I do have experience negotiating sales. In any bargaining situation, both the seller and the buyer each need to have some amount of leverage over the other. The buyer needs to be able to refuse to buy; the seller needs to be able to refuse to sell. Savannah's version gave all the power to the Wa. I'm taking some back.

Savannah watches me for a moment, then turns to Kyon. His eyebrows perk up as she delivers my message. He buys himself some time with a long sip of tea, then answers. "He asks what makes you think that's so."

"Because I'm in touch with the people who took them off the table."

Kyon's mouth puckers. He scans me up and down.

"He asks again who you represent."

I haven't worked out exactly who, yet, though I've narrowed it down to two or three three-letter agencies I don't mind dragging into the mud. I almost went with the Mexican drug cartels, but the people here have recent-ish experience with American spooks. "I'm bringing you a business opportunity in another market. One that should be more lucrative than the one in America, and easier to exploit."

He finishes his tea. One of the teenagers hops to refill his cup. He considers me for a few beats, then growls something.

"He asks why you think he's interested in another market."

"You may not be yet, but you will be soon. The American market is closed to you now. You can't get back in. If you keep trying, the people I represent will be very offended. You won't succeed and things will go badly for you."

"I can't say that to him."

I remember Carson's advice: *they respect strength.* "It gets worse the more he pushes back. Tell him."

She does. Kyon gets very still. He gives me the grimmest smile I've seen since I left PEN. When he finally speaks, it's very slow.

"He asks which market you refer to."

"China. Shanghai."

That makes him straighten a bit.

"He says that's a difficult market to reach."

"But a very lucrative one once you do." At least, that's what Savannah told me last night. "The synthetics"—fentanyl—"have all kinds of downsides, not to mention they're commodities now. You have a unique product. It'll appeal to a whole different slice of that market—the people who want something natural, something predictable, and can afford to pay for it. A luxury good, if you will." The part about luxury goods is all mine. It worked on Bandineau.

As Savannah talks, Kyon sets down his cup and leans his hands on his knees. His eyes dart from her face to mine. I can't tell what his reaction is yet, but at least he's listening.

Savannah says, "He says to go on."

I try to keep my expression as calm as I can. I have a plan for this conversation. "Okay. The premium price also extends to the packaging. The blue-and-white wares"—the Nam Ton pieces—"are very popular in China, unlike in America. You can get a much higher price for them in Shanghai. This means you can give the villagers here a larger credit for those wares and still come out ahead."

Pensri's giving the others a murmured play-by-play. She's the only other one here who can understand what I'm saying. I'm trying to pitch this to her as well as Kyon. She's the one who'll have to talk the chief out of throwing me a blanket party.

"He wants to know who these people in Shanghai are."

"It doesn't matter right now. They're interested in doing business with you. You need someone to do business with. You'll make more money with less effort. They'll make money. The people here will make more money. My people will be pleased that your product isn't coming into America anymore. Everybody wins."

Savannah murmurs, "I hope you know what you're doing."

"Of course I do." *Not.*

Kyon grimaces when Savannah starts translating. Probably the "you don't need to know" part. His mouth softens when she gets into the win-win part.

"He asks if you control the people in Shanghai."

"We have an understanding with them. They'll be… *reluctant* to go against our interests. Especially with the upside they'll enjoy from this deal."

The colonel rocks back on the stool and crosses his arms. His eyes narrow. He talks for what seems like a long time for him.

"He says you've mentioned 'your people.' You've said they'll stop him when he re-enters the American market. Who are 'your people' exactly? Why should they concern him?"

He's finally forcing the issue. What we've done so far was easy; now it gets harder. I have to convince him I have the hammer without being specific about who owns it.

I take a moment to finish my tea and set the cup on the ground next to my stool. "The people I represent have… let's say, *global* interests. I assume you're aware my country and China compete around the world. Politically, economically, militarily, socially. They don't always play fair and, frankly, neither do we. Chinese synthetics are causing us a lot of trouble." It's a good thing that I read the L.A. *Times* every day at work. "It's in our interest to make sure the Chinese have a similar headache to deal with. Why should you care? You have a problem. We can present you with a solution that furthers our goals. Can we get to specifics now?"

I assume that DVDs of American movies make it to Myanmar—they're everywhere else. I hope Kyon reads between the lines of what Savannah tells him, assumes I'm talking about everybody's favorite American three-letter intelligence agency, then draws some conclusions from the movies he's seen. The long pause after Savannah finishes tells me he's thinking.

"He says he's interested in more specifics."

Phew. Now we're haggling over prices. I know how to do that. One problem: Savannah doesn't know how much a kilo of normal heroin goes for in China. (I know... what kind of art advisor is she?) She knows the maximum price her friends will pay—$32,000 a kilo—but I have to decide where to start the bidding. I haven't got a clue.

I force a smile. "The people in Shanghai will take your entire production for 132,000 yuan a kilo." About $20,000. "You can use yuan in Pangkham, right?" Pangkham's the unofficial capital of Wa State.

Savannah's eyebrows tangle. "That's..."

"The opening bid. Tell him."

He snorts, shakes his head. Clearly, that's too low.

"He says that's less than it costs to buy four Vietnamese women. His product's much rarer than that."

I'm disturbed that he knows the market rate for trafficking Vietnamese women. "No offense meant, Colonel. I'm simply establishing a floor for our negotiations. Perhaps you'd like to suggest a ceiling?"

Kyon purses his lips, rocks a little, frowns.

"He says making a product like his is very expensive. He can't make an acceptable profit at less than 260,000 yuan."

A bit shy of $40,000 a kilo, which I figure out because his offer's almost double mine. Now's when I wish the yuan traded at a whole-number multiple of the dollar.

"I appreciate that you have expenses, and I want each side to make a fair profit. Of course, trucking your product over the border to China will be much cheaper than shipping it across the Pacific to America. The bribes will be lower, too. In the interests of fairness, I'm sure the people in Shanghai can pay 145,000 yuan a kilo." That's $22,000.

Savannah says, "You're not buying rugs, you know."

"Same idea. You do this for your clients, right?"

She grinds her teeth a bit, then relays my offer. "He says he hopes your people in Shanghai have the resources to sell his product to their customers. It concerns him that they can pay so little. Maybe they're new to the business and need help getting started. He thinks he may be able to reduce his price temporarily to 250,000 yuan." Around $38,000.

On it goes. We each mildly diss the other's last offer and ratchet our next one up or down by a grand or two. It's all very calm and polite. Only my stomach reminds me that we're dickering over superpowered heroin that'll soon be blowing off the tops of people's heads in a megacity 1600 miles away. I never, ever thought I'd do something like this. Funny how your ethics change when freedom and survival are your goals.

After more tea and more back-and-forth, we reach what should be the endgame: I'm at $29,000 a kilo, he's at $33,000. It's my move. I should go to $31,000, splitting the difference, and he should take it. Except he didn't move off his current price after my last offer. That's a bad sign—he thinks he's at his floor or wants me to think that.

I say, "You know you can't go back to the American market."

"He says he remembers you telling him that." Savannah motions for me to lean toward her. She whispers, "Are you really doing this? He'll walk away."

"He won't walk away. He needs a new customer."

"Don't turn this into some penis-size contest. Give him what my friends offered. They'll still make plenty of money."

"He'll wonder why I'm caving. It'll show weakness. Predators like that."

She sighs. "Are you *sure* you know what you're doing?"

Sort of. "You want this to stick, right?" I sit up and smile at Kyon. "Look, we both want to make a deal. I'll go to 200,000 yuan." A smidge over $30,000. "That's as far as Shanghai can go. What do you say?"

Kyon rocks a little on his stool. He looks like he's sucking on a lime slice as he stares at me. He knows it's on him now. He gets to decide whether we make a deal. I normally don't like to give that power away, but I'm aiming for a different outcome than usual.

"He says that you told him he has a unique product, a luxury good. He wonders if you mean that when you try to lower his price the way you are. He understands that a luxury good comes with a premium price. Perhaps you should reacquaint yourself with that concept."

The colonel stands and talks some more.

"He says this has been very interesting, but unfortunately you and he can't come to an agreement. He thanks you for demonstrating that his product is worth more than he's been selling it for. He'll make his own arrangement with people in China. He wishes you a pleasant journey home."

Savannah twists to glare at me. She hisses, "What did you *do?*"

Exactly what I set out to do: I tanked the deal.

Kyon offloads his gifts on one of his posse, then says goodbye-sounding things to the chief and his relatives. Savannah tries to punch holes in me with her eyes, but I've been death-stared at by pros and she just doesn't have the knack.

When Kyon and his merry men head down the path toward the river, Savannah scurries to Pensri, who's in deep discussion with the chief. They slip off for a sidebar. Their hand gestures get choppy, and Pensri shoots increasingly dark glances my way. Savannah must be blaming me for what happened. It's fair—I did it. But for a good reason.

The chief barks at the village guards, then points at me. Before I know it, I have two guys with rifles flanking me. They drag me off the stool and march me up the hill through the village.

My gut tells me they're not going to throw me a party.

Chapter 54

The house they put me in last night wasn't very comfortable, but at least it was a house with a floor. This time I'm in a house in the middle of the village, tied to a post downstairs on the dirt where the animals live. The smallish pigs peek around the corner of their enclosure at me, and the black chickens keep their distance. Maybe they know I'm not popular right now.

I'd more-or-less prepared myself for the guards to haul me into the forest and shoot me. Not my preferred outcome, but at least I wouldn't go out a major drug trafficker with the blood of thousands on my hands. There aren't a lot of things I won't do with the proper motivation, but that's one of them.

Instead of an instant execution, I get time to think about it. That may be part of the punishment. The second-guessing and self-recriminations start almost immediately after the guards wander off toward the village's center. Should I have just played along? Not if I ever want to sleep again.

Should I have talked to Savannah about this? No—if she knew what I was up to, she would've changed what she told Kyon and made the deal work.

I screwed up her plan instead. I can't blame her for being pissed; if it'd worked out, it would've been her first steady income in seven years. Is she sore enough to let Pensri's goons feed me to the Wa?

All this keeps me occupied through the afternoon and into early evening. A guard returns a couple hours after he left me here, parks himself on the stairs to the porch, and watches me between smokes. People walk past in both directions but hardly anybody looks my way.

I should be scared, but I'm not. Maybe I really did come to terms with death while they marched me here. Maybe it's not real to me yet. Maybe I'm just too tired to care. Whatever's going to happen, I just want it over with.

Savannah strides up the path when the clouds turn fuchsia in the sunset. I recognize her outfit, but I also recognize her walk. It's the same one she uses on a city sidewalk when she's wearing designer dresses and heels, nothing like the local women's flat-footed, functional gait.

She swings through the gate in the fence surrounding the yard, murmurs a few words to the guard, then squats facing me. "I won't untie you this time." Her face is dark, borderline angry.

Great. My butt's asleep and my shoulders are seizing up. "What're they gonna do with me?"

"They're still deciding." She scowls. "What were you thinking? Why did you do that?"

I had plenty of time to think through this conversation, so I have an answer ready. Not necessarily the real answer, though. "To save you from yourself."

Her eyebrows launch. "What does that mean?"

"When we talked last night, it sounded like it would be you, me, and Kyon. Then it turns out we have half the village watching. What part of negotiating a multimillion-dollar drug deal in front of witnesses sounded good to you?"

"Witnesses? Do you really think anyone here will tell anyone about this?"

"I learned something a long time ago: somebody always talks. *Always*. And there's always somebody around to listen. You can't afford to create witnesses who don't have as much to lose as you do."

Savannah makes an exasperated noise. "Who would they tell? There's no law up here. The closest thing they have to law is Kyon."

"What about the Chinese?" That gets me a sudden frown. "You think they're gonna let this super-smack come in and not do anything about it? First they'll squeeze your friends for their connection. Then they'll come here and hunt down everybody who knows about it. Somewhere along the line, they'll hear about the white guy and the blonde who made the deal with Kyon. They'll get your identity from Pensri one way or another. Then what do you think happens?"

She snaps, "They won't try to extradite me. They don't do that."

"Maybe not. There's no extradition treaty between them and us anyway. But do you want to spend the rest of your life wondering who'll meet you at the airport when you fly to Shanghai or Beijing?

Or, remember those bookstore dudes they kidnapped last fall? I think they nabbed one from Thailand, right?"

"Yes. Pattaya." A leak opens up in the anger balloon she carried into this. "Couldn't you have at least told me you were going to do this? We could've talked about it."

"It didn't come to me until you went to sleep and I had time to think. You kept me pretty busy 'til then. Also, I figured if I warned you, you'd go ahead with your plan anyway."

She growls and bolts off the ground. "So you sabotaged me."

"No, I saved you."

She glares over her shoulder at me.

"Now we have witnesses who can say we failed to make a deal with Kyon. However his heroin gets into China, it's not our fault."

"But it won't be my deal and I won't get my share. You cost me a lot of money. How are you going to repay me?"

I sort-of expected her to say this, but it disappoints me anyway. "You really are your father's daughter, aren't you?"

If I'd shoved a plate of *pad thai* in her face, she couldn't look more disgusted. "How can you say that? He was a monster."

"Yeah. And you're pissed that I kept you from poisoning thousands of people for money."

Savannah stares at me, jaw set, breathing hard, arms folded tight. She finally turns her head away to watch the eastern sky fade to purple.

"Look, I get it." I dial my voice down to *understanding*. "You need the money. I've been there. It's easy to justify it to yourself. Nobody'll get hurt, or the people who'll get hurt don't matter. But you'll finally figure out it's not true. They come find you when you're asleep and they don't let you forget." This part I know.

Her jaw slowly unclenches. "What did you do?"

"Dumb stuff. It doesn't matter now. Doing this is how I make up for it." No answer. She just keeps staring at the sky. "You know, you can still do a deal that won't keep you up at night."

She finally looks at me. "What are you talking about?"

"The pottery. Nam Ton wares. Have your friends buy them direct from Pensri's people. You won't get paid as much, but it'll be something, and you won't turn into Lady Macbeth. The village'll get a ton more money. You'll be a hero again."

"What about you?"

"We're a package deal. I got Nam Ton untangled from the heroin. Now it can become a real asset to them."

She sniffs, shakes her head. "I'm supposed to save you from them? I don't know if I can. I'd have to be a 'hero,' as you put it, and I can't do that until I set up the deal for the ceramics. I'll have to go back to Arunothai to do that."

"Why?"

"So I can make a call. Our phones don't work out here, remember?"

"Your iPhone may not. I'll bet that blue Huawei of yours does."

Her eyes practically explode. "You went through my *bag?* How *dare* you! How could you—"

I snap, "The same way you went through the drawers and cabinets in my house and tried to break into my office. Twice. You got no room to complain."

She sputters and grimaces and storms back-and-forth on a short line until she finally gets it out of her system, or until she figures out that what I proposed isn't completely insane. I'm kinda surprised she hasn't thought of it before now. She finally stops to glare at me more. "Okay, let's assume I can even make that deal. Tell me why I should rescue you after what you did."

It's a rational question, but it worries me that she has to ask it. "Because I'm cute and you like to play with me?" That gets me a dark look. "Because I got you here?" The dark look doesn't go away. "Because I just saved your soul?"

She snaps, "Did you?"

"I'm not sure. We'll see whether you leave me here to *them.* If you do... well, I'll guess I didn't."

A lot of silence follows. A little gray pig snuffles at my feet. Pigs eat dead bodies; a wonderful thing to think of right now. It'd take a lot of these guys to get rid of me.

Savannah stands in the corner of the yard with her back to me and sighs a lot. She turns to give me a less-dark look than before. "I have to talk to Pensri. Wait here."

As she walks away, I say, "Like I'm going anywhere?"

It gets dark. The windows in the nearby houses become orange eyes. I can smell frying chicken and simmering spices, but nobody brings me any. Why waste food on a dead man?

My whole body aches from sitting on the ground and not being able to move. I haven't had any water since the new guard took over a couple hours ago, and I can't vouch for how clean that was. Maybe they'll shoot me before I get dysentery. The pigs eventually give up on me and the chickens settle in for the night.

Somewhere along the way, I drift off. I'm too tired to dream.

Somebody kicks me awake. The guard looms over me like a dark tree.

Pensri's voice says something in what sounds like Thai. The guard unties me. When I don't move immediately, he kicks me again.

I snarl, "Just fucking get away from me. This' gonna take a while." Making my body work again is hard and painful and I can't get on my feet without the guard hauling me upright.

Savannah steps in front of me. "Come on. We're leaving now. You can thank me later."

Chapter 55

I say, "I thought you said it's dangerous to drive at night."

"It is." Savannah's eyes are on gimbals and her head's on a swivel trying to keep track of the things coming out of the dark at us. The light from the dash picks out the veins bulging in her hands.

Savannah's driving us south on Highway 45 as fast as the night lets us. It's just past midnight and pouring. We honk our way through the flatbeds and minibuses jostling along the road, playing chicken in the dark.

I say, "What did Pensri say to you back there?"

"When?"

"At the river, when we were leaving." They spoke so quietly I could barely hear them, and then all I heard was Thai. The body language looked like there was a cold front between them.

Savannah concentrates on skirting a pothole the size of a volcano's caldera. "Well, for one thing, she asked me to never bring a guest again."

If she's fishing for an apology, she won't get one. "Anything else?"

"She thanked me for making the deal with my friend in Shanghai for the ceramics. She and Htun are already working out a way to hide the extra money from the Wa. Those are the only parts that concern you."

There's still a cool front between me and Savannah, too. Her long navy-blue dress is buttoned from top to bottom, and she's been in speak-only-when-spoken-to mode since we left.

She glances at me, looks away. "How do I trust you now? After yesterday?"

"How do I trust *you?*" *After the first day we met.* "You set me up, made it look like the heroin deal was mine, not yours. Before that, you were running me around up here when you knew all the time where we were headed. Were you stalling us, too? Burning time until Kyon could get to the village? It's just too coincidental that we arrived the evening before he was supposed to visit." A thought blinks into my head. "Did you call him that last night in Arunothai?"

"I talked to Pensri. She set up the meeting."

"Great. You lied to me—to everybody—about not knowing where Nam Ton comes from. Over Memorial Day weekend? When we were searching the maps? You told me to forget Myanmar. On purpose, I bet."

A long pause. "Uh-huh."

I try to say something but only manage a growl. And *she's* questioning *me?*

She stabs my thigh with an index finger. "You lied about who you are, about your work, about your house. What was that big meeting you put on the day Jim arrived? Was that even real? How did you get the mayor to just drop by that morning?" Her jaw sags. "He wasn't the mayor, was he? He was some kind of actor. I've never felt so conned in my life."

I need to get her off that track. "You know how you said you got me into bed because you wanted to find out more about me? That's not quite true, is it? You were ready to go at the Tonga Room, *way* before you ever saw my house. When did you decide I was rich enough to sleep with? That first day at Achara? The lunch with Jim and Lorena?"

Savannah clenches her jaw and locks her eyes straight ahead. The bones and veins pop on the backs of her hands.

We plow through the silence for what must be three or four miles, playing dodge'em with every truck driver and oxcart in eastern Myanmar. About a third of the northbound trucks aren't using their headlights; one almost takes off our side mirror. Once we get to a relatively clear stretch of road, I notice a strange sound coming from the driver's seat.

It's Savannah. She's giggling.

"What's so funny?"

She claps a hand over her mouth, which doesn't stop the giggles but helps muffle them. A bark of laughter escapes. "Oh, god. We were doing the same thing to each other."

I snicker despite myself. "Takes one to know one, doesn't it?"

"Uh-huh." Now she laughs out loud. "This is crazy! This' *never…*"

I really don't want to laugh, but she's right—the situation's nuts. We've both been lying our asses off to each other. We're absolutely perfectly matched. "Who's ahead?"

Savannah tries to stifle a guffaw and ends up making a noise like rubbing a balloon. "I think we're tied." She palms tears away from her eyes. "Pulling over. I gotta… I gotta…"

We shoehorn ourselves onto what passes for the shoulder and dissolve into a collective fit of laughter. Passing trucks splash water on the Hilux and rock us like little earthquakes. After everything we've been through over the past few days, all the tension, all the maneuvering, it feels amazing to let it out until our guts hurt. The drivers going by must think we're dying from nerve gas.

We finally get to that point where the belly-laughs turn into sniggers. Savannah rubs away her tears, then gives me a really dopey smile. "Hiii."

"Hi yourself."

Giggle. She holds out her right hand. "I'm Savannah. I used to be an heiress, but now I'm broke. I do all kinds of crazy things for money. And I'm really fun in bed."

I almost trip into another fit but pull it out in time. I shake her hand. "Hi, Savannah. I'm Rick." Honesty goes only so far. "I don't have much money, but I've got good clothes. I lie really well."

"Hi, Rick. I'll bet you're fun in bed, too."

"You think?"

"Uh-huh." She pecks my lips. "Let's get out of this country."

Chapter 56

EIGHT DAYS LATER

I slip out of the king-size bed, grab my phone off the long, black headboard, and pad to the sliding glass door looking out on our private balcony. It's almost seven. Savannah's just a long lump under the bright white duvet. I can see through a screen of trees to the Ping River, dappled by raindrops. The muted morning light filtered by the clouds turns the outside into a pastel.

We checked into the X2 Chiang Mai Riverside Resort the day after we left Myanmar—we overnighted in Arunothai to rest and clean up—and we've been here ever since. There's a pool and gym on the roof, a Michelin-star chef in the hotel restaurant, and a spa. I hope Talbot and Medina don't mind paying for all this.

After all, they told me to keep track of Savannah.

I sent my report to them (via Allyson) when we arrived in Arunothai and I could use my laptop again. I told them about Kyon and that the Nam Ton wares aren't going to be a problem anymore in the U.S. Talbot replied (also via Allyson) by the next morning: he had what he needed "and more," whatever that means. He also told me to stick with Savannah "for a few days" and keep checking my mail. I've been doing that ever since.

When it hasn't been raining, Savannah's taken me to see the sights—the temples, the Night Bazaar, a couple expeditions out of town. We've stayed close to the hotel during the downpours. Our shower's the size of a studio apartment; the bed is very supportive; and when we're both vertical, we've eaten enough at Oxygen, the hotel restaurant, to regain the weight I lost in Myanmar. Guarding Savannah is hard work.

I check my email. One message from Olivia, with a link to the "News" page on the website for the U.S. Attorney's Office for the Northern District of California. About what I expected. I switch to

Artnet News; a new post about the continuing "Nam Ton scandal" saga elaborates on the USA's news flash. This crosslinks to the Association for Research into Crimes against Art blog, which has a pretty accurate recap of the story so far as well as some unflattering comments from Burmese officials insisting they're shocked, *shocked*, that such a thing could happen on their watch.

I sigh. Today's the day.

A warm, soft body presses against my back. Warm, soft arms circle my waist. "Whatcha looking at?" Savannah, sleepy voice.

How do I do this? "The river."

"On your phone?"

"*And* my phone."

"Hmm." I feel her shift to peek past me. "Pretty." She snuggles tighter.

I run my palm over her smooth, bare hip while I try to work out how to bring up the morning's Topic A. It's hard to think when her hands go exploring, like they are now.

She murmurs, "Come back to bed."

"I'm not sleepy."

"Who said 'sleep'?"

That makes it hard to think, too. "Not yet."

Sigh. "Okay. Still wanna go to MAIIAM today?" It's a museum on the other side of the old city that features contemporary Thai artists.

This is the best lead-in I'll get. "No. Change of plans. The airport."

Savannah slides around until she faces me. Her mouth turns down. "The airport?"

"Yeah." Deep breath. "It's time to go home."

"But… why? We're having such a good time." Her voice is awake now, even if her eyes are still a bit squinty.

I have to concentrate extra hard to not get lost in that warm, soft body now pressed against my front. "Yeah, we are. I need to go home. There's things I need to do." I don't sound very convincing even to myself.

"What about me?"

Here it comes… "You can't go."

She peers up at me for a twenty count. "Why not?"

"Grab your phone and look at Artnet News."

I could've let her use my phone, but I need some space so I can restart my big brain. And frankly, I can't pass up what might be my last opportunity to watch her walk away from me naked.

She unplugs her iPhone and sweeps it off the nightstand built into the headboard. "What am I looking for?"

"You'll know it when you see it."

The light from her screen turns her face and shoulders the color of skim milk. "Let me guess—'New Indictments in Nam Ton Scandal'?"

"That's the one."

Her index finger slowly drags the post up the screen, then stops. She blinks, swallows. I know exactly what she's reading.

> In a further widening of the scandal that has already snared almost a dozen art world figures, the U.S. Attorney for the Northern District of California announced today that a federal grand jury has returned an indictment against Savannah Kendicott, a San Francisco art advisor. The indictment, which has not yet been publicly released, specifies multiple counts of smuggling, trafficking in protected antiquities, customs fraud, money laundering, and tax evasion...

"*What?*" Her voice is a strangled shriek. She swivels enormous, shocked eyes at me. "What *is* this?"

"Keep reading."

Savannah's finger shakes as she pulls up the text. "Omigod. Omigod." After a moment, her knees go out from under her and her butt slams onto the edge of the bed. It takes all my willpower to not lunge forward to try to catch her if she falls.

She's past hyperventilating and turning crimson when she skewers me with her eyes. "How much did you tell them?"

"Some. I told the feds that you negotiated a deal for the Nam Ton wares to go to China. That should make them—"

"You did *what?* You bastard!" She hurls her phone at me. I catch it after it smacks into my breastbone, which hurts like hell. "Paint a target on me, will you? They'll think I control the wares!" She bolts off the bed and rushes me. "Do they know where the village is?"

I check to see that she doesn't have anything sharp in her hands. "Yeah. That was part of the deal."

"You son of a bitch! *Nobody's* supposed to know that!" She takes a swipe at me that I manage—just barely—to duck. "I told Pensri she's safe!" Another swing connects with the forearm I'm trying to shield myself with. "You betrayed me *and* her! Why? To save yourself?"

I skirt around her and back toward the bathroom. "It was the deal. I tell the feds what I see and hear over here. It's your fault you're up to your eyeballs in this mess, not mine. Besides." I hold up her phone screen to face her. "You read all this? Not all of it came from me. Jim and Lorena did a lot of talking. Your 'friends' sold you out."

She scoops the TV remote off the headboard and flings it. It hits the wall beside me and explodes batteries and plastic bits. "I *expect* that from them. They're weak. But *you?* I expected *better* from you!" The wooden Kleenex box whistles over my head and clatters off the verdigris-stained wall behind the bed. "I thought you'd understand. I thought you'd protect me. Not... not... *this!*"

"Oh, that's cute coming from you." Her anger's catching. I feel my face warming as I stutter-step her way, sending her skittering back a couple paces. "You set me up. You were gonna feed me to the Wa. And you expect me to cover for you? You're—"

"*Damn you!*" The only thing she can reach is a throw pillow, so she throws it. I slap it away. "You bastard!" She hurls herself at me, starts pounding my chest and arms. "You destroyed my life!" Her voice cracks. "I can't go home!"

I catch both her arms before she draws blood and hold on tight. She tries to shake herself free but her strength runs out along with her breath. Tears and little broken sounds eke out of her. I try to pull her against me—both to hold her and to keep track of her—but she shoves me away and crumples face-down on the bed, sobbing into the comforter. She flings off my hand when I try to touch her shoulder.

I lean back against the wall and watch her bawl. I have to fight my instincts so I can just stand there and not try to comfort her. I hate that I've hurt her like this, but I remember what she was prepared to do to me, and it dulls the pain.

Savannah eventually sits up, grabs another king pillow and crushes it in a hug. I find the Kleenex box, plop it next to her, then step back before she can take a swipe at me. But she's too far gone for that. She piles up a small mound of tissues as she mops up the tears and snot pouring down her scarlet face. She finally chokes out, "Are you... supposed... to take me home?"

"Yeah."

Her body sags like someone just cut all her strings. She holds up her arms, wrists together, like I'm going to slap cuffs on her.

I perch on the end of the bed, ready to bolt if she decides to beat me to death with the phone receiver. "I was supposed to keep you from looking at the news so you'd come along with me and walk into their handcuffs at SFO. They even know what flight we're going to be on."

"How?"

Me. "Long story. But you screwed up the plan. I guess you woke up in the middle of the night and couldn't get back to sleep. You looked at the news on your phone, saw the story, packed in a hurry, and left. I woke up in an empty bed."

Add confusion to the anguish on her face. She hugs the pillow again. "You're... letting me go?"

I try on some answers but finally go with, "Yeah."

"Why?"

"I remember something you told me that first night in the village, after I'd found Pensri looting her own site. You said, 'I was trying to do something good.' I know what that's like—trying to do right and having it turn to shit." I squeeze her knee. "You see, there's something I didn't tell them. Something important."

She snuffles, wipes her nose. "What?"

"I didn't tell them the Nam Ton wares are fake."

Her eyes grab onto mine. They're bloodshot but wary. "You say that why?"

"A bunch of little things. Coulson must've brought hundreds, maybe even thousands of pieces into the U.S. up until a couple weeks ago. They had to come from somewhere. Pensri tried to convince me there was nothing left to steal, but the area she said she'd excavated hadn't been touched for years. Then there's the tests I had done at the Getty. They said 'inconclusive' on the TL analysis, which is real convenient. The dig I saw behind the village? Before that dude brained me, I noticed a bunch of Nam Ton wares next to the hole. They were clean. Since I didn't see a way for Pensri to clean them at the site, they didn't come out of the ground. And did you look at the cups the tea girls gave us? Same kind of work, same colors, almost brand new."

Savannah doesn't say anything, just hugs her pillow tighter and stares at the TV remote's corpse.

I say, "You already knew."

Long, long pause. "Uh-huh."

"For how long?"

Long, deep, shuddering breath. "Since they ran out of real ones. Four or five years ago."

I wasn't sure until she said that. It was a theory, but only a theory. "I guess they should add fraud to that indictment. What happened?"

"What Pensri told you? It was almost right, it just took longer. By then the villagers couldn't give up the income. Pensri decided that saving the village was more important than scientific integrity. She'd already figured out how the original wares were made. They used the same clay, the same glazes. She even rebuilt one of the original kilns. It's almost like experimental archaeology." She frowns. "If roughly the same people make the same product the same way with the same materials, are they fakes?"

The last place I want to go is philosophy. "Why does she bury them?"

"It screws up the TL curves. She seasons them for about a year underground. They return the same confused signatures as the older wares. They do beautiful work, don't they?"

"Yeah." That's the hell of it—the pots are lovely, and (almost) completely authentic, and the money goes for a good cause. It's pretty hard to get mad about being conned.

"You really didn't tell ICE?"

"I really didn't. I take it Jim and Lorena don't know?"

She shakes her head. "Lorena was faking the provenances, but she thought the wares were being looted."

"She has a history of that."

Savannah nods sadly, sighs, then climbs off the bed to pace to the sliding glass door.

I watch her stand there hugging herself as she looks out at the rain. It's all I can do to keep from hugging her myself. "So that leaves you. If you go home, ICE or the DEA will get it out of you eventually. Everybody thinks the wares are eight hundred years old. If you spill the secret, they'll decide the pots are trash. The pots won't have changed, only the way the owners think about them. The villagers would lose their income. What's the point?"

"Thank you." She says it so softly that I almost don't hear it. Big breath. "Now what happens?"

She wears goose bumps well. It's easy to get lost counting them. I look at the dark flatscreen TV so my big brain has a chance to think. "You were telling me it's cheap to live here if you stay out of Bangkok. So live here."

Savannah peers over her shoulder at me, rubbing her biceps like she's cold. "Really?"

"Why not? You know the language. You like it here. You haven't broken the law in Thailand as far as I know. The way things are between the U.S. and the government here, I doubt they'd extradite you." I shrug. "Unless you have a better idea."

"Hmm." She turns back to the view. "I could find a little guest house someplace. The money from my Chinese friend should start coming in two or three months. It won't be much, but..." She turns to me, her face serious. "Would you tell them where I am?"

"You talked about heading for Phuket."

"Perfect. I hate that place." She looks at her folded hands. "Sorry I called you all those terrible names."

No she isn't, but we can pretend.

After watching me thoughtfully for a long while, Savannah slides onto my lap and threads her arms around my neck. "Come with me. We'll have fun. There's a lot to see here, and I'd love to show it to you. Maybe I'll teach you a little Thai. And we can play all we want."

Sitting here naked, with a very warm, naked woman perched on my lap caressing me, makes all this sound good. *Really* good. But maybe I'm finally immune to Savannah's reality-distortion field, or I'm just tired of humidity, but my big brain won't turn off. "You're forgetting the part about how we don't trust each other and we've been lying to each other since we met."

She waves that away. "That's business. But this"—she points to me, then herself—"is us. We know each other now. We know what we're getting. We don't have to get married and have a flock of kids and do the 'forever' thing. We stay together as long as it's fun. When it's not fun anymore, you go home and I go… wherever." She kisses me. "Is there anything at home that you really need to get back to?"

I was doing okay until she asked that question. The truth is, there isn't. Slinging coffee, being poor, riding the Big Blue Bus before sunrise, sleeping on a broke-ass sofabed.

Living in the best climate in the world with Chloe, the nicest person in the world.

Being in a place I know and understand. Where I belong.

On the other hand, I can go anywhere I want now. As long as Talbot keeps his promise, I go to one court hearing, I get back my passport, buy my PO a so-long drink, and I'm free.

Every woman I've been close to who wasn't a blood relative has been more-or-less unreliable. I'm drawn to them. They're fun, they're exciting, they're a challenge. I get hurt in the end, but that's part of the experience, too. Maybe that's what I deserve.

Savannah's just the latest. Okay, maybe she's on the more-unreliable end of the scale—she did try to get me to do a big drug deal for her, and she was going to let Pensri's people kill me. That's like a warning, right?

But she's pretty and smart and uninhibited and a ton of fun. I don't trust her, but at least I now know why. She'll eventually hurt me. But until then…

Is there anything at home that you really need to get back to?

Savannah snuggles closer. So warm, so soft. "Come on. Say yes."

Chapter 57

NOVEMBER

I watch two of the most important women in my life sipping tea across the street from my blond-wood table on the sidewalk outside Rosprasert Muslim Food in Chiang Rai. They sit on tall metal stools at a no-name place across Isaraparb Road from me and a couple doors down. We're all in the shadow cast by the big Darulaman Mosque on my side of the street, an imposing stone building with a jade-green central dome and minarets topped with roofs that look like the hats the local farmers wear.

I'm not hiding—just giving them their space.

Savannah sits facing me, her elbows on the metal tabletop between them, cradling a teacup. I know she can see me; she winked at me when she sat down. She's been absorbed with her drinking companion ever since.

We've been shuttling around northern and central Thailand since July, staying in hostels or little guest houses for a couple weeks at a time, then moving on. We covered a lot of territory, but moving so often is hard. We've been here in Chiang Rai in far northern Thailand for nearly a month. It's a good central place: five hours by bus from Chiang Mai to the south, ninety minutes or so from Tachileik on the northern border with Myanmar. We're going to Tachileik tomorrow to renew the Thai tourist visa in my brand-new passport. *My* passport, not Hoskins'.

My hearing in federal court in San Francisco happened on September 14th. It lasted less than twenty minutes. I stood; the USA's staff lawyer read the motion to amend my supervision order; the judge said "So ordered"; and we were done.

Len, my PO, handed me my (then expired) passport when we met the next day for drinks at Rocco's in Westwood Village. He rasped, "Guess I can drop that employment audit I started on you."

When we shook goodbye on the sidewalk, he said, "Don't fuck up. You end up on my desk again, I will *personally* twist your head off. Understood?"

I got the first $72,077 of my agency pay on July 30th. That's for my work until June 17th, when the project switched to ICE and DEA sponsorship. The other $18,800 dropped at the end of September. Most of it went to paying off an elderly student loan and one of Janine's old credit card debts.

The rest is helping keep Savannah and me away from the real world.

I shovel down some more very nice chicken *khao soi*—I've gotten pretty good with chopsticks over the past few months—and chase it with a swig of Coke. It's a soup featuring both crisp and boiled egg noodles, meat chunks, ground pepper, and a coconut milk-based curry that I've come to like. At only fifty baht (less than a buck and a half), it's easy on the wallet, too.

Savannah pours herself another cup of tea. Back in August, she chopped off nearly all her hair and let it grow back in its natural medium brown. It's now a long pixie cut that looks good on her. Today she's wearing her ankle-length, sky-blue cotton dress with big white buttons from her throat to her hem. I miss her designer dresses and heels, but there's not much call for them here.

Since September, I haven't had to report to anybody or get permission to live. I can go where I like, when I like, and do what I like. The people in my life—Chloe, my Starbucks boss, Mom—don't have to deal with random drop-ins and interrogations. It's been years since I've been this free. I didn't realize how much I've missed it until now.

Freedom means making decisions again, good and bad. Which is deciding to stay with Savannah? Not sure yet. I've seen a lot of things and I've learned a lot. Savannah's fun to be with. It's like she left her inner deb back in San Francisco and she can finally let loose. And we are, after all, two of a kind.

But she still calls me "Rick," even though she knows it bugs me. "I like Rick," she tells me. "He's the guy I ran away with." I still watch my back around her, too. I haven't forgotten Myanmar yet.

Everybody else has, it seems. The "Nam Ton Scandal" is already becoming background noise. They're at seventeen indictments and twelve arrests, including Bandineau, Lorena, and over half a dozen collectors, including the client. If this goes the way the Ban Chiang case did, the first trials won't happen for years. Talbot told me I may need to testify "someday." If everybody flips on everybody else, maybe nobody'll go to trial. So it goes.

Savannah laughs. I can't hear it over the traffic, but I can see it, hear it in my head. Her drinking buddy may be laughing, too. Then they stand and shake hands briskly. I've been wondering what they had to talk about for almost an hour. At least they didn't scratch each other's eyes out.

Allyson turns and marches in my direction. To talk some sense into me?

I wasn't surprised when she found us. I *was* surprised when she said she wanted to speak with Savannah. That's why we're here today.

Unlike every other woman in eyeshot (perhaps in the whole city), Allyson is, as usual, dressed to make an impression: a crimson sleeveless lace shell over a knee-length black pencil skirt and heels. Everybody stops to watch her pass. The three workmen-looking guys at the other outside table nearly dislocate their necks when she parades up to me. "Mr. Friedrich?"

I stand and shake her offered hand. "Ms. DeWitt."

She scans me up and down. She sees board shorts and a half-unbuttoned camp shirt. I haven't had a haircut in two months. I still shave, though. Usually. "You're enjoying your… *interlude* here?"

"I am. Thanks for asking."

Allyson glances inside the café—half a dozen tables, wall- and ceiling-mounted fans trying to move the damp air around, a steam table by the missing outside wall, the mobile ratcatching unit (cat) slinking through the chair legs—allows herself one nose-crinkle, then turns back to me. "When will you return home?"

"Staying thousands of miles away from the train wreck sounds pretty attractive."

"You're aware of the results of your election, then."

"Unfortunately, yes."

Allyson suppresses a little smile. "I've spoken with some of the new people. The last time I met so many potential clients with so much money and so much to hide, I was in Russia."

"Funny you should say that."

"My point is, I believe the agency is about to enjoy a huge

windfall. I need all our associates available and ready to work. I'm also recruiting new associates." She tosses a wave over her shoulder. "Such as Ms. Kendicott."

"*What?*"

Her eyes are pleased by my surprise. "We need more staffing in Asia. She has a perfect skillset for the sort of business we expect to be coming our way. Your reports were quite enlightening."

If Savannah is a perfect fit for the agency, am I overqualified or underqualified? What kind of business is Allyson trying to get? "I'm taking some time off."

"I know." Allyson's face becomes serious. "Mind that you don't take too much. I'm inclined to make your temporary promotion permanent. If I do, I'll need you to be available for assignment very soon."

Great. The promotion's nice—€500 extra a day adds up fast—but I'm not sure it'll pay for enough disinfectant to sanitize myself after rolling in the swamp with this new bunch of whack jobs. "How long is 'very soon'?"

"Certainly not later than the end of December."

Another six weeks. "Do I really have to go back? Last I checked, there's an airport in Bangkok."

Allyson's lips compress for a few seconds, then recover. "I'm aware of that. I doubt you'd be effective here given your limited Asian language skills. The cost to send you to a project in Europe or Latin America would be time- and cost-prohibitive. I imagine you could relocate to Europe, though I doubt any of the desirable nations would welcome someone with your... history." She gives me a second once-over. "Central or Eastern Europe, perhaps. Their standards are *significantly* lower."

"Gee, thanks." I guess the Thai I've learned—mostly words for food or body parts, or euphemisms for bribery—doesn't count for much. "I'll think it over."

"Very good. When you tire of your... *idyll* here and settle someplace, please inform Olivia. I'm certain I can provide you with as much work as you wish now that you can travel without restriction. I may be able to... broaden your horizons, shall we say? I believe you have skills we haven't yet tapped." She extends her hand again. "Good day, Mr. Friedrich."

I watch her stride toward the main street. So does everybody else around me. When I turn away, I find Savannah heading for me. The working guys' necks get another workout as she sways up to me, wraps an arm around my waist, then kisses me. "Did she tell you the good news?"

"Yeah. What's your employee number?"

"Three-eighteen." She gives me a squeeze. "Maybe we can work together. Wouldn't that be fun?"

Absolutely not. Doing the I-don't-trust-my-partner thing once was enough.

I glance back at the main road in time to see Allyson slip into the back of a black Audi A6. Would she stick me with Savannah on a project just to teach me a lesson? What exactly would that lesson be?

When I switch back to Savannah, she gives me a Cheshire Cat smile.

The Adventure Continues ...

Miss Carson? Try…

<u>ZRADA: The First Carson Action Thriller</u>

Two priceless paintings. Two million euros. A civil war. What could go wrong?

A brutal betrayal leaves ex-cop Carson far inside war-torn eastern Ukraine with a suitcase full of cash and a huge target on her back. Now she has to survive the only way out.

Buy ZRADA today at your favorite online bookselling site!

Like What You Read?

Share your experience with friends! **Leave a review** on your favorite online bookselling site, on a readers' social network (such as Goodreads) or promotion site (such as Bookbub), or just on your blog or Facebook wall. Someone told you about this book; please pass on the favor.

About the Author

Lance Charnes has been an Air Force intelligence officer, information technology manager, computer-game artist, set designer, *Jeopardy!* contestant, and is now an emergency management specialist. He's had training in architectural rendering, terrorist incident response, and maritime archaeology, but not all at the same time. Lance's Facebook author page features spies, archaeology, and art crime.

Official Website
https://www.wombatgroup.com
Sign up for Lance's newsletter! Be the first to find out about new books, special deals, and the occasional giveaway.

Facebook Author Page
https://www.facebook.com/Lance.Charnes.Author

Goodreads
https://www.goodreads.com/lcharnes

The DeWitt Agency Files

Matt Friedrich has a very particular set of skills that he learned while working in a crooked L.A. art gallery, and other knowledge that he gained while hanging out in federal prison with Wall Street types who had bad lawyers. He's out on supervised release and working for $10 an hour at Starbucks to pay off over half a million in debts and restitution.

Matt's the DeWitt Agency's newest employee. The Agency "fills needs" for not-always-honest people and organizations. When a client has a need to fill that involves art in whatever form, Matt gets the project.

Follow Matt around the world, where he sees new places, meets new friends, avoids new enemies, and discovers (or pulls off) new scams. If he plays his cards right, he can make a lot of money, pay off his debts, and build a new life. All he has to do is not screw up...which is much harder than it sounds.

Praise for the DeWitt Agency Files

"*The Collection* is a breezy read in the way the very early Leslie Charteris' Saint novels were breezy: entertaining with an underlining of grit below the surface..." – *Criminal Element*

"Interlacing storylines give this series its charm... It's nice to have some modern *It Takes a Thief* escapism to slip away to in this world gone awry. Suffice it to say, I can't wait for The DeWitt Agency Files #3." – *Criminal Element*

"A brilliant heist story filled with fascinating art history reminiscent of Dan Brown or Steve Berry. Only better." – *Seeley James, author of the Sabel Security thriller series*

To learn more, go to your favorite online bookselling site, or to https://www.wombatgroup.com/dewitt-agency-files/.

The DeWitt Agency Adventures

Carson used to have a life. Then a crooked superior in the Toronto Police Services framed her for corruption, her husband turned out to be a serial cheat, and her father didn't pay back the millions he borrowed from Gennady Rodievsky, a Russian *mafiya* godfather.

Now Carson (that's only one of her names) answers to two masters: the DeWitt Agency, which "fills needs" for not-always-honest people and organizations; and Rodievsky, the criminal she tried to take down as a detective.

Follow Carson as she shuttles around the world, dealing with friends and enemies, victims and tormentors, fighting to do the right thing in places where even the right thing may be wrong. Someday she may pay off her debts, work out her demons, and be free of a life that can kill her in an instant... but will there be anything left of her when she does?

Praise for The DeWitt Agency Adventures

"A breakneck tale where enemies and friends are often indistinguishable and the heroine's life is literally minute-to-minute. Highly recommended." – *DP Lyle, award-winning author of the Jake Longly and Cain/Harper thriller series*

"Charnes, a capable writer, crafts an exciting and alluring storyline...The author provides enough breakneck action and unexpected circumstances to keep readers entertained, while the Ukrainian backdrop is well conceived." – *The Booklife Prize*

To learn more, go to your favorite online bookselling site, or to https://www.wombatgroup.com/dewitt-adventures/.

Thrillers by Lance Charnes

<u>DOHA 12: An International Thriller</u>

Jake Eldar's and Miriam Schaffer's names may kill them.

An assassination in Qatar thrusts twelve innocents into the crosshairs of a hit team bent on revenge. But two of them refuse to die quietly.

> "*Doha 12* is an exciting and hard-to-put-down read of fiction, not to be overlooked." – *Midwest Book Review*

Buy DOHA 12 today at your favorite online bookselling site!

<u>SOUTH: A Near-Future Thriller</u>

Luis Ojeda owes his life to the Pacifico Norte cartel. Literally. Now it's time to pay.

In 2032 America, ex-coyote Luis Ojeda must get FBI agent Nora Khaled into war-torn Mexico with her family – and a secret that will rock the U.S. government.

> "*South* is a riveting work of action/adventure suspense that is a real page-turner… Lance Charnes demonstrates a truly impressive knack for deftly creating a complex and thoroughly engaging story…" – *Midwest Book Review*

Buy SOUTH today at your favorite online bookselling site!